A LIFE IN BOOKS

The Rise and Fall of Bleu Mobley

A LIFE IN BOOKS: The Rise and Fall of Bleu Mobley
Copyright © 2013 **Warren Lehrer**. All rights reserved.
Published by GOFF BOOKS, an imprint of ORO Editions.
Distributed by Publishers Group West.

ISBN 978-1-939621-02-3
Library of Congress Control Number: 2013943652

A LIFE IN BOOKS: The Rise and Fall of Bleu Mobley
is written, designed, and illustrated by Warren Lehrer.

Some illustrations were made in collaboration with
Melina Rodrigo Smyres. Dimensionalizations by Donna Chang.
Jonathon Rosen collaborated on the cover art.
Additional illustrations were made in collaboration with
Michelle Martynowicz, Tatyana Strarikova Harris,
Melissa Medina Mackin, James Monroe, and Noah Woods.

The poem *If This Scar Were A Ladder* was written
in collaboration with Chenits Pettigrew.

Printed and bound in China on acid-free paper by ORO Group Ltd.

This project was made possible in part with support
from the New York State Council on the Arts, the Queens Council on
the Arts/NYC Department of Cultural Affairs, and a Joseph Leff Senior
Faculty Research/Distinguished Professorship Award
from Purchase College, SUNY. A project of EarSay.

A LIFE IN BOOKS

The Rise and Fall of Bleu Mobley

an illuminated novel written + designed by

Warren Lehrer

goff BOOKS

NOTE FROM THE EDITOR

I first became aware of the Bleu Mobley prison tapes from a *People Magazine* article about the bestselling author's ongoing legal battles. As I hastily cut out the article to

MOBLEY STILL MUM ON SOURCE

After nine months behind bars for refusing to reveal the name of a confidential source, well known author Bleu Mobley remains mum. His bestselling exposé on alleged presidential indiscretions, "as told to him by a former White House cleaning person," has become a cause celeb for writers and journalists around the globe seeking protections on behalf of their confidential sources, many of whom claim that their lives, their livelihoods, and sometimes the lives of their families would be at risk, were their names to

put in a clippings file (for my Ethics of Writing seminar), a sentence in the next to last paragraph caught my eye: "According to a source close to the author, Mobley started and then aborted writing a memoir in prison." This piqued my curiosity more than the legal story. I read on: "'Due to a bad case of carpal tunnel syndrome in his writing hand,' the source said, 'Mobley began making notes for his tell-all apologia by whispering into a tape recorder during sleepless nights.'"

After reading the article, I contacted Bleu Mobley through his lawyer to ask if I could listen to the tapes. To my surprise and delight, permission was granted. Although Bleu and I had met a handful of times through the years and expressed interest in each other's work, I can't say we ever knew each other well. When I met with him to pick up the tapes, I told Bleu I was surprised to read that he'd even considered writing a memoir—after hearing him speak so convincingly about never wanting to make himself the focus of his writing. He told me not to believe anything I read in trashy magazines. "Anyway, I'm done writing books," he said as he handed me the microcassettes in a manila envelope labeled *The Rise And Fall Of Bleu Mobley: A Life In Books.* "Hope you find what you're looking for."

Upon reviewing the tapes, I discovered that they weren't made during "sleepless nights," but over the course of one sleepless night –February 7th, 2008—in the darkness of Bleu's prison cell. It was an exceptionally lucid six-and-a-half hours of recollection and reflection, beginning with his memories of learning how to use the letterpress printer in the basement of his junior high school, all the way to his becoming a high-profile detainee. But there were gaps in his story.

I met with Bleu again to talk about an idea I had for a book that would be one part Bleu Mobley memoir (based largely on the tapes), and one part retrospective (documenting all of his published books including selected excerpts). "And, uh, for the memoir part," I bumbled, "would it be all right with you if we did one or two interviews to help me fill in a few gaps?" He smiled, shook his head and said, "What's the matter, Warren? Don't you have better things you can spend your time on?"

I admitted to him that I was going through a personal/professional crisis of my own, and the idea of basking inside his work (which I had long admired) and his story (which I was fascinated by) could be a lifesaver for me. He asked for a little time to think about it and talk it over with his family.

A week later Bleu agreed to let me edit a book about him, as long as:

- nothing about his life was included if it didn't in some way connect to his life in books
- his share of royalties went to the *Cell By Cell Prison Writing Workshop* that he started at the federal detention center.

I happily agreed to these terms.

The one or two interviews I had requested turned into six multi-hour conversations with Bleu, who graciously shared candid behind-the-scenes stories and insights about many of his published books. I feel particularly grateful to Bleu for this, given his well-known aversion to nostalgia and talking about his past work.

[See *There Never Was A Good Old Days* pp. 224, and Bleu's description of his 'post-publication depressions' pp. 138-139.]

As editor of this book, I took the liberty of weaving together content from the prison tapes with content from our taped conversations. The resulting narrative is an intimate self-portrait of one of the most prolific and controversial writers of our time. Since so many of Bleu's own books are written as interior monologues that take place over the course of one day, it seemed appropriate to try to capture the real-time experience that I had listening to the prison tapes—of one man, during one night, retracing his life and career and the chain of events that led him to the center of a national literary and political scandal.

The retrospective catalogue of his books—including some of the miniature pamphlets he "composed" as a young teen (reproduced here for the first time), all his published books, and book-like objects—represents the most comprehensive overview of Bleu Mobley's career to date. With such a wealth of material to choose from, selecting the text excerpts was probably the most difficult part of this project. A complete Bleu Mobley Reader (not including his articles or blogs) would run more than 28,000 pages! In the interest of making sure each text excerpt reproduced here could stand on its own, I sometimes found it necessary to graft a sentence or paragraph from other parts of that same book, or to combine two or three shorter excerpts into one. When

I asked Bleu if this was okay with him, he made it clear that he trusted me. "Do whatever you want, man. It's your friggin' book."

I considered including testimonies of Bleu's friends and relatives, enemies and critics, former colleagues and assistants, as well as putting in my own annotations. In the end, I decided that my job was not to contextualize or judge, but to step aside and give you the man in his own words. His truth, his memories, his voluminous writings and the multitude of voices that speak through them—even his deceptions and contradictions—are plenty of perspective for one book.

Is Bleu Mobley an important man of letters or a sellout, a book visionary or an inspired fool, a person of principle or an opportunist, a champion of the voiceless or an elitist? Does the truth about Bleu Mobley reside within his fictions, within his non-fictions, in what he confides to a tape recorder inside his prison cell, or in his actions and personal relations? Is America a beacon of democracy or an out-of-control empire, and is Bleu Mobley its conscience or an ungrateful traitor? Is this story a parable of the rise and fall of a culture, or a swan song for the book itself as a medium?

I won't be offering up any answers to these questions myself, or making any claims to being objective about the work or the life of Bleu Mobley. My job is done here. The book is in your hands now.

Warren Lehrer

A NOTE ON THE BOOK FORMAT The approach to putting this book together is inspired by Bleu Mobley's "book composing" techniques, including his idiosyncratic approach to typography, use of pictorial devices, and reproduction of facsimiles.

Memoir
Composed entirely of his own words, Bleu's memoir is a composite of his prison tapes and the one-on-one interviews with Warren Lehrer.

Chapters
A Life In Books is divided into nine chapters.

Book Covers
The books reproduced here are of Bleu's own copies, which he used for public readings, interviews, and scrawling revision ideas. (Whether out of superstition, loyalty, or laziness, Bleu never replaced any of his original author's copies with fresher ones. He also holds onto old clothes, shoes, cars, and friends.)

Sample Page Spread

2
SANDBOX

As a journalist, it was my job to cover what is. As an ex-journalist, I felt free to imagine *what if.* With a good deal of time on my hands between paying gigs, I ended up speculating about any number of things—including the blood-boiling enmity of polar opposites that I kept finding in nearly every sphere of life, not only in the war zones I'd recently come home from, but in politics, in workplaces, and in families. *What if* all these "enemies" somehow got their wires crossed, even for only one day? *What if* flashes of light lit up pockets of acrimony and misunderstanding around the world? Could embittered hearts be opened, or would it make no difference at all?

I didn't write my peculiar first novel with any purpose in mind, least of all to have an effect on the way people behaved toward each other. I didn't even know for sure if what I'd written was actually a novel. *The Switch* was an experiment played out in the sandbox of my imagination. If I hadn't bumped into Ron Hodamarsky at an upstate printer's flea market, *The Switch* might still be an unread manuscript resting peaceably in a file folder somewhere.

A former High School of Printing classmate of mine, Ronald owned a garage-based small press in Middletown, New York. Although the list of his Jewel Weed Editions focused exclusively on books of poetry written by Ronald's wife, Pat Hodamarsky, Ronald really dug the premise of *The Switch* when I described it to him in the flea market parking lot. Without even reading a word of it, he offered to publish the book if I would pay for all the printing and binding expenses—including the cost of having his small secondhand offset press fixed. I agreed if I could do my own typesetting and design the cover. (Having a hand in the design of my books and book covers became a habit I couldn't shake.)

Published in an edition of 300 copies, my first novel received reviews in two obscure literary journals—favorably in one and very unfavorably in the other. The reviewer who panned it (perhaps my first faceless enemy) particularly disliked the book's structure:

It is dizzying enough slogging through a novel where every character is simultaneously someone else, but then halfway through *The Switch,* the reading orientation flips 180 degrees, forcing the reader to physically turn the book upside down. Once vertigo sets in you realize this device is nothing but a cheap trick to get you to notice the book's palindromic cover design that forms a face from both orientations. Cute, but it doesn't make up for the preposterous premise and the altogether convoluted read. *Switch it off!*

A NOVEL BY BLEU MOBLEY

THE SWITCH

excerpt

Shortly after waking up, you realize that you are in the body of your number one nemesis. You look in the mirror. You see your enemy, you think the thoughts of your enemy, but somehow your own consciousness is still there too, as a quiet witness. You won't like embodying this person throughout the day, but there is nothing you can do to stop it. Should you encounter this person during the day, you'll have a chance to see exactly how they see you because your nemesis has become you for the day as well, witnessing everything you deal with on a daily basis. On this day, switches like these have occurred all over the world.

A Zionist from Tel Aviv finds himself at a café in a Palestinian section of the West Bank, smoking shisha, speaking in Arabic to some friends he's never laid eyes on, cursing the stinking Jews for imprisoning him for eight months without charge and killing his father. In Tel Aviv, a Palestinian man discovers he is standing guard in an Israeli army

THE SWITCH

The Switch A NOVEL
One morning, a woman wakes to find that she's living the life of her archenemy. She experiences everything he sees, does, and thinks throughout the day. Her nemesis has been switched with her as well. On this particular day, switches like these are happening everywhere. Author Bleu Mobley, in his ingenious debut novel, chronicles a day in the lives of five sets of switched enemies: three pairs who come face-to-face every day, and two pairs who have never met but despise the very thought of each other.

1979, Jewel Weed Editions, Middletown, NY

Catalogue Copy/Genres
The copy used here, in most cases, comes from original catalogues or prospectuses advertising first editions.

Publishers & Pub Dates
The name and location of publisher, and the year of the first edition.

Articles/Letters
When Bleu refers to articles, reviews, or letters, every effort was made to find and reproduce the original.

Book Excerpts
This edition of *A Life In Books* includes text excerpts from more than one-third of Bleu's books. Excerpts can run anywhere from one to eight pages in length. In some instances they are reproduced directly from the original. Most often the text has been reformatted for this book. Some excerpts that were not included in this volume are available at www.alifeinbooks.net (along with other archival materials related to Bleu Mobley and his life in books).

CONTENTS
BLEUBLIOGRAPHY

My glow-in-the-dark watch tells me it's 12:04 a.m.

I hear faint cries and murmurs. I hear penance and denial and all variety of whispers, snores, groans, prayers, belches, farts, and toilet flushings. Basking in the odors of 450 grown men, most prominently my own, I close my eyes and imagine a laser beam drilling through cinder block, past razor wire and time. All these nights—waiting. Waiting for the throbbing disc pain (L5S1) to synchronize itself to the beat of my heart, then fade to a dull ache and disappear. Waiting for careening thoughts—of books yet to be written and choices made and remade with the benefit of hindsight—to tire themselves out. Waiting for dreams to come and have their way with me. Waiting for windowless morning, for the guard's footsteps at the end of the tier, the turn of his key in the master lock box, the lock mechanisms flipping over in sequence— *chckachckachckachckachcka*—the cell doors opening from one end of the block to the other, the mad cavalry of feet running onto grated metal floors. Waiting for the second buzzer of the morning, peeling the blanket from my eyes, facing the unforgiving fluorescents. All these nights waiting for a merciful guard with the key of keys to come tell me it's all been a terrible mistake and I can go home now.

The federal prosecutor thought I'd crack after one week. "All we need is the name of your source." The grand jury looked on. *Just give it to him*, they pleaded with sympathetic eyes. I refused. So the judge—bless his wholly owned, technocratic soul—sanctioned me to this federal detention center. (He thought my *silence* showed contempt of court. Imagine what he'd think if I'd spoken!) Two escorts paraded me down the courthouse steps in handcuffs past a gauntlet of barking reporters. One of the marshals placed his hand on my head and pressed, as if I didn't know how to angle myself into a car. For the sake of my daughters, I smiled at the cameras like I wasn't petrified.

Convinced that words—my only means of defending myself—would be of no use to me in a place like this, I prepared for the worst. From the minute I arrived, my pathetic physical condition made me feel like a walking target. Only a handful of inmates seemed to recognize me. To most, I was just the lanky new guy with the limp and thick glasses, jittery as a boiling teakettle. I might as well have been wearing a sign that said:

By my eighth day here, the person I thought myself to be no longer existed: I couldn't work, I was separated from my family, my lawyer was on vacation in Belize, and my cause was uncertain (to say the least, though I dared not mention my doubts to anyone). I had backed myself into a corner, very publicly. Between one soul-piercing buzzer and the next, without any plan or forethought, I stripped my cot of its single sheet and tried tying it into a noose. Having never been a boy scout, I found myself ill-equipped to pull off the deed. My new roommate, Chester, a solidly built kid with spiky blond hair and rattlesnake tattoos spiraling down both arms, walked into our cell in the midst of my fumbling. He gently rescued the sheet from my sweaty hands and patiently showed me the proper technique. Instead of rolling the sheet like a joint, he twisted it. He showed me how to make a knotted loop and how to run the tail of the braided sheet through the loop. And *voilà!* The noose he sculpted in less than three minutes looked like the genuine article, only made from bedsheet instead of rope. It was truly a thing of beauty.

Chester was pleased that I was pleased. We both looked up at the seamless gray cement ceiling and windowless cinderblock walls. As he pulled out the tool kit he kept stashed inside the secret compartment of a Bible, he assured me with a wink that every problem had its solution. He did all of this without a shred of judgment, and I realized that in Chester I had met a true friend. Curious about what made this young cellie of mine tick, I decided to put off trying to kill myself.

After managing a few hours of sleep that night, I woke up feeling a tiny bit grateful for being alive. I remember thinking, *If I had committed suicide, I would have deprived myself of the ability to regret it.* All I had to do was hold out ten more days until my lawyer came back and she'd surely get me out of this cage.

Several weeks later, our appeals were "hung up" somewhere. I imagined a cobwebby office where lunch hours lasted weeks and stamp pads had all dried up or gone missing. Since I wasn't about to cooperate with the grand jury, I had little choice but to begin my acculturation to the alien universe I'd gotten myself into.

Perhaps the hardest adjustment to prison life was accepting the help of others. As someone who grew up with no father and a mother who needed her one and only child to take care of her, I'd grown accustomed to relying on myself. But when I lost my freedom at fifty-four, I became a child again, a wobbly-kneed kid in a strange and frightening new world. Only much to my amazement, some very capable people have been willing—even happy—to offer me their guidance and wisdom.

An unlikely mentor, Chester is in for shooting up his TV with a semi-automatic in his dorm room at college. Unrepentant, he insists the TV was private property; his step-dad paid for it with his own hard-earned money. "Whatever happened to property rights in this country anyway?" Chester often asks in his Texas twang. He says he shot the TV because it was spewing nothing but violent trash. It was an impulse thing at the time, but then he saw it as an act of cultural production. "I was taking this media studies class and I decided to hand in the shot-up TV as my final paper." Instead of getting an A in the class, Chester got kicked out of school and sent back to prison—facing five to ten for violating parole from a prior armed robbery conviction.

For someone still in his twenties, Chester offers lots of advice:

> "Some guy ever tries to mess with you, make sure to let him bruise you a little first. That way if you have to kill him, you can prove it was self-defense."

> "Be straight with people in here. Nothing impresses a con man more than someone who is totally honest with him."

"Only way to survive in the joint besides cultivating an aura of complete and total fear around you is to have *a craft*. Tattooing. Computer hacking. Meth chem. Shank design. Bible or Koran study. Whatever it is, if you do it better than anyone else, it could be your ticket to getting out of here in one piece."

Chester's craft is leatherworking. You should see his wallet: the cobra head, the Aztec patterns, the hand-sewn trimwork, the secret compartment with the head of a vampire flap, the picture holders, and the huge letter **C** that stands for Chester. It's the most amazing wallet I've ever seen. He took a leather workshop the first time he was locked up. Now he boasts of being "the best leather-crafter in the whole god-damn correctional system." If you're a guard or part of the medical or recreational staff, he'll make you anything from scratch, offered the right incentive.

I told Chester straight off, "I don't think I can survive in here. I couldn't lift a ten-pound dumbbell without triggering six months worth of back spasms. I don't have a craft. *I'm a book guy.* All I know how to do is write." Chester looked at me for about a half-second before breaking out in that enormous gold-toothed smile of his.

I let it be known that my writing services were available, free of charge. For two months I became the prison scribe, helping guys write letters to their kids, their lawyers, and all their exes. I wrote scores of letters to ex-wives, ex-lovers, ex-gang members. But the ghostwriting service got way too dicey (after a few of the letters I penned triggered unintended consequences), so I shut it down and started running a writing group. It's the best writing group I've ever been in. Actually, it's the only writing group I've ever been in; the very idea of writing groups used to turn my stomach.*

*From a 1994 Writer's Craft interview with Bleu in the *Bellingham Review*

Q: Have you ever been part of a writing group or writing circle of any kind?
A: The whole idea about writing is to be ALONE with your thoughts—not only to get down what's on your mind, but to find out what's in your mind, and your heart. Writing isn't a team sport. It's not about consensus or agreed-upon notions of good. I don't begrudge anyone who needs a support group for whatever reason, but the last thing I'm interested in doing is to write a book, or write any-thing—by committee.

Chester was the first to join. He compared it to playing three-card-monte. "To get a crowd, you gotta start with a bluffer who makes the game look easy. In no time, suckers are drawn in like flies to flypaper." We're sitting around a table in the rec room, just Chester and me. He takes out his wallet and shows me pictures of his two fathers and asks me to guess which one's the real one. I guess the wrong one, then he tells me his fathers are brothers. His uncle is his step-dad. I throw a pad and pen on the table and ask him to write about it. He says, "Nobody wants to read about this. Most people can't handle it."

"If you can *live* it," I tell him, "the least anyone else can do is *read* about it." Soon as I hear those words coming out of my mouth, I correct myself. "Forget anybody else. Just put down *My uncle's my step-dad* and keep writing. Whatever comes to you. Don't stop." In one sitting Chester wrote about both his dads and a good deal about his mom, whom he calls Mama Aunty. (She divorced his father then married his father's brother, "which was great for her because she didn't have to change her last name.") He only scratched the surface of what he could remember before running out of paper, and sure enough there was a crowd around wanting to know what he was writing, *"your life story or something?"* That was on a Tuesday. By Friday there were four guys sitting with me at the table writing without worrying about making a masterpiece or a best-fucking-seller. Within a month there were sixteen guys in the writing group, and then the warden caught wind of it and made me an offer I couldn't refuse—a room with a table, an ergonomic chair, a computer, all the ice packs, paper and pens I needed, twenty-seven desk-chairs, and unrestricted access to the library.

I've since edited a book of writings by my fellow inmates that is due out in the spring. All proceeds will go to fund the writing group. First thing—they can hire someone to run it after I'm gone. I'll still come and visit—volunteer once or twice a month from the outside. But to come from the outside, I have to first get out of here.

My lawyer admitted to me yesterday, she's hit a brick wall with our appeals. They've all bounced back **DENIED!** I thought I'd be here one night, *a week* at the most. This is my 297th day and none of the judges have blinked. What do they care if I die of cell-rot without even a trial? They're not beholden to justice; they're political appointees who know exactly where their bread is caviared.

All this time I've kept mum, defending the principle of confidentiality. I don't want to let anyone down, but I'm dying to see my wife for more than five hours a month, out from under the watchful eye of the Unit Officer. I long to be with my daughters even on odd-numbered days—when I'm free, I'll treat every odd-numbered day like it's a holiday. I'm ready to give back my orange jumpsuits, my sanctioned footwear and all the triplicate request forms. I'm ready to eat food that doesn't taste like the cardboard box it comes in; ready to take long walks again, listen to the sounds of the ocean, get caught in a traffic jam, change a flat tire, have *irrational* fears of getting my throat slit—instead of reasonable ones.

"As long as you answer all their questions truthfully, they have to release you." That's what my lawyer says. The only problem is. . . the principle of confidentiality is just an excuse. The real story, *the truth*, will disgrace me. They'll leak what I say. They're not supposed to, but they will. It's a hard bargain to make: Freedom for Disgrace. My shame, raw meat tossed to the chattering boob-tube bloodsuckers and the finger-licking blogiacs. I'll tell them only what they need to know.

But I owe my readers a lot more than rumors of a reluctant confession, especially those of you who took the time to write to me after I got locked up, and all the authors and journalists around the world who looked to me as some kind of stalwart soldier, and my editors and assistants who (for the most part) kept my confidences, and my beloved wife,

Aconsha, who for some unfathomable reason hasn't given up on me yet, and my daughter Frida who says she's so proud of me, and my younger daughter, Ella, who rightfully feels abandoned by her dad. I owe each and every one of you an explanation. I am not the hero some have made me out to be, that I made myself out to be. I violated a sacred trust. If only I understood better myself how I let this happen, and when exactly I started losing my way. I'm still trying to puzzle it out—*how a life writes itself*. How one thing leads to another without a plan or a map; how a simple compulsion to tell stories—turned into something else, twisted this way and that.

I never wanted to write a memoir. Certainly not a fallen-celebrity memoir, whispered into a microcassette recorder in the middle of the night from the wrong side of freedom. All these years, I preferred to write about *other* people, real and imagined. Looking past my twice-broken nose out into the world has been far more rewarding to me than gazing endlessly into a mirror of negligible returns. But my current circumstances and too many sleepless nights leave me no choice but to reflect on my own life. If I begin at the end, you'd probably close the book on me forever. You'd shake your head, thinking, *What an idiot! Why should I believe another word he has to say?* That's one reason I need to begin at the beginning. And maybe by coming to grips with my story and putting it in a book, I can set myself free of it. For mine has been a life in books (101 of them, I'm told). Books have been my oxygen, my fix, my wings, my armor and fortress, my bread and butter, and now the cause of my demise. And if the story of my life in books can be my last book, I might (finally) be able to start a new chapter.

1

THE INVISIBLES

I was inadvertently introduced to writing in the basement of the prison-like Joan of Arc Junior High School on the western edge of Queens, New York. In between the mandatory math, science and English classes, those of us tracked as terminally working-class were herded into subterranean rooms to learn how to work with our hands. If you were a girl in 1966, you took typing and home economics. If you were a boy, it was shop. Shop teachers initiated us with stories of careless boys chopping off their hands on metal cutters, slicing off fingers on band saws, electrocuting themselves into comas. I was quiet, skinny as a chopstick, and allergic to almost everything. Terrified by the prospect of losing limbs or consciousness, I was drawn to the print shop, where the mild-mannered Mr. Guy Gutiero presided (a lonely king in an ink-splotched robe crowned with a green see-through visor).

I fell in love with that kingdom on the first day of seventh grade. It was terribly outdated—no offset presses, linotype or even mimeograph machines. No phototypositors or stat cameras. It was simply a carefully preserved letterpress shop—*á la* Gutenberg—with lead and wood type, which meant you had to set every word of a text by hand, one letter at a time. The only shop that required no real mechanical or physical prowess, The Print Shop, otherwise known as "Letterpress," was more akin to playing with blocks. I loved the feel of the wood furniture used to square up type to the press, the smell of typewash, the sound of properly inked-up rollers "like the purr of butter in an iron skillet on a low flame." I loved all the terms and expressions Mr. Gutiero used to describe the craft he had once practiced at places like *The New York Post* and *The Herald Tribune*. I loved that type*faces* came in *families*, and individual *characters* were made up of *eyes*, *ears*, and sometimes *tails* with finial swashes, and pages had *headers* and *footers* set into galleys that got chased to the bed of the press and locked up with a key, and image blocks could *bleed* off the edge of a page or across the gutter, and using just the right amount of padding made a *kiss impression* on the paper, like lipstick on a cheek, as opposed to too much pressure, which *bites* the paper. However old-world this world was, it was a new world to me, full of corporeal letters and aromatic solvents.

While the school band provided live music at many Joan of Arc events, and "Art Squad" students created most of the school's signs and murals, those of us heavily into the print shop were charged with putting out the bi-weekly school newspaper, *The Oracle*. Mr. Gutiero taught me and the only other self-selected print-shop geek, a black kid named Barry

Freewell, secrets of the news trade from picas and points to the tenets of good journalism. No matter how insignificant our junior high school rag was, as far as Mr. Gutiero was concerned it was nothing less than the first draft of history. He kept a framed copy of the first amendment hanging on the wall over the galley racks and asked us to consider why it was the *first* amendment and not the fourth or twenty-fifth. "These amendments are not just words on paper. They represent *rights.* Whatever we print needs to serve the public's right to know."

Gutiero instructed us to keep careful notes, seek multiple sources, offer confidentiality to those who need to be protected, and fearlessly question certainties. He lectured us on the differences between reaching an objective conclusion and having a personal opinion. The expression of opinion was only to take place on the editorial page. Above all, Mr. G. pressed us to "dig for the truth" and do more than feed "the masses and the powerful" happy or trivial news. Barry and I rolled our eyes at the "masses" bit, since most students and hardly any teachers even bothered to pick up *The Oracle,* let alone read it. By "the powerful" we assumed he meant the principal, Mr. Collingsworth, whom Gutiero clearly detested.

I took up the challenge and wrote a front page article questioning Mr. Collingsworth for removing a student painting of two dogs having sex. The headline read:

INDECENT CENSOR
A MATTER OF PRINCIPAL

I wrote exposés on the accounting teacher who helped parents with their investments at a "special parent discount," the assistant principal who spent hours a day on a treadmill in his office, and the drama teacher whose rehearsal "method" was suspiciously hands-on when it came to "the student body."

Gutiero started catching heat from Collingsworth about all the muckraking going on in *The Oracle*. He suggested I consider writing about "ordinary" people and recommended that I keep a notebook with me to write down stuff I came across on a daily basis. "You have the *got you* thing down pretty good. Now try covering the kids who never run for class president or become stars of the basketball team, the parents who are working slobs doing whatever they can just to make ends meet, the never-beens and wouldn't-want-to-bes, the losers and little heroes that we rarely hear about. Find out *their* stories. Everybody's got a story, Bleu. See what you can come up with."

Taking Gutiero's new directive to heart, I approached people I barely knew, total strangers even, asking them to tell me their stories. I started a column in *The Oracle* called "The Invisibles." Every other week my column featured the story of a different unsung someone I had met in the Queensbridge Housing project where I lived—and beyond. There was Maricella the Cuban soothsayer who talked telepathically with her twin sister, the only sibling of eight who refused to leave the island after Castro took over the family farm. There was Butch, the one-eyed garbage collector who earned his distinctive red, white, and blue eye patch from a chunk of shrapnel in the Korean war. There was Henry, the super of our apartment building, whose grandfather had been a slave in Alabama—and Henry had the chains to prove it. One column Gutiero especially liked was about an old lady who made and sold dolls:

THE INVISIBLES
Sarah The Doll Lady

By BLEU MOBLEY

Sarah sells her colorful hand-sewn dolls on a bench in the park at my housing complex, if you can call concrete walkways with two-foot wide strips of grass a park. Sarah does. "I love it out here in the park. My husband was younger than me but he was sick in bed for twenty years and I'd sit out here making a living. It's four months since he passed away and here I am talking to people, sitting. I have friends, but they're also poor people. Most of them can't buy a doll for twenty-five or thirty dollars. But some people have the money. Usually they come from outside the project. They can tell me what color, what kind—Raggedy Rita or Big-Eyed Bonnie or the Persian doll. I've been making the Persian doll a year already. Whatever they want, I make. I used to be a beautiful girl myself. You wouldn't believe it if I showed you the pictures. The second my husband saw me he scooped me up. I was twenty-three but I looked sixteen. Now I make up my dolls instead. Did I introduce you to my Flapper doll? Isn't she something?"

Like forsythia, Sarah pops up in the park every springtime, only with her you're never quite sure if she made it through the winter until you see her out there with your own two eyes. From a distance Sarah looks small and shriveled and her dolls don't sit up straight on her bench, but once you sit next to her and get to talking, she's as big as a movie in a widescreen theater and her dolls spring to life just the same. Sarah tells me I'm not the first reporter who ever wrote a story about her. "*The Daily News* did an article years ago and then everybody started coming around. They printed a picture of me with a man doll, the French one with the sequin hat. For a while, that was the only doll people wanted because it was *famous*. I haven't been able to make that one lately. I'm working on a new doll, but it's going slow. I'm so mixed up with my husband passing and the funeral. I'm the oldest in my family. They're all dying before me. I'm naming the new doll, Hairy Harry. That was my husband's name—Harry. Every one of his organs went to pot. Just like his father he had bad organs but a full head of hair to the very end. Whenever someone dies, I try to make a doll in their memory. Even if most people don't buy any, they see the dolls sitting on the bench with me like we're a family. It puts a smile on their day and that makes me smile."

After writing a dozen or so of these columns, it dawned on me that my mother qualified as one of these "invisible" people. According to my Aunt Chloe, my mother was "born with a paintbrush in her hand." For years I took this much-repeated description literally, until I was old enough to understand that it was only an expression. "Ever since I can remember," Aunt Chloe told me, "your mother was drawing and painting pictures. Whatever she did, she had tons of talent—singing, dancing, making friends with boys." Apparently, her contagious joy for life attracted many suitors, several of whom proposed to her after their first dates. Yet, she never married. I could have written an "Invisibles" profile of her as a single mother, a much more unusual phenomena in those days. But she never drew attention to her single parent status, never uttered the phrase or complained, probably because her mother raised her own kids almost entirely by herself. My mother did have a father, knew him, even revered him, but he wasn't around very much.

My grandfather was a Jewish rag merchant/entrepreneur/socialist who did business in Mexico under the alias Jake Mobley. His real name was Mordechai Jacobson. When he wasn't in Mexico, Jacobson had a whole other life and a whole other family on the Lower East Side of New York. By all accounts he adored my mother (his second Mexican-born daughter). He showered her with affection and brought her art supplies and exquisitely printed art books whenever he visited. After my grandmother had a miscarriage seven months into her third pregnancy, she fell into a severe depression; Jake, impatient with her doldrums and her inability to bear him a son, left for New York never to return to their house on Reforma Boulevard. Not about to be left high and dry after all those years and a thousand promises, my grandmother, Monique, turned her sadness into anger and determination—brought her two daughters to New York in search of their father, only to find out that her two-timing, deadbeat husband had died of pneumonia shortly after abandoning her.

Instead of going back to Mexico, Monique Mobley found a job at a girdle factory on the Lower East Side and an apartment within walking distance. On weekends she worked as a barmaid at a former speakeasy in the West Village in order to have enough money to continue raising her daughters the way she was accustomed to, the way they deserved. She sent the gifted younger child, Rose (my mother), to drawing classes at the Art Students' League until she was fifteen. Then Rose attended the High School of Music and Art, and as soon as she graduated she took her portfolio and her infectious charm and got herself a job as a sketcher with Claire McCardell, one of the top-flight fashion designers of the day.

In a box my mother hid in our Queensbridge apartment—behind my baby blanket on the highest shelf in the linen closet—were dozens of black-and-white photographs with Rose Mobley looking as glamorous and radiant as any movie starlet, in wide-brimmed hats and slinky low-cut dresses, mixing it up with other artists, jazz musicians, writers, intellectuals, and left-wing political types. The pictures were all dated from the mid-1940s up until 1950 when she turned twenty-two—and her first mental breakdown landed her at Creedmore State Hospital where she was diagnosed with schizophrenia. (The doctors later downgraded their diagnosis to manic depression, but back then, if you disappeared for a while and came back not quite right in the head, people just called you crazy.)

Throughout the years, my mother's psychotic breaks were interspersed with periods of lucidity. During one of those periods when she was twenty-four, she met the man who fathered me. I never met my father or knew anything about him except what Aunt Chloe once divulged to me—after she'd had one too many gin and tonics—about him being. . . *a very decent. . . a very famous. . . a very important man. . .* who was married and had a family of his own, but had nonetheless fallen head over heels in love with my mother and carried on a secret love affair with her for four months. Even after he realized she had serious problems, according to Chloe's glassy-eyed recollection, he still loved her, but he was very married and very much in the public eye and traveled so much that he and my mom, "tragically, were never meant to last."

"And who was he?" I asked.

Chloe looked at me—after I asked this simple question—as if I had woken her from a dream. She answered my question with question.

"Who was who?"

"My father!" I said. "The man you were just telling me about."

"A lot of men went out with your mother. She was always the one men went after."

"Just tell me his name."

"Whose name?" Chloe asked.

"What you were just telling me. About my *famous* father."

"I wasn't saying anything of the kind, child. You're imagining things again. You're a lot like your mother sometimes."

"Am I like my father?"

"In ways, yes."

"Aha! So who is he?"

"Who is *who*?"

Chloe was a stone wall on the subject after that.

All her life my mother kept the identity of my father a secret. As far as she ever let on, my daddy was a stork, a whisper in the night, someone whose name she just couldn't remember, a good man like you, dear (don't worry yourself about it), a divine intervener, a seed depositor, a good for nothing, a drifter, a hobo, a fly-by-nighter, a dream, a dreamer, a nightmare, a song, a songbird, a one-act play, a one-note samba, a freedom fighter, a saint, a ladykiller, a nobody—a constant change of subject.

Nearly half the time, my mother was on the upside of the bipolar roller coaster ride that shaped most of her adult life. When I was very young, her mood swings and delusions frightened, confused, and sometimes mesmerized me. As I grew older, my expectations of her ever being a normal parent dissipated. Her inappropriate behavior and excitability became, at worst, an embarrassment. Sometimes I'd pretend not to know who she was. She spoke too loudly (alternately in French, English, Spanish, Yiddish, and Polish). She hugged and kissed too hard and laughed and cried like a child. This supposedly grown-up person frequently rearranged the furniture in our apartment, or gave away all the money in her wallet to a homeless person, or walked gleefully down the middle of Queens Boulevard (one time), telling the policeman she was just looking for God; had he seen or heard from Her by any chance?

In her own scattershot way, my mother did provide for me. She made sure I always had a roof over my head and some kind of food to eat every day, was enrolled in school, had a library card, clothes on my back (including some very peculiar-looking shirts and sweaters that she lovingly stitched together with her own hands). And most of the time she had back-up care for me when she was in the hospital or in a bad way. For all her flaws, there were times my mother was pure magic. We lived in the largest public housing project in the country—a complex of thirty-four near-identical six-story apartment buildings— in a small, dark apartment that looked out onto other brick buildings. But to Rose Mobley our "home" was a kind of Eden where we could discover the wonders of nature, science, and art. We chased wasps, roaches, and mice around the apartment for hours until we caught them in jars or boxes, then set them free in the park. I remember one time it was raining for two weeks straight until one morning we were eating breakfast and the clouds must have parted and a single ray of sunlight hit my glass of orange juice causing fan-shaped rainbows to rake across the kitchen wall. That's when my mother explained to me that all colors come from white light, and she and I watched the spectral shadow play for a long time until the screen again became a kitchen wall, in need of painting. And I'll never forget the incredible drum solos she heard in the clanking polyrhythms of the radiator with her eyes closed and her long swirls of hair shaking side to side and her fingers jabbing the air pointing out the off-off versus the off-off-off beats.

Though she never returned to working as a fashion designer, my mother filled up scores of sketchbooks through the years, and when there wasn't a sketchbook or a sheet of paper around (and she was in a manic period), she'd draw or paint on anything: newspapers, shoe-boxes, envelopes, or occasionally the walls of our apartment. I was just about the only person who ever saw my mother's art, which was passionate and colorful, often unfinished, and more and more childlike as she got older.

I wrote a draft of an "Invisibles" column about my mother, but it didn't feel right exposing her in the school newspaper since she was such a private person. So I composed the story into a miniature-sized book with no names attached, printed it on one sheet of paper folded down to a single sixteen-page folio, and bound it with the saddle-stitcher Mr. Gutiero kept in the back of the print shop.

Measuring just three-and-a-half inches tall, my very first book was titled:

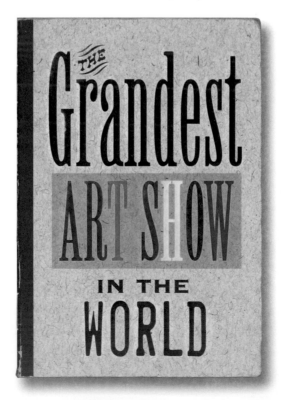

the complete text

Mother is a famous artist that no one knows about yet. You can see her work in our apartment, but for some reason, nobody except the few people we already know are allowed in. She does most of her artwork at home or around the neighborhood, but from time to time she goes to the South Shore of New Jersey to draw

or just to look around.

———

One time when I was nine years old, she took me to a New Jersey marshland not too far from Staten Island. I'll never forget, it was a Sunday, late afternoon, middle of winter. We sat there freezing in my Aunt's gold Rambler station wagon that my mother borrowed for the day. There was no heat on in the car and my mother's window was three-quarters open because we were there to watch the sunset. *Together.*

———

Shortly after we got there, my mother looked up at the sky and said, "Today is going to be a good one. I can tell by the atmospheric conditions and the moisture and the wind velocity" and all this meteorological terminology that I had no idea my mother knew. She was definitely pumped for the occasion and excited to share it with me, her only son. "We're going to have a fantastically colorful sunset today! It's going to be quite a show." Well that was just about the last thing a nine-year-old kid wants to be doing on a Sunday — sitting in the freezing cold in a dumpy car with his mother watching the sunset. But at the same time, I have to admit, it was kind of amazing. It was like this huge planetarium light show, only there was no technology involved except for my mother's stop-watch and her sketchbook and watercolors. Actually, she never touched the sketchbook or the watercolors that day, but she did keep looking at the stopwatch. "In three seconds the shadows over there are going to change from Prussian blue to magnesium blue and then to a kind of luminescent mauve." Sure enough the sun went down a few more degrees. Then she said, "These clouds up here are going to turn like a florescent orange-pink," and she was right! I looked up at her and I noticed her eyes weren't blinking at all, I think so she wouldn't miss even a fraction of a second. And then I saw her body was shaking and it scared me a little because I knew she wasn't shaking from the cold but from the beauty of watching the sun go down. And then I was shaking too, not so much from the cold (because I didn't feel cold anymore), and not so much from the beauty of the sunset, but from looking up at my mother, almost in shock, wondering how she knew *in advance* what the sky was going to do before it happened. It was as if my mother (who you might think, if you saw her on the street, is just an ordinary person) had orchestrated the grandest art show in the world, and I was the audience.

Anonymous
© 1967

I printed four copies of the book: one for my mother, one for myself, one for Barry Freewell (who helped with the binding), and one for Mr. Gutiero, who inspected the typography on the cover and put it up to his nose to smell the freshness of the ink. Before opening it, he asked if it was fiction or non-fiction. I asked him why it mattered. He said it was important to know if a book is true or made up. I asked him, "If non-fiction is *the truth,* why is it defined in the negative? Wouldn't it make more sense to call true stories just that— *true* stories—and call novels and other made-up stories *non-true* stories?" Gutiero looked at me like I was asking an interesting but ultimately useless question. "I think it has something to do with fiction having more longevity than things you read in the newspaper or even in history books, which are always being revised."

I persisted. "Why would *non-true* stories have more longevity than *true* stories?"

Gutiero scratched his bald head. "Maybe because non-fiction is held to such a high standard of accuracy, it's considered a more restrictive medium than fiction, where the writer is free to make stuff up."

I thought to myself, *What kind of world allows truth to play second fiddle to fiction?*

"If I answered you that my book was fiction, would that make you more interested in it?"

"No. As a newspaperman and history buff, I prefer non-fiction. But I've got to tell you, Bleu, a hell of a lot of people—like *my wife* for instance and most of the English teachers at this school—swear by fiction."

Seeking a more straightforward answer, I went to a source that never equivocates.

> **fic·tion**. *noun.* **1.** The act of feigning, inventing, or imagining; as, by a mere fiction of the mind. From the Latin *fictio,* meaning shaping. **2.** An invented narration or story that is "made-up" by the author, whether oral or written. **3.** A story told in order to deceive; a fabrication; opposed to fact or reality. **4.** Lie. Falsehood. Fictitious.

> **non·fic·tion**. *noun.* **1.** A literature that is not fictional. **non·fic·tion·al**. *adjective.*

Feeling even more perplexed, I consulted my mother who admitted to not being an expert on the subject, but guessed that "by being free to invent characters out of their imagination, fiction writers can probably get at more of the truth than news reporters. Like in art, don't you prefer pictures that aren't so perfectly realistic?" I looked at the watercolor she had been painting by the window. There was a lot of emotion in it, but very little resemblance to the scene outside.

I handed her a signed copy of *The Grandest Art Show in the World.* She read it and cried, kissed both my hands one finger at a time, and told me it was the most precious gift anyone had ever given her. A week later the book disappeared from the apartment.

By my last year at Joan of Arc, I was composing stories completely from scratch and printing them into books. I use the word *composing* because I used a *composing stick* to write these stories. An essential tool of any letterpress shop, the composing stick is a rectangular metal tray that you hold in the palm of one hand as you pluck alphanumeric characters from a case of type with your other hand. The first time Mr. G. showed us a composing stick he demonstrated how the old-time printers used it to set the writer's copy into type. Then he stood up from his stool, barely able to contain his excitement, and declared, "But *you're* going to be both the writers *and* the printers, like Benjamin Franklin and William Duane were in the early days of America."

I wrote and edited my little stories at home using a secondhand manual typewriter, then I set them in the print shop, until one day by accident I discovered the real power of the composing stick. I had written an "Invisibles" column about a neighbor of ours who had suffered a very bad stroke; the woman had to learn to speak all over again like she was a baby, even though her mind still had the knowledge and memories of a seventy-one-year old. For some reason I forgot to bring the typewritten story to school, so I grabbed a composing stick, opened up a drawer of nine-point Garamond type, and began plucking out

        l e t t e r s,

                  a n d

                       t h e

                            l e t t e r s

                                  f o r m e d

                                        words,

                          and the words

                formed sentences,

           and by the time the bell rang

               I had composed a little story about a mother and daughter in Vietnam who got hit by a mortar shell on their way home from working in the rice paddies. The eight-year-old girl only had minor injuries, but her mother was unconscious for weeks. When the mother finally woke up, it became apparent that she had lost her ability to speak. Over the next few years the little girl taught her mother how to pronounce letters and words and put sentences together just as the mother had taught her.

I printed a cover, sewed it up, and titled it:

In composing this little book, I violated several rules I had set for myself, most notably: *Never write about any person you haven't met or any place you haven't been to.* Not an altogether bad rule, but now I had a new rule: *Don't become a prisoner to rules.*

I composed a whole suite of miniature books letting the composing stick lead the way. Using the key Mr. Gutiero gave me, I'd come into the print shop after school hours, turn off all but one set of lights, pull a few drawers of type out of their cabinets, sit down on a stool, and begin my journey into I knew not where.

The books I called *My Famous Fathers* came out of this period. Ever since I can remember, I've dreamed of the father I never knew. I imagined him teaching me how to ride a bicycle, taking me to ball games and concerts, telling me about girls and the ways of the world, and imparting words of wisdom about what to believe and who not to trust. After Aunt Chloe spilled the beans about my father being a famous man, my fantasies sharpened. That he also may have been married and traveled a lot narrowed the field of possibilities too.

For my *Famous Fathers* series, I used a rare binding I saw diagrammed in a musty old manual in the print shop. The do-si-do binding, used most often to pair editions of the Old and New Testaments, forms a Z, allowing two separate volumes to be bound into one. On the one side, I described what each of my "famous fathers" did to transform the world. On the other, I portrayed the kind of relationship that particular famous father might have had with me had he followed his lust with responsibility. I focused my fantasies on heroic figures—great artists, entertainers, athletes, scientists, journalists, revolutionaries, statesmen, and outlaws—who could have conceivably been my father: were famous enough, old enough, in some cases married or entangled enough, and could have come through New York in the winter of 1952. I didn't limit my *Famous Fathers* to any particular race, creed, or color. I already saw myself as the by-product of generations (perhaps centuries) of love affairs and lies, of conquerors and conquered, of talent and madness. The *known* ingredients of my gene pool being part Jewish, part Polish, part French, and part Mexican already made me an indefinable American hybrid, free to imagine myself as anything. And for lack of an actual, physical father, free to make him the father (or fathers) of my dreams.

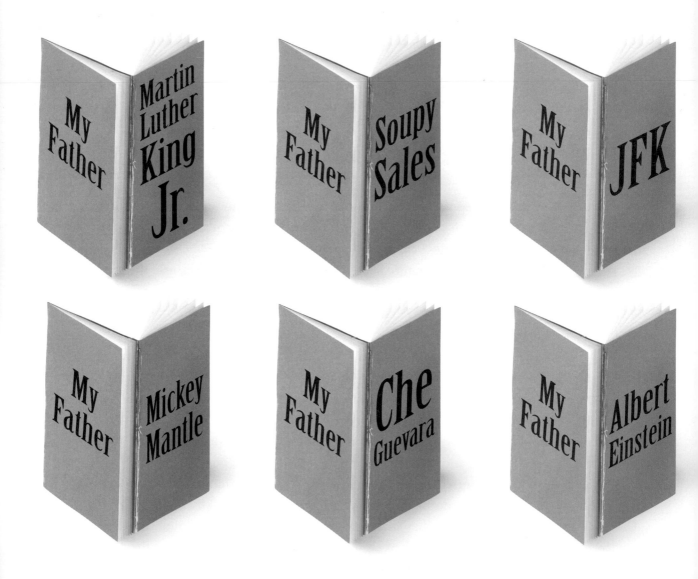

There are no known copies of the *My Famous Fathers* books still in existence. These simulations are based on a sketch Bleu made for this publication.

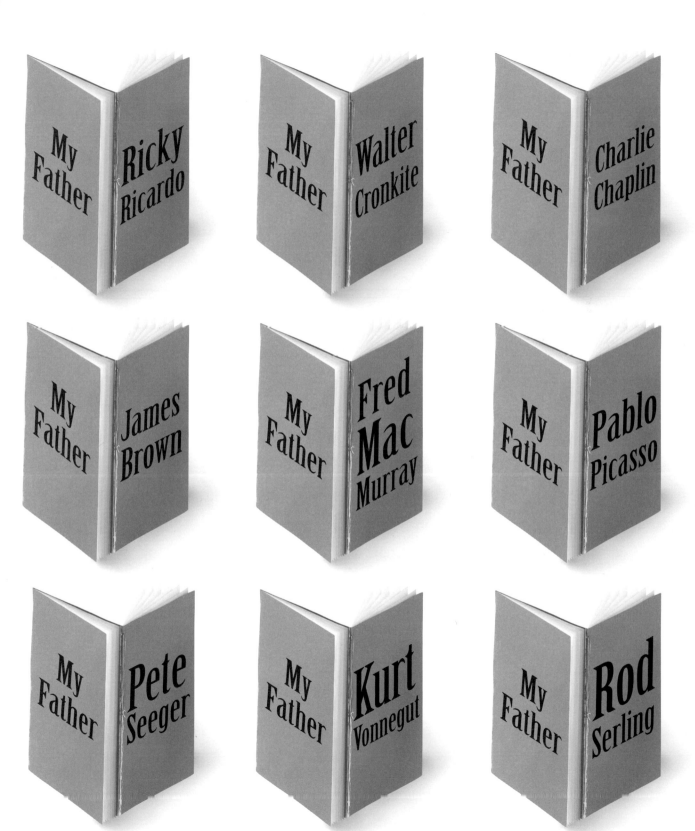

 My Father Groucho **Marx**

 My Father Woody Guthrie

 My Father Orson Welles

 My Father Timothy **Leary**

 My Father **Dr.** Jonas **Salk**

 My Father Steve **Allen**

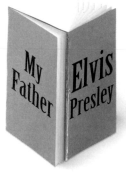 My Father **Elvis** Presley

 My Father **J.D.** Salinger

 My Father Salvador **Dalí**

 My Father Leonard Bernstein

 My Father **Red** Skelton

 My Father Chuck **Berry**

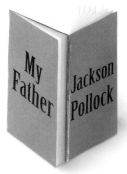 My Father **Ray** Bradbury

 My Father Jackson Pollock

 My Father **Dr.** Seuss

My Father **Jean** Shepherd

And finally, even though he died seven years before I was conceived:

No other man provided for me and my mother like Franklin Delano Roosevelt did. We lived in a federal housing project built in 1938 to provide affordable housing for poor people. My mother received a monthly Social Security check due to her mental disability, and I knew that one day when I was old I'd receive Social Security retirement checks— all because of FDR. He was THE MAN, even though he couldn't have been *the man*.

A week after completing the printing and binding of *My Famous Fathers*, Martin Luther King Jr. was assassinated. I'll always remember the chill that went through me watching Walter Cronkite announce his murder on the evening news, hearing the screams and cries reverberate throughout our housing complex as the word spread and almost everyone at Queensbridge—which was majority African-American by then—spilled onto the streets. Shaken by what she was seeing, my mother started turning channels, but it was the same on every station—spontaneous riots breaking out across the country, images of the balcony at the Lorraine Motel, images of people weeping in Memphis, weeping in Atlanta, weeping in Chicago and Detroit and Birmingham and Boston and San Francisco, as public officials called for calm. A few times in the past, the television had been the purveyor of apocryphal "messages" beamed at my mother—leaving her understandably wary of the boob tube's authority. On the night of April 4th, 1968, watching those pictures flash across the screen, hearing our city within a city begin to shake, she probably didn't know what was real and what wasn't. She turned off the television, slinked into her bedroom and wouldn't come out. I had no way of knowing what was going on in her head. All I knew—she once told me that Martin Luther King Jr. was the closest thing to a prophet she'd seen in her lifetime. And now the prophet was dead. I wanted to go outside and join the crowd of angry mourners, but Walter Cronkite had said that a well-dressed white man was seen running from the site of the shooting in Memphis. For the first time in my life it hit me that I wasn't just me: I was a white guy.

The following night, I took all my *Famous Fathers* books to what I thought to be a well concealed spot under the Triboro Bridge, dumped them in a trash can, and burned them. Somehow, I got it in my head that my audacious act of setting into print a fantasy that

Martin Luther King Jr. could have been my father had something to do with his being assassinated. When I came home my mother was still locked inside her room. The next night she was hospitalized and didn't return home for five months.

Instead of advancing to a high school with a good writing or journalism program, I ended up going to a vocational school dedicated to training the next generation of printers. Unlike many of my High School of Printing classmates who went on to work at commercial print shops after graduating, I had my sights on college, and after eighteen years of living with my mother in our meager apartment, I desperately wanted to go *away* to college. It didn't matter to me if the college had a pretty campus or ivy covered buildings or even much of a reputation. As long as it was out of commuting distance to Queensbridge Housing, I was ready to enroll. But the City University of New York was the only college we could afford—it was tuition-free.

During the summer of my junior year, I interned at *The New York Daily News*, even got a few of my own bylines. They dispatched me to the Bronx to cover a missing baby, to Brooklyn and Harlem to cover broken fire hydrants, and all over the city to cover the graffiti problem. The only problem I had covering the graffiti problem was I didn't see any problem with the graffiti. I sneaked a whiff of that opinion into the article, and for some reason it didn't get edited out. After I graduated, the *Daily News* hired me as a stringer for the city desk, and I began my career as a professional writer.

In the fall of 1975 New York City was on the verge of bankruptcy, crime was rampant, and racial tensions were heating up. Assigned to write about the onslaught of homeless people panhandling on the Lower East Side, I wrote a day-in-the-life story about a home-less family and the ways the parents managed to create a sense of normal for their two kids. Assigned to write an article about welfare mothers draining the city coffers, I ended up focusing on the drain of middle-class tax dollars caused by waves of white-flight to the suburbs. Emboldened by the publication of the white-flight article, I asked my editor if I could do a series of stories on life in the suburbs called *Tales in a Cul-De-Sac*. My request was denied with a skunk-eyed stare that said, *You haven't even begun paying the kind of dues needed to propose a series of your own.* Assigned to chase fire trucks and ambulances, I quit.

Still convinced that being a reporter was one of the best ways to change the world for the better, I applied for a job with *New York Newsday*, which had longer articles and a more literate, left-of-center readership than the *Daily News*. For a little more than a year I worked for the city desk writing about sanitation slowdowns, Son of Sam slayings, bomb-ings by Croatian and Puerto Rican nationalists, and the often sleazy machinations of a federally bailed-out city government. I met some amazing gumshoe reporters at *Newsday*, real heroes with guts and passion. I also discovered layer upon layer of political gamesmanship going on at the paper, not only between labor and management but also between hard-nosed reporters with swollen egos who by any logical measure should have been best buddies. The two reporters I looked up to the most hated each other's guts.

Restless to finally get out of New York and away from the paper's disheartening interpersonal conflicts, I requested work with the overseas bureau. Little did I realize that with the granting of my request I would be graduating from the locally disheartening to the globally devastating.

For two years I worked as a foreign correspondent, reporting from the West Bank on the first Israeli settlements, then from South America and the Caribbean reporting on U.S.-backed despotic regimes and anti-leftist guerrilla insurgencies. I should have been scared out of my skull going to the places I went, meeting face-to-face with people who could have killed me and my photographer in a second if they decided we were spies. But I'd do almost anything (back then) to get the story behind the story. The greater the intensity of the conflict, the greater the turn-on. Fueled more by competition than bravery, coated in the protective shield of youth, I convinced myself that I was immune from the dangers that surrounded me, and if I simply wrote the truth, I could nudge history in a better direction.

Maybe I didn't feel scared because I ended up liking most of the people I met; even if I knew that someone was a 'bad guy,' more often than not I could find strands of truth in his side of the story. And the more I learned about what was really going on, the harder it was for me to flatten out the story and squeeze it into 1,200 words. That's what finally burst my bubble of idealism for the job. While working on a series of articles from Haiti, I ran into difficulties with my New York editor who accused me of *editorializing*, even worse—of writing *poetry*. This is a transcription of our last phone conversation, which I happened to tape record for purely professional reasons:

> **By Bleu Mobley**
> HEBRON, (WEST BANK) — "The Giant Who Had Three Sons. That's the original meaning of Kiryat Arba," Eliezer Levinger told a group of grade schoolers in the fledgling Jewish settlement, citing The Book of Joshua, Chapter 14, Verse 15. "Sure, the Palestinians have deep roots here. I won't deny that. But we aren't foreigners either."

> **By Bleu Mobley**
> SAN SALVADOR — "Do you think this is a problem of bad math?" a supporter of Ernesto Rozeville asked me in an armed encampment north of the capital. His wry question and the anger inside it reflect a growing number of credible witnesses from sixteen districts claiming that the populist UNO candidate won last month's election by a resounding 75% of the vote. Election officials here certified his opponent, General Carlos Humberto Romero, the victor.

> **By Bleu Mobley**
> PORT-AU-PRINCE — After losing her job with a mainstream newspaper, an award-winning photojournalist—who spoke to me on condition of anonymity—took a job with an opposition newspaper. When their offices were burned down, she took a job with another opposition newspaper. When the editor-in-chief of that paper was killed

EDITOR: First of all, we're cutting the lead. We can't start a news article 'Behind mountains, there are more mountains.' Why would anyone reading a newspaper article want to keep reading? It says nothing.

MOBLEY: It's a well-known saying in Haiti: *Dèyè mòn gen mòn*.

EDITOR: Well, you're not writing for Haiti. You're writing for a New York readership, for an *American* readership.

MOBLEY: Haitians are American.

EDITOR: Don't get smart with me, Mobley. We've been through all that before.

MOBLEY: Okay. How about we cut the French and go straight to the English translation.

EDITOR: The French was already cut before this conversation started. Now we're cutting the English.

MOBLEY: In the very next sentence I explain what the expression means.

EDITOR: Yes, I can read. 'Behind every mountain there is another, the darkest one nearest you, and back and back lighter and lighter; behind every story, many stories. Behind every invasion, rebellion, and installation of a president-for-life; generations of invasions, rebellions, coups, and installations of presidents-for-life. Behind everything you think you know about Haiti, there is always a more complicated explanation. Behind every man or woman, well, it all depends how much time you have to explore.' This is a newspaper, Mobley, not a poetry magazine.

MOBLEY: Okay. So you're cutting the first paragraph. Let's move on.

EDITOR: I don't see why you need to get into the doctor's whole family tree.

MOBLEY: I think it's relevant and interesting that Pierre was taught his lineage by his parents going all the way back to Africa, to the 1790s slave rebellion, up to his being born, and everything else I wrote in that paragraph. In this *one man*, you've got the entire history of Haiti. Most Americans couldn't tell you their family history two generations back. I can't even tell you who my own father is!

EDITOR: This isn't about you, Mobley. And uh, did I hear you say *most Americans*? Don't you mean most people who live in the *United States* of America?

MOBLEY: Oh cut the *shit*, L_____. You know what I'm saying.

EDITOR: All right, I'll cut the shit. But I'm also cutting the second paragraph. Now let's get to the meat and potatoes. Basically, what you're saying in this article is that this doctor was simply doing his job practicing medicine. Whoever came to him for his services, he tried his best to help. And then he was arrested and tortured for patching up a woman whose tongue was cut out, *you say* because she spoke out on the radio against the not-so-secret secret police, and what they did to her husband. Now *that* is a great story. *That* is what we're paying you to do. But you make some leaps here. You write, 'Pierre looked into the eyes of his captors and saw children who a few years earlier had nothing. No jobs. No future. And they were offered food and a chance to become a part of something—a king's army—and were ordered to *disappear* civilians, many of whom they knew growing up.' Now, you and I know that the Duvaliers are thugs. But what proof do you cite that the doctor's captors, specifically, were ever ordered to disappear civilians?

MOBLEY: What is this, my twelfth article from Port-au-Prince? I'm simply drawing conclusions based on my reporting. Do I have to prove and re-prove in every article that Baby Doc and his Macoute are ruthless murderers?

EDITOR: You need to corroborate accusations like this. You have *one* source in this entire article. I take that back. You have two sources! You've got the doctor and his wife, who is a known member of a leading anti-Duvalier guerilla group.

MOBLEY: *She's a photographer.* She records what she sees onto non-partisan film.

EDITOR: This isn't getting us anywhere. I don't know what's happened to you. You were becoming such a good reporter. Now you write these *portrait* pieces with these long metaphorical sentences. And when it's not poetry, or... or *book-writing*, it's political diatribe. You have an axe to grind, man. We can't do that here. This is a reputable newspaper. I like you, Bleu. Your heart's in the right place, and you've got guts. I'm going to give you one more chance. You either clean up your act or...

I quit before I got fired, freeing myself from having to report every day on the cruelty and futility of undeclared wars without being able to say how cruel and futile it all was; freeing myself from having to report from the hot zones of the cold war without having the space or permission to connect the dots for the reader who might not be paying very close attention; freeing myself of a growing addiction to being at the center of these hot zones, and all the savagery, heroism, and life and death intensity brewing inside them.

I came back to New York, got a part-time teaching gig at Brooklyn College, earned extra cash painting interiors of renovated apartments, and began working on my first full-length novel, *The Switch*.

2

As a journalist, it was my job to cover what *is*. As an ex-journalist, I felt free to imagine *what if*. With a good deal of time on my hands between paying gigs, I ended up speculating about any number of things—including the blood-boiling enmity of polar opposites that I kept finding in nearly every sphere of life, not only in the war zones I'd recently come home from, but in politics, in workplaces, and in families. *What if* all these "enemies" somehow got their wires crossed, even for only one day? *What if* flashes of light lit up pockets of acrimony and misunderstanding around the world? Could embittered hearts be opened, or would it make no difference at all?

I didn't write my peculiar first novel with any purpose in mind, least of all to have an effect on the way people behaved toward each other. I didn't even know for sure if what I'd written was actually a novel; *The Switch* was merely an experiment played out in the sandbox of my imagination. If I hadn't bumped into Ron Hodamarsky at an upstate printer's flea market, *The Switch* might still be an unread manuscript resting peaceably in a file folder somewhere.

A former High School of Printing classmate of mine, Ronald owned a garage-based small press in Middletown, New York. Although the list of his Jewel Weed Editions focused exclusively on books of poetry written by Ronald's wife, Pat Hodamarsky, Ronald really dug the premise of *The Switch* when I described it to him in the flea market parking lot. Without even reading a word of it, he offered to publish the book if I would pay for all the printing and binding expenses—including the cost of having his small secondhand offset press fixed. I agreed if I could do my own typesetting and design the cover. (Having a hand in the design of my books and book covers became a habit I couldn't shake.)

Published in an edition of 300 copies, my first novel received reviews in two obscure literary journals—favorably in one and very unfavorably in the other. The reviewer who panned it (perhaps my first faceless enemy) particularly disliked the book's structure:

> It is dizzying enough slogging through a novel where every character is simultaneously someone else, but then halfway through *The Switch*, the reading orientation flips 180 degrees, forcing the reader to physically turn the book upside down. Once vertigo sets in you realize this device is nothing but a cheap trick to get you to notice the book's palindromic cover design that forms a face from both orientations. Cute, but it doesn't make up for the preposterous premise and the altogether convoluted read. *Switch it off!*

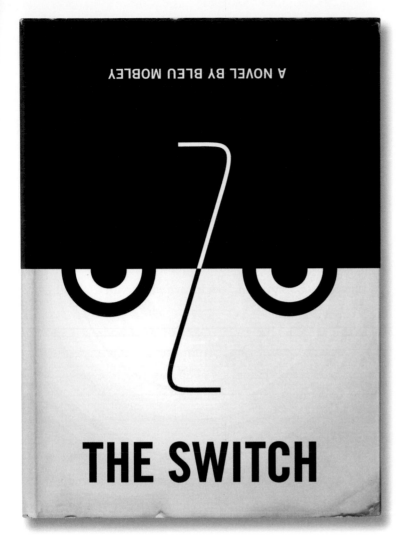

The Switch *A NOVEL*

One morning, a woman wakes to find that she's living the life of her archenemy. She experiences everything he sees, does, and thinks throughout the day. Her nemesis has been switched with her as well. On this particular day, switches like these are happening everywhere. Author Bleu Mobley, in his ingenious debut novel, chronicles a day in the lives of five sets of switched enemies: three pairs who come face-to-face every day, and two pairs who have never met but despise the very thought of each other.

1979, Jewel Weed Editions, Middletown, NY

Shortly after waking up, you realize that you are in the body of your number one nemesis. You look in the mirror. You see your enemy, you think the thoughts of your enemy, but somehow your own consciousness is still there too, as a quiet witness. You won't like embodying this person throughout the day, but there is nothing you can do to stop it. Your nemesis has become you for the day as well, witnessing everything you deal with on a daily basis. Should your nemesis encounter you during the day, you'll have a chance to see exactly how they see you, and vice versa. On this day, switches like these have occurred all over the world.

A Zionist from Tel Aviv finds himself at a café in a Palestinian section of the West Bank, smoking shisha, speaking in Arabic to some friends he's never laid eyes on, cursing the stinking Jews for imprisoning him for eight months without charge and killing his father. In Tel Aviv, a Palestinian man discovers he is standing guard in an Israeli army uniform outside a dance club that was fire-bombed a month earlier. In a suburb of London, a very gay man wakes to find himself in the body of a very homophobic man who is lying in bed next to his very square, albeit very nice wife. A few blocks away, the homophobic man opens his eyes from an unusually restful sleep, only to find himself being spooned by a rather hairy, well-toned male lover. Across the Atlantic Ocean, in Rochester, New York, a die-hard, bible-thumping "pro-life" activist finds herself switched with a die-hard "pro-choice" feminist escorting a sixteen-year-old girl through a phalanx of protesters into a women's health clinic for an abortion. On the South Side of Chicago, two old friends turned archenemies—one black, one white—wake up feeling not quite themselves. Each man, shaving, sees the other in the mirror, razor in hand. And then there's Helena and George—two high-powered L.A. lawyers who show up to work switched with each other…

George, in the person of Helena, feels the buoyancy of a body forty pounds lighter than his own. Through her eyes he sees himself—George—coming down the gray-carpeted hallway. It's not pretty. Helena decides to keep walking, say good morning to George, maybe ask him how his dad is doing or something about the Anderson case.

Helena, in the person of George, witnesses George's decision to avoid a hallway encounter by ducking into the stairwell, as is his way.

Two people disliking each other is not a serious problem in and of itself, but it is a serious problem for George and Helena: they are both lawyers at Bennett and Bennett and have no choice but to see each other five days a week. Truth is, George doesn't care for ninety percent of his colleagues. He considers most of them immoral, shiftless hypocrites. But he would never leave the firm, because it's pretty much his whole life.

Helena dreamed of working at Bennett and Bennett ever since she was a pre-law student reading about the firm's landmark class action suits against pharmaceutical companies. It's not the largest firm in Los Angeles, but it has an excellent reputation, and her partners let her take on as many *pro bono* cases as she likes. Still, she often considers quitting, primarily because of George. Helena is a mediator by nature and considers it a personal failure that she's never been able to reach some kind of common ground with George. She loses sleep over the conflict and has named a deepening worry line in her forehead after her nemesis.

At the morning partners' meeting the two can't help coming face-to-face. Looking at themselves through the eyes of the other, Helena and George wonder if the Switch happened both ways or if this freaky phenomenon is asymmetrical. Either way, they're both sure that whatever is going on is

HELL ON EARTH!

And they both are praying (neither of them prone to prayer) that this is a one-day thing and they'll each get their own lives back by tomorrow at the latest.

Nine years earlier, George had thought he was next in line to become a partner at Bennett and Bennett when Helena leapfrogged him, becoming the firm's first woman partner. His objection to her becoming a partner, he wrote in a letter to the Bennetts (never sent), had nothing to do with Helena being a woman or "because she may turn out to be more talk than action. It simply is a matter of seniority." Three months later, Helena cast the sole vote against making George a partner, "not because of his textbook passive-aggressive behavior or because he's a chauvinist pig, but because of his poor organizational skills." These deeply ingrained memories are revelations to each switched observer.

Where to sit? The goal for both of them is to keep eye contact to a minimum. It's a game of musical chairs. In this particular meeting they're nicely shielded, seated on the same side of the table with two other partners between them. But like clockwork, Helena and George find themselves at opposite ends of every agenda item. Helena views cases in political terms. Who's in the seat of power? Who's being taken advantage of? What are the demographics? George thinks every case needs to be seen on its own merit, "not through some politically correct lens or checklist." Helena likes to process every little thing; George wants to cut to the chase. Helena seeks to dispel conflict through dialogue; George designs ways of ripping his opponents to shreds. Helena thinks of herself as having a purpose; George considers himself a professional with a job to do. Helena sees human consciousness as evolving, very very slowly, and she is a catalyst working to jog it forward; George thinks the best days were long ago, and the most he could possibly hope for is to channel some of the high standards from back then. Usually Helena dominates these meetings with her well-articulated arguments, while George (bursting with opinions) barely ever says a word. But on this day, for some reason, Helena is relatively quiet, and George is the one blabbing away like someone slipped truth serum into his coffee. The barbs and daggers of the two sparring partners—normally kept behind the scenes and between the lines—ricochet in full view all over the conference room. Yet, by the end of the meeting, the two actually break though a seemingly intractable impasse and reach an agreement on a preliminary approach to the Anderson case. A consensus is reached to continue the discussion after lunch.

Going down for their respective lunch breaks, George and Helena meet up accidentally in the elevator. The awkward eye contact already made, there's no use pretending they didn't see each other. George notices for the first time that Helena's eyes droop down at the corners. They are sad eyes. Helena asks how George's dad is doing after his colon surgery, which is strange because Helena didn't even know George's dad *had* cancer.

"He's actually doing a lot better. Thank you," George says, feeling oddly appreciative of the question but also baffled by it. The elevator door opens. Helena and George hurry through the lobby, step out onto the street, and take off in opposite directions.

Put me across a table from someone with a story to tell, and I am all ears. My inclination is not to doubt anyone's version of their story. After all, it's *their* story.

My grandfather, Mordechai Jacobson (a.k.a. Jake Mobley), was known as a captivating raconteur. "Being with your grandfather was better than being at the theater, and it was often just as hard to get a good seat," an acquaintance of his told me once when I was researching my roots. However entertaining Mordechai might have been, his stories proved over time to be more theater than reality. Yet there were several people who to their dying day refused to believe that my grandfather took *any* liberties with the truth, especially because of the precise details in his stories. Year after year he referred to the same ensemble of characters from his youth—the facts of the stories never changed, they were only embellished upon with each telling. "And the look in your grandfather's eyes," a former neighbor of his told me, "that look could transport you to whatever time and place he was talking about. It was as if you were back there with him. Even his stories of hardship—coming home from school one day to find his family's house burned to the ground, or walking all the way from Warsaw to Paris, then escaping to this country as steerage on a cruise liner—were filled with fantastic personalities and bizarre sexual encounters. I can still picture Big Lula, the 3oo-pound wife of the ship's head chef, nearly crushing your sixteen-year-old grandfather when her elephant legs wrapped around his slender body. As excited as he was being surrounded by so many hills and valleys of female flesh, he was terrified that after everything he'd been through, he would perish at sea, crushed by Lula and her pulverizing pelvis."

I never met my grandfather, but I've been haunted by him all my life, and have often wondered how much of him is in me, or in other people I've met throughout the years.

When I returned to New York from the West Indies, I rented an apartment on the Lower East Side in a building that turned out to be one of the buildings my grandfather lived in with his New York family. The coincidence was eerie.

I got a break on the rent in exchange for occasionally painting apartment interiors— met a lot of my neighbors that way. It was a building full of characters; and sometimes, as I stood transfixed by a story I was hearing from one of them, I'd wonder if maybe I was talking to the reincarnation of my grandfather, even though I don't believe in reincarnation.

My soon-to-be best friend, Samir Braxton, had two apartments on my floor. It was hard not to notice this five-foot-four, brown-skinned, uproariously wavy-haired man with his six-foot tall, fair-skinned, blond-haired wife, running between the apartment they lived in and the one they used as a workshop, either very excited or very upset about a momentary success or wrinkle in their latest entrepreneurial pursuit. Samir would stomp his feet in ecstasy or rage and knock on my door to celebrate a breakthrough or to calm down from a disappointment. Almost anything was reason enough for him to take a time out, roll a cigarette, reflect and savor. Carla, his devoted Chilean-American wife and business partner, was a cancer survivor who wouldn't tolerate his smoking, so I kept him company on the fire escape or up on the roof.

Samir inspired *The Book of Lies*. His fantastic tales—of growing up a privileged mixed-race kid in Kenya before its independence from Britain, going into exile with his mother, becoming a pothead in Pakistan, a street performer in Amsterdam, a communist in London, a carpenter in Moscow, then settling in America and becoming an inventor and entrepreneur—fill my 564-page tome. I titled it *The Book of Lies* not because I thought the stories Samir told me were fabricated, but because he often called the world *a book of lies*, in which he provided a few rays of truth.

Since Samir wouldn't allow me to use his real name or call the book a biography, I took the liberty of writing it in the first person and changed the narrator's name to Sadiki Jones. I didn't feel comfortable calling it fiction since it was based on a real person and his true life stories, so I called it *A True Fiction*. "You must disguise my identity," Samir instructed me. "No one should know who it's about except for me and Carla." He refused to read the manuscript. "When it comes out, I'll read what you wrote and see if you got it right. If you did, we'll still be friends. If you messed up," he said with a devilish smile, "it was nice knowing you."

A year after the book came out, I received a letter from a woman claiming to be Samir's sister, Yvette. She wrote that a friend gave her a copy of *The Book of Lies*, thinking she'd find it most interesting. By the second page she knew that Sadiki was really Samir. She said that I captured the voice of her estranged brother to a tee, and she went from laughing to crying the whole time she was reading it. Her letter went on to say how hurt she was that there wasn't even a mention of a sister, though she recognized herself in some of the stories:

```
    I understand that you've fictionalized names and places, but still it made me
feel like I never existed. My brother and I had a falling out a long time ago.
I can't even remember what it was about. At least he didn't talk about the lies
of his sister. But how could he? If anything I'm honest to a fault. We were both
very honest with each other, and that can bruile feelings. The thing is, Mr.
Mobley, I love my brother, perhaps m're than I've ever loved anyone. I've come
to realize that throughout my life I've been looking, unconsciously, for men who
remind me of my brother, who aren't afraid to share their deepest feelings, and
can bring out the happy side of my personality which also has a morose side.
The times he and I spent together are the happiest of my life.
```

The letter ended with a plea for me to send her Samir's address and phone number. In the PS, which was nearly as long as the letter itself, she asked me to call him Oonie Que and see how he reacts.
```
But whatever you call him, she wrote, do call him, and let him
    know that his sister is sorry. Whatever it was I did or said, tell him I apolo-
    gize. Tell him his sister still adores him and thinks about him all the time.
```

When I told Samir that I got a letter from his sister Yvette, he stomped, he refused to see the letter, and denied having a sister. "The letter," he said, "was addressed to you. You should never divulge the contents of a personal letter to anyone." (Samir often came up with rules out of thin air, which I attributed to his being the son of a rule-obsessed father. *Protocol at every turn*.) He wouldn't even let me describe the letter to him. He called it "a letter of lies" and insisted that I burn the letter in front of him. Ever since I told him about burning my *Famous Fathers* books, I think he took me for a pyromaniac.

I played along with his theatrics and told him to meet me on the roof of our building in five minutes. I went to my apartment, took the letter out of the envelope, replaced it with some empty sheets of paper, and went to the roof. I held the envelope; he lit the match. As we burned this blank letter on the rooftop where Samir and I spent so much time together, and the autumn wind swept the ashes toward the East River, I wondered: How could he keep something as important as having a sister from me? What else did he keep from me? Could it be possible that this person claiming to be his sister was a con artist? I advocated on behalf of the alleged sister, suggested he let go of whatever came between them—have a reuinion with her, or just meet for coffee. He sneered at me. I let it go. Who was I to judge? I hadn't written a book based on the story of *my* life. And if I had (though there wasn't much to write about), I'd have probably left out any number of things.

Before heading back downstairs, Samir put his arm around me. The smell of ash lingered in the cool night air. Without saying a word to each other, we looked out onto the charcoal haze that enveloped the city. The only thing that is *real* in this life, I thought, if anything is real, is the direct experience you have with another human being. The stories you share with each other. The time you spend together losing track of time. *That's* what's real. If I were still a journalist, I'd be obliged to pursue the sister's side of the story. But I was no longer a journalist. I was an obscure writer, writing obscure books about obscure people, and I could happily continue along that path for as long as I kept my aspirations modest, was a single man with no family or responsibilities, living in one of the Lord's precious rent-stabilized apartments.

excerpt

What a chorus: "He's dying, Sadiki. You don't have to talk to him if you don't want to. Just write him a letter. If you can't forgive your father, just send him a message saying you're okay." *Reconciliation*. That's the word of the week. They don't understand what it means to keep a promise. At least my wife respects my choice never to talk to him again.

That's what I thought anyway, until tonight. Before Olivia fell asleep, she whispered in my ear, "Did you *always* hate him?" I pretended like I was already asleep and didn't hear the question. Looking out the window of our apartment I wonder: Do I owe my father anything? What harm would it do to break the promise I made my mother eighteen years ago?

The Book of Lies *A TRUE FICTION*
Brought up in a world he says is founded on lies piled on top of myths, Sadiki Jones speaks the truth about the deceptions of his father, his tutors, his bosses, and most of his other role models who in their own way helped make him the fiercely independent man he's become. A devout atheist born to a Christian Kenyan father and a Muslim Indian mother, Jones embarks on a four-continent quest for the genuine. Along the way he befriends a colorful cast of fellow runaways and expatriots, is radicalized, becomes an anti-colonialist Marxist, a circus artist, a carpenter, an inventor, and born-again capitalist. Bleu Mobley's second book is *a true fiction* that whispers and shouts the faithless gospel of an incendiary yet strangely loveable narrator.

1980, Jewel Weed Editions, Middletown, NY

Before he became an operative for the British government, my father worked at his father's lawnmower repair shop in Nairobi. Even in Africa the British had beautiful gardens, and the gardens needed to be mowed, and the lawnmowers needed to get fixed. My grandfather never went to school, but he had a mind that enabled him to take anything apart and put it back together again. At eleven years old he was fixing white people's lawnmowers out of a street cart. Ten years later he opened a lawnmower repair shop in downtown Nairobi where he would eventually pass everything he knew onto his son. When my father came of age he expanded the business to bicycle and motorcycle repair. Practically anything that had moving parts, the two of them would fix—which is how my mother became part of the family. She walked into their shop one day with a broken toaster and left very impressed by this refined young man who was able to guess—while re-wiring her toaster—that she was an Ismaili Muslim and she and her family came to East Africa after India was partitioned.

After my grandfather died, my father inherited enough money to build a palatial house for his beautiful Indian bride. At the time, it was one of the nicest houses owned by a black man in all of Kenya. I was conceived in that house, and it was there that my mother showered me with unconditional love and my father showed me how to fold origami and construct bridges out of popsicle sticks and complicated marble runs out of just about anything.

I grew up having the best of the best—private nannies, private tutors, a beautiful garden, fancy cars—at a time of great turmoil in Kenya and throughout Africa, when most dark-skinned people were still fighting to get out from under the heels of their colonial rulers. But my father lived this charmed bubble existence, with good friends amongst the British and Portuguese and the few affluent blacks, Indians, and coloreds who either were royalty, or like him had made themselves indispensable to the ruling class. Except for the occasional racist comment or sideways glance, I lived in the bubble too, and accepted the explanation that we lived the way we did because without my father, all the white people's gizmos wouldn't function. It made sense he was appointed to a position in the British government in Nairobi. He had earned their trust through his miracle repair shop and his unthreatening personality. And it made sense they made him chief censor for the film bureau since he loved movies and had a reputation as a squeaky-clean family man with puritanical tendencies. It was his job to review all new films, splice out any indecent or controversial scenes, and when necessary censor entire films he deemed beyond the pale. Even to his family, the job seemed fitting for a man who repaired lawnmowers in a suit and tie; looked askance at the growing permissiveness that was spreading throughout the world; insisted that silverware be laid out properly and that tea time was tea time; and despite his being Christian, liked having a wife who covered herself with a scarf in public.

I was only four when my father became a government censor. It made little difference to me. He went to work. He came home. He brought me presents. We traveled. He showed me how to make things with my hands, and he continued to be a stickler for the rules, the tough cop to my mother's good cop. Did I always hate my father? *No.* I loved him. I felt lucky to be born of my parents and raised in that modern castle house. As I grew older, there were more and more uprisings and states of emergency in the city. A revolution was taking place in Kenya, but I was shielded from most of it, happy to have nannies and tutors who made me feel like one of their own, happy to have a baby brother when he entered the picture, and no shortage of cousins and kids of my parents' friends to play with.

One day when I was ten, I was playing hide-and-seek in the downstairs playroom with my cousin Naima. After looking all over the basement for her, I gave up. She came out from an alcove under the stairwell. "But I looked there!" I said, dumbfounded that I had missed her. Naima took me by the hand and showed me a secret door—behind a chest of drawers and a map of the world—that led to a small room filled with books, film canisters, envelopes with film strips, and boxes full of photographs. The odd thing about this collection of images: all of the people in them were either naked or in varying degrees of undress. Most of the pictures were of naked women. Some were of a woman and a man doing things to each other, or a woman with another woman, or a man with several women. Some were of many men and many women, and a few were of men doing things to other men. We thought it was all very bizarre and hysterically funny, and we agreed not to tell anyone about what we'd found.

For two years, Naima and I would sneak into that room when the coast was clear. We became increasingly curious about those pictures and the resemblances we saw in them to our own ever changing anatomies. We'd take off our clothes, hold a film strip up to the light or spread photos across the floor and mimic the poses. As we both approached puberty, what once seemed like innocent exploration started feeling naughty, and my father's skeleton closet became our skeleton closet, and our sins became inextricably linked to his.

I never told my mother about my father's secret room, though she must have caught him with more than just pictures, this very proper father of mine, because the shit did hit the fan one night when she came home all furious about something. My father didn't apologize or make excuses. He was just furious that *she* was furious. After that, a coldness set in between them. They slept in separate rooms. He drank more and became abusive in his language. We stopped eating together as a family. Before long my mother asked for a divorce, but my father refused, insisting they keep up appearances for the sake of his job and the kids. In the middle of all this, my father thought it very important that I be versed in all the new movies. Since he knew every movie, he gave me recommendations (and cash) to go to triple feature matinees. When I'd seen every movie, he gave me money to see them again so I could watch for the foreshadowing and figure out all the filmmaker's devices. I thought he was grooming me to become a filmmaker, but I realized later he just wanted me out of the house so he and my mother could fight.

My mother's palace became her prison. The people who had been hired to help her were replaced by goons hired to keep an eye on her. She dreamed of escaping to another life, starting a career of her own, but it took years before she came up with a plan and the courage to carry it out. I was seventeen when she handed me our passports and three plane tickets and asked me to hide them somewhere out of the house. In two weeks we'd be leaving Kenya and I wasn't to say a word to anyone including my girlfriend Sonia.

Sonia was my first true love, and I knew in all likelihood I'd never see her again. I swore her to secrecy, then told her my mother's plan. We'd always wanted to go on a beach trip together, so the day before departure day, we took a bus down to Mombasa, found a secluded spot on Nyali Beach, smoked a joint, and made love for the first and last time—under the spell of an unusually tranquil Indian Ocean. A cop woke us up asking to see ID. I suppose we looked conspicuous, this colored boy and white girl, buck naked, curled around each other in broad daylight. We didn't have ID. The portly white cop searched through our stuff with his stubby fingers till he found the bag of pot in my backpack. He told us to get dressed. "You're coming with me." This was not possible. We couldn't have the cops contact Sonia's family because her dad was the head of the drug enforcement administration. And we couldn't get my parents involved because it would ruin my mother's escape-to-freedom plan. I gave the cop all the money in my wallet, 200 shillings. He looked at me like it was the lowest bribe he ever saw. I offered him the pot. He asked Sonia to empty her purse. He took a pair of earrings, a watch, then he looked at Sonia and raised his eyebrows. I shook my head, *No way.* He made a face, pinched Sonia's ass, and said, "Okay, Go."

We hitchhiked back to Nairobi and tearfully kissed each other goodbye. The next morning after my father left for work, my mother, my brother, and I took a heart-pounding cab ride to the airport. My five-year-old brother wanted to know what was going on. *Where are we going? Where's Daddy?* After two weeks in London, we were still telling him that it was only a vacation.

My father tracked us down to the house of my mother's aunt where we were staying. Through a door, he begged my mother to take him back. I remember him saying how he would change, how much he loved her, how different life would be—he'd stop drinking, she could go to school if she wanted to. When she said, *No, never,* he threatened to kill her. Two days later, with hardly any money left, we flew to Karachi. My mother changed all our names and made us promise *never, ever* to speak to our father again.

I have always resisted classifying personality quirks and out-of-the-norm behaviors in terms of disease or disorder. Where others see madness, I frequently find prismatic personality; sometimes even wisdom. But every so often I am forced to come to terms with the fact that someone I love is exhibiting signs of pathological or destructive behavior. It's with a similar reluctance but sense of urgency that I felt compelled to write *Narcissistic Planet Disorder.*

In the winter of 1981, I read an article about research being done on "a space-based defense system" that could one day shield the United States against intercontinental missiles. The Cold War seemed at its zenith, but a new president named Ronald Reagan was eager to ratchet it up even higher. According to the article, think-tankers at the Hoover Institute had visions of ultra-precise laser beams zapping Soviet nukes into nothingness from platforms high above the earth's atmosphere. Coming just four years after the first *Star Wars* movie captured the imagination of many Americans (including their new B-grade Hollywood actor *cum* president), the militarization of space had a disturbingly romantic appeal. The idea of an actual "star wars" system that would expand the arms race into the heavens seemed crazy to me, yet somehow inevitable; could we possibly resist inserting our warrior selves into the final frontier?

However timely *Narcissistic Planet Disorder* may have been (in its own allegorical way), it was difficult convincing stores to carry a book that stood twenty-eight inches tall. I remember one book buyer offering me a deal. "If you can find one shelf in this store that your book will fit on, I'll buy your entire edition." I searched the store for fifteen minutes but couldn't find a spot for my hot-off-the-press behemoth.

Too depressing for a children's book (the one genre that accommodates ridiculously oversized books), and too unwieldy an object to be taken seriously as literature, copies of *NPD* languished for years in storage. (I finally decided to rent a storage space after one bookseller took his time looking at every page of *NPD* with great interest and admiration, then handed the book back to me and said, "Fabulous! Come back when you're dead.")

Narcissistic Planet Disorder

UNPOPULAR PSYCHOLOGY

There once was a planet that thought it was the center of the universe. Without a care in the cosmos for anyone but itself, **planet e** is now on the verge of going completely out of control. Channeling an expert with four billion years of experience, Bleu Mobley uses **planet e** as a case study to help identify the core manifestations, symptoms, warning signs, and treatment of the newly classified *Narcissistic Planet Disorder (NPD)*—a rare, chronic, and potentially dangerous condition. A must-read for all celestial bodies or anybody who may be affected by this debilitating malady. *Oversized.*

1981, Jewel Weed Editions, Middletown, NY

We all have to deal with difficult planets: worlds imploding in on themselves; reeking gaseous globes; old rocks set in their ways. Fact is, we can all be pretty difficult. Heaven knows, I've had my bad days. But every once in a blue moon you come across a planet whose behavior amounts to something more than just "difficult." Should you ever come near the orbit of one of these planets, it's important to recognize the difference between normal planetary difficulties and serious planetary disorders.

Consider, if you will, the behavior of **planet e**. From its very beginnings, it exhibited a grandiose sense of self-importance without having done anything to justify it. Sure it's a picturesque planet, and the atmosphere (after long periods of hot and cold volatilities) is relatively hospitable. But nice scenery and decent air do not a superstar make. Yet for century after century, **planet e** has been consumed by fantasies of its own unmatched power, brilliance, and beauty. It assumes that it has a uniquely special place in the universe. This bloated sense of entitlement manifests itself in a continuous need for admiration and a lack of empathy for other planets. Ask **planet e** and it will no doubt reply: *What* other planets? Right there you have more than the minimum number of symptoms required for an unambiguous diagnosis of *Narcissistic Planet Disorder*.

But what, if anything, should be done in a situation like this? Excellent question. What **planet e** does to itself is its own business. If it chooses to cut down its trees to spite its air, poison its oceans, and suck all the oil out of its core, so be it. If its inhabitants make up stories about being the center of the cosmos and continue to come up with more and more lethal ways of slaughtering each other in the name of Peace and God and Freedom, well, that's sad, but what can you do? It's a free universe. A much graver problem arises when **planet e** or any planet starts acting out *beyond* its own atmosphere, dispersing its garbage and weapons and toxic technology, and spewing lots of big ideas about what to do in "outer space." Interplanetary exploitation (taking advantage of other planets and stars in order to achieve its own ends) is a more dire manifestation of *NPD*—one that requires intervention.

Before I begin to describe the various forms of remediation and intervention that are possible, let me explain why I consider myself an expert on **planet e** and *Narcissistic Planet Disorder*, despite having no formal training as a planetary therapist. I am the moon of **planet e**, and have (for better or worse) been in a position to observe its behavior for four billion years, give or take a billion. Granted, I am not a completely neutral observer. But, as an only moon, I am in a unique gravitational relationship with my parent planet. And in my opinion, being both distant from and connected to **planet e** affords me a perspective like none other.

The very first thing you learn growing up in the shadow of a narcissistic planet is that the narcissist is everything and you are next to nothing. For eons, my planet didn't know what to make of me. It feared and then romanticized me. When it finally sent some of its inhabitants to visit me, it made a huge spectacle out of the trip. There were a few follow up visits, and then nothing for years. Not even a phone call. This is typical of narcissists. They place you on a pedestal for as long as you are unattainable. Then when a real relationship is within reach, if you are not willing to simply be a mirror or an audience for them. . . *banishment!* In all these years, I have received no real expression of appreciation for:

- regulating my planet's tides
- inspiring its lovers
- or providing the most dependable source of night light for centuries on end at absolutely no cost.

A lifetime of such neglect instills a lack of confidence and feelings of shame. *Why am I not good enough to deserve my own self-sustaining atmosphere? Why am I so small? Why am I covered in pock-marks?* The moons of narcissists often assume that their impossible-to-please planets are one of a kind. This causes the moon to feel even lonelier than it would orbiting a normal planet. Frequently the moon of a narcissistic planet blames itself for being the cause of the planet's irrational behavior, when the fact is the planet is sick. The planet is suffering from a disorder. The planet needs help. And as the saying goes: when planet gets a cold, moon catches a fever.

I wrote *38 Feet, One Year* soon after getting my full-time teaching job at a state liberal arts college on Long Island. I replaced a very popular professor who had just been awarded tenure "by acclamation." A week after getting his tenure letter from the chancellor, the newly minted associate professor up and vanished. With no notice, he abandoned his classes, his home, his fiancée and his health-care and pension plans. Rumor had it that he moved to Oregon to live in a cabin in the woods, though others believed he got caught having an affair with a student and was forced out. Still others simply said, "drugs." All I know is, I became obsessed with this man who escaped the life I had just signed up for.

The publication of *38 Feet, One Year* put my name on the map as someone who wasn't afraid to write a book devoid of intra-character tensions, action, violence, sex, or even plot. The claim of a 365-page sentence also attracted attention. I never said the book was one sentence—that was the publisher's conceit! I wasn't even thinking sentences. I was thinking more about writing a book that functioned like a Japanese scroll painting moving without interruption through the seasons, capturing the flow of the mind as it migrates from one observation to the next.

The debate between those who hated *38 Feet, One Year* and those who heralded it as something new and exciting caught me by surprise. On one side were critics who complained that the book wasn't actually a sentence, and those who labeled the writing "verbal diarrhea," "word vomit," and other such regurgitations.

In *The Iowa Review*, Henry Blum wrote:

> Here are three reasons why the reader doesn't care to know about every thought Mobley's simpleton protagonist preoccupies himself with:
> 1. He never did anything that anyone would care to know about.
> 2. He has neither saved anyone (including himself) nor done any measurable harm to anyone.
> 3. Combine reasons one and two with nothing happening for 365 pages and welcome to Snoozeville!

Another critic wrote:

> **as compelling as watching paint dry!**

On the other side, Jill McAllister of *The Kenyon Review* wrote:

> At long last, a book about nothing that reaches toward everything. It may not get there, but it's worth every bit of the ride.

> In his own solitary way, Jeremy Boyce is irresistibly familiar. I await the sequel.

New Letters:

> I couldn't put this book down. If I was reading it up on a ladder like the kind Jeremy Boyce is on throughout the book, I'd have fallen off by the tenth page because all else disappears once you open its cover.

The big prize for me (or so I thought at the time) was the two-sentence mention in the *New York Times Book Review*'s "New and Noteworthy." Here is one of the two sentences:

> In Mobley's *38 Feet, One Year*, words take on thought's very form, bringing the experience of bearing witness to the reader as directly as ink on paper can allow.

The original publishers, Neil and Gabriel Forester, were a well-meaning couple living on an island off the coast of Maine. Gabe had a passion for "daring new fiction" and Neil was a trust-fund baby with family connections to the publishing industry, but they never had an answering machine and only checked their post office box every couple of weeks. Even with all the write-ups, very few people were interested in reading the ruminations of my soul-searching back-to-the-earther until after I became a bestselling author and *38 Feet* was resurrected as a "pivotal" early work.

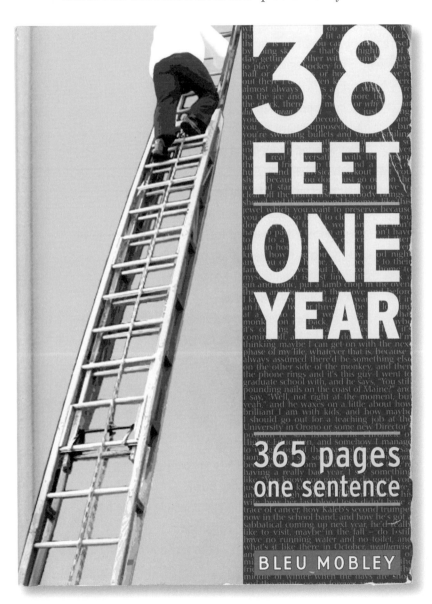

38 Feet, One Year

INTERIOR NARRATIVE

38 Feet, One Year inhabits the mind of one man over the course of a few hours. Bleu Mobley's protagonist, Jeremy Boyce, PhD, ditches a promising career as an academic to live a hermetic life in Downeast Maine in a cabin with no plumbing, earning a meager living doing odd jobs like mowing lawns and painting houses. Throughout this one-sentence, 365-page novel, Jeremy stands atop a thirty-eight-foot ladder in autumn, painting the red trim of a red barn red, looking out on the changing seasons and into some of life's existential questions, as well as back on his checkered past and ahead to the coming year. This extended interior monologue captures the rhythms and interstices of a mind at work as it observes, remembers, ponders, and hopes.

1982, Awanadjo Books, Sedgwick, ME

up on the very top rung of the ladder
thirty-eight feet above the ground
right hand resting
left hand painting with my favorite five-inch flattop brush
painting the trim of a red barn—red
"how about white?" i asked mrs. lowry
"red clapboards white trim?"
"keep it just the way it is please" she cawed
"you got it mrs. lowry"
customer's always king
red trim red barn red everything
i've scraped sanded and primed
now i'm painting
if the sun's out for three hours
work like hell for three hours
once it drops below forty-five degrees i'm down
that's my rule of thumb
could have used a roller
hell of a lot faster
but there's something about using a brush
that feels more honorable
and—i charge by the hour
dip
dip
left to right
feather it
a gust of wind hits the back of my neck
glance down
paint can dangling on the hook
one rung down
tarp all the way down on the ground
oh jesus
both feet steady
breathe
focus on the barn
solid as a rock
well-built barn

old barn

nice barn

lowry barn

favorite paint brush in hand

breathe

everything's fine

don't look down

don't look back

monkey's hardly there

heart rate almost normal

don't look up at the cloudless sky

don't look out at the spruce tree farms getting

their buzz-cuts for christmas

or down at the blueberry fields covered with doilies of frost

don't look anywhere but straight ahead

you want to check out the view

build a scaffold

you want to get the job done and live to see the superbowl

just keep painting

used to be afraid of heights

then i learned how to scale a cliff at outward bound

you fall there's a rope around your waist

get back up and keep climbing

after a while you stop being afraid

and focus on getting to the top of that rock

the top of that barn

no rope

one step

one foot

followed by the other

dip brush into paint

very simple task

not like writing an exegesis on the dialectical intentionality

of self in foucault's early post-structural period

something you can drive by and see next week

next year

say "i painted that trim"

every once in a while think of applying for a job

some go-for-an-interview-type job

then i look at the suit in the back of my closet and go *nah*

i don't even think i fit into that thing anymore

dip   left   right

follow the grain

keep looking for a sign to show me what's next

maybe there is no next big thing

writing a letter to a friend and mailing it—*that's something*

planting a garden

life!

that's a full-time job—what about that?

gearing up for winter

that's a job in itself

smell of wood stoves starting up again

don't look down

winter's coming alright

better have my wood and my gas in order

and enough money to make it through to spring

because there's almost zero money-making work in the winter

tommy used to say "it's a grand experiment living up here

not having a paycheck coming in at the end of the month

going for just what you need versus all that you want"

always looked up to my adventurous older brother

then i came here and i couldn't find him anymore

except behind a bottle of scotch

i can picture tommy standing at an AA meeting a year before he died

shaking his fist saying "this higher power stuff is a bunch of crap"

he never believed in anything he couldn't grab a hold of

whereas i always knew there had to be something else

besides all this naked-eye-stuff

something higher

dip

dab   dab

wonder if i heard that kid right in central park that day

after i handed over the keys to my apartment

and i went to the park

not knowing where i was going to sleep that night

let alone what i was going to do for the rest of my life?

the sun was shining and everybody had that look of *being from somewhere*

like they knew *exactly* where they were going

and life was *exactly* the way it ought to be

and there i was sitting on a bench without a clue in the world

then i saw this woman walking with her two-year-old kid

maybe he was one-and-a-half

i smiled at her and i smiled at him

and the kid looked me straight in the eye

his mouth opened

and these words came out in this strange voice

"follow your blood"

and i was like *whoa mama what was that?*

and the mother bent down and said

"what did you say?"

to her kid

because she couldn't believe it either

i don't even think the kid knew how to talk

it wasn't the kid talking

the kid was a messenger

and the mother and the kid walked passed me

and i just sat there on the bench for a long time trying to figure out

what *follow your blood* meant

until i decided it meant **go to maine** because that's where

what's left of my family—my brother tommy—was

only i'm still not 100% positive it was *follow your blood*

because the kid

the voice could have said

swallow the flood

or

borrow from HUD

or

wallow in mud

but i'm pretty sure it was *follow your blood*

and that it meant i needed to come here for some reason

I fell for Aconsha the very first time I met her. She barely noticed me. We met at a Halloween party thrown by a friend of Samir. I wore a third leg. She wore wings and a skin-tight bodysuit with a sepia feather pattern. After spotting this short-haired, South-Asian, winged woman with dark, penetrating eyes, I shimmied over to her and muttered something about her costume. She said, "No. I'm not an angel. I'm a bird of prey." Her face had a seductive combination of mischief and vulnerability. She asked why I wasn't wearing a costume. I pointed to my third leg.

"It's the only costume I could think of where I didn't have to disguise myself."

"Don't you like role-playing?"

"I get to role-play all the time in my writing. In real life, I'm more comfortable being myself."

"So you're a writer."

"Well, I was. Now I grade papers."

"So you're a teacher."

"I guess you could say that."

"You teach writing?"

"I teach people."

"What kind?"

"Of people?"

"Of *writing*. Fiction or non?"

"A little of both. They have me teaching a short story class, but I'm self-taught when it comes to creative writing. I don't know the rules, so teaching it feels kind of fraudulent. Enough about me. Let me guess. You're a... *dancer*."

"That's amazing! How'd you know?"

At that point in our conversation, a black lioness came over and gave Aconsha a whiskered kiss on the lips. "Nice meeting you," Aconsha said, as she and her furry feline scampered to the back room to dance.

I couldn't help but watch the two of them for a while. Aconsha led the lioness in what seemed to be a well-rehearsed duet, but was most likely improvised. At one moment they were moving their hips like accomplished belly dancers. A moment later they were doing tango thrusts, spins, and turns. Within minutes everyone who had been dancing was on the sidelines watching. The way they changed tempo from fast staccato rhythms to slow and graceful ones, the lusty tease of their approaching and withdrawing, and the back-and-forth play between traditional and spontaneous moves made their performance at once sophisticated and primal. Whatever vulnerability I thought I had seen in this woman had transformed into power and ecstasy. Moved as I may have been by her dazzling grace, I couldn't stomach watching the two of them together.

I managed to speak with Aconsha once more that night on line to the bathroom.

I complimented her dancing and asked if she was a professional. She said she was really just a tormented soul. *"That's* what I am," she laughed, "and if I didn't dance, if I didn't keep my body in motion, I'm afraid I would fall to pieces." She roared with laughter as she said this, but I sensed she was serious. Suddenly it was her turn for the bathroom. While I stood there next in line imagining her behind the door peeling out of her feathered bodysuit, I asked myself what it was that so attracted me to tortured souls. I left the party crestfallen that the first woman I had the hots for in months was a lesbian.

The next morning I had Samir call the host of the party, inquiring about the bird of prey. This was the scoop: Name, Aconsha Battacharjee. Age, late twenties. Born in India. Moved here with her family when she was young. Dances with the Pico Davis Dance Company. Is not strictly a lesbian (most likely bi). Doesn't have a good track record maintaining long-term relationships, probably because *she's a handful*. Lives to dance (workaholic). Used to be a chain smoker (now intolerant of anyone who smokes). The lioness is a sculptor and amateur dancer named Jasmine Dodgling. The two of them have been seeing each other on and off for a few months, but are *not* living together.

I put off calling Aconsha for over a week, knowing all too well that the longer I put it off, the more difficult it would be to make a connection. I weighed the improbability of a relationship with her against the glimmer of hope:

ON THE IMPROBABLE SIDE:

> She was not exactly single. She was clearly comfortable being with women. As a dark-skinned Indian woman going out with a black woman, she most likely identified as "a person of color"—and whatever I was genetically, most people consider me "white" even when I'm sporting a tan. She was way too physically fit for me: all muscle, perfect posture, probably ran ten miles a day. If we ever were to go dancing, anything we had going for us would be over after a few steps.

ON THE HOPE SIDE:

> If she really was tormented, maybe she'd be interested in a man who wasn't afraid of a little mental illness. She'd confided in me, exposing a glimpse of what lurked beneath the party animal. I had guessed that she was a dancer, and that impressed her. Her face, although very attractive, was not perfectly symmetrical: her left eye had some kind of astigmatism and was the tiniest bit higher than the right one, and while her lips seemed very inviting to me (what I wouldn't do to see them, feel them right now!), they did point downward at the corners when she was in repose, forming more of a frown than a smile, making her imperfect enough to not automatically put her out of my league.

When I called, Aconsha remembered me and agreed (somewhat reluctantly) to meet for a drink. Within a month the lioness was out of the picture. Within six months Aconsha and I were seeing each other almost every night, sharing practically everything—our bodies, our dreams, our fears, even our clothes. She warned me that she didn't get attached, that she was still experimenting with her sexuality, that she was on the road a lot with the dance company. None of this scared me. I felt happy just being in her presence, revelling in her earthy intelligence, her joy and pain. I could listen to her talk all day long about dance, her childhood in India, coming to the U.S., and everything about her family, even though she wouldn't introduce me to them. "It's not you, Bleu. It's them. They're very traditional. It's hard to explain."

One Sunday morning, after a round of lovemaking, I said to Aconsha, "You know, if I was a normal person and I believed in marriage, I would ask you to marry me." Without blinking an eye, she said, "Well, if I was a normal person and I believed in marriage, I'd probably say yes." We both got dressed. I went off to write. She went off to dance. Neither of us brought up the topic again for a long time.

In Aconsha I had found both friend and lover. She was as preoccupied with her work as a dancer and choreographer as I was composing my books. We are both rebels—she rebelled against being the subordinate Indian girl her parents raised her to be; left to my own devices growing up, I bucked authority and took no set of rules at face value. In many other ways we were (and continue to be) very different. She experiences life through physicality; I am a head attached to a body. She is *of* the world; I am a witness to it. She is gregarious but tormented, and shines in a crowd. I only get depressed episodically, and am most comfortable one-on-one or alone. She screams when she gets mad, gives strangers the finger, or tells them to go fuck themselves; I'm reluctant to make a scene. She stews and cries but sleeps soundly; I think of myself as generally content but toss, turn, and grind my teeth. She always looks put together; I do my best not to look too disheveled.

Despite our differences, we felt at home with each other. Without making a decision to do so, we ended up living together in my fifth-floor walk-up. Wary of laying claim to another human being as one's own, fearful of ruining a good thing, neither of us spoke of marriage again, until a year later.

I wasn't aware of the connection back then, but I'm pretty sure my fascination with my neighbors Joey and Frances Jordon peaked around the time Aconsha and I were toying with the idea of getting married. Not having been raised by two parents, I was always intensely curious (if not a little dubious) about married life. Why was it that most of the interesting couples I'd known had split up, while so many couples who seemed not to like each other stayed together? An exception to the pattern, Frances and Joey's inspirational relationship and spirited tales spanning half a century captured my imagination.

Aconsha and I used some of our wedding gift money to publish *Alone Together* under the imprint *Word of Mouth Press*. If you'd like a copy, we've got boxes full of them in our basement.

Alone Together *A DOUBLE PORTRAIT*

Alone Together is a parallax portrait of Joey and Frances
Jordan–married for fifty-four years. Each of them describes
his/her own take on the highs, lows, and in-betweens of their
relationship, being part of the jazz scenes in New York and Paris,
being an interracial couple in both cities, cooking omelettes
with John Coltrane and Thelonius Monk, the good old days
of smoking opium, and much more! This two-volumes-in-one
double portrait by Bleu Mobley is a moving reflection of a
couple bound at the hip yet very much their own persons.

1983, Word of Mouth Press, New York, NY

excerpt [from *Frances*]

When I was eighteen, I was so anxious to get out of my mother's house, I said yes to the first man who asked me to marry him. I didn't love Vince, but he had an apartment and he owned a bar and grill. Within six months I was the bar and he was the grill. At the time I didn't think of myself as a substance abuser. I just thought, *It's here so I'll drink it.* I'd watch people come in and deteriorate in front of me, see wives come in and yell at their husbands. "You're drinking your whole paycheck away. What are we gonna feed the children?" I can't tell you how many fights I saw break out in that bar. With pot-smokers I never saw scenes like that—with marijuana everybody feels good. Opium too. Why would you get into a fight with somebody when you feel good like that?"

Vince always had a jazz band on weekends at the bar and grill. One weekend this trumpeter named Joey Jordan came to play. Our eyes kept meeting in and out of the mirror. (His eyes could melt an iceberg.) Long story short, I ended up spending the night with Joey in his Harlem apartment. I came home the next morning expecting Vince to be at the door calling me a whore or something worse. But he didn't. He seemed calm. I told him I was sorry.

He said, "You went off with that black trumpeter, didn't you?"

I said, "Yeah, I did."

He said, "It's just sex, you'll get over it."

I said, "No, Vinny. It's not just sex. I'm *madly* in love with him."

I didn't lie. I never lied. I don't have the memory for it. I knew a girl who kept a book of all her lies—what she said to whom and when. She had all kinds of lies going, especially with her husband. She'd go out with some guy, and I'd ask her, "What are you going to tell Norman?"

She'd say, "I have to look it up in the book." It was a very intricate web she spun. I told her, "Don't get me involved. If Norman ever asks me anything, I'll just say I have no idea." It's easier to tell the truth. So that's what I did. I told Vince I was sorry and started packing my things.

"You going someplace?"

"I'm moving in with Joey."

Vince was so upset he started to cry. When I finished packing, he stood in front of the door like a cross.

"I'm not letting you out."

I said, "Listen Vinny, if I'm not at Joey's place by two o'clock, he's going to come here. You don't want a scene, do you?"

Vince was a nice guy. He never laid a finger on me. Which made me feel even worse.

Mom had a hard enough time when I married a goy. When she found out I was living with a black man, she nearly had a heart attack. All of a sudden a Catholic didn't look so bad. She called me on the phone, "Frances, you had a good marriage. Why would you walk away from that?"

"Ma," I said. "You wouldn't even come to the wedding!"

As cool-headed as Vince was when I first left him, that's how steamed up he got over time. After about a month, he bought a gun and went to see Joey at a joint he was playing on 52nd Street. Soon as Joey's set was over, Vince went up to the bar and told the bartender he wanted to buy the trumpeter a drink. The bartender told Joey, "That guy down there wants to buy you a drink." Joey knew instantly it was Vince. He went over to him with his hand out. "Good to meet you. My name's Joey Jordan."

"I'm Vincent Parker. I believe you played at my bar and grill one time."

"Be my pleasure to buy you a drink," Joey said. He gestured to the bartender who poured a couple of drinks. They each insisted on paying. Joey was so charming, it didn't take long before they both were laughing and telling each other stories. Poor Vince. He had his hand in his pocket with his finger on the trigger, but he couldn't bring himself to pull out the gun and shoot this guy. *This wife robber*. Vince called me up after he left the bar.

"You know I almost killed Joey tonight."

"You're crazy! What are you talking about?"

"I bought a gun."

He had it all worked out in his head. Joey would come over for a drink and before he sat down Vince would take his gun out and load six bullets straight into Joey's heart. "I don't know why," he told me, "but I just couldn't do it. Aren't you ready to quit this nonsense, Franny, and come back home?" Of course I said no, like I always did when he called me in that state. When Joey came home that night, he said, "Your husband was in to see me."

I said, "I know. He called me."

"I knew it was him right away," Joey said. "Not because I remembered him but because of the sadness in his face."

He didn't say he liked Vince. All he said was, "I felt bad for the man. He was suffering so."

Little did Franny's mother know that the black man her daughter was living with was a Jew. For the longest time Franny didn't want to give her mother the satisfaction, but I wanted to see the look on her face when she found out—see which was worse: her being married to a white goy or living with a black Jew. When we finally told her, she couldn't believe I was Jewish. She never heard of any black Jews. I sang the Sh'ma for her. Then I took out my trumpet and played "Avinu Malkenu." She still didn't believe me. The following week I brought her my tallis and my collection of yarmulkes. She still would not believe it. I showed her pictures from my Bar Mitzvah, all these black Jews from Temple Israel in Harlem gathered around me. *She never heard of such a thing.* I asked her why she didn't know any Jewish prayers. She said, "I was born Jewish, I'll die Jewish," implying if I'm Jewish, I must have converted. I asked her what about *in between* being born and dying? She said, "I consider myself Jewish, but I don't practice. At my age I shouldn't have to practice. I think I know how to be Jewish by now, and that's in my own way. I'm my-own-way Jewish. That's my whatdoyoucallit?"

"Denomination?"

"Exactly!"

"Hey, look at me, I play jazz gigs on Friday nights. Far be it for me to judge how another..."

Then she got all irrational on me. She takes out two candles and a sheet of paper with English transliterations of Hebrew prayers, lights the candles, and recites the prayer for the bread over the candles. I didn't have the heart to tell her. I asked if she'd like to come to my family's synagogue on 125th Street on Saturday. She nearly fainted at the suggestion. That never did happen.

Most white Ashkenazi Jews don't have a clue black Jews exist. I was living in Brooklyn years ago, in an apartment building in Borough Park. Half the building was Hasids and Lubavitcher. The other half was anyone else who needed a cheap place to live. One Friday night, this young Lubavitcher guy from across the hall knocks on my door all dressed in black and white, with the payes curls and the pasty face. "Excuse me for bothering you, sir. My wife left the radio on and it's our sabbath tonight. Could you do us a big favor and turn it off?" It didn't bother him that I was black.

"Oh sure," I said. I go into their apartment and turn off the radio.

"Thank you so much."

"No problem at all. Really."

The next day, he tells the landlady about me helping him with his radio.

The landlady says, "Oh, the black guy in 3B. He's Jewish!"

The man says, "What are you talking?"

The landlady says, "No really, he's Jewish."

Lubavitcher man says, "Nah!"

Landlady: "Yeah."

"No."

"Yes! I'm telling you, his father is a cantor at a shul in Harlem."

Later that night the Lubavitcher man comes to my door all furious. "Why didn't you tell me you're Jewish? *It's a sin! It's a sin!*"

I say, "What do you mean? You didn't ask me what religion I was. You asked me to shut off your radio. You just took it for granted I wasn't Jewish."

He's going on and on. "It's a sin for a Jew to turn off a radio on the Sabbath."

"So if you have a sin," I said, "you have a sin. It's not my problem."

He carried on for quite a while like that. Some of these orthodox don't make any sense to me. They'll kick you out of Israel if you're not the right kind of Jew, but you can't turn off their radio.

With Franny, it's not about me being black or Jewish or a jazz musician. Just for fifty-four years now, going on fifty-five, she sees me as a man. *Her man.* And she's my woman. Whether or not I've had flirtations and whatnot with other ladies is neither here nor there. My *heart* has belonged to Frances since our eyes met in that mirror all those years ago, and there's nothing anyone can say that will change that.

It didn't matter to Aconsha, or to me, that we'd lost thousands of dollars on our first publishing venture. We each had paychecks coming in from our day jobs. Whatever money was left over after paying our modest living expenses went back into our art. If bookstores wouldn't carry my bifurcated book, I'd make a trifurcated book! Same thing with Aconsha. Whatever time she had off from the Pico Davis Company, she spent choreographing and staging her own dance pieces, hiring dancers, commissioning costume and lighting designers, renting performance spaces, and doing whatever it took to fill seats with warm bodies. No project idea was too improbable, no audience too small, and no financial loss too big to keep either of us from following our muse.

When I told Aconsha I wanted to write a book based on some of the people I'd met in Latin America—whose stories of courage in the face of brutality I couldn't do justice to as a newspaper reporter—she said, "You should do it." When I told her that I was as terrified as I was excited about diving back into that material, she said, "That's how I feel ninety percent of the time." Looking down at her meticulously bitten fingernails, she continued,

"Sometimes I wonder, if I *wasn't* terrified, if I'd still be motivated to do the work. Do it now, Bleu, before your memories fade of those people, and your notes lose all their meaning."

Ménage à Trois: a man, a woman, her camera

A TRIPLE PORTRAIT

Born and raised in the same village in Haiti, Philippe and Nadine marry and fight the good fight against the brutal Duvalier regimes. The couple's fearless activities—Philippe in his capacities as a doctor, and Nadine as a photographer—nearly do them in. With no real choice but to leave their beloved island country, they end up making a new life for themselves in Brooklyn, New York with their son and daughter. "Composed" by the author of *38 Feet, One Year*, this multi-perspectival work portrays an enduring love between a man and a woman, and their valiant struggles for social justice and personal trust.

1984, Word of Mouth Press, New York, NY

There is a Haitian saying, *Dèyè mòn gen mòn*—"Behind mountains, there are more mountains." This is the truth in Haiti. Behind every mountain there is another, the darkest one nearest you, and back and back, lighter and lighter. Behind every story, many stories. Behind every invasion, rebellion or coup—generations of invasions, rebellions and coups. Behind everything you think you know, there is always a more complicated explanation. Behind every man or woman, well, it all depends how much time you have to explore.

Philippe was born in his parents' house. His father and mother each were born in their parents' house, and before them their parents... You can trace the bornings back to Philippe's great-great-great-grandfather Azacca Jacinto who was born on a plantation in the house of his mother's master. That same year there was an unprecedented slave rebellion throughout the island that beat back the armies of three colonial nations making Azacca one of the first free children of African descent born in the Caribbean.

From an early age Philippe was taught this lineage beginning with his great-great-great-great-grandmother who could be traced back to Africa, all the way to the time Philippe and his brothers and sisters came into the picture. It was a tree Philippe could see as plainly as the mango tree outside his family's house in the small village not far from Port-au-Prince where he knew every one of his cousins and all his neighbors. When he went to play at his best friend's house, the friend's mother knew his mother because they went to school together. Philippe's grandfather was the friend's father's doctor. Philippe's father was the friend's doctor, and Philippe would grow up to become the doctor of his friend's children and nearly everyone else in the village.

Philippe will always be a son, a brother, a doctor, a husband, a father, and a survivor of both Duvalier dictatorships and their not-so-secret secret militia, the Tonton Macoute, who kidnapped and tortured him for saving lives in a time of death. That was the part Philippe played in the struggle against the Duvaliers—daring to save the lives of peasants who were burned out of their houses; who were shot at by M16s as they ran to the river; whose ears, jaws and noses had been sliced off with machetes; whose mutilated bodies were left to die in dumping grounds. That was his crime—taking up arms with morphine and antiseptic, scalpels and needles, thread and bandages, even though he administered care to *anyone* whether they had a leopard patch or a guinea hen sewn to their shirtsleeve or a rooster tattooed on their chest. The night the Macoute came to Philippe's house—and found him patching up a woman whose tongue was cut out for speaking on the radio, and found a loaded gun under a floor tile next to his bed, and couldn't find his troublemaker wife—he knew that he was facing death.

Philippe looked into the eyes of his captors and saw children who a few years earlier had nothing, no jobs, no future, and were offered food and a chance to become part of something—a king's army—and were ordered to *disappear* civilians, many of whom they'd known growing up. At first, they performed their duties with some misgivings. But after the third and tenth and twenty-fifth time, they no longer saw their victims as human, which is why their eyes had grown cold and lifeless. They beat Philippe till his clothes wouldn't fit, his body swollen like a whale. They asked for names, dates, whereabouts. He said nothing, so they beat him some more.

They could have just killed Philippe. Instead they played with him like a cat plays with a mouse. One of his interrogators said, "When we are finished with you, you'll wish you were dead." This was his punishment: to be kept alive. They offered him a way out, but his confidence was not for sale. They showed him pictures of people, some that he recognized. His eyes said, *I don't know these people.* They showed him a picture of his wife. "Don't you know this woman?" His eyes said, *You know that I know.* For his silence they beat him across his eyes and threw him in a cell.

He was blinded. All he could see was the beautiful, robust face of his wife telling him to be strong, telling him to do whatever he needed to do. He always felt incredibly blessed that Nadine was his partner in life. He could see her in front of him as if she were there in the prison cell. She wrapped herself around him like a blanket of pure acceptance, enabling him to sleep.

When he woke up he could see again, first out of his left eye, then, blurrily, out of his right. He was lying on the splintered floor of a prison cell, his own blood splattered all around. He could hear himself breathing heavily. He called out for help. A guard approached. Philippe looked into the guard's vacant eyes and asked, "Please, get me some help." The young Macoute said, "You are a doctor. Take care of yourself."

One of Philippe's degrees was in acupuncture. At first all he could do was concentrate whatever energy he had left on staying alive. After he gathered some strength he located the pressure points on his body as he would on a patient, then he applied acupressure with as much strength as he was able to muster. This is how he saved his own life. In his prayers he thanked the guard, his enemy, for giving him the suggestion.

A few weeks later he was brought to a hospital. In less than a year, he was "recovered," though he knew, and anyone who had known him knew, that he would never be the same.

When they first moved to Brooklyn, Nadine would dust, scour, and scrub the soot and grime that built up every week on their window ledges. After a while she decided just to cover the dirt with white paint several times a year. Back in Haiti, there was plenty of dirt, but the dirt was *earth* and you could simply dust it away. The dirt of New York City is a different kind of dirt altogether. Sometimes Nadine wishes she could paint over everything in her life and start over. But she is not a painter, she's a photographer, and she's not one for wishing everything was different. By nature Nadine is not a brooder. Philippe says Nadine's optimistic disposition, her *joie de vivre,* is his religion. Nadine says she doesn't want to be worshiped, only cared for and trusted.

Nadine was fearless about her photography till it finally got her into serious trouble. She was a photojournalist who dared to cast light in a time of darkness. She lost her job with a mainstream newspaper in Haiti and went to work for an opposition paper. When their offices were burned down, she took a job with another opposition newspaper. When the editor-in-chief of that paper was killed and Nadine heard from a reliable source that her name was near the top of a state enemies list, she went into hiding. She moved from house to house, never long enough to endanger the lives of her hosts. The people she stayed with were ordinary people who were part of a movement of Haitians tired of the killing, tired of their children being exposed to every disease that comes their way, tired of the rape of their daughters and mothers, tired of their land being stolen. One time there was to be a meeting at a bus station. As she looked for her comrades, she heard a siren. Before she could do anything, two men in blue jeans and t-shirts grabbed her and forced her into a van full of rifles and more men in blue jeans and t-shirts.

She was interrogated at a "detention center" every day for two months. During one interrogation she was shown photographs that she had taken.

"Did you ever see this?"

"Do you know these people?"

"Where is this place?"

She knew they knew those were her photographs. Some of the photos were cut out of newspapers and magazines, her name printed in small type beneath the picture. Some of the photos were taken from the camera bag she had with her when she was captured, and they had developed and printed them (poorly). Some pictures were taken from her private files. She could tell because her name was stamped on the back with a © sign and a date. She thought, *What a moron I am!* She wondered what good all this picture-taking had done. Had her photographs been used against other people in this way? Almost everything she believed in crumbled into nothingness.

They showed her a few photographs reprinted in foreign publications that she never gave rights to, with captions that described the pictures as the opposite of what they actually documented. The corpse of a young girl slain by the Macoute was captioned "The body of a young Haitian girl slain by anti-government guerrillas."

After six months in detention Nadine was taken out in handcuffs to be transferred to another location. One of the transfer guards recognized her as the wife of the doctor who saved his mother from dying of tuberculosis. Risking his life, the guard set her free.

Under the cover of darkness, Nadine, Philippe and their two children boarded a pontoon boat and fled their home and their extended families and everything they ever knew and loved. Since Haiti was considered a nation friendly to the United States, they didn't have much hope of getting asylum, but they applied for it anyway, and rented a small stucco house in Crown Heights—the only Haitians on an African-American block. For the first year they felt like turtles ripped from their shells (an expression their daughter Chanté came out with after an awful day at school). It wasn't long before the kids adjusted to their new environment, then Nadine fell into a career as a prison social worker, and gradually her faith in the present reawakened.

After five years of never touching it, Nadine dug out her camera and held it in her hands. It was an easy reunion. She splurged on a second hand macro lens, and on her off-hours started roaming the streets of New York searching for small signs of life in the crevices of the city—a few blades of grass breaking through a crack in the sidewalk, a crystalline bubble of ice formed by a balloon that had since deflated, a mound of green and white mold growing around a discarded burger bun. Nadine had no idea what she was photographing till an intern at a downtown art gallery told her that her work was about nature defying the authority of man. Philippe didn't understand these abstract, peopleless photographs, even though he had to admit they were kind of beautiful in their own strange way.

Aconsha was happiest when she was dancing, and that made me happy. I felt nothing but pride watching her mesmerize an audience, and while she may not have read my books cover to cover, I knew she was my number one supporter. She didn't hassle me to go on vacations, or have babies, or spend time together playing cards. We both could drop into bed in the middle of the night worn out by clockless work habits, and neither of us complained. If there was any inkling of competition or jealousy between us, it was kept in check.

That is, until Pico Davis hired a hot new dancer from Hungary, and I came to a performance and saw the chemistry between her and Aconsha, and watched the two of them holding hands—beaming—as the crowd showered them with a standing ovation.

I had accepted the fact that I married a woman whose work involved pressing up against other perfectly toned, gorgeous, sweaty bodies dressed in tight-fitting leotards. But watching her perform this unabashedly sexual duet with this ravishingly beautiful Hungarian woman—seeing them roll around on the stage together, and leap into each other's arms—made me uncomfortable. Ten minutes of dance was an eternity. I didn't say anything to Aconsha at first, other than how great she was.

"And the new girl seems. . . *quite good*."

"You mean, *Lena*?"

"Yes, Lena. She seems very. . . uh, *double-jointed*."

"She's trained as a gymnast."

"I read in the program she was on the Hungarian Olympic team."

"Yeah, but she injured her pelvic bone in the qualifiers. Poor thing. It still hurts her."

For the sake of our mutually supportive relationship, I didn't say anything more. Over the next few weeks I managed to submerge the gyrating images of the two of them from

1983 poster for a performance at New York's Dance Theater Workshop

my conscious mind into my dreams. But when Aconsha told me (in the middle of dinner one night) that she hired Lena to work with her on one of her own pieces, whatever fears I had about my wife's ambidextrous sexuality catapulted to the fore. Instead of accusing her of anything, or admitting my jealousy, I waited for her to go back to her studio, then I walked down the hall to commiserate with Samir.

"Just because Aconsha is married to me doesn't erase the fact that she's bisexual. If she were merely heterosexual, I could confine whatever normal jealousies I have to the men she dances with, and since most of them are gay, it would barely affect me. But my fear of Aconsha desiring women—apparently— is stronger than I realized. And it's making me question any number of things."

"Like what?"

"Like, the voracity of our lovemaking. Like, maybe she just married me to get health insurance, or to throw a bone to her parents who never would have accepted her as a lesbian. Like, maybe I'm just a cover, and she's been having affairs with women all along."

Samir told me to calm down. "First of all," he said, "Whatever relief Aconsha's parents may have felt because you weren't a woman was wiped out by your not being Indian. Second of all, Aconsha is madly in love with you and everybody knows it. Third of all, even if she's having some sex on the side, what's the big deal? *She loves you!* Whatever neurotic fears you have, keep them to yourself or you'll make it worse. If you have to process, do it with me. Better yet, just get over it."

Feeling more paranoid than I was before, I thanked Samir for his advice and went back to our apartment to sublimate my fears into the book I was working on about a Haitian couple who risked their lives battling the despotic Duvaliers. After several hours of frenetic typing, the book developed an unexpected subplot—a love triangle between the husband, the wife, and her work. Instead of writing the chapter about the couple's harrowing journey crossing the ocean on a pontoon boat from Port-au-Prince to Miami, the words hammering themselves from my fingertips were nothing but jealous fantasies.

Aconsha came home late that night, climbed under the covers and fell asleep. An hour later I woke her.

"Aconsha. Are you up?"

"No."

"Can I ask you a question?"

"No. . . Yeah. What?"

"Do you love me, even though I have a penis?"

"What kind of question is that? Of course I love you."

"You do? You're not just saying that?"

"I love you *and* your penis."

"You love my penis. Are you saying you love my penis or you love penises in general?"

"I hate penises in general. I mean, I hate what they represent. As an object I can take them or leave them. But *your* penis, I love it. It's perfect. Now let me sleep."

"Is that why you're with me—because I have a perfect penis?"

"Honey, I'm going to kill you in the bathtub."

"Is that all you're after is my penis?"

"You're a dead man."

"I could just leave you my penis, and the two of you could. . ."

"*Fuck* your penis. I don't give a damn about your penis. I would still love you even if you had no penis."

"Are you saying you wish I was a woman?"

"Bleu!"

"What are you doing?"

"Nothing."

"It doesn't feel like nothing."

"I just want to hold you, that's all."

"*No wait. Wait. Aconsha, stop!* Besides my penis. What about the rest of my body? I know it's not like the bodies of the people you dance with."

"I like you just the way you are. I wouldn't have it any other way."

"I thought you said that you weren't used to being with someone so... what did you say? *Underdeveloped*. Remember when we first started going out, you said that I wasn't really your type, physically. Remember you said that my chest seemed more like the chest of a fourteen-year-old boy?"

"It's just that compared to. . ."

"Jasmine?"

"No. Compared to you, I felt a little *overdeveloped*, that's all. But I don't feel like that anymore. Your body is fine."

"Fine?"

"More than fine. It's perfect, Bleu! It's beautiful. I think you have a beautiful body."

"Is that what matters to you, beautiful bodies? What about my mind, my soul?"

"If you keep talking like this I'm going to get a divorce."

"What do you mean by that?"

"You heard what I said."

"Are you serious?"

"No, I'm just kidding."

"But what did you mean by that?"

"What do mean, what did I mean?"

"Why did you say what you said?"

"Why did you say what you said in the first place?"

"I didn't say anything!"

"Yes you did. You woke me up and asked if I liked you with a penis."

"Is that what you heard? Because that's not what I asked."

"You *didn't* wake me up to ask me about your penis?"

"You're twisting what I said."

"It sounds like you're blaming me for something."

"I'm just trying to tell you how I feel."

"That's the same as blaming me. Now go to sleep."

"But we didn't finish."

"Finish what?"

"Finish talking."

"Okay, what's bothering you?"

"I want to know why we don't make love like we did when we first met?"

"No two people can sustain that amount of fucking."

"*Fucking*. All this time I thought we were making love."

"I swear, Bleu, you're like a woman."

"Would you prefer if I was?"

"Oh God. What is this about? Just tell me what's bothering you."

"Nothing. Never mind."

"Good. Let's go to sleep."

"I can't."

"What time is it?"

"3:24 a.m."

"That means it's time to sleep."

"Not yet. . . *Here*."

"How do you get like that so fast?"

73

"Touch me."

"Over here?"

"Yeah."

"Like this?"

"Yeah."

"How about like this? You like when I do this?"

"Yeah. Yeah."

"Bleu? Remember that thing we were doing a few weeks ago, when you were behind me and I was upside down?"

"Yeah."

"You never did that with anyone else, did you?"

"Um."

"Did you?"

"Umm."

"You did, didn't you? *How* could you? Tell me I'm the only one."

"You're the only one."

"Just me, right?"

"Only you."

"I'm the only one."

"You're the only one."

"Just me, right?"

"Just you."

excerpt [from *Her Camera*]

No longer her primary means of earning a living, Nadine's camera is free of having to carry that burden for her. It can feel the difference in the way she holds its body (with greater ease, with more joy, at odd angles), and only on days off or (like a secret lover) occasionally during lunch hours. Now in exile, Nadine's camera is also free of the weighty expectations of having to save the world or at least the battered, suffering poor of Haiti, which is nearly everyone who lives there. Together with her husband, Nadine still works for change in Haiti, but her camera is free of that responsibility. And, being an inanimate object, it's free of the memories that continue to haunt the photographer.

Or is it?

Nadine believes that her camera keeps a little piece of everyone and everything that it photographs. She isn't the only one who thinks this. The language of photography is filled with allusions to theft, violence, even spirit catching. The photographer *takes aim, lines up her target in the crosshairs, zeroes in,* steadies herself. Without permission, she *fires away, captures* otherwise private moments with her camera. Photographers share the methods of spies. They *surveil, scope out a scene, crouch,* hide behind drapes and bushes. They *shoot,* and inspect a contact sheet with a magnifier searching for secrets. The camera comes off the assembly line an innocent. Over time it becomes an accomplice to the act of picture-taking.

Nadine and her Japanese-made 35-millimeter camera collaborated for two decades framing pictures of Haiti. Does the camera remember any of it? Does it recall the scenes of sugar caners and cotton pickers silhouetted against steeply folded mountains; of children riding donkeys on the edges of Highway 3 into the blazing sun? Does it remember the pictures it took of stunted-looking pigs and scrawny dogs loitering outside two-room huts with banana frond roofs; the hungry-eyed water refugees of Peligree Dam; the young girls sewing Mickey Mouse dolls in sweltering factories; entire villages of people wandering through forests, cutting down trees to sell as charcoal; congregations standing outside churches, dressed in their Sunday best; the ecstatic dancing of voodoo priests; and the tapestry of coloreds, blacks, and whites dancing together at Carnival in Port-au-Prince?

Nadine wonders if her camera also has trouble sleeping at night. Can it hear the gunshots like it was yesterday? Does it see the battalions of khaki-camouflaged soldiers parading through town squares; the countless funerals of outspoken priests, could-have-been politicians, nosy reporters, and fair-minded judges; and any number of massacres and executions that enabled Nadine to amass her considerable portfolio of horrors?

Her camera may or may not retain the scenes of the Haiti years in its hollow chamber, but it senses things have changed. Nadine doesn't go out in the world and aim it at people like she used to. These days she spends most of her camera time taking close-ups, prowling against walls or crouching curbside. The only human subjects she photographs anymore are her husband and their two kids. Even though she promises not to exhibit the photos she takes of them, Philippe isn't pleased with all the picture-taking.

One morning he is awakened by the mechanical slap-clacking sounds of Nadine's single lens reflex.

"It's not even 9 a.m. for God's sake!"

"Sorry, you just looked so beautiful to me. I couldn't resist."

"I'm not shaved yet. There's crud in my eyes."

Nadine tried to explain:

"My camera helps me understand the world I live in, and you and the kids *are* the world I'm living in. This family is my culture, my community. Turn toward me.

Hold it.

No, just like you were a second ago. *Perfect!*"

"Sweetheart!" Philippe said raising his voice. "Can't you put that thing down for *one* second? This is our bed! Is nothing sacred anymore?"

Philippe knew he was out of line as soon as he said those words. She is a photographer. It's what she does. She said he looked beautiful to her. How can he argue with that? He apologized. Then Nadine conceded, maybe she'd crossed a line with her early morning shutter-snapping. She promised not to disturb his sleep like that again. They made love, quietly, so the kids wouldn't hear.

Having both faced death, Nadine and Philippe share an unusual appreciation of life and of each other. They make love more than most couples married twenty-plus years, more often than some newlyweds. But Philippe is not the same confident man he was before he was tortured. He loses his temper and has bouts of paranoia, and Nadine's rekindled passion for photography has brought out a possessive streak in him.

Several weeks ago he confronted her after she returned home a few hours past dinnertime. "Where were you tonight, sweetheart darling?" Philippe's sarcasm sent a shiver down Nadine's spine. She married a tender man, a genuine hero, but recently his tongue could be as sharp as one of his scalpels.

"I know you left work at four this afternoon. It's eight-forty-seven."

She smelled alcohol on his breath.

"I was out shooting the old rail yards on the west side."

"That's fantastic, Nadine. For someone no longer earning a living as a photographer, you spend a lot of time with that thing. Would you like to know what part of your children's development you missed tonight?"

Nadine reminded Philippe that he worked full-time as a medic at the hospital for three years while going to school at night so he could re-earn his doctor's license. "And now that you spend most of your weekends playing soccer, I don't think you're in any position to criticize, Mr. Glass-House-With-A-Stone-In-Each-Hand. So lay off."

They argue like this a lot these days.

Just last night they both were reading in their living room when Nadine took out her camera and snapped a few shots of Philippe. She loved the gesture his long fingers made holding the book, and the way his left leg slung over the footrest like an apostrophe. The second he heard the shutter snapping, he dropped the book in his lap, turned toward the camera, and said, "Can't I just *be* in my own home without that thing going off?"

"Hold it just like that for one second. Beautiful! You know you're a lovely man, Philippe, even when you're upset."

He asked Nadine if her camera had a name. She didn't respond. He asked again.

"Tell me, is it a he or she, that thing?"

"Don't be ridiculous!"

"You know, you can see every pore in my skin with your precious Nikon lens. Every wrinkle. Every nose hair, twitch, and awkward glance. All I see is something's between us, and my own reflection in the eye of a machine."

There are plenty of objects that occupy Philippe's attention that Nadine could be jealous of—the gun he bought after his run-in with some Macoute guys in Prospect Park (an object he keeps polished and loaded under their mattress), the clock-radio he listens to till the wee hours of the night, all his soccer paraphernalia, and his curvaceous Ibanez guitar that she often finds him sleeping with on the living-room couch. But she's happy for him that he has things other than medicine and his family to distract him from the plagues of uninvited memories. Instead of making that case to him, she said, "If you want me to stop taking your picture, I will." Touched by her offer, he almost said yes, but held his tongue, worried about the repercussions.

It's 4:30 in the morning. Philippe wakes from a bad dream, reaches out for Nadine— reaches,

reaches.

He turns on the light. She's not in bed.

He bolts. She's not in the bathroom or the kitchen. His heart is racing. He doesn't know where she is, until he finds her safe and sound in the red light district of her basement darkroom. "I got so worried. I thought something *happened* to you." Nadine sees the panic in her husband's face and pulls him close. For the first time in nineteen years together, she sees him weep. He's weeping like a baby. She takes his hand and walks him up to their bedroom. They lay down and hold each other till they fall asleep cheek-to-cheek on his side of the bed, the gun hibernating under the mattress, the camera resting near the pillow on her side of the bed, the kids sleeping down the hallway two hours from having to get ready for school.

Over the years, I tried to visit my mother at least once or twice a month. But life gets busy. One time after not seeing her for three or four months, I paid her a surprise visit.

She greeted me at the door with a tremendous smile and welcoming hug—a shell of the woman I knew. Her mood seemed expansive, but her body was emaciated, almost like a concentration camp survivor. Her skin—white as a ghost. I stepped inside.

As if the sight of my skeletal mother wasn't shocking enough, her living room and kitchen were covered with floor-to-ceiling drawings made directly onto the walls with pencil and ballpoint pen. Human figures of all sizes and forms, imaginary creatures, animals, fish, insects, plants, planets, squiggly lines, geometric and biomorphic shapes animated the room. The total effect was of an all-over pattern, but unlike wallpaper, her drawings didn't blend into the background and nothing repeated. It was the most astonishing and frightening thing a grown son could behold walking into his mother's home.

"Are you feeling manicky, Mom?"

"No, sweetheart. I'm feeling absolutely marvelous. How are *you* feeling?"

"Have you eaten anything today?"

I opened her fridge, saw a bag of coffee grinds, a can of tomato juice, and a lot of white light.

"I'm not really hungry, but you go ahead and eat without me."

After my initial shock, I had to stop and marvel at this woman. It wasn't the first time she had transformed her sad apartment into an amazing work of art. One time she draped dozens of strings from one end of the living room to the other. It looked like a drunken cats cradle. Hanging off of the strings from clothespins and paper clips were Chinese spirit papers, coupons, cancelled postage stamps, scraps of metal and wire mesh, clumps of thread, pieces of candy, shards of ceramic, broken toy parts, orphaned buttons—hundreds of ordinary discards lovingly enshrined into an installation intended to be seen by *no one*. If I had dropped in on her a day later, she might have already taken it down and put everything back into the fastidiously categorized and labeled boxes she kept things in.

Another time I came unannounced, there was no answer when I rang the doorbell, so I let myself in. The living room seemed oddly barren. I called out, "Mom?" There was a faint reply, "Oh, I'm in here, sweetheart." I went into the bedroom and saw that she had taken almost every object from the apartment—her bed, the kitchen table, shelves, the couch, dresser drawers, chairs, blankets, curtains, curtain rods, stacks of papers, framed pictures, pots and pans, dishes, books, shoes, shoe-boxes, hats, a glass vase, some jewelry, a thimble—and balanced them according to size, one on top of the other in the middle of the room to form a totem that nearly reached the ceiling. It looked like she'd been sleeping on the floor next to it and I'd woken her. She sat up and smiled. The scene rattled me. I sat down next to her and looked up at the totem. For someone considered to be unbalanced, she did a remarkable job balancing all this stuff! I put my arm around her and asked the question without having to say a word. She shrugged and said, "I was curious to see if it could be done." I burst out laughing. We both sat there laughing for a long time.

I should have been used to my mother's apartment transformations, but for some reason, this all-enveloping, wall-to-wall drawing took my breath away like nothing she'd ever done before. To this day, I can think of no work of art whose image is as etched in my memory as my mother's living room masterpiece. I remember thinking to myself, *She's the real McCoy, my mother. She doesn't make art for the sake of getting reviews, or making money, or to get tenure. She doesn't even call what she does "art."*

"Can I get you some tea, Bleu?"

"Yeah, sure. And then I'll order in some lunch for us."

While my mother prepared tea in the kitchen, I went to the bathroom and sat on the toilet with the bathroom door open a crack so I could peek at her doodled phantasmagoria. With a tap of my foot I opened the door all the way, and then I saw it. This seemingly cacophonous drawing wasn't just a random collection of marks. From where I was sitting I could see that the long wall of the living room formed one very large, very round face—with two eyes, a nose, a smiling mouth, a chin. *It was the big round face of a man.*

I pulled up my pants and stood in the bathroom doorway looking out. It wasn't just a generic face—it was the spitting image of Hoss Cartwright, the rotund son on the 1960s television western *Bonanza!*

I sat back down on the toilet and tried to remember the actor's name. I closed my eyes and recalled the opening credit sequence. I heard the theme song and saw the map of the *Bonanza* plantation and the branding mark of the sponsor, *Chevrolet*, then one at a time over the character's face came the actor's name.

DAN BLOCKER

That's who played Hoss Cartwright.

I wondered: *Could Dan Blocker be my father? Hoss wasn't the smartest bulb in that cast. Would Mom have gone for a guy like him? He wasn't like his swashbuckling brother, Michael Landon, adored by everyone, or their strappingly handsome father, Lorne Greene—now, He was a father! Hoss was a brother, a son, a supporting actor, an oafish kind of guy—not a father. Dan Blocker. . . Fuck. Well, he's somebody. A face. A perfectly fine face. I'll take it!*

I sat down at the kitchen table and asked my mother to sit. She handed me my tea.

"I see the face, Mom." She looked at me like, *What face?*

"The face. The man's face. I see it."

No reaction.

"It sure looks like Hoss Cartwright from *Bonanza*. Don't you think?"
She looked at me as if she had no idea what I was talking about.

"Did you *know* Dan Blocker, the actor?"

She shook her head no, disturbed by the question.

"Come on. We used to watch *Bonanza* together when I was a kid."

"I vaguely remember. It wasn't very good. A cowboy family with no mother. Did you think it was a good program? I remember the cook. What was his name?"

"Hop Sing."

"Yeah, him I liked. But why are we talking about this, Bleu? Are you feeling nostalgic today? Because today I'm not feeling nostalgic. Today I'm feeling *wonderful*. I'm feeling full of creative energy—and when I feel this way it makes me want to be totally *in the moment*. We can be together now if you want to be in the moment with me. Otherwise, I'm going to have to ask you to leave, and we can talk about old TV programs some other time."

I always felt horribly conflicted calling my mother's doctor at times like these. But she wasn't taking her medication, she wasn't eating or sleeping or bathing, and she wasn't going to listen to me. If I didn't want her to die of malnutrition or exhaustion, I had no choice. And as usual in extreme periods like this, the doctor had no choice but to commit her till she stabilized.

After seeing her so waiflike, so within her own world and withering away, I began to worry that I would visit my mother one day and not be able to find her. She'd be some-where, lost inside her apartment. Lost to me anyway and to the rest of the world.

The Doodler *A NOVEL*

Security guard and lifelong doodler Marla Lockhausen lets loose her tenuous reigns on reality and falls inside one of her intricately penned doodles. Terrified at first, trying to navigate the densely packed fantasy world of her own creation, Marla eventually finds her footing, even her wings, then has a decision to make. Author Bleu Mobley ventures outside his modern realist style of *38 Feet, One Year* and *Ménage à Trois*, with this surreal tale of misunderstanding, solitude, and imagination.

1985, Famulus Press, Stockbridge, MA

The more anyone expressed concern about her doodling ways, the more Marla doodled. When she went to the movies, she doodled in the dark. When she ate, she doodled over napkins and place mats. At ballgames, over scorecards. At plays and concerts, over programs. At the doctor's office, over questionnaires. During school tests, in and around multiple-choice boxes. By the time Marla was a young adult, if you were talking to her you could see in her unfocused gaze that she was imagining spiral patterns across your cheeks and forehead, devil's horns coming out of your head, and every other tooth blackening.

Even though her head was almost always in a book, Marla never seriously considered going to college. She looked for ways of earning a living that required little or no interpersonal contact and had plenty of downtime. A desk security guard was the nearest thing to the perfect job. The graveyard shift, even better.

On weekends she'd often go to tag sales and flea markets to buy used books. At a yard sale a few blocks from her parents' house, Marla met a man named Ernest who collected old bottles: medicine bottles, whiskey bottles, his favorite—blue glass. He struck up a conversation with Marla while holding a blue vase up to the sun, marveling at how perfect it would be for his collection. He admitted to even liking *faux* blue glass as long as it was the right color blue. At one point in their conversation he whispered a question in Marla's ear: "How can they call this a yard sale when everything for sale is on the driveway?" Marla chuckled at Ernest's way of putting things. She wasn't really interested in giving him her phone number or going out with anyone, even for coffee, but Ernest was persistent. Like Marla, he was a person of few words, and there was something about the way he smiled that reminded her of Jason Nahimo, her third-grade crush.

Their relationship shifted to a higher gear when Ernest figured out what made Marla happy, and started bringing her books instead flowers, and it became evident that he had no problem with her doodling ways. After two years of dating she agreed to marry him. When he made love to her she doodled across his back and through his hair with her fingernails. He liked that very much, and he'd reciprocate. In many ways they seemed content together. It was a marriage not unlike many marriages. They cut familiar grooves in each other's lives, reinforcing familiar patterns in familiar ways. He adored her. She was comfortable with him. By their tenth year of marriage, two of the five rooms in their apartment were being used as storage space for all the books, catalogues, and magazines she'd shrouded with ink. Marla had no interest in what she'd already doodled, but Ernest couldn't bear to part with a single page of it. Next to M.C. Escher, she was his favorite artist.

As the years went by, Marla grew more distant from worldly things, including Ernest. Despite her self-absorption, she had always been considerate of the few things

Ernest asked of her. She would never doodle on his papers from work or on any of his favorite newspaper sections till after he read them—until one Sunday morning when she covered most of the articles in *The Week In Review* before he even had a chance to see the paper. It was the week of the G7 Summit and Ernest was looking forward to reading about the meeting of world leaders. Marla turned the headlines into slave ships, the articles into sky-high tombstones, and the photos of the president of the United States and the next six most powerful men in the world into fire-breathing Vikings. Until that day, Ernest had never once raised his voice to Marla. But his frustrations must have been mounting, because when the dam burst it really burst. He flew into a rage, very much like the kind Ernest described his father flying into when he was a kid: foul-mouthed, neck veins bulging, sapping all air from the room. Less than five minutes into his fit, Ernest stopped himself and apologized. Without Marla having to say a word, he promised never to yell at her again. She accepted his apology. Marla figured most men, left to their own devices, were wild animals. At least Ernest made an effort not to repeat the sins of his tyrannical father.

When Marla began doodling across the walls of their apartment, Ernest really started to worry that she was fading away somehow, somewhere. When he made love to her, her fingers went limp. The only thing that captured her attention in the fall of 1980 was a public television series called *Cosmos* hosted by the scientist Carl Sagan. Whenever Dr. Sagan showed animations of things like the big bang and black holes, Marla stopped doodling. She loved the way Sagan cut through technical mumbo jumbo, explaining the cosmos with such clarity and warmth. One story he told was about a Western traveler who asked a Chinese philosopher to describe the nature of the world. The philosopher told the man that the world is a big ball resting on the flat back of an enormous turtle.

"Ah," said the Westerner, "but what does the world-turtle stand on?"

"On the back of a still larger turtle," the philosopher told him.

"Yes, but what does *he* stand on?"

The philosopher said, "It's no use continuing with your questions, it's turtles all the way down." Then Sagan looked into the camera and said, "In the cosmos, it's galaxies, quasars and quarks all the way up and down."

Marla was so enraptured by these stories, Ernest thought maybe buying her books about outer space could be a key to getting her back down to earth. A pragmatic man, Ernest was ready to try anything to get his wife back to her old lovable self. He went to a bookstore and bought Marla a textbook called *The Known Universe.* That was the doodle-saturated book they found face open on the security desk in the Natural Science building the morning of Marla's disappearance.

Tobias Drummond, a senior professor in the literature program and my official mentor at the college, insisted I have something to drink. He pulled out a bottle of tonic water from the mini-fridge he kept under the desk in his office, poured me a glass and took a long swallow from his own glass (wrapped in a suede covering that matched his brown corduroy jacket), then he leaned forward in his chair, looked me in the eye and said, "The problem with you is, you're a grasshopper. You keep jumping from one thing to the next. Take my advice, Bleu—be more like a turtle."

It was only 11 a.m. and I could smell vodka on his breath. On the wall behind his thinning gray hair was a dust-covered plaque that read: *Chancellor's Award for Excellence in Teaching, 1970*. Next to the plaque hung a framed picture of a still youthful-looking Drummond surrounded by attentive students. I sat up in my creaky chair, curious to hear more about turtles and grasshoppers and how they related to the mysterious inner workings of the college. Even though Tobias was assigned to be my mentor, I sensed he genuinely had my best interest at heart.

"You can use this job as a lily pad if you want, and jump to something better, but if you're interested in getting tenure at this godforsaken place, I think it's time for you to pick a pad and stay on it."

"You want to be a biographer? Fine. Pick a *famous* person to write about (not these nobodies), someone with a built-in following, preferably someone who's been dead long enough they can't sue you. After you have three biographies like that under your belt, then you can branch into something else. If you'd rather stick with Fiction, I recommend you slow things down. Write some short stories. Submit them to the story magazines—then come out with a story collection. Once you have that under your belt you can take on a novel. Even if it's really your second or third novel, you can still call it a debut novel. People do that kind of thing all the time. Believe me, there are worse oversights a person can make. When Ginger and I went to get married at City Hall, they asked if either of us had been married before. I said no. (I hadn't told her about my first wife.) The clerk is typing our names into her computer. She says, 'Oh, Mr. Drummond. It says here you were divorced in 1968.' Let me tell you, this was a very bad way to start a marriage. But you don't have to go to City Hall to publish a novel, so don't worry."

Tobias reached under his desk to replenish his glass.

"And whatever you do, make sure your next few books can fit on a shelf, you know, *one spine* per book—this weird format stuff is not helping you. Once you get your tenure you can make books with wings for all I care, or make nothing at all. Look at me! I haven't published a book in twenty-three years, though I've been tinkering with a collection of poems—*modern sonnets*. Soon as I finish building the extension on our country place, I plan on getting back to them, maybe print up a little chap book. Hey, do you think sometime you could show me how to run that printing press you got for the students?

"Anyway, I thought you should know that there are people around here... I'm not naming names, but some of the faculty are, how should I put it... *uncomfortable* seeing you come out with these big fat books year after year. They wonder, *How does he have time to produce all those?* We've got some real bean counters in the department who have nothing better to do than add up how many committees their colleagues are on, how many senior projects they have, and external commitments. People know you have a little cult following. But this isn't a cult. This isn't the avant-garde. This is an *academy*. If you want to advance within the academy, it's good to get an article or two published in an academic journal.

"And don't assume being popular with the students helps you. In many cases being loved by students is a strike against you, the thinking being that any candyman can get on the good side of kids. It's great you've got such favorable student evaluations, but there's a concern—and I'm only the messenger here—that your classes are straying from the curricular goals of the department, and if they get any further afield, nobody here will be able to quantify your student outcomes.

"By the way, have you given any more thought to getting a masters degree? The more I think about it, the more I think it makes sense for you. And while you're at it, maybe you should go all the way and get started on a PhD. Personally, I think these higher degrees are a crock of shit. I only have a bachelor's myself. Of course in my day, you could get a job teaching college if you had real world experience in your field and were interested in educating young people. Nowadays it has nothing to do with real experience or what you can impart. The academy isn't about teaching and learning anymore, it's about propping up the academy. It requires you to have an alphabet soup at the end of your name in order for you to teach in the academy. And who *enables* you to get those letters at the end of your name? The academy is like this multi-headed monster that produces all this waste, and then it feeds on the waste and gets bigger and bigger and full of nothing but its own excrement coming out of its ears; all it can hear is the sound of gurgling. Its nose so full of regurgitation it can't smell anything. Its eyes blinded by too much inward looking. It contorts itself more and more every year, and when May rolls around it congraduates itself with its own honors. Then in September it starts up all over again in a way that's one more step removed from reality than the year before. *Oh Hell*—I'm fifteen minutes late for my class! Well, I hope this has been of some help to you, Bleu. We should have more of these conversations."

Another piece of advice Tobias gave me early on, "Get away in the summers. You have to get yourself far enough away from the college so that coming in for mid-summer orientations and emergency meetings is an impossibility."

One of our colleagues went to a Greek island every summer. Another summered in Bali. Spending the summers in Downeast Maine wasn't as far away as either of those, but the ten-hour drive pretty much did the trick. Being in Maine also put me in contact with nature—something I barely experienced as a kid. The closest thing to a swimming hole I ever knew growing up in Queensbridge was the fire hydrant we used to open for relief on those torturously humid summer days. We didn't actually swim, but we would bum-rush the hydrant's gushing mouth, let its frigid waters drench us with spasms of ecstasy.

For the first nineteen years of my life I'd barely been anyplace you could call *the country* other than the marshlands of New Jersey (with my mother) and a hike up Bear Mountain one time (with some friends) that ended in our getting rescued by park rangers and a helicopter. Then one summer during college, my girlfriend Sharon and I hitchhiked across country with packs on our backs and a plan to hike the tallest peaks in as many mountain ranges as we could. We made it to the top of Elk Mountain in the Poconos, up Mount Davis in the Alleghenies, then we got a ride all the way to Colorado. When I first saw the Rocky Mountains it felt like this cork that had been stuck inside my chest my whole life just popped and I could breathe with my entire body for the first time. We hiked up Mount Elbert, then up Grand Teton, and when we got to California and made it to the top of Mount Shasta, it felt like I had found the place where heaven and earth came together, and I was cured of my total urban immersion for good.

A few years later I was in Maine hiking through Acadia National Park, and the combination of sheer rocky cliffs and roaring ocean reminded me of the California coastline—I was hooked. When I returned to Maine for my first full summer out of range of the college, I rented a cabin with a distant view of a river named Bagaduce in a compound owned by six lesbians, one of them a former lover of Aconsha's. They assured me that their well, which had been poisoned by local homophobes the first year they moved there, had been redrilled and the water tested three times since the poisoning.

The cabin I rented was off a long dirt road, tucked into the woods. It was just me, the black flies and the mosquitoes for three months straight, except for the few weeks in August when Aconsha was able to join me. For seven summers I drove up to that cabin in Maine, and I'd compose my books with few interruptions in this bucolic setting where I could hear myself think, and could go for walks in the woods and along the shore. On Friday afternoons I'd venture out to play non-competitive co-ed softball with a bunch of back-to-the-landers and Maine natives. After the games, we'd eat and drink beer at a new-age pizza place called Pie In the Sky. That's where I started catching wind of the complicated feelings year-rounders have about summer people like me (*some are people, some are not*) who come up from the big cities and love the beauty of the place but bring their city ways and their city needs, and become associated (fairly or not) with encroaching development.

As ruggedly beautiful and rural as Downeast Maine was at that time (and in many ways still is), I came to find out that a lot of its forests had already been ravaged for pulp, lumber, and subdivision. Despite my desire for seclusion and keeping a laser-like focus on my work, I found myself going to more and more meetings and writing press releases and op eds as an unofficial member of a group of activists fighting to preserve the rural lifestyle and environment. The way these politicized schoolteachers, farmers, nurses, and grandmothers fought for what they believed in made a lasting impression on me. No matter what uphill battle they happened to be waging, they didn't seem to care how much time it took from their lives, how silly they may have looked, or how detrimental their actions might have been to their careers or reputations as law-abiding citizens.

Spit Sonata STORIES

Bleu Mobley's first collection of short stories features interior monologues of people in very high places, including: Alexandria atop her fire-watch tower on Lookout Point, Rafael the roofer re-slating a four-story Victorian, Frankie the phone guy up a pole in the Poconos, Vladimir the cosmonaut on rotation in his Soviet space station, and Corrie doing a tree-house sit-in to save the forest on Turtleneck Hill. In all, *Spit Sonata* portrays a dozen elevated yet down-to-earth perspectives on family, work, "progress," and the phases of life.

1986, Terra Firma Books, Providence, RI

2nd Grade Teacher
UP A TREE

Covington. A woman dressed as a sunflower climbed a 105-foot pine tree today on a forested patch of land known as Turtleneck Hill, now owned by the RITE AID Corporation. Corrie McKinnon, 59, a member of RAGA (Rite-Aid-Go-Away) says she will stay in the tree "until the drug franchise packs up its attaché cases and leaves the peninsula."

Mark Hallworthy, a spokesperson for RITE AID, says tomorrow's groundbreaking ceremony, co-sponsored by the Covington Chamber of Commerce, will take place as scheduled. Ms. McKinnon, a schoolteacher at Covington Elementary (currently on sabbatical) and an amateur poet, answered reporters' questions via a walkie-talkie from her 105-foot perch. "This is not a matter of what I want to do. The ancient spirits of Turtleneck Hill have compelled me to keep this vigil," she said.

The "Hill," known for its great views of the Bay and much of the peninsula, was purchased two years ago by RITE AID. The sale was approved by the Town Council, over which Corrie McKinnon's sister Lorrie McKinnon-Chase presides as First Selectperson. Despite the town green-lighting the project, RAGA and other environmental and small business groups vow to continue their battle against what Corrie McKinnon calls "the mallification of rural America." The 10,000 square-foot drug superstore is slated to open sometime next spring.

Sitting in a full-lotus position, Corrie McKinnon, dressed in a sunflower costume, begins the first morning of her 105-foot-high vigil like most other mornings, with an affirmation meditation.

There is so much I have to be thankful for, I almost don't know where to begin. I guess I should start with the most obvious: I AM THANKFUL THAT I AM EVEN ALIVE TODAY. That I am able to sit here, after a night like last night, and count my blessings. I heard Mom saying (even before I got here, I heard her saying), "Corrie, there's no damn need you going up that tree in weather like this." Even without my sunglasses I could see a huge circle around the sun, which meant the air in the upper stratosphere was loaded up with moisture. And the Bay wasn't just calm, it was greasy calm. Mom taught me those were sure signs a big storm was on its way. But I acted like I didn't see. I just knew if they did this groundbreaking without something to counter it, we would lose for sure. Wasn't three hours after I made it to the top, those dark cumulus clouds started blanketing the sky. I could hear Mom calling out to me, "You should know by now, Corrie," just as clear as if she were alive. Soon as the tree started bending in the wind, and I could see the tide getting choppy and the lightning coming closer and closer, I knew I was in for one hell of a night. Once the rain really started coming down, Janice walkie-talkied up to me. "This is last call, my love. Are you really going to stay up there tonight or you coming home with me?" Felt like changing my mind as I watched her yellow poncho get smaller and smaller toward the road.

Should've known better than to listen to the hippie radio station for the weather. They're usually talking about some wonderful or horrible thing from the sixties, like it just happened yesterday. Maybe their weather reports are from the sixties too. Once the rain started going sideways, I began singing "Jesus Savior Pilot Me" and "Throw Out The Life Line." All those hymns I learned as a kid. Made up some new ones too. "Quake Not My Darling Self." And "Hold Fort With The Tremors Of A Love-Sick Owl." When the storm let up a little, I turned on the radio, and the man on the hippie station was saying, "Haven't seen rain like this since Woodstock!" But alright, I am alive and pretty much intact (except for a sore throat and a few cuts and bruises). Took the tarp down soon as the sun popped out from behind the clouds. *Thank you, goddess.* Sun sure feels nice on my eye-of-the-flower face. Finches are chirping, warblers are warbling, squirrels are spiraling up and down the trunk, and beads of water are all over the branches lit up like pearls. If I sit real still, I can hear the pine cones whistle and taste the tears of the ancient wood. Look! Janice is back down at the base of the tree waving newspapers in the air, calling on the walkie-talkie, describing the photo of me climbing the tree on a front page, and another one of me and her on page three building this little tree house. Latoya's down there too and Maureen and a half-dozen other RAGA women each taking turns on the walkie-talkie telling me how crazy I am and how grateful they are. I am grateful for them too, and I'm grateful for their gratefulness. There's Norbert Sanger from *The Star Ledger* and two TV crews.

Mostly there are a whole lot of businessmen I never saw before shaking hands with Town Council people and thirty or forty other misinformed citizens who think RITE AID will bring all these jobs and all this tax money into the community. And oh look who's just arrived, my beloved sister the First Select*person*. I asked her once, "Why don't you just take the leap and call yourself Select*woman*?" She snarled at me, "Not everything in this world is a matter of *gender*." What is she wearing? Oh my goddess, she almost fell. Those high heels are not made for walking on pine needles, dear. A TV reporter is trying to ask her a question. A bunch of reporters are circling her. Janice is there too. She's got the walkie-talkie on so I can listen in. They're all asking her what she thinks about her sister's protest. She gives a succession of "no comments," and weasels out of their net. Surprise, surprise. Whenever my sister hears of the things I do, she usually is embarrassed to no end. She didn't even acknowledge I was her sister. It was like, *What woman? What tree?* Oh, how I love my sister. One thing we have in common, we both like keeping our relationship clean—which means very little contact. I'm thankful for that. I don't expect her to carry a sign saying:

> MY SISTER IS A LESBIAN
> WHO GETS DRESSED UP IN FUNNY COSTUMES.
> MAYBE SHE'S EVEN A WITCH AS FAR AS I KNOW.
> BUT I JUST LOVE HER TO DEATH.

I don't expect anything like that. After all, a Town Selectperson has appearances to maintain.

Looks like they're moving the ceremony down toward the shore so the cameras don't focus on me the whole time. Only problem is, the cameras are not moving. With all of RITE AID's high-priced, velvet-tongued public relations people, *we* are the ones who came up with imagery the cameras want to shoot. I know for a fact they're not building where they have their shovels pointed. This here is the footprint for the site and everyone knows it.

Daryl Marlin from Channel 5 shouts up to me, "Just a couple of questions, Corrie." I do the interview with him, then an interview with *The Weekly Packet*, a real short one with the all-news radio station, and a long one with the hippie station, which was the best so far because I just took over instead of waiting for questions. A lot of these reporters seem more interested in how I poop and pee up here than the devastation of the forests and the water table and the local economy. Norbert Sanger from *The Ledger* sends his camera up in a bucket so I can take pictures of myself for a feature he's doing about two sisters on opposite sides of a political battle. I snap a few pictures with the self-timer, but insist, "This is not about me or my sister." Norbert says he understands that, "but just one last thing—how does it feel going head-to-head with your baby sister?" I yell down, "Norbert, you're not getting a cat-fight sound-bite out of me. This interview is over!" Sarah Lambert writes a wellness column for *The Packet* called "Positive Outlook." Using Janice's walkie-talkie, Sarah says, "Okay Corrie. There's something I've been meaning to ask you. If you're so sure the world is heading for ecological disaster, how do you maintain such a *positive* attitude?"

I walkie-talkie back, "I inherited my mom's conviction that 99% of people on this earth are basically good at heart. They just aren't very well-informed. That's all we're trying to do here is get some better information out to the people. Truth is, Sarah, I'm not feeling very optimistic these days. But what's a sunflower to do? Sit around and mope?"

A reporter from the Bellmore College newspaper is climbing up the tree to do a face-to-face. Turns out the young lady is a business major, thinks I'm nuts. Thinks a totally free market is the answer to the world's problems. Says I remind her of her mother, who's also a fruitcake. I notice she's wearing a Red Sox cap, so I change the topic—tell her how my Grandpa Macky took the mailboat off the island, then hitched a ride down to Boston to see Babe Ruth pitch against the Cubs in the fourth game of the 1918 World Series. The girl didn't know Babe Ruth ever pitched, let alone for the Red Sox. "Oh yeah. He won *both* games against Chicago." I tell her how Grandpa Macky treated me like his grandson, taught me everything about baseball: the proper way to hold a bat, throw a knuckleball, score a scorecard. He'd say, "The only things that brought the fishermen and the carpenters and the artists and the believers and non-believers together on the island were storms, fires, births, deaths, and baseball games." My young reporter friend is a bit of a baseball freak herself. We both complain about people being cynical about baseball. I say, "To me, being cynical about baseball is like being cynical about trees. I have no patience for it." This comment elicits a reluctant half-smile. I decide to tell her how the last four years, on opening day of the baseball season, no matter where I am I wear my authentic 1930s baseball outfit. "And if somebody asks what I'm wearing, I say, 'Don't you know? Today's the opening day of major league baseball. Isn't it great! Baseball's being played all over America again!'" Crystal thinks that's pretty cool. That's her name, Crystal. (No wonder she resents her mother.) Before she leaves, she recommends I ditch the flower get-up if I want people to take me seriously. She promises not to be too hard on me in her article, then she climbs down the tree. The next generation—they're our only hope. That's something to be thankful for—young people with open minds. There's *plenty* of things to be thankful for: St. John's Wort. This tree and the spirits that are in the tree. Shouldn't have to give a name to everything. Leave a few things unnamed and just *feel* them for a change. Maybe throw an unnaming party! Go around unnaming things so we can experience them directly.

Thankful that Mom died in her sleep, didn't suffer much. Soon as she died I called the *Same Day Cremation* man, 2:30 in the morning. He said, "It'll take three hours to get there." Lorrie looked anxious, "What are we going to do for *three hours?*" I took a deck of cards out of my bag. "Let's play Pitch." Lorrie said, "Yeah. That was Mom's favorite game. It reminded her of being out on the sardine boat." We sat there next to our mother's dead body playing round after round of Pitch.

"Mom would like this."

"Yeah, she would." Didn't say much else. We were both so stupefied from staying up four nights in a row. When the *Same Day Cremation* man finally came, he was one of these high-strung ectomorph thin-as-a-rail types, looked like Anthony Perkins. I whispered in Lorrie's ear, "Oh my goddess. The man from *Psycho* has come to cremate our mother." That was the last close moment my sister and I have had in three years. That's something to be thankful for—memories, while I still have them.

I wonder what to do with my body. Better leave instructions. Never know when some car will just… or a comet… or an aneurism… *anything* can happen. I always assumed I'd be cremated. Let whoever wants a part of me, have some. But if I die intact, it would be fun to have an open casket, be buried in one of my costumes. Have Janice dress me up in my baseball uniform. Either that or the cowgirl outfit and my whip. Not sure which. Maybe let Janice decide. Write: *Whatever you think is more fitting. Just make sure people enjoy the viewing.*

The groundbreaking festivities have been over for a while, but there's some kind of commotion going on down there. Focus the binoculars. Janice is trying to get a word in with the sheriff who's aiming a megaphone up at me.

"CORRIE! THIS IS HANK. I DON'T HAVE TO TELL YOU THAT YOU'RE TRESPASSING ON PRIVATE PROPERTY. MAKE YOU A DEAL, CORRIE. YOU COME DOWN HERE RIGHT NOW AND I'LL TEAR UP THIS WARRANT, WHICH HAS, LET'S SEE. . . FOUR, FIVE, SIX MISDEMEANORS AND YOUR NAME ON IT. COME DOWN NOW, CORRIE! PARTY'S OVER."

I have nothing against the sheriff. Never voted for him, but his wife Megan sings with us in the *Laughing Gull Chorale*. Decent people really.

If I wasn't a Virgo, I'd tell Janice to dress me up in the baseball outfit *and* to put the whip in my hand. But I'm too precise for that kind of mixing and matching. It's got to be one or the other. *Mmm.* Looks like the sheriff's sending up Deputy Hawkins to come talk to me. Dwayne was a student of mine fourteen years ago. He was a sweet boy.

The baseball uniform would really be neat. It's about gamesmanship. It's about physical strength and team spirit and individuality and tradition. It's about Grandpa Macky, and being a tomboy. All kinds of good things. Whereas the cowgirl outfit...

I hear Dwayne losing his footing about halfway up. Poor kid. Always had two left feet. "You alright Dwayne?" The things they make you do when you're a rookie cop. By the time he makes it up, he's huffing and puffing like an old goat. Dwayne grabs my hand and climbs onto my four-foot-square platform.

"You want some water?"

"No thank you, Ma'am."

"What's this *Ma'am* business?"

"Come on, Miss McKinnon. Come down of your own free will. *Please*. Nobody wants a scene." I've got nothing to say to this child.

The cowgirl outfit would be such a hoot—mother-of-pearl buttons, shiny studs, long suede fringes. I always liked fringes. The cowgirl outfit is about power and being exotic. Of course it's really the whip in my hand I keep picturing. The whip is like a...

What's that sound? Is that... Oh my goddess. That's a state police helicopter up there. It's heading this way! I look down and see my sister hiding behind the sheriff as the Chamber of Commerce people and the RITE AID people look up at the helicopter hovering over me. *These people are crazy!*

Fold back into full lotus. Straighten my green stem spine. Sing "Oh, Beautiful This Tired Grove." Arms in an X across my chest. Sing "Fill My Lungs With The Proud Queen Courage Of Highest Things." Face ringed by golden petals, calm but defiant. Sing "The Burning River Out Of Its Flames." Mom's picture in my breast pocket. Eyes dead ahead.

"I'm not sure which is worse," Aconsha wondered aloud, "the Indian upbringing that trains you to be obedient and leads you to poverty and slaughter, or the American corporatocracy that only cares about the almighty dollar."

We were in Samir and Carla's apartment, eating Mexican take-out, drinking margaritas. There'd been other occasions when Aconsha expressed her gratitude for being part of two great cultures, but on this night back in 1984, she could only see "the oppressive structures, hypocrisies, and lies" of both. Three days earlier, her cousin Partha died in the Bhopal gas leak disaster.

Samir agreed with Aconsha about the hypocrisies and lies, but not about the corporatocracy. "After I left Kenya, I became a staunch anti-colonialist, pro-Marxist spewer of all the same slogans and platitudes that you spew. That's why I went to live in Moscow—to experience socialism first hand. I visited Cuba and went back to see what the great socialist pan-African liberators had made of their countries. That's when I became a rabid anti-communist. America is the *best* country, the *best* system in the world. What did Winston Churchill say: 'Capitalism is the worst system on earth, except for all the others'"?

Sidney Lewiston—another friend from the building, and perhaps the oldest living communist in America—guffawed into his margarita. "That's the problem with you right-wingers," he said looking at Samir. "You're always confusing capitalism with democracy. What Churchill actually said was: '*Democracy* is the worst form of government except for all the others.'" Sidney was beginning to have trouble with his short-term memory, but anything he knew from fifty years ago, he could remember like it was yesterday.

"Okay, I stand corrected," Samir conceded. "The point I was trying to make (and I feel *terrible* for your loss, Aconsha, you *know* that—but you shouldn't blame America or capitalalism): It's *human fallibility* that killed your cousin and all those people."

Reeling, Aconsha fired back. "It's not *fallibility* when Union Carbide's own scientists warned that this could happen—and they did nothing to prevent it. It's greed!"

I stood up, walked behind Aconsha's chair to massage her neck. She continued venting. "Four years ago Partha told me about accidents at the Bhopal plant. Five workers were hospitalized after a cyanide storage tank leaked, and one of them died. Two years ago some kind of pump thing failed and twenty-five workers were hospitalized. In today's paper they're saying that the leaks were so frequent, they turned off all the safety sirens. Now three thousand people are dead. Maybe millions will die prematurely over time. That's not fallibility. That's *mass murder*. That's your wonderful corporate system at work. And the local and national authorities in India are accomplices to the crime."

"Religion has been the people's opiate in India for a long time," Sidney said, never letting his sketchiness about a subject keep him from speaking about it, "but you can't eat religion. You can't dress your children in the parables of the Bagava Gita."

"The *Bhagavad* Gita," Aconsha injected, correcting Sidney.

"Exactly! After centuries of meditating in nothing but loin cloths, and bowing down to cows, a lot of people in India started looking at Americans, thinking why can't *we* have blue jeans and cars and color television sets? You can't blame them! So companies like Union Carbine came…"

"Union Car*bide*." Samir and Aconsha said in unison.

"Right. They came to India, these men in their three-piece suits, pockets bulging with American dollars, saying, 'Oh we have all these great jobs we can give you people so long as you let us build these chemical plants in your population centers—*state of the art*. They never explain, we're going to pay two cents on the dollar. They never say, oh we love countries like yours that have little or no safety regulations."

Aconsha patted my hand to stop massaging her. She was restless, fuming. "Yeah, but India is not a child, Sid. It happens to be swarming with engineers and scientists. We even have newspaper reporters and people who write and read books over there. Not just naked Brahmans. The local authorities knew what was going on, but they did nothing."

I asked Aconsha if she wanted to call it a night. She shook her head, making it clear that she'd rather fight misconceptions than lie around grieving.

Samir took out an already rolled cigarette from his shirt pocket and gestured for me to go up to the roof with him. "Oh terrific!" Aconsha quipped. "You can go outside and *choose* to kill yourself, one cigarette at a time, but my cousin didn't have a choice. None of those people had a choice." Out of respect for what Aconsha was going through, Samir put the cigarette back in his pocket. Aconsha thanked him with a smile, then turned to Sidney. "While we're on the topic of smoking, there's something else you might want to know about India, since you're becoming such an expert."

Sidney raised an eyebrow.

"Poppy is a major crop in India, and millions of people smoke opium there as a part of everyday life. So you really shouldn't use opium as a metaphor when you're talking about India. If anything, you might want to say: in India, opium is the opiate of the people."

"Okay," Sidney said, putting his hands up like he got busted. "Now *I* stand corrected."

Samir never considered a discussion over until there was a declared winner, preferably himself. He steered the conversation back to the question of culpability." I still don't think it's fair to blame American capitalism for a horrible accident that happened in a third-world country. I grew up in the third world too, you know. This has nothing to do with American capitalism. You think an accident of this magnitude can't happen in a communist country? I'm sure it already has. Plenty of times. But China and the Soviet Union are so secretive we never hear about it."

"The truth is," Sidney exclaimed, his seventy-six-year-old index finger pointing up toward the empirical truth he was about to state, "what country you live in or economic system it supposedly adheres to is becoming irrelevant. It's only a matter of time before there'll be no more nation-states or municipalities or even ethnicities or religions. There'll be no such thing as America or New York, India or Bhopal, no tribes, sects, or governments. All those identifiers will be meaningless. There will just be corporatelands. People will live and work in places called Union Carbideland or Walmartland or Boeingland. Instead of your country's flag, you'll put your hand on your heart and pledge to a corporate logo and sing your corporateland jingle. Unless there's some kind of worldwide revolution to reverse this tide (which I don't see happening), you can mark my words."

Boxland *A NOVEL*

In *Boxland*, The Corporation has super-seded all other jurisdictions. Notions of town, county, state, nation—even continent—exist only as hearsay. Free of having to pay government taxes, keep up with a whole lot of bad news, or vote for indistinguishable politicians, Boxlanders live and work for The Corporation in a relative state of contentedness. Recently promoted to a plum Vice Assistant Manager of Receiving position, Camilo Rios (also a devoted husband and first time father of a newborn baby girl) has every reason to feel fortunate. Yet he's consumed by a feeling of dread. This cautionary tale by the author of *38 Feet, One Year*, is a portrait of a suddenly sleep-less man living in a narcoleptic world.

1987, Halcyon Press, Charlotte, NC

As Tobias Drummond leaned back in his office chair, I could see long linty hairs sprouting from his nostrils. He warned me, if I didn't improve my file within the year, my chances of getting tenure were only fifty-fifty. In order to raise the odds, all three areas of criteria—teaching, community service, and professional achievement—needed to show marked improvement. As far as teaching was concerned, Tobias recommended I stop proposing new courses. "Every new elective you teach and get special funding for means somebody else (perhaps someone serving on your review committee) has to teach another one of your required classes. In the abstract, program innovation is a great thing. In reality, too much of it breeds resentment. The same goes for *how* you teach."

Whatever decent reputation I enjoyed among students was offset by the one or two complaints waged against me every year by disgruntled students and parents objecting to my unorthodox methods.

My very first day as a college professor, a student asked me what my attendance policy was. Since I'd never given it any thought, I made something up. "It's important that you be present. I mean, have *presence* of mind, presence of heart while you're in attendance. Otherwise, you might as well stay home." The student looked at me like, *What kind of answer is that?* "Alright," I said formulating a policy as I spoke, "you have to come to every class. But if one day you come to class and you learn nothing, then you're entitled to miss the next class. But you must be honest when you ask yourself, *Did I get something from today's class?*" A young man with a ring in his nose and four smaller rings through his bottom lip raised his hand. "What if you're sick or have a family emergency?"

"What if I'm sick?"

"No—*us*. Most professors allow a certain number of absences."

"Well… Since this is a writing class, if you're out sick… your assignment will be to write about being sick. What does it feel like to be sick? Describe the dreams you had while you were sick. Are they different from dreams you have when you're well? Did anybody take care of you while you were sick? Who did that for you? Why did they take care of you? What was it like being cared for?

"If you miss a class because someone in your family died—knock wood—write about it. It's *terrible* if a grandparent dies or an aunt or uncle, but it's important to go back home and attend the funeral. Feel the senselessness and the randomness of death, or whatever it is you're feeling. If you were at your uncle's bedside before he died, write about that. If he recovered and you reverted back to not really liking the guy, write about it. If he almost died but recovered, and you see a noticeable change in the man, or change in yourself, write about it. If you have to miss a class because, I don't know… your parents are getting divorced or they're selling their house, and you come back to clean out your room and stumble across something that you'd forgotten all about, write about it! Or, if after all that, your parents decide *not* to split up or *not* to sell the house and that leaves you feeling confused, you don't know whether to be happy or angry or sad—your make-up assignment is to write about it."

By the end of that semester it occurred to me that the best papers were from students who missed classes for one reason or another. Whether they were about death or illness or being hungover or falling in love, or just your run of the mill college debauchery, those papers stood out as very raw and honest, or at least as well-spun lies, which gave me the idea for my first elective course offering.

In "Field Writing," students had to engage the world outside the classroom and beyond their own navels. Every week, I'd drive the class somewhere—to a cemetery, a forest, the middle of Harlem, a hospice. Three hours later I'd pick them up. The following week they'd hand me their edited writings in the van ride to that week's site. The most popular class I ever taught, "Field Writing" also generated the most complaints.

In "The Fake Class," I admitted to the students that I had only taken one creative writing class when I went to college, and I really didn't know the proper way to run a writing class. I told them that I often feel like a charlatan, like I'm getting away with something, and I know some day I'll get caught and have to get a real job. There were always a few students—when I said things like that—who'd look at me like I was out of my mind. But my confession would ignite a spark of recognition in the students who worried that they were fakes too, that their thoughts were insignificant, their voice inconsequential, and it was only a matter of time before they would get caught. If we were indoors, I would close the door so we could all safely be fakes together. Outside, we'd take note of the fake world around us: brands blazoned across t-shirts projecting the spirit of a sneaker cult or carbonated drink, the different masks we put on in the daily costume party that is our lives. Then we'd set out in search of the real. "I know what *I* do in my work and in my life," I'd tell the students. "I'm an expert at being my imperfect self. What I have no expertise in is what *you're* interested in doing, what kinds of things you want to write about. But I'm here to help you figure it out."

"I am not paying for my daughter to learn about *fakeness* from a man who admits he's a charlatan!"

a very red-in-the-face father told the dean while I looked on. The man's embarrassed daughter sat next to him, still wanting to take the class. The father insisted not only that the dean *un*enroll his daughter from my class, but that the entire course be shut down. "It won't look good if *The Daily News* or *The National Review* runs a story about a state college teaching students about fakeness." Fortunately, Dean Lipsky was big on curricular innovation. She understood what academic freedom meant, and was skillful at mollifying pedestrian complainers.

After Lipsky left the college we got a new dean, a priggish fellow named Lambert

Worthington, who was much more responsive to parental pressure. When a kid in my
"Composing Book" class complained about *the alchemy project*, Worthington convened
a meeting with the dean of students, the college ombudsperson, the student, his parents,
and me. The young man's family happened to be very religious, and when he told his
parents about a classmate who bandsawed a biography of Billy Graham into the shape of
a cross and spray-painted it gold, all hell broke loose. To add insult to heresy, apparently,
I had told the class that the re-done Billy Graham book was *brilliant*. "Isn't this supposed
to be a creative writing class?" asked the exasperated father. "Why are you telling students
to *destroy* books? Are you a Nazi?"

"No," I explained. "I have family who were killed by the Nazis. I'm only alive today
because my grandfather escaped a pogrom in Poland. Most of his family perished in
Auschwitz." Shaking her head in dismay, the mother asked, "Then how could you require
students to desecrate books?"

Believing that fear is mostly rooted in misunderstanding, I tried to explain the goals
of my course. "I start the 'Composing Book' class with a series of *un*doing projects as a way
of shaking up the baggage students bring with them about how to write and what a book is.
Did Martin tell you about the Dada poems he made?" Martin shrugged. His parents started
to go numb. The dean of students looked at me nervously as I explained Dada poetry to
these born-againers. "That's what we do during the first two weeks of 'Composing Book'—
disassemble things that already exist and remake them. That's the purpose of the *alchemy
project*. Not to destroy books, but to make them more of what they actually are, or transform
them altogether. One student constructed a model of an apartment building out of cardboard and mounted a book about urban gardening on the roof, then he rototilled and
fertilized the book's cover, and planted a miniature garden. You've got to see it! Someone
else in the class who happens to be a survivor of childhood leukemia, took her favorite
book, which she described as *pure medicine*, very carefully unstitched the binding and
folded each section into the compartments of a pill box so she could parcel her readings
out into daily dosages. Another student picked a book she didn't like at all. I think it was
called *Administrative Behavior*. She took it to a laundromat, washed and dried it several
times till this stiff, foreboding book turned into something soft and lovely.

"Once they've shaken things up in those first exercises, wiped the slate clean of expectations and rote ways of doing things, they begin to build language up from nothing, starting
with a few words at a time, working up to sentences, then paragraphs, stories—until they're
composing their own books from start to finish, treating the form and the content as one
thing. It's really amazing what the students come up with by the end of the semester."

As my passion for the subject and the students became evident to the parents, their
outrage turned into bewilderment. "I sure wish Martin could be a part of this year's final
exhibition and reading that the class puts on for the school. But if you're uncomfortable

with the course, I'll sign the withdrawal form right now." I took a pen out of my pocket and removed the cap. Martin and his parents looked at each other. The mother said, "We'll discuss it some more with Martin and let you know what we decide." As Martin and his family backed out the door, the dean of students looked at me disapprovingly. Holding back a smile, the ombudsperson muttered something about the college needing to avoid another lawsuit. Worthington didn't tell me to change the way I taught, but his body language made it clear—if I didn't watch myself he could do me in with the stroke of his pen.

The following year I was able to get a commercial printer to donate a letterpress, a few cases of type, and some bookbinding equipment to the college. I converted my office into a print shop and mounted "The Artist/Writer Workshop," a hands-on course that students seemed to really appreciate. But two faculty members in the visual art department complained to the Curriculum Committee that I was teaching studio art, which, they said, was *their* area of expertise. When and if I received a terminal degree in visual arts, they would entertain the possibility of my teaching an art course. Until then, the committee felt they had no choice but to discontinue my class.

A similar controversy did in my "Writing Across Campus" course. The project that created the biggest furor was called *Campus of Dreamers*. In the outdoor evening presentation, close-up photographs of mouths and eyes were projected onto the large south wall of the Performing Arts Center as detailed descriptions of the students' dreams echoed through the campus. Some patrons of the Performing Arts Center walking from their cars to see a performance of *Swan Lake* got scared that extraterrestrials had landed. When they found out that it was part of a student art project, a few of them complained that they could have died of heart attacks. There were also complaints about the broadcasting of explicit and inappropriate sexual encounters. Two days later, I was called into Worthington's office and given the choice to either censor the students' projects before they went public or discontinue the class. I chose to discontinue.

As for the "community service" portion of my file, I was already on four departmental and two campus-wide committees, and was a union delegate. But Tobias thought I needed one more very visible feather in my cap. When the Humanities division received word from the state that its application to offer a graduate program in creative writing was finally approved, Worthington called me into his office and asked if I'd like to be the program's first director. I knew I didn't want to do it, but I told him I'd give it some thought. When I mentioned the offer to Tobias, he explained to me that Worthington wasn't really *asking*. I had no interest in heading up a graduate program, especially since I never went to graduate school myself. But I got the message and accepted the honor, which had no salary increase or release time attached to it.

If I went by the old adage "publish or perish" (having published nine books in nine years), I'd have thought "professional achievement" was my strong card. But Tobias convinced me that my publications, "however inventive and novel," had little standing in academia. So I decided to bite the bullet and go for a master's degree. Luckily, I discovered a way to do it without having to attend classes or subject myself to assignments and tests or the kinds of critiques my students had to endure.

The University Without Walls, "dedicated to individualized learning," is physically located in Burlington, Vermont, though I only had to go there one time—to meet with the president in her small fifth-floor office in an old commercial building on Main Street. President Bailes, a woman in her early to mid-sixties with long ghost-white hair and a very youthful-looking face, asked me to please call her Randy. On the walls of her office surrounding her various degrees and certificates were framed photographs of her shaking hands with Jimmy Carter, holding a plaque of some kind next to Joseph Campbell, arm in arm with Maya Angelou, and group photos of her with the likes of Linda Ellerbee and Vladimir Horowitz. There were no pictures of students walking with books through a campus green, no graduation scenes, no architectural plans for new buildings.

A stack of my books and the binder full of reviews that I sent with my application were piled on a table near her desk. She explained to me that a lot of their students were already college professors and accomplished professionals. Then she urged me to go for a combined masters/doctoral degree. I could do it all from my home in as short as three years. I would develop my own program in consultation with an advisor of my choosing. I'd never even have to meet this person. My doctoral thesis would evolve organically out of my individualized program and would require two additional outside readers.

I wrote Randy a check right then and there. We shook hands, both pleased by the deal struck. Then we redid the handshake and the smile for the photo she took of the two of us using the time-release gizmo on her new camera.

The Codex Coup:
How Gutenberg's
Invention of
Moveable Type
Helped Destroy
the Oral and
Pictorial Roots
of Storytelling

Bleu Mobley PhD Candidate

Before leaving Vermont I drove my rented car to Calvin Coolidge State Forest in the Green Mountains. For ten dollars I got a wilderness site—a concrete lean-to on Shrewsbury Peak, listed as having panoramic views of three states. Even though it was rainy and foggy the whole time and I barely could see past my feet, it was a perfect spot to reflect on the direction of my life and map out my individualized learning plan. I would continue to write and compose my books the way I was used to, but I'd back up whatever I did with theoretical papers, using whatever academic lingo was necessary to get the degree.

Three-and-a-half years later I completed my doctoral thesis: *The Codex Coup: How Gutenberg's Invention of Moveable Type Helped Destroy the Oral and Pictorial Roots of Storytelling*. It was never published.

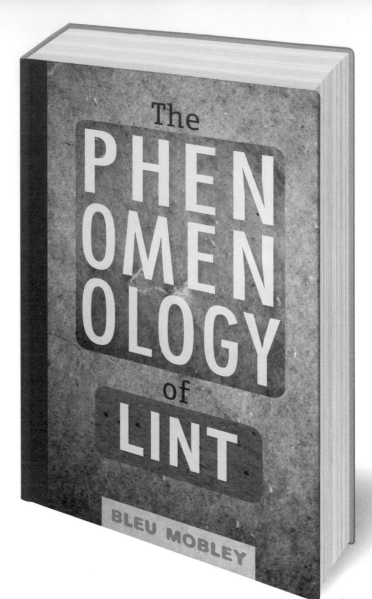

The Phenomenology of Lint *A NOVEL*

Originally from a small village in Northern Pakistan, Sultana Farook grew up handwashing and air-drying her family's clothes. Now a twenty-six-year-old interdisciplinary doctoral student at New York University, Sultana is obsessed with those colorful patches of lint that get trapped in washer-dryers throughout the industrialized world. Sultana's fascination with laundry lint inspired her thesis project—*The Phenomenology of Lint*. Its premise: If a society can be judged by the way it treats its prisoners, perhaps an individual, family, or even an apartment building can be better understood by its laundry lint. Using volunteer residents of her apartment complex in Queens as her population base, Bleu Mobley's hardworking protagonist compares lint specimens with oral histories only to discover hidden truths and unexpected friendships.

1989, Tellurian Editions, Brooklyn, NY

excerpt

At first, Sultana was surprised that the homeless man who sleeps on the third-floor hallway volunteered for her lint project. Then she realized it was a way for him to get his clothes cleaned. (On her flyer she promised to wash participants laundry as part of the trade). She also slipped the man some cash in exchange for his oral history, and made him a home-cooked dinner. Sitting across from her in clean clothes and freshly washed hair (she let him use her shower too), Sultana *saw* the man for the first time. No longer was he just the hairy homeless guy, a smelly shadow that sneaks into the building late at night when it's cold and sneaks out before most people leave for work in the morning. He was actually a rather handsome man, curiously familiar looking, with deep-set green eyes, a fine long nose, and a sweet laugh that bubbled up out of nowhere and made her small, sparsely furnished apartment feel warm and not so claustrophobic.

Norman had been a professional man, working as a typesetter at a newspaper for twenty-five years till they switched from hot type to cold, and he fell through the cracks and never resurfaced. He's got three kids out in the world somewhere and an ex-wife who's remarried to a banker. His only sibling, a brother he looked up to all his life, died a little over a year ago. That was the hardest loss of all. It only took two follow-up questions before it came out that Norman sleeps outside apartment 3N because the man who used to live there—who was taken away in an ambulance in the middle of the night six months ago and never seen again—was Norman's older brother. *That's why he looked so familiar!*

After Norman said good night and thanked Sultana for the excellent dinner and the "exquisite" company, and she thanked him for his generosity in sharing his story and his lint, Sultana closed the door, washed the dishes, and went back to her word processor. Her doctoral presentation was only three weeks away. Picking up where she left off, she typed:

Subject profile 64:
Dilip is a thirty-four-year-old man who came to the United States, he says, because India was no place for a gay man to feel in any way free. "Hiding. Always hiding." An aspiring actor, Dilip mostly does clerical temp work and volunteers as a docent at the Museum of Natural History. The walls of his ground-floor, one-room apartment are covered with photographs of loved ones and movie stars from Bollywood and Hollywood. Peacock feathers, beaded necklaces, hats, and colorful scarves hang off his closet door and around his oval, wood-framed mirror. The smell of fruit-scented candles and sandalwood incense permeate the air.

Lint description and interpretation:
Dilip's mauve, heliotrope, and chartreuse garments produce shimmering, prismatic lint specimens. Fluffy beach towels, silk pillowcases, and chenille scarves give these specimens a velvety, almost luxurious tactility. [It should be noted that Dilip carefully discards all pocket matter, hair, paper, coinage, and granules of dirt from his clothing before depositing them into the wash. In fact, he treasures cleaning out his own lint trap and has kept a lint collection of his own for years before he ever knew about my lint study project.] Microscopic observation of Dilip's laundry lint specimens reveal a topography that resembles the Himalayas, the land where the subject is from, a land of incredible variegated peaks, plateaus, and valleys, a land the subject tries but finds hard to put behind him.

- -

Subject profile 65:
Recent arrivals to the United States, Dalila and Kofi Samaddar are refugees from Zaire. They live in a studio apartment on the seventh floor. Trained as an electrical engineer, Kofi works as a salesman at a sneaker store.

Trained as a teacher, Dalila works as a gardener. She is four months pregnant. Kofi's face reveals a profound sadness, while Dalila possesses a bubbly personality and a full-bodied laugh. Dalila and Kofi fled their home country due to a military dictatorship and political persecution.

Lint description and interpretation:

The Samaddar lint specimens range in color from a lavender gray to saffron gray. To the naked eye, the surface textures are unremarkable in their density and pattern, although microscopic observation reveals a wide range of substrate matter. In between the coarse fibers of burlap and globular grains of garden dirt and shredded bathroom tissue—embedded into shirtsleeve, cotton hanky, and flannel pillow case fibers—I found evidence of tears. In and around the finer fibers of hair, linen, and rayon, also signs of tears. Much to my surprise, nearly 100% of the salty, bottomless-pit-variety tears are traceable to Dalila Samaddar.

I approached Ms. Samaddar, delicately, with the picture of sadness the fibers painted, and asked for a second interview. She agreed to tell me more of her story:

"I was not a political person growing up, except that I knew I didn't care for this man Mobutu Sesu Seko who rules our country with fists of iron for all my life. Two months before graduating from the university there was a big demonstration, students marching through the campus calling for democracy in the country, setting government cars on fire. I had no idea what was going on. I just knew that I couldn't get to my class. A few weeks later, government soldiers stormed into the dormitory, searching rooms and arresting people. They wanted to arrest me too, so I ran. Four soldiers chased after me until I fell on the ground. They beat me over the head so hard with their belts, and they kicked me. When you are on the ground and you see a soldier's boot coming into you, the boot is very big and very hard. They threw me in a bus with other students and drove us to a secret place to ask us what was our involvement in the demonstration. I told them, 'I know nothing about it.'

I won't bother you with all the details of what they did to me, but I will tell you that I was taken to the hospital in a coma. When I woke up, I promised myself that one day I will make them pay for what they did to me. They can't do these savage things and get away with it. I was a simple, happy-go-lucky girl who wanted to become a schoolteacher, and they turned me into a fighter for democracy. That's how I met Kofi. He was a student leader of UDPS, an underground opposition party fighting against the military dictatorship.

Kofi and I had a baby boy. It was an unplanned pregnancy, but

```
we loved the boy with all of our heart. Kofi had a govern-
ment job. Underground he worked against the government and
above ground he worked for the government. There were no
other places for him to work as an engineer except for the
government, and we wanted to save enough money to send our
son to a private school run by Jesuits. It was a dangerous
double life for Kofi, but it was the life he led until one
day he got caught leaving a UDPS meeting. By the end of that
day we lost everything including our little boy.

If I could swim across the sea of tears you found in your
microscope and reunite with my son, I would do it (even though
I am not a very good swimmer). I would do anything to get him
back. We are having another baby soon, but he or she will never
be a replacement for our first son. I hope I answered your
question. Now you'll have to excuse me."
```

As Sultana types her thesis, thoughts of her dinner conversation with Norman reverberate inside her head. Is there anything else she could do for him? She's only a teaching
stipend away from being homeless herself. To lose your whole family and your job and
home and your identity as a contributing member of society must be unbearable. How
much loss can one person endure? She knows what it's like being displaced not of your own
choosing, but it's hard to imagine the kind of displacement Norman has to live with. Such
a refined man, she had no idea. Still typing, her mind wanders to other homeless people
she steers clear of going to and from her building every day. What are *their* stories?
What secrets would their lint specimens coax out of their hiding places?

Unable to concentrate, Sultana stops typing and puts on a clean pair of white cotton
gloves. Curiosity has overtaken her normally disciplined adherence to her to-do list. Very
carefully, she takes Norman's sinewy swath of lint out of its clear plastic bag, extracts a few
fibers with a pair of tweezers, places them onto a glass slide, slips the slide on the mounting
stage of her microscope, then places her eye on the eyepiece and focuses.

Sidney Lewiston and I are at a bar on the corner of 3rd Street and the Bowery. It's a
bright, sunny, early afternoon, December 1986. We're not alcoholics. We're there to watch
live television coverage of the Senate Intelligence Committee's first inquiry into the Iran-
Contra scandal. We *are* drinking, slowly. Scotch on the rocks for Sid. Lite beer for me. To
news junkies like us, this is a much anticipated event. We are giddy at the prospect of watching these White House mercenaries get their comeuppance (which is terrible when I think

about it now, considering the thousands of people who died because of Iran-Contra).

Dressed in a highly decorated marine uniform, Lieutenant Colonel Oliver North stands, raises his right hand, looks into the camera with the righteous pride of a self-anointed crusader, swears to tell the truth and nothing but the truth, then proceeds to take the Fifth.

"More than anyone," he says, stiff-jawed, oozing with pious earnestness, "I want to tell the American people the whole story." If only Congress would give him immunity, he'd be happy to tell the committee everything he knows. In the spirit of watching a ballgame at a bar, I shout at the TV: "Yeah, like how you subverted the Constitution, an arms embargo, and the Bible in the name of protecting the American way of life."

Regardless of North's silence—and the silence of John Poindexter, his boss at the National Security Council—the story is coming out that the U.S. government, or an off-the-shelf cell within the government, secretly sold high-tech weapons to Iran (an avowed enemy) as part of an arms-for-hostages deal, then funneled the profits (via Israel, Swiss banks, and private third parties) into an illegal and gruesomely violent guerilla war waged against the democratically elected (socialist) Nicaraguan government and anyone thought to be their supporters. Sidney and I are horrified by what they did, but we are not shocked.

Another NSC cog (whose name escapes me) refuses to answer questions about the president's conflicting statements until he is given security clearance to hire a lawyer.

A woman sitting next to me at the bar grumbles, "*Ah.* They'll never pin the tag on the Gipper." Sidney laughs. "That's why they call him the Teflon president."

"Plausible deniability," I say.

"What's that?" the woman asks.

Sidney turns to her. "You *don't know* what plausible deniability is?"

"No," she says. "I've been busy raising four kids the last fifteen years."

Sidney looks up at the rack of wine glasses hanging upside down above our heads. "Plausible deniability is when there's a, uh... nefarious, uh... a covert... How would you explain it, Bleu?"

"It's a euphemism for making sure that the head of an organization (be it the mafia or the chief executive of, say, the federal government) is shielded from any paper trail that could tie him to criminal activities."

Sidney brags on me. "This guy knows *all* this stuff. He used to be a reporter. He knows everything they'll never show you on TV. Tell the lady about the drug-running our government is doing, selling cocaine *in this country* to fund the Contras."

I press my finger against my lips to shush Sidney.

"You're right!" Sidney says under his breath. "What was I thinking? I don't know who this woman is. Any of these people could be FBI."

I say to the woman, "My friend here is referring to a rumor I heard. I'm not sure what it's all about. Let's see if any of these senators ask about it."

Sidney leads me by my shirtsleeve to a table in the far corner of the bar. He's paranoid all of a sudden that we're surrounded by spies. "You're right, Bleu," he whispers, cupping my ear with his hand, "we really do have to be careful. I just read in *The Socialist Worker* about the Feds reviving their domestic infiltration techniques. You know, bringing back the same kinds of shenanigans they used against political dissidents in the seventies. What was that called? Co and-something?"

"COINTELPRO."

"Yes, COINTELPRO! Witch hunting, breaking into people's files, like that organization they raided that works with poor people in El Salvador. What's their name? C-something?"

"CISPES. The Committee in Solidarity with the Peoples of El Salvador. You know they're suing Reagan for violating their..."

"Man oh man! I should really know better than to shoot my mouth off in public. I grew up with the FBI skulking around my Uncle Zalman's place. In those days they were easy to spot. Today they're more sophisticated. And it's not just the FBI anymore; the CIA has spies. The NS, uh, Oliver North's agency—whatdoyacallit?"

"The NSA."

"Yeah, they have their own spies. And the other NS-something?"

"NSC."

"And the INS. Even the Army has spies."

"Actually, every branch of the military has its own intelligence. Even FEMA is a spy agency under Reagan. That's what he means by *emergency management*. Forget about hurricanes—it's the environmentalists and the peaceniks we have to protect ourselves against."

"Did you ever request your file?" Sidney asks, looking around to make sure no one hears.

"My tenure file?"

"Your FBI file!"

"I can't imagine there'd be much of a file. All the reporting I did is in the public record, and all I've been doing since are oddball books that very few people read. Why would they waste their time keeping a file on me?"

"You're talking on the phone with this reporter friend of yours all the time, right? You got fired from your newspaper job because you were too radical, right? All I'm suggesting is, you put in a request with the freedom of, uh. . . you know, the information uh. . . whatdoyacallit?"

"A Freedom of Information Act request."

"Exactly!"

Later that night when Aconsha comes home from a rehearsal, I tell her that I'm requesting a copy of my FBI file. She bursts out laughing. "I'm sorry. I love you, honey, but you flatter yourself. If you lived under a fundamentalist regime or in an Eastern Block country or in India where writers and poets are taken seriously as dangerous threats to the system, I could understand your being worried. But you live in America where nobody, least of all the government, cares about the books you write—about old couples and men painting barns and doodlers falling into their doodles."

"You're right. They have bigger fish to fillet." I tell her it was Sid's idea.

"Ha! Two delusional men deluding themselves about how important they are. I love it! My husband—one of FBI's *most wanted.* Don't worry, baby, you'll always be number one on my most wanted list. Come here."

Fourteen months later I get a slip in my mailbox telling me I have a certified package. I race to the post office before it closes and give the slip to the clerk. She hands me a box, return address **U.S. Department of Justice / Federal Bureau of Investigation**. Outside the post office, I rip open the package and take out a five-inch-thick file dashed by redactions.

After the initial shock, I catch myself feeling a little bit flattered that there *is* an

FBI file on me—and of such heft. I bring it home. Aconsha can't believe her eyes. Her hands shake as she leafs through the pages. I try to calm her. "At least *someone's* been paying attention to what I've been doing all these years." She laughs. I love making her laugh. Ever since we first met, I've told Aconsha that I was sent down to earth with an assignment to keep her laughing.

Once we start reading the file and see how detailed and personal and wildly inaccurate it is, neither of us find much to laugh about. It's hard to fathom why the FBI bothered compiling 99% of that stuff. I can understand their making transcripts of wire-tapped phone conversations between me and my editor at *Newsday*, but what use could articles I'd written for the Hunter College student newspaper be to anyone? And long passages from *Ménage à Trois, Boxland, The Switch?* And pages and pages of information on Aconsha: names and addresses of former lovers, long passages about her uncle's involvement in the Communist Party of India, even a letter to the editor I helped her write about the Bhopal disaster?

Aconsha came to this country when she was twelve, and has very few illusions about what America is and isn't, but I can see in her face that this invasion of privacy comes as a blow. She thinks we should call the authorities, file a complaint.

"This file is *from* the authorities."

She doesn't think it's funny.

The file describes my friendship with Sidney Lewiston, who they refer to as a "communist leafleteer." They know that his youngest son is "homosexual" and HIV-positive (news to me). They know that Sadiki Jones (*The Book of Lies*) is based on Samir Braxton, which is also an alias. They know that I am a union delegate and that I once organized a human chain of 1,100 students, parents, faculty, and administrators spelling out the words  as a protest against the governor's proposed cuts to the state university. Throughout the file, words, phrases, entire paragraphs, even full pages are blackened out for no apparent reason. It's as if they gave my file and a black magic marker to a chimpanzee and said, "Enjoy yourself."

Horrified by what's in the file and frustrated by not being able to do anything about it; Aconsha seeks escape, digs out a bag of pot she's kept hidden in an old tabla drum that was a gift from an uncle. Even though I quit smoking pot years ago, I share a joint with my wife. It's the first time we've ever smoked grass together. Through stoned eyes, I see that Aconsha is at once more ravishing and more pained than I had realized. I turn back to the file and begin noticing all the beautiful patterns that make up my redacted life.

The next day I make a copy of the file and use the photocopies to wallpaper our kitchen. When anyone accuses me of holding something back from them, I point to the wall and say, "Don't look at *me*. I have no secrets. I'm an open book!"

A few weeks later I apply for a National Endowment for the Arts grant under the category "Artists' Books." I propose making an 'artist book' inspired by my FBI files. I indicate on the form that I have a fine arts degree in visual arts from Hunter College (a bit of stretch since I actually got an interdisciplinary BA with three concentrations—journalism, philosophy, and art). In the Artist Statement, I write:

```
My goal is to create a book--working title, My Redacted Life--that
will give nobody something to read and somebody nothing to read.
It will be an interactive book in the sense that the reader will
have to do much of the work, not only trying to read between the
lines but simply trying to read the lines. In the end, I hope that
the reader will do as I have done--take a step back and observe
the larger picture. Our lives needn't be defined merely by words,
names, places, dates. Perhaps we are more readily understood by the
patterns we make as we crisscross and get crossed out through time.
```

Nine months later I receive a certified letter informing me that I'm the recipient of an NEA Artist Fellowship. Walking home from the post office, I know that at least two federal agencies have active files on me.

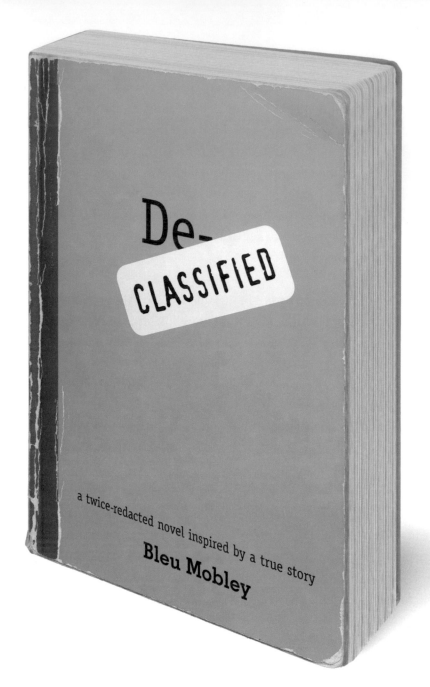

De-Classified *ARTIST BOOK*

From the author of *38 Feet, One Year*, this twice-redacted pictorial novel is inspired by the true story of a former foreign correspondent who requests his FBI files only to discover things about himself he never knew.

1989, Visual Studies Workshop, Rochester, NY

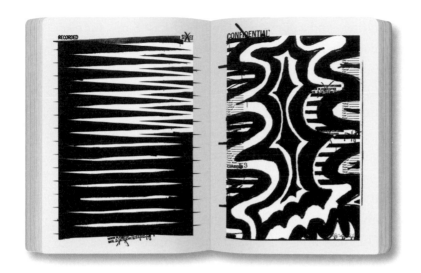

As our marriage matured into its seventh and eighth years, Aconsha and I became known throughout our apartment building—and a portion of the Lower East Side—for our blowout arguments. I'd never been much of a screamer. This may have something to do with disposition, but it probably has more to do with growing up in a building with sixteen apartments on a floor, becoming conscious at an early age of how family feuds seep under doors and through paper-thin walls and become the source of free entertainment.

Aconsha grew up in private houses, in a hot-blooded family whose everyday mode of conversation was shouting. After we got married and Aconsha felt more and more at home with me, the volume and intensity of our conversations ratcheted up proportionally. It took a while for me to understand that what seemed like fighting was for her a normal way of communicating, if not a sign of intimacy. I'd often ask Aconsha, "Why are you *yelling*? We're just talking about money." It didn't take long before I adapted to high-decibel discourse, and like most things, when you practice enough, you get good at it. By the time Aconsha told me that she was pregnant and had decided she definitely was keeping the baby, I didn't calmly ask her to consider my feelings on the matter—I simply went berserk.

When we first met, Aconsha expressed no interest in being a mother. Like me, she loved children—worshiped their spontaneity and directness—but felt no compulsion to have any of her own. Raised in a strict home, one of seven children, she rejected the life her parents planned for her—bearing lots of kids with the Hindu businessman they arranged for her to marry years before we ever met. She forswore that life so vehemently, she came to equate being a mother with succumbing to the will of her parents. At times, the ferocity of her aversion to having kids struck me as adolescent, but I never pushed the point since I also didn't want kids.

Sometimes, while visiting one of her sisters or brothers and their house full of kids, Aconsha would whisper in my ear that she couldn't wait to get out of there—always an instant turn-on for me. We didn't consider ourselves superior to couples whose lives centered around their adorable tots, we just felt happy about our own choices, and quietly reveled in our freedom. We could visit the children of friends and relatives, babysit to our hearts' content, and then leave. As aunt and uncle, mentor and teacher, we felt like we had plenty of impact on the lives of young people. The slightest insinuation that Aconsha was selfish for not fulfilling her biological destiny as a woman, could get her to say things like: "You want to know what I think is selfish? Bringing one more defenseless child into this crazy, overpopulated world—*that's* the irresponsible thing. *That's* the selfish thing."

And that was pretty much her tune on the subject for the first five to six years of our relationship. Soon after she turned thirty the tune started to change. No matter how physically fit Aconsha kept herself, sustaining a full-time career as a dancer—especially as the principal dancer of a company known at that time as the most physically demanding on the contemporary dance scene—started to wear on her. As Aconsha's sense of physical immortality waned, she began sprinkling our conversations, even our lovemaking, with second thoughts about having a baby. My retorts were usually sarcastic quips about our lives being ruined and the kid growing up to resent us for not really wanting to be parents. I'd improvise scenarios in which our teenage son or daughter legally divorces us and returns one day (armed and loaded) to mercilessly seek revenge. Aconsha reminded me of a promise she said I made before we got married, to leave the decision of having a child to her, since babymaking was ultimately a woman's choice. I told her I didn't remember making that pledge (though I knew I had).

According to Aconsha, I had confessed to her (before we were married) that the very thought of being a father terrified me. Having never had a father myself, I couldn't even model my approach to fatherhood in *opposition* to having had a bad one. Nevertheless, if sometime in the future, for some reason she were to change her mind, I promised (because of my unequivocal love for her) that we could have *one* kid. And if it came to that, I'd try to be the best father I possibly could.

Once it was made clear to me in couple's therapy that the future was indeed upon us, I agreed to stop the sarcasm and approach the topic of having a kid more seriously (while secretly hoping that the serious talk would scare Aconsha into dropping the subject). But the subject didn't get dropped, and we began attempting to get pregnant.

Several months after beginning our contraception-free sex, Pico Davis received a MacArthur Genius Award. With the money, she bought a building for her company in Brooklyn and began working on a gargantuan dance-theater piece that would be performed a year later on three continents (simultaneously). It was all very exciting, even though I could tell there was a part of Aconsha that wished *she* had gotten the Genius Award, and it was her company buying a building, turning fantasy projects into realities. With three years of advanced bookings suddenly on the calendar, and assurances from Pico that she was central to the company's future, Aconsha decided we should put off trying to have a kid. Though I never expressed it out loud, I secretly felt that *I* was the one benefiting the most from Pico's award.

Then Aconsha got pregnant.

I freaked out. She refused to get an abortion. I refused to make good on my promise. Our fights thundered across Fourth Street, and I became the screaming shithead who didn't want anything to do with his child.

We separated.

The only times we saw each other during our separation were at funerals. Within four months, three people we knew died of AIDS: Sidney Lewiston's youngest son, a dancer in Pico's company, and then my oldest friend in the world, Barry Freewell. I'd seen Barry a few times after he found out he was HIV-positive, but I wasn't aware that his health had deteriorated so quickly. Barry wrote an article for the *Village Voice* in '85, excoriating Ronald Reagan for never once mentioning the word AIDS since it was identified by the Centers for Disease Control in 1981. **REAGAN'S SILENCE=OUR DEATHS** He compared Reagan's silence and inaction to Pope Pius XII's silence and "neutrality" during the Holocaust. The article, which paired Pope Pius' anti-Semitic quotes with the Reagan administration's homophobic statements, has since been reproduced in countless

More than one historian has cited Barry's *Village Voice* article (and the editor's title for it) as an inspiration for ACT UP's Silence=Death campaign, mounted two years later.

books and referred to as a seminal text in the literature of AIDS. Inspired by Barry's outspoken militancy, some of the speakers at his funeral said they weren't going to accept his death as the will of God, or destiny. They were indescribably sad but also angry as hell, and would do whatever it took to get people to wake up and get serious about extinguishing this plague. Barry's lover, Gordon, led the charge.

"There's *no reason*," Gordon said in a defiant eulogy, "that Barry had to die. Not yet anyway. He was murdered by a culture gone deaf, dumb, and blind."

Over five hundred people came to the funeral including Guy Gutiero whom I hadn't seen since Barry and I graduated from Joan of Arc. He walked with a cane, and the few hairs he had left on his head had gone from gray to white. We hugged and both expressed disbelief that Barry could actually be dead.

Mr. G. told me he'd been following my writing career. I asked him *what* writing career, and if he comes across it again, could he give me a call and tell me where it is. "All kidding aside," I told him, "I'm having doubts about writing." I wondered aloud about becoming a social worker or a doctor—something that could actually be of benefit to people. My old teacher gently tapped his fist to my chin. "Just stay true to yourself, Bleu. Write with honesty. Report what you see, and you'll have an effect on people's lives." He looked over my shoulder at Aconsha who had just come up behind me and was starting to be visibly pregnant. I introduced them to each other. Aconsha shook Gutiero's hand, "I've heard so much about you." He looked at her protruding belly, then looked at me. I nodded. He broke into a broad smile. "*Congratulations!*" Aconsha thanked him. He wished us great good luck. Aconsha took me by the hand, and we walked together in silence from the Judson Memorial Church back to our apartment.

these words *SCROLL*

It's the middle of the night. The writer can't sleep. He's in his pajamas typing nonstop on a manual typewriter, onto a roll of paper that feeds directly into a trash bin on the other side of his desk. He hates his day job writing ad copy equating sexiness and genius with a particular brand of beer. His marriage is in shambles. His closest friend recently died of an infectious disease and hardly anyone seems to care that millions more are infected with the same deadly virus. Filled with feelings of impotence and self-loathing, the writer rails against the very words he's typing. At 6:30 a.m., he rises from his chair, walks downstairs, and gets ready to go to work. Bleu Mobley (author of *38 Feet, One Year*) rescues the roll of paper from the writer's garbage, reads it, and decides to publish the unedited text as a limited-edition scroll, available only by mail order.

1990, Word of Mouth Press, New York, NY

excerpt

THESE WORDS

these words cannot be splashed against a wall of indifference / these words cannot scream / these words cannot shout a lion's roar into the winds of deafening silence / the voice is the mother of the word / but i cannot hear this tongueless combination of letters / they have no larynx / no throat (sore from fits of rage) / no bloody phlegm will regurgitate from out the walls of their blistered mouths / these words cannot sing the blues or croon heart-tugging melodies / this erect architecture is but a façade / push it over and you will d_____ only another set of words / words that cannot smash_____ a hardwood floor / shattering its rickety form_____ess / these words cannot turn you o_____ould never be / these words cannot cry_____sspool of dissonant relations / these _____house / this city / this moment and its stratosphere and have it boomerang back_____ / a radiant and healthy love / an understa_____ love / these words cannot whack a fist into chin_____ plexus or an endlessly resilient punching bag / all th_____ in the world cannot shake the blinded populations into clea_____ sightedness / no constellation of words could be written (or spoken) or thought / that could break the chains of ignorance / greed / or neglect / these words cannot do that! / these words haven't the slightest ability to liberate themselves from the regiment of line after line after line / these words cannot give me the strength to defy the forces of gravity / to fly through the clouds with herculean strength lifting this monolithic tombstone of text above my head in order to

Three of my books were included in the huge survey of what the catalogue called "the best of contemporary word-art," which included work of the Letterists, the Situationists,  concrete poets, Fluxus artists, and other avant-gardists known for blurring the lines between art and writing. Aconsha and I flew to Paris to attend the opening at the Georges Pompidou Centre. The curators of the exhibit (so excited to meet me) injected my faltering ego with a much-needed booster shot. (It was good to know there were people in the world—other than the FBI—who knew my work, even if they didn't read English.) The trip to Paris also gave Aconsha and me an excuse to take a second honeymoon—our last chance to travel together before becoming parents.

At seven months pregnant, Aconsha's very pronounced, bulbous belly jutting out from her remarkably thin figure made her the focus of endless attention. It didn't matter that we were strangers in a foreign country and could barely speak the language—wherever we went, from a jazz club on the Left Bank, to an outdoor café on the Champs Élysées, to opening night at the Pompidou exhibit—women, men, boys, and girls of all ages asked if they could touch her swollen belly; Aconsha almost always accommodated, as did Frida (a real ham in utero), moving every which way, producing bulges that could be seen through dress, shirt, and sweater. Our fetal Frida got such a kick out of being in the most romantic city in the world, we shortened our trip from ten days to six.

On the return flight, looking at Aconsha sitting in the seat next to me—shifting from side to side, trying to sleep for two—I decided to do whatever it took to be the best father and most attentive family man I could possibly be. With only one income and another mouth to feed I wouldn't be able to spend most of my time and half my salary creating books that made little or no money. I would give up the dream of being a writer and become an internationally renowned word-art star. (As if there were such a thing.)

The 100% cotton envelope with its rubber-stamped persimmon-red Ada Editions logo stuck out from the bills, solicitations, and returned manuscripts that crammed our jumbo-sized P.O. box. I assumed it was another rejection letter, then remembered I hadn't sent anything to an Ada Editions. I'd never even heard of Ada Editions. The letter had two signatures. I turned it around and saw ink from the signatures bleeding through. It wasn't a form letter!

I did some research and found out that Ada Editions was a small press owned by a lesbian couple, funded by dividend money Mary Neal earned as a copywriter with Microsoft. She and Cassandra named their Seattle-based press after Ada Lovelace, who was the daughter of Lord Byron, but more importantly is considered to be the mother of computer programming, and in her day had to publish under a male pseudonym. All Ada Editions' authors were women, and most of their books had something to do with the lives of women.

Cassandra had earned a reputation in the '70s as a lesbian separatist reporter and columnist with a barbed sense of humor. Her bylines vanished for a decade and no one knew what happened to her until she came out with her first novel, a work of comedic science fiction that takes place a few thousand years ago in a year not specified as BC or AD because Jesus never existed, nor did Caesar or Adam. In the earth scenario of *Without Him*, no men are necessary, biologically or for any purpose, since evolution, in Her glorious wisdom, never stumbled into that particular chromosomal mutation. *Without Him* was published in 1987 to little notice. In 1988 Cassandra and Mary Neal had a baby boy.

I had no idea what their proposition was going to be. Maybe they needed a sperm donor.

We met for lunch at an Italian restaurant close to where the Women's Lit conference was taking place. Cassandra and Mary Neal turned out to be a dynamic duo who seriously loved books but didn't take themselves too seriously. Mary Neal ordered a bottle of Venetian wine and an antipasto platter for the table. It was obvious from her perfectly fitted, pin-striped suit and the take-charge way she spoke to the waiter that she was the business partner. Eyes full of emotion and mischief, Cassandra—dressed in blue jeans, a white button-down shirt, and a blazing floral scarf—was clearly the literary soul of Ada Editions. "I'm sure you're wondering what we're up to," she said right off the bat. "Kind of curious," I said. "But I always enjoy meeting new people." We toasted to meeting new people. "You know, I don't read much of anything written by men," Cassandra admitted. "Why should I when I could spend several lifetimes reading women writers and still only scratch the surface?"

"I see what you mean."

"I used to feel the same way about men in general. I mean, even *being with them*," Cassandra elaborated.

I feigned ignorance.

"I had good reasons to avoid dealing with men, but righteous anger can only last so long."

"Especially if you're an open-minded person like my sweetie here." Mary Neal's squarish face softened as she ribbed her partner.

"Thing is, I kept meeting men that I couldn't help but like. I'd say to Mary Neal, 'Well, Victor is *different*. Ram is different. George is different...'"

Wanting to keep the conversation on point, Mary Neal placed her hand on Cassandra's arm. "Tell him about reading 'Vigil on Turtleneck Hill.'"

"Mary Neal bought a copy of *Spit Sonata* at a flea market that sells books by the pound," Cassandra explained. "A few months later I was home flipping through books—flipping, reading, flipping, reading—till a voice caught hold of me."

Mary Neal interrupts. "The voice was Corrie's from 'Vigil on Turtleneck Hill.'"

"She reminded me of an old friend, and your story let me hear her talking to herself."

"She *really* loves that story," Mary Neal said, rolling her eyes slightly.

"When I finished reading it, I looked at the back cover and saw that the author was a he. I hadn't noticed the author's name, or if I had I might've thought Bleu was a woman's name. All I know is, I was taken aback that Corrie could be written by a man. Out of curiosity I read the rest of the book. Then I read it again to see if maybe the humor was mocking. But the characters only seemed more sympathetic and authentic the second time around. I don't know if you realize, but out of eleven stories in *Spit Sonata*, women are central characters in eight. That's very unusual for a male author."

"Why do you think you write from a woman's perspective so well?" Mary Neal asked, gesturing to the waiter to bring a second bottle of wine.

"I have no idea. Maybe it has to do with growing up the only son of a single mother."

"You don't need to know why," Cassandra said. "Just keep doing what you're doing."

"Actually," I said, looking into my newly filled wine glass, "I do have a theory, though I've never thought of it in relation to my writing because, really, if you did a statistical analysis of my books, I'm sure I've written as many male characters as female. My theory has more to do with why as a kid, for the longest time, I wished I'd been born a girl."

Before getting into my theory, I told them about my secret doll collection that I kept hidden in the back of my closet when I was a kid, and how Frank Mulroney and his gang from Building Twelve used to call me a girl whenever they made me their target—tied me to a flagpole, poked me with lit cigarettes, broke my nose with a baseball bat. Did they do these things because of the odd colorful clothes my mother made for me or because I was slender and leggy and skipped as I walked? I'll never really know.

I talked about the High School of Printing being ninety-percent boys, and how my years there got me thinking that if there was a hell, it would probably be ninety percent male.

After Mary Neal refilled my wine glass for a fourth time, I admitted to having always associated sex with love; my wife being the one who brought the toolbox and the weight-lifting equipment into our apartment; and making sure to watch the last quarter of the Superbowl every year so I have something to talk about with Men in the year to come.

"And your theory?" Mary Neal prodded, nervous about being late for the conference.

"Do you know what DES is?" I asked.

"Yes of course, Diethylstilbestrol," Mary Neal said, looking at me quizzically.

"The so-called wonder drug," Cassandra continued, "prescribed to millions of pregnant women in the '50s and '60s to prevent miscarriages, that turned out to be a disaster..."

"Because of the reproductive disorders," Mary Neal picked up the saga, "and vaginal cancers it caused in the female offspring."

"Did you know the drug companies knew about the side effects for decades?

"Oh yeah, we published a book on DES daughters a few years ago. The whole thing's outrageous. But what's it got to do with..."

"Well, when I was thirteen, my aunt, Chloe, handed me a newspaper article about DES and said, 'I'm pretty sure your mother took this when she was pregnant with you. Now don't blame her, Bleu, because doctors were prescribing these pills to women back then like they were M&M's. Thankfully, you're not a girl so you don't have as much to worry about.'

"After I read the article (which focused on the health effects of DES on daughters, but also mentioned higher rates of urinary problems and testicular cancers in sons), I probably scratched my head, went outside to play, and didn't give it another thought. In the intervening decades I've had time to think about the chemical effects that *daily dosages* of synthetic estrogen equal to seventy times that of the birth control pill could have on a male fetus. Imagine, day after day for months on end, you're a teeny but growing male fetus exposed to huge amounts of female hormones sluicing into your bloodstream. Now jump-cut twenty, thirty, forty years later, and you've got millions of estrogen-laced men roaming the earth bending gender stereotypes, wondering why they don't understand the whole freaking battle of the sexes. That's my theory. Nobody's tested it as far as I know, but I really do think that DES—as terrible as it was for many people—had something to do with the breakdown of rigid gender differences, which affected the peace and justice movements and the whole creative explosion of the sixties that placed human values, *female* values, over the values of domination and destruction."

"That's a fascinating theory," Mary Neal said. "You should write about it."

"You should write about your whole experience growing up," Cassandra added.

Suddenly feeling a need to change the subject, I said, "Yeah, but generally I prefer not to write about myself. Maybe one day I will, but not yet."

"That's perfect," Mary Neal said, happy to redirect the conversation, "because we'd like to give you a $2,000 advance to write a book of stories entirely of female narrators."

Stunned by the offer, unsure what to say, I told them it made me a little uncomfortable, my being a man and all. Inside I was bursting with pride that these two women, these *lesbians* trusted me (a bearded, cock-sure fool) to write from the vantage point of a woman. They explained that it was a difficult, even risky, decision for them, one that had a lot to do with getting beyond their own prejudices, and probably those of their subscribers. I told them I was flattered and would start on it right away. "Maybe I'll write a story about being pregnant and giving birth, because my wife and I are about to have a baby."

"Congratulations! We recently had *our* first. His name is Conor." Mary Neal took out her wallet and showed me a photograph of a beaming baby boy.

"He's adorable!"

"He'll be a year-and-a-half next month."

"As far as the book goes," Mary Neal said, looking at her watch, "you can write anything you want, as long as women are central to each story."

On the subway ride home, whatever feelings of pride I felt began to deflate. I wondered if I was being used as part of an experiment or as the subject of a dare. Or was *I* the one putting something over on them? Everything I said at our lunch was true, but I had definitely been pandering—bragging about my girlish ways, while never mentioning that I nearly abandoned my pregnant wife a few months earlier, and was freaking out about anything and everything to do with becoming a parent.

excerpt [from the title story]

The best thing of all is the silence. To be at home *without* the radio on or a record playing or a saxophone blaring or drums snaring or bands rehearsing the same song dozens of times in row—this is a gift my solitude brings me every single day. After forty-six years of one man or another controlling all the sound waves in the house, I can finally hear myself think—or *not* think if that's what I want to do. I can sing in the shower without being criticized. I can put a piece of music on that isn't the *best* whatever or the *first* or *most* sophisticated. Just to listen to an ordinary piece of music as background—what's the crime in that? No crime. Look both ways. No sound police. Silence. Peace of mind. *Freedom.*

The only one who gave me any space for myself was Freddy, the violinist. When he asked me to marry him, he swore he was a family man. What he forgot to mention was— he had another family across the river in New Jersey. He'd tell me he was out of town for a gig, but mostly he was with his other wife and their two kids. When I told him I knew, he didn't deny it. He just swore that I was his *true* love. The only reason he stayed in Jersey more of the time was because my mother lived in our basement and he couldn't stand her hyperactive personality. He used to say, "If they took out your mother's thyroid, the thyroid would live on its own for five years." Mom had medication to slow her down, but she never took it. So when Freddy was around her *he* took medication. Soon as dad passed away, mom kept coming upstairs and Freddy couldn't handle it. He'd drop in two weekends a month or whenever "the bitch" was out of town, which was hardly ever. I resented being the part-

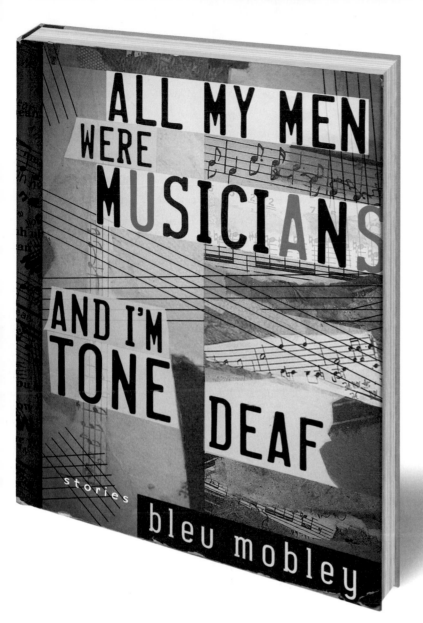

All My Men Were Musicians and I'm Tone Deaf *STORIES*

Mobley's second volume of short stories erupts with joyous, scathing, uproarious, and tender portrayals of women, ages sixteen to ninety-six, as they approach the light at the tunnel's end of childhood, marriage(s), child-rearing, and being a professional woman in a testosterone-laden world. "A male author writing in a woman's voice seldom gets it right. Perhaps what is most extraordinary about Mobley's collection of nine stories—he gets it right nine times!" Majora Peer. *Bloomsbury Review*

1990, Ada Editions, Seattle, WA

time wife until it dawned on me one day that I liked it better when he was away.

My first husband (the accordionist) was an emergency wedding. My mom had diarrhea, she was so upset her little girl got knocked up "by a stranger." The night before the wedding, she was throwing dresses on me from her closet till something fit. The Justice of the Peace asked if anyone knew of a reason we shouldn't be married. The nine people in the room all looked like they had plenty to say, including Sam and me. But nobody said a peep. Sam kissed the bride, and within five years we had three kids.

Don't get me wrong, I loved raising my kids (mostly), and still I love them (mostly), but now that they're all married and have kids of their own and no one else is living in the house but me, I can't tell you how nice it is having a bathroom all to myself. Heaven must be having a bathroom all to yourself. If I want to stay in the bathroom all day, light candles, take a bubble bath, put a mud pack on my face, pluck my eyebrows, read a book sitting on the toilet, write my own book if I want to—*it's my prerogative.* My last husband, Ralph (the sax player), said to me once, "Brenda, you've got the gift of gab. You should write a book." I laughed, "I don't know the first thing about writing." He said, "Aw, nobody cares if you're a writer these days. As long as you got a good story to tell. And you've got plenty. All you need is a title. Then you can write your book." Eight years later, as Ralph lay in bed dying, I was looking at pictures of me with all my exes, and a title came to me. It took Ralph six more months to die. In between feeding him and wiping his bottom, I'd look at my photo albums and write down whatever I could remember.

It'll be a year next Thursday since Ralph passed away. I've been a nurse for thirty years and I never saw anyone die of wet brain. Not like that. Dr. Imersohl said, "Brenda, your husband has more booze than blood in his brain." His legs started giving out, so he had no choice but to quit performing. Before too long he quit everything. He just sat home all day in his ratty green recliner watching videotapes of his concerts. Came a time you couldn't tell where the recliner ended and he began. It just became one big green blob sinking closer and closer to the floor. Once he was confined to the bed, he kept one eye on me and one eye on the TV. Got to where he only had three things left he could talk about and he'd rotate them: the first time he saw Dizzy Gillespie play with Chano Pozo; his Holton bass saxophone that was stolen in Philadelphia back in '63; and why I wouldn't go walking with him anymore up at his family's cabin (Because you can't stand up, Ralph! But that didn't make a difference). One thing he never talked about was drinking. *That* he had to sneak. He always said, "Aw, I can quit." After he split his head open on the edge of a piano, I begged him to quit. He said, "Yeah, I will. I promise."

He had a drink the day he died. Sixty-two years old. A drink and a chocolate chip cookie he had tucked under his pillow. Ralph's insides were rotting away. You could smell it all over the house. For six months our bedroom was an intensive care unit. I was in the middle of changing his IV when he asked me to shut the blinds. Said he saw his brother (who suicided three years back) and it spooked him. Later in the afternoon he asked to see out the window, says he's not afraid no more. I opened the blinds, popped in his favorite Billie Holiday tape, kneeled down on the floor beside him, and whispered, "Why don't you go be with your brother up at the camp? You can go if you want to, Ralph." Five minutes later he was dead. I don't know if he was going to die at that moment anyway, if his brother's spirit came and took him away, if Lady Day lightened his load, or what. All I know is he had a little smile on his face when he went.

Then I did like he asked and brought his ashes up to the pond. Ralph never liked the thought of being stuck in the ground forever. He said to me one day, "I want you to put some of my ashes in the North Inlet and some in South Inlet so I'm flowing in and out of the pond to the river." I did him one better and got a few fellas from his band to come, and his kids and grandkids. We took three boats and headed to North Inlet. It was a rough, windy day and a bunch of the grandkids were smoking cigarettes, their smoke blowing in my face. When we got to North Inlet we stopped the boats and Ralph's son Jimbo decided to take a leak off the back of his boat into the river. That gave everybody a case of the giggles. Then Emory, Ralph's long-time sideman, took out his trumpet and started blowing a soulful blues to the rhythm of the tide lapping against the boat. Carlos started playing his clarinet, and Ralph's daughter Linda, her harmonica. That's when I knew it was time. I opened up the coffee can with Freddy's ashes. I could see the grandkids thinking, *Holy shit, that's our grandpa in there.* I was standing in front of the boat trying to steady myself. Ralph's kids in the middle, grandkids in the back. I reached into the can, grabbed a handful of ashes and flung it away from the boat, not in the least bit thinking about the wind, which blew all the ashes back onto my white overalls and into the faces of Ralph's whole family. Kira shook her head laughing, "Daddy's not gonna let us get rid of him that easy."

We rowed down to South Inlet, put some ashes in there and on the beach by the cabin, all while Ralph's band played a romping New Orleans-style funeral march. I remember thinking to myself, *This is good. The two things Ralph loved the most: being by the water up at his cabin and making music with these guys. He's everywhere now. On the ground. In the wind. In the river and all over his family.* All I had left were a few handfuls to send to the sister in South Carolina. The grandkids started tying up the canoe that Ralph built to the dock when a man came by admiring the canoe. "I like your boat!"

Eleven-year-old Nikki proudly blurted, "My grandfather built it."

"Well, you tell your grandfather he made a really fine boat."

Nikki picked up the coffee can with the ashes and shouted into it, "YOU HEAR THAT, GRANDPA, THE MAN LIKES YOUR BOAT!"

Later that night, after everyone had either left or gone to bed, I was sitting on the couch reminiscing with Emory. Out of nowhere he let it be known—should I ever be interested—he's always had an eye for me. And he's sure Ralphy would'a liked nothing more than for his wife and his best sideman to get together and keep each other company into their golden years. Emory's a sweet soul and not bad looking, but I couldn't help but laugh. And then I cried, and then I laughed some more. "Have you lost your mind, Emory? Not only did we just finish spreading Ralph's ashes, and now we're in his cabin on his favorite couch, but you want to know something else, Emory? I've been married four times to four different musicians, raising their kids, doing everything to make them happy even after they're dead. So please don't take it personal when I tell you: the *last* thing I am ever going to do is get shacked up again with anyone, least of all to another musician. *My Lord!*"

Thinking about it now, I know that is one pledge I am going to keep.

Aconsha went into labor two weeks early, on route to a video shoot for Pico Davis' *Earth Marks* extravaganza. Six months earlier, Pico reluctantly accepted Aconsha's resignation in a letter affixed to her last paycheck. "I have no choice but to give you my blessing. Go, my friend. If you're half the mother you are a dancer, your child will be very fortunate."

A few weeks after sending the letter, Pico called with an idea to videotape Aconsha for the five continent *Earth Marks* piece. "You'll be performing a central role as the embodi-

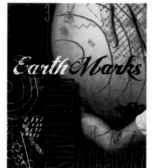

ment of fertility—sensual but maternal, modern but timeless, muscular, wise, slowly transforming before audiences around the world—all while you're at home blissfully breastfeeding your baby." Pico's idea was to do three shoots, one during each trimester. Aconsha said yes even though she was wary of her former boss' surprising idealization of the pregnant woman.

The day before she was scheduled to do the final video shoot, Aconsha felt some mild contractions. Jody, our midwife, assured us there was no dilation and gave us the all-clear for the trip to Jersey. I was straphanging—

on the train to Newark—looking down at my pregnant wife sitting below me, when I saw her face tighten. She let out a bellowing fart that rose in pitch like an off key opening to *Rhapsody In Blue*. What would normally be subject to scorn and giggles was instantly forgiven by our fellow train-car passengers, since there was no doubt about the source of the flatulence. Feeling a trickle of wetness between her legs, Aconsha hoisted herself from her seat and a flood of water gushed onto the floor. Soaking from midsection to toe, she announced,

"IT'S HAPPENING!"

Pico and her videographer were waiting for us at the station in the company van. They wanted us to go to a hospital in Newark, but Aconsha said, "No way! Our birth plan is in the City where all our people are. Who's in New Jersey? C-section doctors. Knives everywhere. To the midwifery unit at St. Vincent's Hospital, please!"

Aconsha lay down on the floor of the van, enduring every agonizing bump and pothole, listening to radio reports about bumper-to-bumper traffic into the city, calculating the time between contractions. "I don't understand. This is a *first birth*. It's supposed to take longer than this." Aconsha had read every book about birthing she could get her hands on. We'd done Lamaze classes together, watched the videos, rehearsed everything frontwards and backwards. Getting stuck in a traffic jam on the New Jersey Turnpike—with four minutes between contractions—wasn't in any of the contingency plans.

By the time we made it to Saint Vincent's, the OB and the midwife were there, but the contractions had receded to barely perceptible. After ten hours, the OB was ready to induce labor—Aconsha wouldn't allow it. She tried visualizing, vocalizing, taking warm showers, even herbal induction. After fifteen hours, she was only up to four centimeters. Despite all the years of serious endurance training, and a hardcore determination to give birth in a completely natural way, Aconsha's tolerance for pain finally reached a breaking point. She let the OB give her a little something for the pain, and then a little something to induce labor (the dreaded Pitocin). As they administered the I.V. pump, the fetal monitor and the epidural anesthesia, all our birth plans unraveled. A tremendous sense of relief washed over Aconsha. Suddenly she could care less if Pico's videographer taped the birth. All good, except for one thing—Frida wasn't ready to make her film debut.

By day two, friends, colleagues, and relatives gathered in the waiting room taking turns popping into the delivery room. Aconsha had given strict orders not to let her mother know that we were in the hospital, but one of Aconsha's siblings spilled the beans and both Aconsha's parents appeared in the waiting room. "What am I supposed to tell them?" I asked. "Don't say anything," Aconsha ordered. "She doesn't even acknowledge your existence."

"They know that *my* mother is here," I said, smiling at my mom, who accepted Aconsha from the start without condition and was turning out to be a very reassuring presence in the delivery room. "And you can't let your father in without your mother." Aconsha loved her dad despite his being such a wimp in his marriage.

As the epidural dosage increased and delivering the baby superseded all else, Aconsha flung open the doors of resistance not only to medical intervention, but also to her mother.

Both soon-to-be grandmas were in the room for the final two hours of labor. My mom kept Aconsha's legs up. Aconsha's mom massaged her spine. I held her hands. After practicing for months with squeeze-balls, Aconsha was squeezing my hand so tightly, she nearly broke it. I kept thinking the ordeal was about to end, but Frida continued to resist coming out. "Did Aconsha like being in the womb this much?" I asked her mom.

"She really had no choice, since she had to wait for Prasad to come out. He was the stubborn one. Once he was out, Aconsha just followed." These words floated around me for a few seconds before they registered. Prasad was Aconsha's brother; the one no one in their family ever talked about. Whenever Aconsha mentioned Prasad, she referred to him only as an older brother who died as a child in an accident. She never mentioned that he was older by just a few *minutes*. The dots connected themselves in my brain as Aconsha continued squeezing my numb hand. I wasn't sure whether I felt worse for her, having lost her twin, or for myself, having married a woman who would keep something so important from me. All I knew was—this was neither the time nor the place to pursue it.

The OB kept coming in and out of the room, prepared to do an *internal*, or a *C*, or to incise the opening. But Aconsha's formidable will and powerful abdominal muscles wouldn't give in. Jody kept saying, "PUSH! Just a little more. Push!" Aconsha responded, "Arrrrrrgggghhhh! *Mother*FUCKER!"

To my surprise, both grandmothers seemed unfazed by this language. Soon as I saw the top of our baby's head, Jody said, "Okay Aconsha, she's crowned. Now put your chin to your chest, your hands under your legs and push for ten counts… Now do it again… One more time…" Using whatever strength she had left, Aconsha propelled little Frida down through the birth cavity. "PUSH! PUSH! PUSH!"

*"I'm PUSHING. Goddamn it!
What does it look like I'm…
Arrrrgghhhhhhhhhhhhhhhhhhhhhh."*

Frida entered the world beyond the womb, wrinkled and gray, covered in placenta goo. "Is she okay?" I asked, petrified that the protracted ordeal had done irreparable damage to our baby. Jody smiled and handed me scissors to cut the umbilical chord. "Are you sure?" Barely able to hold anything, my right hand did what it was told. After a few seconds, our little Frida took a breath on her own. Her body inflated and her color went from gray to a beautiful bronze. Aconsha's mom, who years earlier swore she'd have nothing to do with a child of ours, looked at her granddaughter with a smile that said, *The white man's genes couldn't keep this girl from being Indian.* Instantly, I was no longer persona non grata. Jody placed Frida on Aconsha's belly. Frida coughed out her first commentary on the situation— music to Aconsha's exhausted ears. The nurse took Frida for her first bath, first eye drops, and whatever other firsts they did to her. The room cleared. Aconsha and I held each other, weeping and laughing with joy, pride, and an indescribable sense of relief.

We had no intention of ever moving out of our rent-stabilized Lower East Side apartment. Within walking distance, Aconsha and I could eat cheaply at a different ethnic café or food stand every night for a month and not eat at the same place twice. We could fill ourselves up with art exhibits, poetry readings, music, dance, and theater performances of every kind if we cared to or had the time, though I mostly imbibed on the theater of the streets—talking to grizzled old-timers, cantankerous stoop philosophers, scatological stoners, pierced runaways, curbside gardeners, guerilla squatters, sit-down comedians, and the off-the-cuff bards of the sleepless, muse-oozing night.

But when a baby comes into your life, and you're walking up five double flights of unswept stairs with three bags of groceries hanging off one arm, and your precious twelve pound poop-drenched-bundle-of-crying-joy secured to your chest with the other arm; and you're trying to get into your triple-locked door, and your wad of keys pops out of your mouth and down the steps, and you're standing there, lower back aching, trying to figure out what to put down first, the bags or the baby; and the car alarm out on the street—a noise you have prided yourself for never letting get on your nerves—is giving you a headache; and you realize you've left your wallet at the Korean market, either that or it was pick-pocketed in the crush between subway and newsstand; and you begin smelling pee mixed in with the poop—a thought can pop into your mind: *Maybe it would be nice to have a car you could drive to the market in and a carport you could pull into a few feet from your kitchen which looks out on some grass where a chipmunk climbs a tree and a robin sings; and other than that, there are no sounds, no distractions, just the smell of fresh cut grass and the taste of peace and quiet.*

I painted the picture to Aconsha of moving to Long Island—more space; a safer, cleaner environment for Frida; closer to nature, better public schools; in-house washer/dryer, and a shorter commute to the college for me. She could see us in that picture, so we bought a used car and moved to a split-level rental house on the North Shore that was listed *Water View*, though you could only see the faraway swath of the blue-gray Long Island Sound in the winter when the leaves were down, and only if you stood on the toilet in the upstairs bathroom and pressed your head against the window. There were other things we discovered about suburban living that didn't live up to the picture I'd painted. Still, it was a nice change of pace and nearly perfect for raising a child during those all-important formative years.

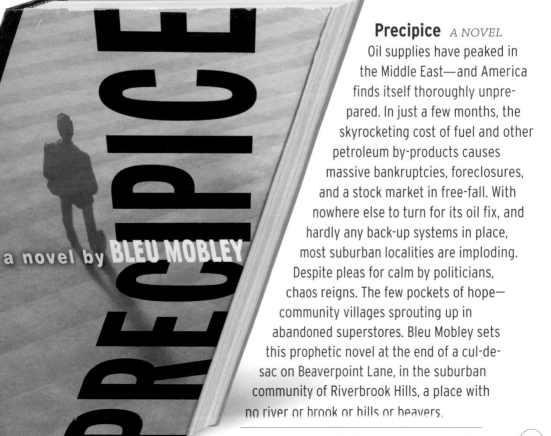

Precipice *A NOVEL*
Oil supplies have peaked in the Middle East—and America finds itself thoroughly unprepared. In just a few months, the skyrocketing cost of fuel and other petroleum by-products causes massive bankruptcies, foreclosures, and a stock market in free-fall. With nowhere else to turn for its oil fix, and hardly any back-up systems in place, most suburban localities are imploding. Despite pleas for calm by politicians, chaos reigns. The few pockets of hope—community villages sprouting up in abandoned superstores. Bleu Mobley sets this prophetic novel at the end of a cul-de-sac on Beaverpoint Lane, in the suburban community of Riverbrook Hills, a place with no river or brook or hills or beavers.

1991, Raucous Kindle Press, Port Jefferson, NY

"The problem with you is, you're fixated on the negative," Tobias said as he signaled the waitress for another shot of whiskey. "You have so much going for you, Bleu: a precious daughter, a beautiful, talented wife. You got your tenure, your health, your whole life ahead of you, but you keep writing these morose books. You moved from that roach-infested walk-up into a nice house in a nice neighborhood, and what do you do? You write a book about the suburbs erupting into chaos. You have the kind of job security people would kill for, and now you're writing a novel about an unemployed screenwriter. *I don't get it.* You say your daughter is your guru, right? The only teacher you ever completely surrendered to. Why don't you write a book about her? Call it *My Daughter, My Guru.* Put that photo of Frida looking like a Buddha baby on the cover. That's a book you can make money with. Then buy your wife a house for her birthday. Don't be paying someone else's mortgage. If I had your talent, I'd try to make something tangible with it.

"I never was a good enough writer. I faced that fact a long time ago. You know that saying, 'Those who can't do, teach.' I know who I am. And in two more years—I'm retiring. Marge and I are buying a Winnebago and driving around the country till we tire of it. Then I'll come back and spend my last years making model airplanes—just like I did when I was a kid. Complete the circle. Who knows how much time I have left? Already had a triple by-pass. If I make it to California in our Winnebago, and croak looking out on Monterey Bay, I'll die a happy man. If I die right now, I'll die a happy man. You can put that on my tombstone.

"Maybe if I had your imagination and your abilities, I'd be a miserable son of a bitch too. It's a gift what people like you have, and if what you have to offer goes unrequited, it must be terribly painful. So you end up teaching. And what you have, you can't teach."

Tobias ordered another whiskey. "The thing I don't understand: you write all this bummer, glass-half-empty stuff, but you don't seem like a bummer-kind-of-person to me. You strike me as a glass-half-full person. What do you think that's about?"

Now that I had tenure, Tobias was no longer officially my mentor. There was no reason to keep meeting him at the Cornerstone Bistro the first Thursday of every month—except I'd grown quite fond of the old codger. He was what you call a 'functional alcoholic.' His teeth were in terrible shape, he smelled, the soles of his shoes were worn down to nothing, his two corduroy sports coats both had elbow patches sewn on top of their original ones, and more often than not his eyeglasses were held together by a paper clip and electrical tape. The best thing he had going for him was his second wife, a former student who was younger than his oldest son. Together, he and Marge had two kids of their own, who got a lot more love and attention from their dad than his first set of kids, who all hated his guts. No one in their right mind should have taken advice from Tobias Drummond, but that didn't stop me from playing the part of his mentee.

"I'm not sure why I write the things I do," I said, trying to answer his question. "My mother says she named me Bleu not because I was a sad baby but because I was literally blue when I was born, and I turned blue in cold weather. Why did I go to triple-feature Ingmar Bergman films when I was in high school and come out of the theater feeling exhilarated? I can't tell you. There was just something about all that gorgeous black-and-white brooding that made me feel not so alone. Why did I ride my bike all the time to the Masbeth Cemetery when I was a kid? I'm not sure. But I remember how peaceful I felt lying on my stomach, looking through the blades of grass up at the tombstones that mimicked the Manhattan skyscrapers in the distance. I must have found sanctuary in those meandering pathways, felt glad to be alive knowing that one day I'd be buried under the feet of some adolescent daydreamer. You can say I'm a *flip-sider*. If it's the middle of the day, I know that on the other side of the world it's the dead of night. I know that good times for some mean bad times for others. When I was young, I wondered why bombs had never been dropped on New York City like they had on other cities around the world. I imagined a day when we'd get ours, and the sound of jets flying overhead would trigger fear in our hearts too. Sometimes when I look at Frida, I picture what she'll be like as a grandmother. You can call that morose. I think it's just the flip-side of the story. One twin dies in an accident as a kid. The other one lives with a hole in her heart. Some child's parents sleep soundly through the night. Another child's single mother gets whisked into an ambulance for taking a midnight stroll down the middle of the Boulevard in her PJs. Same day I received my letter from the chancellor awarding me tenure, Aconsha's uncle lost his job at the company he worked for most of his adult life. *You and I* may be doing alright, at the moment, but we're in the biggest economic downturn this country has seen in years. Aconsha's uncle worked for a highly reputable corporation nobody ever imagined would go belly up. There were other opportunities he could have pursued through the years, but he remained faithful to the company that lured him here from India. He found out his plant was closing by watching the evening news! They didn't mention that the CEO got a golden parachute while Aconsha's uncle and 2,600 other employees got nothing but pink slips. Just this morning I heard a money advisor on the radio saying what a good investment that company is because they're freed from all their fiscal obligations. Someone has a windfall. Somebody else gets clobbered."

The crowd at the bar erupted into cheers. Don Mattingly hit a triple on the television set, scoring the go ahead run for the Yankees against the Red Sox. Tobias dipped a fried clam into his second serving of tartar sauce. "Have some. They're delicious."

"Thanks."

"Hey, I'm not trying to tell you what to write. All I'm saying is, you could make real money if you ever decided to write something more. . . *upbeat. Something people want to read.*"

"I appreciate the confidence, but I couldn't write anything commercial if my life depended on it. It's just not in my DNA. Hey, speaking of my life depending on it, I got a family waiting for me."

"Oh Jeez. Me too."

"Let me drive you home, Tobias."

"No, I'm fine."

"It's no big deal. I can drive you to your car in the morning."

"No, really. I'm fine."

"You sure?"

"Positive."

"Alright, man. But drive carefully."

"See you next week."

"No, I'm seeing you tomorrow morning."

"Tomorrow morning?"

"Yeah, we have a Human Subjects Committee meeting at 8 a.m."

"Holy crapoly! How could I forget that?"

excerpt

.....LADIES AND GENTLEMEN! DON'T WORRY— I'M NOT ASKING FOR A HANDOUT. I'M JUST AN UNEMPLOYED AUTHOR LOOKING FOR HONEST WORK. ONE DOLLAR, I'll write your story. Then *you* can be an unpublished subject. *Ha ha ha!* Tell me your story and I'll write it into a poem, FIFTY CENTS. FOR A DOLLAR I'll make it rhyme, every other line. FIVE DOLLARS, every line will rhyme, and you'll feel fine. TEN DOLLARS, an epic poem. Imagine you—a modern epic. No question about it—each and every one of you has the seeds of something great, or at least something interesting, I'm sure. I see it in your faces. TWENTY-FIVE DOLLARS, you're immortalized in a short story. Make it a short short story. FIFTY DOLLARS, a novella. Make that a HUNDRED a novella. TWO HUNDRED, I promise to make it a classic, nothing less. What's the matter, nobody here dreams of immortality? I know—nobody reads anymore except maybe the funnies and the TV Guide. Okay, THREE HUNDRED DOLLARS, you got

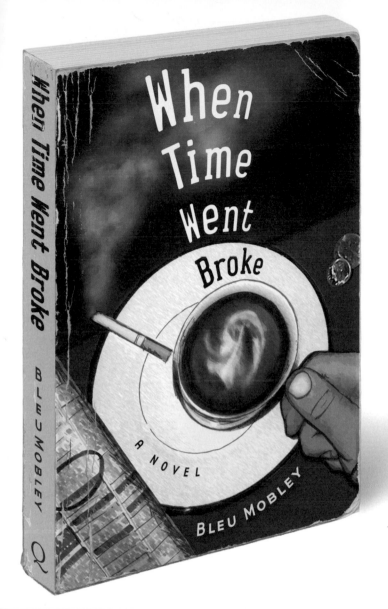

When Time Went Broke *A NOVEL*
An out-of-work screenwriter barks from a subway platform offering to write up people's stories for cash. Only two years earlier, Jack Grossman was a hotshot in the entertainment industry. Time was money. Then time went broke. In this disturbing, at times hilarious extended monologue, Bleu Mobley's down-on-his-luck, seasoned protagonist says what's on his mind as he confronts the commuting public and imagines what's on their minds.

1991, Raucous Kindle Press, Port Jefferson, NY

yourself a screenplay. THREE-FIFTY, a teleplay. You're the hero, the super hero, the war hero, the Christ, the anti-Christ, the lover, the comic everyman, the wronged person out for revenge. Whatever you want. Sci-fi, chick flick, remake. Yes, I do possess the abilities to remake you bigger, brighter, better. *Just give me some cash!*

Doesn't anybody have a story around here needs to be written? Don't worry, you don't have to be a fascinating person. Everybody has a story to tell. At least one story. That's my *specialty*. I used to write biopics for TV, building up heroes, then tearing them down in two hours (minus twenty-six minutes for commercials). All the sordid details of the rich and famous. But I've renounced all that. Or it renounced me. I won't burden you with *my* story. The good news is I got a second lease on life. Now I'm into *ordinary*— THE EXTRAORDINARY ACTS OF ORDINARY PEOPLE. LET'S DO THIS THING!

Okay, *just look right through me, lady*. Pass me by like I don't even exist. I'm giving you the opportunity of a lifetime here. Used to write for Lifetime. Showtime. Time Warner. All the Times. Swear to God! I can show you my reel. Choice is yours. You can drag your weary self into your quiet life of, well, you know, *desesperanza*. You can live that cliché another day, or you can call in sick. Happily sick! ONE MOTHER-FREAKIN' DAY your boss can spare you; we can meet for an hour or two over coffee and a sandwich. Just you and your personal biographer. You tell me all you care to share. Then I'll do my magic. COME ON PEOPLE! Somebody. Anybody. Be the first one on this subway car. *Everybody* in the last car was doing it! You know, I'm not just any shlub off the street looking for a panhandle. I'm a professionally unemployed writer! I got two Emmy nominations and I won a Cammy for a very famous dog food campaign. I'm sure you remember the *Low Cal Puppy Chow Now Now Bow Wow It's Low Cal Puppy Chow* jingle! If I can write about crap like that, I can write about you. Trust me, I will draw out aspects of your story that NOBODY ever cared to ask you about. Even *you* don't know the things about you I can come up with. LET'S GO PEOPLE. TAKE THE LEAP. I'm cheaper than a shrink, less honest than a mirror. Give me a chance, I'll show you why TV Guide called me the *most* talented writer working in the industry. Or was it the most prolific? Or most ambitious? Whatever it was, it was a nice thing they wrote. You probably read it. What was it five, six years ago. Maybe it was ten. Whenever it was, I was top of the heap. *I'm a professional!* Not something you throw away like a paper towel. For a quarter, I'll write you a haiku, sight unseen. COME ON PEOPLE! You want me to cut off my ear? I paint too you know. I'm an interdisciplinary loser. What do you want, ad copy? How about a personal ad? Whatever you're looking for: true love, weekday trysts, couple swapping. Maybe you need to send a card to somebody. What is it, April? Mother's Day, just around the corner. You haven't spoken to your mother in six months? I'll make it right in three stanzas. She'll put you back in her will. *That's* an investment you can't beat. You need a condolence card? A letter of reproach to an old friend? A letter of forgiveness? A letter of resigna....

Oh, no thank you Ma'am. I don't take handouts.

Yes, I'm positive. I'm just here looking for some honest work.

No really, Ma'am, I don't accept charity. I'm a *working* man. Like the sign says: **YOUR STORY FOR MONEY.** I could help you write yours.

Yes, I'm sure you do. I can tell. You have the face of a *thousand* stories.

All right, Ma'am. No, I understand. I don't want to make you late.

No, *I'm* sorry.

Oh, you too, Ma'am. Nice day. Yes, you too.

OKAY FOLKS! THIS IS YOUR LUCKY DAY. For the next ten minutes I'm running a very special special. First two volunteers, I'm offering creative control of the ending of whatever I write about you. That kind of control I never gave to anybody. Not to Spielberg. Not to Puttnam. Not to my own mother, may she rest in peace. NOBODY's going to match an offer like this. C'mon, I see you smiling. Put this undeniable charm to work for you. Make it *your story* that changes someone's life. *Your story* that offers hope and inspiration. Twenty minutes of your time and I'll find the ray of hope inside your story, however dark or desperate you think it is—I'll find the light. *Money back guarantee!* I'm the Sherlock Holmes of hope. I always find what I'm looking for. And right now I'm looking for a sign, some sign of hope. This isn't about me, people. I'm just a witness, a vehicle, an empty vessel. *You're* the star of this. Use me for the only thing I'm good for. C'mon, *be* the hero of your own life. MGM, Columbia Pictures, NBC—those are just a few of the top-tier institutions I no longer work for. If you don't try, you'll never give yourself the chance of getting rejected by the movers and shakers who make and break hearts, minds, and careers with a single nod of the head. If you don't try, you'll never know. Once you stop trying, that's the beginning of the end. And we can't have that now, can we? You're worth more than that. *So come on.* BELIEVE IN YOURSELVES. Who wants to be first? Don't all jump up at once. COME ON PEOPLE! Be the first. It just takes one.

I swear, I never meant to write a bestseller. I set out to write a book about waste and consumption, through the eyes of an old garbage collector. But I had trouble getting it off the ground (reams of false starts filed in the trash; much doubt about what I was doing). If it wasn't for Frida, a three-year-old at the time, I never would have found my way in that book.

One of the reasons I dreaded having a baby—I like people I can *talk* to. Soon after I agreed to splitting the child-rearing responsibilities fifty-fifty, I made Aconsha a proposition: "How about you take the first nine years, and I take the second nine?"

To my amazement and delight, Frida and I were having conversations shortly after she was born. She was like the John Coltrane of babies—overflowing with things to say in her own beguiling language. She taught me so many things when she was a baby. Not only Fridaspeak. She showed me how to live in the moment, and how to play and experience life through all the senses. Watching her discover the world of a thousand million sensations, by inspecting it with her nose, sucking on it, gurgling into it, grabbing onto it, and looking at it with wide-eyed wonder or squinty-eyed fear, was my post-doctoral education. By the time she was a year old, there was a lot of storytelling going on. I'd make up stories with Frida in her language, much like she told stories to our dog, Einstein (Eyesigh), in his language. She told stories to flowers (flalas) in a language she and the flowers both seemed to understand. Her toys and stuffed animals also seemed to enjoy Frida's verbose tales.

As she grew older and the stories we told each other had more real words in them, it became clear that she made no distinction between human beings and other animals, even inanimate objects. Since she would empathize with just about any noun in a story, I needed to be careful that the insects as well the dogs, birds, boats, *a rickety chair* didn't end up abandoned or irreparably harmed. At the same time, Frida needed stories to have lots of twists and turns. I couldn't get away with telling her a story about a man painting a barn. Stuff had to happen, and it had to happen with flair. She didn't want anyone to die or get hurt, but she demanded tension—the *possibility* of danger. She'd put her hands over her ears or hide under the covers when a story would approach the edge of a cliff or the stroke of midnight. But then, she'd lift her hands or peer out from under the covers, challenging me to tell her what happened next in the split second before she covered up again.

After one such story session with Frida, I returned to my desk, which was covered with piles of false starts from the garbage collector book. I placed my hands on the keyboard of my computer and started typing what turned out to be *Buy This Book Or We'll Kill You*.

Buy This Book Or We'll Kill You

A NOVEL

Unable to find a publisher for their book, *Talking Trash: An Oral History of Garbage*, Marsha and Neil Metcalf concoct a scheme to blackmail an editor at a large publishing house. In this high-wire romp of good intentions gone awry, Bleu Mobley makes a compelling case for desperation being the mother of desperate acts. "One part Studs Terkel, one part Buster Keaton, one part Bonnie and Clyde." ***Kirkus***

1993, Maelstrom Limited, Chapel Hill, NC

There is very little in Marsha and Neil's past that prepares them for what they are planning to do this morning. Neither has a criminal background, though no one who knows them would say they're the most straight-laced people in the world either. They both took drugs when they were younger, snuck into concerts, and lost their virginity before the age of fifteen. Marsha twice jumped subway turnstiles when she was a teenager, and once as a young adult she got caught shoplifting at a Pathmark supermarket. She didn't intend to shoplift. She simply ate a bag of cashews and raisins while waiting on the checkout line with a cart full of groceries. After paying for everything except the nuts and raisins, she got nabbed by security and brought to the manager who gave her a choice: "Either I call the police and show them the surveillance tape, or you sign this letter pledging never to shop in a Pathmark store for the rest of your life." She signed the pledge, and in nine years she hasn't once violated her fugitive status at the supermarket chain.

Neil's background is somewhat more transgressive. When he was an undergraduate, he slept in the basement of the NYU library. He finally got caught when a reporter for the student newspaper found his diary and published excerpts under the headline "Confessions of a Library Squatter." Neil also got thrown out of a couple of bars as a young man, the first time for making a pass at the bartender's girlfriend. The second time was on a date with Marsha at a bar/jazz club, over a salad bowl. The waitress said the bowl was empty, but Neil refused to give it up until he finished eating the remaining (two or three) leaves of lettuce. A tug of war ensued over the bowl, which the waitress succeeded in prying loose. Then Neil decided to hold the empty onion-ring plate hostage. Voices were raised, the jazz trio was interrupted by the ruckus, and a 300-pound bouncer ended up tossing Neil onto the snowy street followed by his jacket and boots. This incident and others like it *did* worry Marsha, but she ended up marrying Neil because she loved his passion more than she feared his volatility.

After eight years of marriage, their life is a lot more sedate than it was when they were younger. Neil is a college professor now, up for tenure in a year, and Marsha has a part-time job as an archivist at the Central Park Conservancy. Her work as an oral historian (published occasionally in journals and self-produced cassette tapes) is all about outcasts: people who are homeless, mentally ill, in prison, destitute, or work unglamorous jobs. Neil is a garbologist (a branch of archeology that studies garbage as a way of understanding culture). Their first collaboration, *Talking Trash,* fuses the study of garbage with the methods of oral history. The 700-page manuscript is the result of two years traveling the country interviewing and photographing hundreds of garbage collectors, street-sweepers, recyclers and dumpmasters; an additional year writing and editing; and nearly all of their life's savings.

Eighteen months and twenty-three rejections after beginning the search for a publisher, their agent asked if they would consider a university press. They said, "Sure. One way or another, this book has GOT to be published." Why is it so important to them? Because:

— (as they write in their introduction) "*Talking Trash* tells the story of what the mightiest country on earth discards by the millions of tons on a daily basis; and in all that trash—and the gritty but wise ruminations of those who haul and process it—is nothing less than a pellucid reflection of a nation consuming itself and the planet it inhabits…"

— they owed it to all the people who so generously laid bare their stories to them

— Neil needed to have at least one book published by a legitimate publisher in his tenure packet or he was a goner

— and Marsha dedicated the book to her father and wanted to give him a bound copy before he dies.

Every Saturday when she was growing up, Marsha rode in the pick-up truck with her father and mother collecting trash from homes and small businesses in a rural county in Pennsylvania. Her mother drove the truck. Her father collected and disposed of the garbage. And Marsha, starting when she was four years old, looked for the envelope with the two or three dollars in it, and when there were no envelopes to be found, she knocked on doors and asked for the money. What an irresistibly adorable bill collector Marsha was as a little girl. And as she got older she became irresistible in other ways that helped her father attract even more customers.

So many kids who grow up working in their family's businesses end up resenting being used as free labor. Not Marsha. She loved Saturdays because she cherished her father, and the fifteen stories he told over and over, and all the laughs and good times they had together—the three of them, and then the two of them after her mother died of lymphoma. Marsha stuck up for her old man too, if she heard kids making fun of him for being the trash collector of the white trash's trash. A student of karate, she'd give macho boys a kick in the shins or a black eye for thinking they were better than her because their dads were farmers or shopkeepers or worked at the mill.

Most human beings are hard-wired not to like the smell of garbage, but Marsha finds a sweetness in the aromas of waste. She prefers the smell of rotting meat or moldy fruits and vegetables to odorless garbage full of synthetic substances with half-lives of forever. And now that her dad is in failing health, the smell of old-fashioned garbage is like roses to her.

In many ways, *Talking Trash* is much more than a book project for Marsha and Neil. It's come to encompass their entire professional, political, and personal lives. It validates their past and gives hope to their future. They've even convinced themselves that the future of the planet rests on the publication of their book. Their marriage, originally a coming together of two individuals of different backgrounds, dreams, and fields of study, has turned into a melding of two people into one entity. They use one business card with both their names printed in small type under the words **TALKING TRASH**. Their phone machine says, "Hello. You've reached *The Talking Trash Project*. Leave a message." They talk *Talking Trash* when they eat, when they shop, before, during and after making love, the first thing in the morning, and the last thing before they fall asleep. They even dream *Talking Trash*.

And together, they dreamt up this harebrained scheme to rescue their project from the jaws of oblivion.

The idea of blackmailing an editor at a major publishing house started out as a joke. For at least the first year of their search for a publisher, Marsha and Neil maintained a healthy sense of humor, fantasizing what they might say in their Pulitzer Prize acceptance speech, play-acting interviews with talk show hosts, and thinking up publicity stunts like having the book launch at the landfill on Staten Island or producing a music video with hundreds of garbage collectors singing *The Talking Trash Blues*. When the rejections started coming in, they kidded around about things they could do to force an editor or publishing company CEO to publish their book. At first it was in good humor, but after the third- and fourth-tier publishers all said no, and finally their agent told them there was nothing left she could do for them, their predicament was no longer a laughing matter.

Using her skills as a researcher, Marsha began snooping around for dirt on publishers and editors. After only a few weeks she had a desk full of potential scandals to pick from. She and Neil zeroed in on Darcy Wolf, an editor with her own imprint within a large corporate publisher. Wolf only published 'authors' who could generate vast amounts of publicity. The only real writers she worked with were ghostwriters who, it turns out, had lots of scurrilous stories to tell, not only about Wolf, but about the movie stars, fallen politicians, sports figures and scandalized provocateurs they wrote in the name of. Wolf didn't care whether the well-known person was a victim or victimizer, or which side of the political spectrum they were on. As long as the mere spelling of their name could sell large quantities of books, she'd publish them. Without a doubt, Wolf was an industry whore— someone who wouldn't have to sacrifice a single scruple in order to save her own skin.

Marsha and Neil followed up on the rumors about Darcy Wolf, gathering as many first-hand testimonies as they could, much like prosecuting attorneys gather depositions before a big trial. Or, you could call what they were doing *oral history*, or *investigative journalism*. Call it what you will. Marsha and Neil called it "our last resort." Their distorted interpretation of karmic law goes something like this: *We kept our end of the bargain— wrote a damn good book. Now it's time the universe gave something back to us.*

The breaks of the Manhattan-bound number seven train screech to an abrupt stop. The doors open. Marsha and Neil step onto a packed subway car. The train lurches forward. For nearly everyone around them, it's just another Monday morning, getting joggled and bobbed on their way to work. For Marsha and Neil it's a momentous day that will either put an end to their streak of bad luck or make it a whole lot worse. Every boundary separating right and wrong, logic and passion, sanity and madness has been swept away by the blind momentum of necessary action. Whatever happens, come tomorrow, their lives will not be the same. The pack on Neil's back (the same one he used when he squatted in the NYU library) is filled with rope, duct tape, a walkie-talkie, a week's worth of camping food, a change of clothes, a cassette recorder, two tapes full of incriminating testimonies, and three blank tapes. The other walkie-talkie is inside Marsha's pocketbook, along with a camera and an alarmingly real-looking toy gun. Marsha whispers into Neil's ear: "Remember hun, there's no need to get macho. Just play it cool. We've already picked up the garbage. Now all we have to do is deliver it to the dump."

Buy This Book Or We'll Kill You didn't get much of a reaction when it first came out. Then somebody gave a copy to a friend, who lent it to somebody who was an acquaintance of Carrie Richardson (the independent filmmaker), who called me up one day asking if anyone had optioned *Buy This Book* for a movie.

When her film adaptation of my book came out, it made a shitload of money, especially for a low-budget film made on the fly. And on the coat tails of her blockbuster, the book became a bestseller; my first.

In the literary lunatic fringe and academic circles I was trudging in at the time, having a book on a bestseller list was practically an embarrassment. It meant either you weren't a serious writer or you had sold out. For the hundreds of thousands of people seeing my name for the first time dissolving in and out of a big blue sky on a wide screen under the words BASED ON THE NOVEL BY , I was synonymous with Carrie Richardson's madcap adventure comedy.

Of all the books I'd written up to that time, the one that made me "an overnight success" was the one I felt most ambivalent toward.

Buy This Book Or We'll Kill You is a silly book that (in hindsight) does a disservice to its more serious underlying themes. I made sure to stress those themes in my first meeting with Carrie Richardson. She pressed me on which theme I felt was *most* important, "because you can't expect an audience to follow too many things in a movie." I described my book to her as a tapestry. In one direction you have the story of these two people whose good intentions get tripped up by their aspirations. Faced with failure, they risk everything they ever believed in. In the other direction, you have the stories of the garbage workers, who— though ignored, even despised by the society they clean up after—turn out to be shamans. They provide a mirror to a culture of waste. By the end of the book, and I hope the movie, both these threads are inextricably linked on a path that seems bound for destruction."

"And at the same time," the purple-lipsticked filmmaker said, looking sincerely interested in my motives, "It's a *love* story. Not only between Marsha and Neil but also between Marsha and her father. Two very different kinds of love stories."

I couldn't disagree with that.

"Above all," Carrie said, "I think this movie has to leave the viewer with a question: What will be America's most enduring legacy? Its ingenuity, or the garbage left over by its ingenuity? And if it does end up being its garbage, what and who will have been discarded?"

Carrie was saying all the right things, yet a part of me didn't trust her. Her fast-paced, action-packed films were heralded as "guy flicks made from a woman's perspective." The films I usually like are slow moving and introspective. But I was desperate to find a way out of having to teach, so I signed over the exclusive movie rights to her and her company. The boilerplate contract gave me the right to see the screenplay, but no veto power over any aspect of the movie.

My book has no sex scenes, and events don't spiral out of control for the main characters till the last three chapters. In Carrie's screenplay, characters are out of control from the beginning, the pace is roller coaster start to finish, and there are three sex scenes including one on a kitchen table between Marsha and Neil with the abducted and apparently bisexual Darcy Wolf tied to a chair looking on making lascivious glances. My book also doesn't include a car chase, drug addiction, a murder (inadvertent or otherwise), or a happy ending. I tried fighting some of these, but it became apparent that if I wanted to have any influence over the making of this film, I had to choose my battles carefully. I dug in on two points: the screenplay's portrayal of heroes and villains, and the use of humor.

Admittedly, certain characters in my book are more sympathetic than others, but there are no clear-cut good guys and bad guys. Even the Darcy Wolf character has likeable qualities. If Darcy had turned out to be the calculating bitch Marsha and Neil imagined her to be, it would have been much easier for them to pull off their plan, and for the reader to come along for the ride laughing at Darcy the entire way. But in the book, the sure-headedness of their plan begins to waver once they find out that Darcy is raising a severely autistic son, and she and Marsha have that talk about losing their mothers to cancer.

I found myself sticking up for my fictional characters like an overprotective parent who suspects daycare workers of manhandling his children. Carrie Richardson is no dummy, but too often she succumbs to a lowest common denominator approach to getting laughs. I threatened to scream bloody murder in a very public way if she didn't make certain changes. "Feel free to be as funny as you want. Make the culture of consumption look ridiculous, pull the pants down on the inanities of academia, the publishing industry, and the way we measure success, but don't poke fun at the expense of these characters. You can laugh *with* them, but not *at* them."

To this, Ms. Richardson accused me of being a prima donna and kicked me out of her office. On my way out, I accused her of being a parasite, and asked why she bought the rights to my book if she was going to change everything I'd written. Well aware of our contractual obligations and the ability of each of us to sabotage the project, we both apologized the next day, and then kept re-locking horns and making up until the movie was in the can.

In the end, Carrie Richardson made a very entertaining, suspenseful, somewhat thought-provoking, occasionally tender, undeniably funny movie that bore very little resemblance to my book.

For the second edition of *Buy This Book*, the publisher, Maelstrom Ltd, wanted to play up the 'synergy' between the book and the hit movie. I agreed to redo the cover art so Marsha

was in front of Neil and she was holding the gun, as Carrie had done in the movie poster, but I refused to replace the drawing with a photograph of the actors. I also compromised on the book jacket's tagline. Instead of *Now a Hit Comedy Motion Picture by Carrie Richardson*, I agreed to *Now a Film by Carrie Richardson.* But I slammed my foot down on the request to revise my book to include scenes Carrie put in her movie. As furious as this request made me, and as adamant as I was about it being out of the question, there was something very tempting about the prospect of doing a rewrite.

Whenever a book of mine is released, I experience a post-publication depression. It's one of the reasons I envy painters. When a painter labors over a painting, then decides that it's finished, she can live with it there in her studio for as long as she wants. She can decide it's not finished and continue painting. She can exhibit it, even have a postcard made of it, then take it home and keep reworking the canvas. She can knife it to shreds if she wants, or paint a whole new painting over it. With a book, once the writer says it's done, and thousands of copies get printed, you pretty much lose control. You know you've done the best you could, and have little choice but to accept that the thing has begun a life of its own. All you can do is wait to get your first bound copy. And when it finally comes, if you're anything like me, you're terribly disappointed.

While you're working on a book, it lives in the boundless realm of the imagination. Ideas and characters can take off on their own and surprise you at any moment. Once the book is printed on paper, captured between two covers, summed up by a catalogue description, and branded by a cover design, it becomes just one more finite object in the world, riddled with flaws, susceptible to mildew, floods and misinterpretations.

A package arrives from the printer with your new book. Once it's in your hands, you know it's out of your hands. You open it, crack the spine and begin reading. You see it objectively for the first time. It's like looking in a well-lit, overly-precise mirror. Suddenly all you see are the open pores, the wrinkles, and a sickly look in the eyes. Your heart sinks. You're filled with self-loathing at the very time you're supposed to be out on the stump talking with great enthusiasm about your great new creation. Right away (if you're anything like me), you begin marking up that first bound copy, which you superstitiously never replace with another. By the time you're doing your first public readings, you've already taken pencils and pens, scissors and glue to it. Within the first two weeks, the pages of this new old book of yours are already covered with handwritten notes—revised word choices, scratched-out sentences, arrows pointing to new insertions, notes climbing up the margins and around corners, newly typed paragraphs pasted in, and entire pages ripped out.

The thing is alive again!

Every reading you give is different, because the text keeps changing. Anyone following along with their copy of the book very quickly finds scant resemblance to what it is they're hearing. Within six months of its publication, your copy looks more like an ancient scrapbook, soiled and weighted down with more ballpoint pen and paste-ins than printer's ink. But you never bother to send in these changes for subsequent editions. You got so used to not having subsequent editions, you've long since given up on the idea. Anyway, it's your nature to *move on*. Not long after the initial post-publication blues, you usually manage to crawl out of the abyss toward the next project in an attempt to reach for something closer to the truth, better crafted, less riddled with imperfections. If one day you ever do finish something that you're really satisfied with, you might just throw in the towel and become a normal person. And that would surely kill you. Thankfully, you're still happily dissatisfied with everything you do.

Instead of submitting a revised manuscript, I took stock of the money I made from *Buy This Book Or We'll Kill You* and submitted a request to my dean for a one-year leave of absence from teaching. After handing in my grades in May, I looked out at an uninterrupted horizon of time—an entire academic year and two summers with no teaching obligations. If during that time I wrote another bestseller, I wouldn't have to go back to teaching. At the very least I knew I had fifteen months to be more of a husband to my wife, more of a father to my daughter, more of a son to my mother, more of a friend to my friends, and I could sit in a chair composing my books for months on end like I'd long dreamed of.

A wonderful plan, except for one thing. I couldn't sit. I couldn't stand. I couldn't do anything but lie in bed due to a debilitating disc disease that finally caught up with me.

3

The orthopedic surgeon gave me two choices: "I either admit you into the hospital right now, and put you in traction for a week; or your wife drives you home, puts you in bed, and you will lie there for as long as it takes to recover. If you choose to go home, there'll be no getting up to go to the bathroom, or eat, or sit at your computer. I'm talking bedpan. I'm talking lying flat on your back doing nothing till you're well enough to begin physical therapy. Either way, you'll need to completely overhaul the way you live your life. And if that doesn't work, we're talking surgery."

For two years, my chiropractor, Dr. Mapleleaf, had assured me that my problem was not a herniated disc. He was right. I had *three* herniated discs! All his kinesiological adjustments, vitamins, homeopathic potions, and therapeutic magnets he sold me over the years did nothing but make my back worse. And he wasn't the only one who misdiagnosed me. The acupuncturist (a former opera singer who had to refer to his manual of Chinese medicine before inserting each needle) didn't get it right either. Neither did the polarity expert and her energy fields, or the massage therapist and his willingness to go as hard and as deep as I wanted, or the osteopath who yanked my bones this way and that and took me into his closet, with a special light, to show me how the mucus in my nasal passages was the actual cause of the sciatic pain running down both my legs.

It took Aconsha forcing me to go to an orthopedic surgeon before I found out the real story of my back. She could no longer sit by and watch me:

- pop sixteen Motrin a day
- invent excuses why I couldn't lift Frida (unless we were in a pool or the ocean)
- drive my car with the seat pushed back to the most reclined position
- go to bed with ice packs and heating pads, silently writhing through the night.

"This is madness!" Aconsha said one day after finding me in the bathtub soaking in Dr. Mapleleaf's herbal bubble bath, scribbling onto a waterproof writing tablet, a half-empty bottle of naturopathic painkiller lying next to the tub. "You have a body, and it's trying to tell you something. *Fuck* all this alternative medicine crap! I'm taking you to a *real* doctor."

I didn't understand how Aconsha could say such a thing. She was the one always railing against Western medicine and its zap-it, medicate-it, cut-it-out, non-holistic approach to what's supposed to be *the art of healing*. She's the one who told me how her great-grandmother Medha, dying of liver cancer, came back to life after going to an Ayurvedic doctor who cleansed her with herbs and colonics and healing fingers, and brought her body back into harmony with her mind and spirit. Aconsha's the one who inspected Frida's tongue to see how her kidneys were, massaged the bottoms of her feet to ease the top of her head, and poured warm milk on her forehead to soothe her stomach. She's the one who taught me Pranayama breathing techniques, even though I insisted that I already knew how to breathe. And there she was, talking to me about getting CAT scans and going to surgeons.

"I'm *not* a hypocrite," Aconsha protested. "Those people you've been seeing, Mapleleaf and the others—they don't know what they're doing. They're not giving you pure herbs. They're giving you processed nutriceuticals, 'plant products' filled with pesticides and heavy metals. They don't understand the complex system of knowledge that goes with the herbs. For them it's just, 'Here, give me money for this bottle of ashwaganda extract or ginseng. It's good for everything. See you in two days.'"

"You don't know what they know or what they don't know."

"I know that you've been in pain for a long time, Bleu. And now you can barely walk. I know that I love you and I can't be silent anymore about what you're doing to your body. It's mind-boggling to me that someone as perceptive and aware of so many things could be so blind to what's going on with his own body."

Early on in our marriage, Aconsha and I had made a pact not to say anything about each other's work habits and their potential negative effects on the body. It's true that I live in my head much of the time, and can write for hours on end, oblivious to the rest of my body; whereas Aconsha is keenly aware of her body—the primary tool of her work. But for as long as she danced for Pico Davis, I feared for her health and her life.

Pico calls her choreography "extreme movement." In her promotional materials, she writes: Through my choreography, I confront my deepest fears, the laws of gravity and physics, and the limitations of the human body. Her dancers throw themselves against walls with bone-crushing abandon, hurtle down ropes, crash into each other at great speeds, hang from swinging bars thirty feet in the air, and drop face down onto mats and trampolines. Aconsha never liked the description, but her work with Pico was as much daredevil stuntwoman as it was dancer. To this day Pico Davis is thought of (by some) as running a freak show, although even her detractors acknowledge that her company has the most athletic, hyper-technical dancers in the field. If one of her smashing, crashing, gravity-defying dancers flinging herself across the stage didn't happen to be my wife, I would have probably been one of Pico's staunchest fans. Even though Aconsha knew all the injury prevention techniques, she still came home with bruises and fractured bones. Several of Pico's dancers have had concussions. One broke her collarbone. Another landed on his back and had to have a metal rod embedded in his spine. For eleven years, whenever the phone rang, and Aconsha was dancing with Pico's company, I feared that it was *the call* informing me that something horrible had happened.

We both cringed at the sight of the other at work: her, being dropped from a ceiling onto a metal fence, then ricocheting herself into a brick wall; me, sitting motionless for hours at a time, slouched over a keyboard in various contorted positions. Once we got past our honeymoon period, Aconsha started calling me 'Screens' because I'd go from staring at a computer screen all day to watching a movie or a television show. In return I started calling her 'My Perilous One.' We'd nag each other continuously like that. "*Where* in the canon of Ayurvedic medicine," I'd wonder aloud, "does it say to drink seven cups of coffee a day?" She'd ask me, "If one morning you woke up as just a head with two hands, would you even *notice* a difference?" During the biggest fight we ever had on this topic, I accused Pico Davis of being a sadistic maniac. Aconsha defended her, saying that their company was no more susceptible to injury than a professional sports team. She questioned if I *really knew* what it felt like to be fully alive. "Human beings are *designed* to swing from trees and run and jump and roll around. We're not made to sit in a chair for hours on end, only moving our fingers." When I questioned whether or not she had a death wish, she said, "No. I don't want to die. It's just that, I. . . some of us don't feel alive unless we're facing death. I'm sorry," she said, her eyes filling with tears, "but that's the person you married. You should have married a writer, someone you could sit side by side with, happily typing away till death do you part."

The morning after that fight, we decided to stop trying to change each other. It wasn't easy at first, biting our tongues, swallowing every worry. After a while, we learned the slow dance of acceptance and kept whatever observations and fears we had about each other to ourselves. But by the time Aconsha took me to the orthopedic surgeon, I didn't put up a fight. I was so hobbled by sciatic nerve pain and numbness in my feet, I literally didn't have a leg to stand on.

"You're absolutely right, Aconsha," I said lying in the back seat of the car on the way home from the surgeon. "I've taken my body for granted most of my life and now it's taking revenge on me." Aconsha shook her head like I still didn't get it. "The body is a civilization. And like many civilizations," she said, reaching back and tapping my skull, "there are the upper echelons. And then there are the forgotten classes." She ran her fingers down my legs to the bottom of my worn-out sneakers. "The body can rise up and revolt, but if you listen to it and make the necessary changes, it can also be forgiving."

Tortured Soles *MANIFESTO*

Written from the vantage point of a pissed-off pair of middle-aged feet, *Tortured Soles* gives voice to a heretofore silent subclass that at last is speaking out and rising up. The bestselling author of *Buy This Book Or We'll Kill You* places himself at the bottom tier of the human body only to discover a disquieting manifesto boiling over with resentment and resolve. The order of things may very well change if these emboldened foot soldiers—tethered to a blundering, ungrateful master—get their way.

1994, Syzygy Books, Venice, CA

Aconsha grabbed her copy of the *I Ching*, sat down beside me on the edge of our bed, and showed me how the symbol for crisis 危机 is a combination of danger and opportunity. I'd read somewhere that that was a mistranslation of the Chinese character (more wishful thinking than accurate translation), but I knew what she was getting at—I was given an opportunity to take time out from my nonstop life of making and doing, to just *be*. My body, the doctor, the state university, the money from *Buy This Book Or We'll Kill You*, and the support of my wife and daughter had all aligned to give me the gift of rest and relaxation. But all it was doing was making me anxious. I'd been lying flat on my back for three months, and there was no end in sight to my convalescence.

I lifted up Aconsha's nightgown and rested my hand on her belly. She was five months pregnant with our second daughter. To both our surprise, I put up little resistance when Aconsha told me she wanted to have another child. I agreed, it would be good for Frida to have a brother or sister (recalling my own solitary childhood), and with the infusion of movie money, the prospect of having two kids didn't seem so bad to me.

Seizing on the idea of creating opportunity out of crisis, my hand reached further up Aconsha's nightgown. (We normally have a very good sex life together, but when Aconsha is pregnant, it's outstanding. She is a thin, small-breasted woman, and when she's pregnant her whole figure gets fuller: her hips, her ass, everything. When we make love, it's like I'm having an affair with my own wife—different body, same amazing woman. Then after giving birth, she slims down to who she had been, and since I've always been attracted to *that* Aconsha, it's like she's come back after being away for six months.)

Aconsha straddled my slowly recuperating body, making sure not to put any weight on my spine. She tapped my groping hand down to my side and asked me to relax. Then she pulled down my pajama bottoms and began rubbing herself on me. Unable to just lie there passively, I started massaging her breasts by moving my head in a circular motion. Since Aconsha was already pregnant, we didn't have to bother with contraception (another wonderful side benefit). She was on all fours doing her weightless horsy-ride on me, rearing her head, slowly rocking the two of us toward a frothy climax; when the door opened and Frida hopped into the room, as if right out of Toon Town, raring to play with Mommy and Daddy. With the speed of a sleight-of-hand magician, Aconsha whisked the blanket over our half-naked bodies, and we discreetly buttoned up while Frida told us about the monarch butterfly that had landed on Einstein's nose, probably mistaking it for a flower. She wished we could have been there to see our dog's expression as he looked down the roof of his nose at the beautiful butterfly. "He didn't shake his head or bark or *anything* for the longest time. And then you know what he did?"

"No. What did he do?"

"He sneezed!" Frida thought this was the funniest thing she'd seen in her "*entire life.*"

"And *then* what happened?"

"Then the butterfly flew away."

Aconsha climbed out of bed, kissed both of us on the forehead, and dashed out of the room leaving Frida and me in each other's care.

"Let's play the story game, Daddy!"

The story game was based on the surrealists' *Exquisite Corpse,* a spontaneous writing technique involving two or more people taking turns writing a text. The story we came up with that morning was about the three-legged turtle she'd brought into the house the day before, and how the butterfly from Einstein's nose flew to the Island Of Lost Legs on an emergency mission.

Frida's heart went out to all living creatures, especially those with missing eyes or limbs. It's not easy being the father of an empath. I had to make sure to drive around puddles in the road so we didn't kill any frogs hanging out in their frog Jacuzzis. Injured birds, turtles, moths, caterpillars—we needed to care for all of them, at least until they got better, and then somehow they would tell Frida if they wanted to rejoin their families in the wild or become a permanent part of our family.

I sensed no resentment from Frida that her Daddy was a pathetic creature himself, who hadn't gotten out of bed in months. She enjoyed playing nurse, bringing me food, steaming hot towels, and my pads and pens. I couldn't understand why she was so patient with me—I wasn't patient with myself. Stuck in bed, bursting with ideas; stuck in the suburbs, hungry for the city; I was churning, plotting, uncertain if I'd ever write another book again, or be able to roam the streets meeting people who inspire me to write.

After we completed the story of the three-legged turtle (who turned down the new leg, having come to terms with her three-leggedness), Frida fell asleep curled up in my arms. I put my cheek against hers, and for a moment my worries disappeared and everything seemed exactly as it should be.

The doorbell had been ringing for a while. Frida woke before I did, leapt out of my arms like a tadpole and raced to answer the door. It was Sidney Lewiston. The more my temporary infirmity was looking like a permanent disability, the less I wanted to see anyone, or be seen. But it was good to see Sidney. He handed me an icepack and placed a box of *Whitman Samplers* on the table next to my bed. I smiled at the sight of him and the chocolates, and raised myself to a sitting position. "No, stay down," Sidney said, having been coached by Aconsha. I rolled onto my stomach, put the ice pack across my lower back, and turned my head toward my old friend. He'd lost weight since I'd last seen him, and appeared to be in good spirits. I was half his age and he was bringing me ice packs. Within minutes Sidney had me cracking up as he told stories about all these communists who lost their shirts in the stock market crash of '29. They were all playing the market, had summer homes, and collected expensive possessions. "Materialists, almost every one of them!" My left eyeball rolled up from my pillow to Sidney's wily expression. *There* was the subject of my next book! I didn't have to go anywhere.

Sidney didn't think anyone would be interested in "a book about a nobody," but he was game to come and talk if it made me feel better. He visited a dozen or so times, and gave me and my tape recorder a lot of great stuff just by being himself. I started transcribing the tapes, but I couldn't sit up for long enough stretches to get much done. I tried writing with the pad above my head, but my hands tired quickly. I'd often wake up with the pad on my face, the bed sheet blotted with ink. Writing while lying on my side was productive, but the physical therapist told me not to put myself in asymmetrical positions. I ordered a laptop computer (not cheap in 1994), thinking that a writing machine I could use in bed might be the solution. But my hands cramped from working on what felt to me like a toy keyboard.

I swallowed my pride and called Monica Medollo, one of the graduate students from the college. She was working on her thesis, a novelized oral history based on interviews of the wives of soldiers who participated in nuclear bomb testing in Nevada. I asked Monica how her thesis was going. She'd finished all the interviews and was fleshing out the first few chapters. "Whenever I have moments of doubt," she said, "which are frequent, I remember what you said about 'doubt being an enzyme,' and that keeps me going." I didn't remember saying that, but I had no reason to doubt her memory. Monica asked how I was doing. I told her, "My recovery is going slowly. I'm trying to finish a book, but for the life of me I can't do it on my own. I don't know how to ask this, but. . . do you think there is any way you could help me with it?"

After a few moments of silence, Monica said, "My God! It would be an *honor* to work with you, Professor Mobley."

"Please," I said, trying not to reveal my ambivalence about having an assistant, "if we're going to work together, call me Bleu."

Second Thoughts: Reflections of an American Communist

NARRATIVE PORTRAIT

For sixty years, Sidney Lewiston has been a perennial figure at protest marches and on street corners throughout New York City, hawking communist and socialist newsletters and spreading the gospel of a world free of religion, capitalism, and inequality. Born to Polish-Jewish immigrants on New York's Lower East Side, Lewiston like many first-generation, depression-era Americans, was drawn to the ideals of Marxism and the field of dreams that was the Russian Revolution. While most of his comrade-classmates from City College became disillusioned by Stalin and the promise of communism, Lewiston kept the faith for most of his life. Now eighty, Lewiston reconsiders his devotion to redness in this bittersweet oral history as told to Bleu Mobley, author of *Buy This Book Or We'll Kill You.*

1994, Paradiddle Press, Brooklyn, NY

The people of the earth today don't give a damn about the things an old pinko nobody ever heard of has to say. That's all I am—a has-been dreamer who believed in equal justice and equal pay and all that pie-in-the-sky stuff for most of his livelong day.

I never heard of Democrat or Republican until I was maybe twenty years old. I was too busy with communists, socialists, Trotskyites, Cannonites, anarchists, syndicalists, The Young People's Socialist League, The International Workers of the World. Left-wing ideology was my mother's milk. Not so much from my own mother. Her relationship to the left wing was reading the gossip column in *The Forward*. Both my parents were apathetic Jews who ate kosher-style food. I'd call them gastronomic Jews. But we lived on the Lower East Side where there was a soapbox on every corner, each with a man or woman on top making a speech more radical than the next. I had no idea it was radical. To me it was the way people spoke. My Uncle Zalman told me by the time I was three years old I was getting up on a milk crate mimicking the soapbox barkers. I always began, "Haverim!" [Comrades!] "Soldatim!" [Soldiers!] Then I'd go off into some meaningless crap like I was orating to the masses. Fifteen years later when I was studying Marx at City College, I started getting up on a soapbox for real. I remember one time overhearing two Hasidic men talking about me. "…A zar kluger younger man. Ubber vus hut air gezuct?" [Such a smart young man. What is he talking about?] I was parroting the theoretical aspects of Marxist economics without a clue of how to connect to the people. I remember singing *The Internationale* at my Uncle Zalman's apartment with all his friends after they heard about the Russian Tsar getting turned out by a bloodless revolution. I was only four years old but I could sing *The Internationale* in three languages! My father considered his brother Zalman a bad influence on me. My mother called him a rebel without a cause: "If one day all the world's problems were solved, your Uncle Zalman would still find something to fight against."

By the 1940s, the Communist Party in America went underground, and in the summers they all came to my Uncle's house in the Rockaways. Dr. Dubois, Eugene Debs, Paul Robeson, all the left-wing people. The FBI used to come around too. The neighbors used to say, "Zalman, your *friends* are here." Which meant FBI. They were so easy to spot because they wore turtlenecks in the middle of July. Even the way they walked was false. When the Communist movement split in two, there were members from each faction in my Uncle's house. One half didn't speak to the other, but they all spoke to Zalman. He always said, "Steer clear of the little skirmishes, Sidney. Keep your eye on the big picture, which is the little man." To this day when I think of Uncle Zalman, I think *big picture, little man*.

The Left never needed any other enemy than itself. The Communist Association people fought the Communist Party USA people. The hard-line Socialists fought the Democratic Socialists. Within the Jewish Left, you had Jewish Communist cemeteries and Jewish Socialist cemeteries. Even in death they had to be kept apart. I never liked the infighting. I always thought, *big picture, little man*. When I learned how Stalin threw Trotsky out of the Party, I thought that wasn't right. But it was a revolution, and revolutions are messy. Zalman used to say, "In every family there are skirmishes." When I read about gulags and the murder of dissidents and Jews, I called it propaganda. When I found out a lot of it was true, I wrote letters to the editors of *The Partisan Review* and *The Daily Worker*. When my letters didn't get published, I chalked it up to the price of social evolution. No one wants to see their dirty laundry up a flagpole, especially when they're already getting attacked from all sides. I bit my tongue and kept selling copies of *The Daily Worker* like a good soldier.

Tell you the truth, I wept the day I heard Stalin died. I'll never forget the voice of the man on the radio. "Joseph Stalin died today of a cerebral hemorrhage." I dropped my cup of coffee on the floor, put my head in my hands and sobbed. I knew Stalin wasn't a perfect man, but he fought against fascism and presided over a great social experiment. That's the way I thought of him. It took Nikita Khrushchev evicting Stalin's body out of Lenin's tomb and announcing the crimes of his predecessor for me to admit the man wasn't all I had him cracked up to be. Then when Brezhnev invaded Czechoslovakia, I finally denounced the Soviet Union as not the real deal. But I wasn't going to throw the baby out with the bathwater. If Fidel really quarantined homosexuals with AIDS, I considered it a forgivable sin. We all have blind spots. I banished my son Bernie when I found out he was gay. "You're no son of mine!" I shouted, as I kicked him out of my life. "You can come back after you come to your senses—a handsome boy like you can find a girl if you had more confidence." He kept coming back, but I was stubborn. I didn't look him in the eyes till I found out he was dying. I screamed at him, "How could you not tell your own father?" He said, "Dad! You didn't return my phone calls for seventeen years. How could I tell you anything?"

I was such a schmuck. I wouldn't talk to my own son, but I went around reciting Mao to any stranger who would listen. I still admire many of Mao's sayings, but now I know the truth about what happened in China. This woman in my building, Mrs. Cho, tells me stories of losing her home and the family business during the Cultural Revolution: how she was separated from her children, and her husband's body and spirit were destroyed in a labor camp. This is the other side of the *Little Red Book* I never wanted to know about.

That was my crime you see, my folly. I was a fundamentalist. Only my word wasn't the word of God, it was the word of No God. The word of Marx, Engel, Mao. The word of communal systems and classless economics. That was my opiate. Everything I thought I was opposed to—that's what I became: a didactic, intolerant parrot clutching the shoulder of a falling statue. For most of my life I'd stand on any corner and debate my "ism" against anybody else's. I was the ism king of my block, my building, and my too-small apartment where I lived with my wife and three kids. No one could win an argument from me.

I won all the battles and lost most of the wars. Each one of my kids left home as soon as they could. What good did my isms do them or my ex-wife who didn't have equal anything in our house? Our house wasn't even our house. Now that I'm in the last chapter of my life I'm an anti-ismist. It's my new religion. I practice it with my new ladyfriend. She's six years older than me. Whatever comes up between us that you might call a disagreement, we talk about and then we vote. If I can't sway her and it's a tie, I let her have her way. She told me, "Life is not a book, Sid." She bought me a guest pass to the gym. I told her, "I don't believe in gyms. Why would I want to sit on a bicycle going nowhere at twenty miles an hour?" We put it to a vote. Now I go to the gym three times a week. I got muscles for the first time in my life. Feel that! The world is going to hell in a handbasket and everything with me is changing for the best. There's something not right about that. I should be a basket case, but I've never been happier. Even my kids are coming around to visit their old man, the two who are still alive. They say, "Dad, we can barely recognize you." When my older son became a stockbroker thirty years ago, I stopped talking to him too. Can you imagine? Now he comes for lunch almost every Saturday. We agreed not to talk politics. So I talk to him about the dangers of nuclear energy in terms of economics and slip pamphlets inside his jacket pocket.

Maxed out on home visits, I started going for physical therapy at a factory-style rehab clinic located in the basement of an out-of-business clothing warehouse. At first I cursed my health insurance company for making me drive a half hour each way to such a depressing place. Then I wondered if they were geniuses, putting me around people who were so much worse off than me. How could I complain about a few herniated discs when I was surrounded by victims of serious car accidents, electrocutions, falls, strokes, gunshot and stabbing wounds?

One of the worse-off patients I came to know at the clinic was an old acquaintance of Aconsha's, the actor/storyteller Lars Halloway. Lars had suffered a massive stroke, but was determined to recover and perform again. He'd been an actor in the experimental theater scene for many years until he began telling stories about his own life, beginning in 1977 when the New York City blackout prevented his company from performing their production of *Medea*. The audience had already been ushered into their seats and were sitting in the darkened East Village theater when the city lost its juice. Lars didn't want to tell a hundred people primed for the magic of the theater to go home just because the electricity wasn't working. But this *Medea* was an elaborate production, with a moving floor, motorized props, prerecorded sound effects—all kinds of electricity-dependent bells and whistles.

The company's stage manager was about to announce the show's cancellation when Lars stepped onto the stage with a lit candle in his hand and told a story about the time a lightning storm blacked out his family's house in rural Pennsylvania where he grew up. The storm shook everything in the house, including all four kids and their basset hound, Rusty. Lars described how his father walked up the stairs with a candle in his hand, calmed the kids down, then scared them up again with a story about a man who came back from the dead to sing songs to his widow and children every time a lightening storm blew through town. Lars continued for over an hour—telling tales about growing up on his parent's farm—before he informed the audience of the blackout. Some people were incensed that he didn't tell them about the blackout right away, but most were grateful that he put on such a memorable show, and the word spread about Lars Halloway's unforgettable blackout performance.

Lars had such a good time telling stories that night, he quit the theater group and began a new career telling stories about his life using no script, no props, no costumes; only his body, his memories, and his way with words. Over the next fifteen years, Lars mastered the art of describing every day occurrences in delectable detail. Often his stories would be about something that happened to him earlier in the day, perhaps on his way to the theater, then he'd link that encounter to a story from his past, and somehow tie the two together with philosophical reflections, leaving audiences feeling like they understood their own hard-to-make-sense-of lives a little better.

Ten years before meeting him at the rehab clinic, Aconsha and I had dinner with Lars and his wife at a Ukrainian restaurant on the Lower East Side. I remember thinking how youthful he was for a sixty-year-old, and wondering what I'd be like at that age. After the stroke, Lars seemed ancient. For the first three months he could barely say his wife's name. Through sheer determination and discipline he built up his strength, learned how to speak again, and two years later he performed a monologue at the Public Theater about living with aphasia and what he called his "second life-changing power outage."

Lars inspired me to take my exercises seriously. He told me to "PIC TURE YOUR SELF DOOO ING EX ACT LY WHAT YOU WANT TO DO. WITH RIGHT A MOUNT OF DIS CI PLINE, PAAA TIENCE, YOU CAN GET CLOSSSS ER TO THAT PIC TURE EVVVV ER RY DAY."

I became an exercise fanatic, performing my regimen three, four times a day, doubling then tripling the suggested number of repetitions. I visualized myself giving Frida and Ella piggy back rides, making love with my wife without her having to worry about injuring me, and writing all day without need of assistance.

Seven months into my year off from teaching, I could sit in a chair and write for an hour or two a day. Any more than that reignited the sciatic nerve pain. The physical therapist said, "You can do a lot with positive thinking and exercise, but you also have to face the fact that you have Degenerative Disc Disease."

When I told that to Lars, he said, "FLUSH THAT! BEEE ING DE GEN E RRATE IS NNNOT END OF THE WORLD. IF YOU CAN'T SIT, STAND! WHO EVER SAID WRI

TER HAS TO BE SIT TER?" He also told me, "CAN'T IS A FFFOUR LEEET TER WORD. VAN QUISSSSHHH IT FROM YOUR MIND!"

I went home, put two crates on my desk, raised my computer, and tried working in a standing position, Lars' command singing through me like an anthem.

In less than an hour I needed to lie down. I slumbered into a dream about Samir. Woke picturing him in his workshop soldering, mitering, "inventing solutions for almost any kind of problem." Called him up. He took the train out to Long Island the next day, sized up the situation and came up with a fix. With a little bit of carpeting, a few pieces of wood, and a metal brace, he rigged it so I could lie flat on the floor with my computer monitor suspended above my head, keyboard and mouse at my fingertips. All I had to do was look up at the screen, rest my elbows on the carpet, type, click and drag to my heart's content. The first time I slipped into position, it felt like I had died and gone to. . . Or more like— I was reborn. "You're amazing, Samir!" With zero pressure on my back I could type away for hours on end. Except I kept panicking that the hulking computer monitor was going to dislodge itself from the rig, fall and crush my head into a pancake. If that didn't kill me, the electromagnetic waves gravitating into my bloodstream would. Samir came out again, and without making me feel like a neurotic, he patiently raised the monitor a few feet higher and to a slight angle so if it were to fall (he assured me it would not), my head wouldn't get crushed. But then the monitor was so far away it was difficult for me to see what I was doing. A week later, Samir set up a video projector so the entire ceiling of my workroom became a huge screen. Talk about illusions of grandeur! No matter how much I tried, Samir refused to let me pay him for more than just the cost of equipment and supplies.

The ceiling screen was a great idea, but seeing my words loom gigantic above me proved to be very intimidating, plus working in full recline kept putting me to sleep and that sabotaged my self confidence. *If I'm putting myself to sleep, then. . .*

Reluctantly, I called Monica Medollo and asked if she would help me with another book. She was happy to do it. I asked if she would mind keeping mum about what we were doing. "If I was an architect or a filmmaker, or even a painter, I could hire as many people as I needed to help me with my work. But the book-writing profession doesn't allow for the kind of assistance creative people in other fields have long enjoyed. If word got out that I didn't write my books all by my lonesome, it could easily be misconstrued."

Monica assured me that it wasn't a problem. She was honored to help in any way she could, and that included keeping it on the QT.

I gave her an outline for *Riveted In The Word*, along with comprehensive character studies and full drafts of the first and last chapters. I likened what we'd be doing to the process of an animator who creates the story, makes the character drawings, develops a storyboard, and has an assistant (or five or ten) do all the in-between drawings and coloring.

Monica worked at home, then brought in drafts of the second and third chapters. They weren't close to what I wanted. The syntax was too clean. The rhythm, off the mark. The mood, too-over-the-top emotional. I needed to rewrite almost all of it. Monica is a cheerful-looking person with hazel, raring-to-go eyes and a mane of long dark hair that was pulled behind her ears the day she came to go over the first round of *Riveted In the Word* edits. Looking over her drafts from my chaise recliner, I prepared to tell her that it wasn't working, that it wasn't her fault—it must be incredibly hard to write in someone else's style, let alone a novel narrated from the voice of a stroke victim with severe aphasia. But we got to talking about other things, and I found out that she'd never met anyone who'd had a stroke. Instead of firing her, I took her to meet Lars and a few other people I knew with brain injuries. She was so moved by them and so fascinated by the loss and reacquisition of language, she ended up volunteering at the rehab clinic working with patients and their families.

Together, Monica and I started playacting the voice of the narrator in *Riveted*. One of us would play the Jesse who could think clearly and had a lucid memory and was a fully emotive human being, and the other one improvised the Jesse who had immense difficulty communicating what she was thinking and feeling. Then we merged the two voices.

Monica turned out to be a quick study. Her drafts got better and better, and she didn't mind doing countless rewrites till I got what I wanted. It was a delicate situation, letting someone else into the sanctuary of my work process. Before almost every suggestion, I'd apologize, saying things like, "I'm *sorry*, but Jesse wouldn't be able to put words together in that way…" Or, "S*orry* but, on page 141, second paragraph, instead of what you have there, could you please have Simon say something about…." Monica made me stop apologizing. She knew what the deal was. It was *my* book and I had every right to be picky. Just as long as I thanked her every so often, I could dispense with all the pleases and apologies. She was right. As her teacher, it had been my job to help her find her own voice and empower her to become as independent as possible. But as my writing assistant, I needed her to think like me and become one with my way of working.

excerpt

7:30 a.m. Getting it back. Slow. Hard. Awffffully toe to road. Every day, not easy. It's go ing to be all right. Aaa eeeeeuwww. Maddening! Not productable to think, oh pitiful me. Go ing to be a proud clear day. Sun waking up. Weep ing willow, down to the ground. Old softly bearded tree. Birds fuff ling past window. Glints of light, such soothing relief.

Dreamt I left voice machine on airplane.

Don't know how to say a word—type it out on the machine.

Listen to the sound, Aha! Every day, read. Every day, type type type. One letter. One word. One book at a time. Speech path ol o gist says, "Every day." Chaaaa N ge, e

Riveted in the Word *A NOVEL*

As highly regarded for her word-craft
as her scholarship, Jesse Hanson, PhD,
wrote books and lectured widely on the
Cold War, the arms race and Cuban Missile
Crisis. Prior to finishing her fourth book
(her first historical novel), she suffered
a massive stroke. In Bleu Mobley's revealing interior portrait of Jesse Hanson's
courageous battle to regain command
of language, he captures the infuriating
struggle many aphasia sufferers experience trying to bridge the gap between
what they comprehend and what
they can communicate.

1995, Kinesthesia Books, London, England

is silent. Chaaang[e]. Slowly. Every day. Change, like Charles. English language, so exasper-
ating! Chaucer. Rawde dwa. Italian, Spanish, German, not so bad.

But English, very very...

casserole, all mixed up. Specially vowels. A can be aahh, or aye, or uh. E can be eh,
or eeee, or smooooothly, efficiently. E can be silent. Consonants more like soldiers, steady as
you go. Unless H or X. But all right. Every day, slow, slowly. Started with *Treasure Island*.
One word at a time. Aroma. Aye, ar, ack, ah. Type it out. Listen to machine. Ah-Rome-Ah,
is two things. Rome is one great city, cathedrals, up to the sky. Statues. Rome antic. Also
cooking, Yes! Smell of Manicotti. *Aroma!* Never will forget. Next word. Next book. *Willow
in the Wind*. Choo choo. What's that? Type it out. A B C, Choo. Sounds like a sneeze, or
to make a decision between two things, or like the train a sound makes. Next word. Next
book. *Grimm's Tales. Alice in Wonderland*. Ashamed, grown woman reading kiddy books.
Not fair. But all right, next book... *Narnia*. Next, *D. Day*. Hoo ha! Big fat one. Difficult.

153

Omaha Beach, Patton, History! By instinct, by heart. Diff ffi cult but de light ful. My favorite. Not the war—*understanding* it. Every day wrrrench ing words. Old words, new words. Sometimes ordinary words won't show themselves. They hide in shadows or send decoys. Sometimes diff ffi cult words, *a snap*. Pentimento. Cartesian. Palimpsest. No rhyme or reason. Inside: ninety-five percent. Pictures. Mem ories. Feelings. Vivid as coffee in the morn ing. Then open mouth: garble garble, all jumble up. Black hole mouth. Lipstick lips—not such terrible *looking* thing, pretty, but *inside*, hugely cavernous place for words to hide. Picture in mind's eye: instant recognition. *Whole.* Then reach for word and *Rrrrrrraaahhhhh. Reaching.*

Reaching.

Know it's there.

Can't grab hold of right one.

Sometimes reach for simple word like soap. End up with soup or suppose or pose. Or have to take very way long around, like *pump-thing liquid gooey. Clean!* Where was soap hiding? In pitch-black room. Biggest darkest room I ever live in. All the furn i ture—strewwwn about. Like burglar broke in, wreaked havoc. Some words, I know where they are right away. Some, I trip over (in front of company). *Reach* for the word.

Warm.

Warmer.

Then it slips away, sometimes, back into tun nel of lost words.

I scream ing inside. Anyone would, but Remembering is my life's work. *Arrgghh!* Dr. Barlow says, "You'rrrrre doing vvvvvery welllll." Slow but chang[e]. "Verrrrry good."

Today, first time going on air plane since stroke. Nerve-wracking. Tickets in pouchbag. *Not* pouchbag. *Kangaroo thing.*

Not kangaroo. *Socket-book.* L M N O P. Pah. Ket. *Pocketbook!* On desk. Bags all packed. Key inside. Not to worry. Rita, best friend in world coming with. Keeps saying, "Not to worry. Go ing to do great." One, two, three, *four* hours from now, we get on plane. *Oh boy.* Then to mor row I give lecture, Cor nell University. First big talk in eight years. Or eleven—one of those e numbers. Conference on Cuban Missile Crisis. Title of my talk, "DEFCON 2 Would Turn Any Cold War Hot." Corman helped with title. Said, "Don't thank *me.* It's chapter in *your* book." When the Cor nell man called, I said, "Oh no. Thank you, very kind, but I don't in public any more talk. Cannot even write. Maybe one day. Thank you." Hang up phone. Used to speak all over world. Now, babbling brook, all over my apartment.

What's left inside here? Who am I if not scholar? If not person of language? Mail comes every day with my name on it. Proof of what? Friends come and visit, recognize me. For mer students, colllleagues. Very patient. Very remembering of me from before. Pick me up. Take me to museum or library. Cheryl, Tuesdays, we go shopping. Rita, Wednesdays, brings lunch, sandwiches. Rita said, "Oh, call the Cor nell University man back. You can give speech, Jesse!" Dr. Barlow said, "Can't seeeeee why nnnot. Maybe a fffffriend can commmme and helllllllp you." Dreamt left word computer on airplane. Frightful panic. Got up to speak, sweaty palms, knees knocking. Uh oh. Where's word computer?

Where's Rita? Where's my cane?

Students, professors, *everyone* looking at ghost standing there—me. Hundreds of eyes waiting. Pictures flashing in my head, speech all in my mind, but no words coming out my mouth. Didn't need any words. Like miracle, they under stood! Never more a hundred percent understood by audience. Standing ovation. Only I sorry it was a dream.

In beginning, hospital nurses, doctors, thought I didn't know anything. Inside I was *ninety* percent. Words came in. But not out. Tried to move lips—nothing. Mouth drown ing in itself. Hands useless. Nurse waving toothbrush back and forth, saying "tooooth-brusssshh." Big taped-on smile nurse cradling bowl, saying, "bOwl." I'm, *I know I know*, with my eyes. She didn't see. She waving comb at me. "Comb." Like I'm deaf. Like I'm baby or brain-death. I'm thinking, *Bring me my manuscript so can finish to publisher on time.* Thinking Khrushchev boasting, years before, about "build ing missiles like sausages." Joint Chiefs saying FULL-SCALE invasion only so lu tion or Soviets win Berlin. Kennedy eating po poached egg on toast with McNamara, worried allies will think trigger-happy cowboys.

Simon could tell. He always had great faith I was in there. Something fasss cin ating or infurrrr iating on TV or in news paper he reading me. He could see smile or fury in my eyes. So many ways to trans mit yes or no.

Yes by raising eyebrow or tiniest nod of head, or eyebrow and nod together.
Yes by blinking.
No by two blinks or half-face grimace. Rejecting food right out of mouth—that gets a no across pretty good. Waving off is no. Teeth gnassshing is no.
Few months later, eyes wide open—big em phat ic YES. Squint, luke warm yes.
Eyes slammed shut, *definitely NO.*
Wiggle left index finger, so so. Shoulder up, I'm cold. Knee lift, something hurts.
After months exercising face muscles, learned to lip words sound less ly. Not just yes or no, but—too much, bring paper, turn it off, love you too. Good side of mouth leading way. Tried so hard to get a peep to come out. Nobody could hear. Year later, still mute as a headstone. Never gave up! Always riveted in the world. In the word. Inside screaming, *Arrrrrrggghhhh.* Wanted to rip a word, any word out of my mouth, so bad. So mad. Few more months and one afternoon,

"Chocolate" stumbled out. (The word.)
Simon shook his head like he was hearing things.

155

He was! "Chocolate?" Yes! Yes! I'm nodding C D E F. Fran, fran ti cally moving eyebrow up, down. Bed shaking. So excited. Simon runs downside. Down*stairs*. Brings up box of Rus sell Stof fer. *Samplers!* Simon and me both, *Goody goody!* Give and take in marriage. Love each other like one. Don't know how many years. Then a milli meter blood clot, a milli second, and *Ka plunk*—I forever take and take. Simon all give. Until before he die, give and take again. Two patients we helping the other.

Picture of me and Simon with war buddies. Visiting, furlough in France for Armistice. Only woman there. Always only woman. First woman honorary Wiffenpoof. First woman professor Princeton University. First visiting history professor at Cambridge. Everybody asks, how does it feel being a woman? Like, can imagine being something else? Only me being me. No big deal. But strange, so many years only one in rooms full of suits, ties, mustaches. All those so many meetings. So many men.

Must get going. Roll onto right side.

Left hand under right leg. Drag leg over edge of bed. Left arm out, hand up to drawer handle. Pull rest of body, all my strength to sitting position. . .

8:20 a.m. Velcro—greatest invention. Buttons, next to impossible. Snaps, okay but headache. Buckles, unh unh. Laces, forget. Zippers, snagging. Velcro shoes, Velcro belts, shirts, coats, pocketbooks. Velcro keychain. Velcro life! Can't imagine life without velcro.

Put up water for coffee. Scramble eggs. Toast and jam, raspberry.

[PHONE **RING**.] Oh my goodness.

[**RING**.] Lower flame. Grab cane. Step.

[**RING**.] Step. Step. If they know me, ring and ring till I pick up. If they don't know me, hang up.

"Hello.

Rita!

Yes. It *is* a good morning. Very very.

Both. Ner vous and excited.

Airplane, myself, evvverything. You know.

Very wanting to go. But nervous. Cheerfully making my way. You know.

Ten o'clock! I thought *eleven*. Good heavens.

Okay. Yes, I'll be ready." [HANG UP PHONE]

Time is mathematics. Most diffffi cult of all. Hours of day. Dates. Someone says, "How's the four teenth?" Or "week from next Friday?" Nightmare for me. Counting down, up. Friday. Saturday. Sunday. Never enough fingers. Piano, no problem. Chopin *Polonaise*. Mozart *Waltzes*, flow like water. Hands on keys. Trans pose even, second nature. Up a third. Down a fifth. Look Ma! Old joke. Left-brain dashed. Music never damaged. Carotid art ery clogged, or they don't know what. Right semaphore banished to hell. *Hemisphere!*

Red spot between eyes never goes away.
Dark red spot. Sometimes big. Sometimes (like now) not so big.
Sometimes red spot is blue.

11:09 a.m. Rita says I'm like osprey spreading her wings again. Feel more like chicken. *Pluk pluk.* Rita wheeling me down ramp into airplane. Tell her new idea for book, *The War between My Hemispheres.* History of self torn asunder. Survival story. Send signed copy to doctor who said, "You probably never talk again." Inscribe: *For all your encouragings.* Simon used to say, "Don't need a project to be you, Jessums." Love him forever, but thought of having a project again, sharing what I have learn—is giving me something to live for. Something to have in sight other than red dot. Maybe just meaningless scratches, what I will write. Maybe nonsense, but have to try. Not lazy around till end of my life. End of ramp. Don't need wheelchair.

"I can use cane from here, Thank you."

Seat 7C. Long line of succession. Aisle seat. Could've been worse. Rita next to me in 7B, says, "I love the idea of your book." The fffaith in her voice makes me believe *anything* is possible. Always fffaith in Rita's voice. Not have to be ter ri bly big book. Ask Corman for help. Swal low pride. Need plenty help. Write, "It was a special day. Just back from teaching, Cambridge. Friends throwing one of those fresh bake cornbread welcome home din ner party parties. First course. Consume, very very yellow. One second, *ha ha ha.* Riveted in the world. Next second, right side slack. Blaaaaaaaaahhhhh. Just like that. . . .

My year off from teaching had come to an end. Since I still couldn't sit for long or get around very well, I taught lying down on a trolley stretcher that Samir retrofitted for me with a motor and little steering wheel. It took some getting used to (on everyone's part), but for some reason my classes that semester were the best I'd ever taught. I think the students seeing me lying there must have thought, *If he can come in here like that, think of what we can do!*

As rewarding as those classes were, I'd *had it* with academia, not so much because of the teaching part (there are far less noble ways of prostituting yourself), but because of all the other crap that has little to do with teaching or students, and because of the poisonous climate that had permeated the college's already demoralized workforce.

The State University of New York (like a lot of public universities throughout the U.S.) built many campuses in the 1960s and '70s to accommodate all the coming-of-age baby boomers. By the 1980s, public education became less of a priority as cutting taxes and fighting crime captured the imagination of voters and politicians. New York's famously liberal governor [1982-1994] built twenty-nine new prisons as he slashed the university's budget, slippery-sloping it from a publicly-funded institution to a publicly-assisted one. Fighting to maintain their share of an ever-shrinking pie, besieged programs and their faculties were forced to go at each other's throats, bringing out the worst in otherwise decent people.

And those were the good old days! While I was on leave, the new [Republican] governor went after the university system as if it were an enemy of the state. Within his first weeks in office he proposed cutting the university's budget in half, and appointed a board of trustees who imposed a core curriculum in "western culture" and "the classics" that siphoned resources from programs they considered threats to traditional values, such as women's and gay studies, Afro-American and Asian studies, and classes with weirdo titles like "Freaks, Rebels, Witches" and "The Fake Class." In addition to usurping faculty authority over curriculum, the trustees required faculty to teach more, test more, have larger classes, fill out more paperwork, and conduct more "self-studies" proving that they were actually teaching what they were teaching and students were actually learning what they were learning.

Since our little campus was on a long-standing list of possible campus closures, it was in a constant state of external and internal review. Committees sprouted like weeds choking off time spent with students. The year before my leave I actually got into trouble for teaching when I was supposed to be at a committee meeting. I also got reprimanded for posting an anti-Gulf War flyer on my office door, which apparently violated the guidelines set out by the "Advisory Faculty Door Committee," an ad hoc committee that reported directly to the provost, a guy who long dreamed of being the head of something, *anything*. Soon after he got the job, he decreed that all committees would be called *Advisory*. Under his reign, committees proliferated as the power of the faculty serving on them shrivelled.

One afternoon, while I was sitting on the Advisory Program Review Committee (a.k.a. the Cut Our Own Throats Committee), the provost suggested a new committee that could make recommendations for standardizing syllabi and class bibliographies. This inspired idea inspired me to start a list of other new committees that the campus sorely needed:

> Possible New Committees:
>
> The Administrative Restraining Committee
> The Squaring a Round Peg Committee
> The Lifetime Sabbatical Committee
> The Committee to End All Committees Committee

With practiced discretion, I slipped the list to a colleague sitting to my right, a kindred spirit whose contempt for academia surpassed mine. She looked at it, chortled, and not so discreetly added her own committee ideas to the list:

> The Is It Or Is It Not Too Late To Rebuild Trust Around Here Committee
> The Air Is Toxic, Everyone Must Now Leave The Building Committee
> The Why Isn't There Ever Any Coffee in These Fucking Committees Committee

She passed the list under the table to a colleague sitting across from us. He added:

> - The GUARANTEED BRAIN-CELL ERADICATION committee
> - The You WILL REALLY WiSh You HAD Become A ROCK STAR OR Tennis champion Once You're On This Committee committee
> - The STick A Pin In YourSELF To See If You're Still ALive committee
> - The Committee That Never ACtuALLY Meets committee

He folded the list of new committees into a paper airplane, and (as soon as the provost left to go to another meeting) shot it across the room in the direction of another colleague who was retiring at the end of the year. It's funny when I think about that now, because we use a similar method in here of passing notes from cell to cell.

Later that same day, at the Faculty Clusters Advisory Committee meeting, I doodled across the agenda and daydreamed ways of escaping my much-coveted tenured teaching gig.

Escape fantasy number 116:

It's a Friday morning around 8 a.m., a few days past mid-semester. A number of faculty, staff, and students crowd around the hallway outside the Humanities office in a state of shock. Professor Bleu Mobley is hanging by his neck from a rope attached to the leak-stained ceiling. Nobody there has the know-how to verify it, but the professor sure looks dead. Dangling from a button on his well-worn sports coat, is a manila envelope with a magic-markered message that says:

DEAR DEAN WORTHINGTON,

HERE IS THE OUTCOMES
ASSESSMENT REPORT
YOU REQUESTED

Knowing there was still a little *Buy This Book Or We'll Kill You* money in the bank, I took another unpaid leave of absence. If need be, I'd apply for disability. Whatever it took, I had to give myself a second shot at being a full-time writer.

Samir didn't like taking money from a friend, but he agreed, finally, to let me commission him to make a workstation that I could write in for more than a few hours a day. Instead of asking me what I wanted him to build, he asked what made my back feel the most relaxed. I told him about the aquatic exercises I did at the rehab clinic—how the water took almost all the pressure off the discs and muscles in my back. He listened carefully, made a few sketches, and in less than a month he constructed a fish-tank-like floatation workstation for me. The warm, buoyant water was like a dream come true—very gentle on my back and relaxing. The only problem was it made me wrinkle up like a prune, and the wet suit he got me to prevent pruning caused me to break out in skin rashes.

Undeterred, Samir brought me designs for *The Lean-Back*, a bedboard-like contraption that came up from the floor at an obtuse angle. "It could narrow at the top like an ironing board," he said pointing to one of his maquettes, "or it could flare out wider for more head support. It could be straight or contoured to your back, made of wood or steel or fiberglass. Whatever it's made of, we can attach a little pillow at the top to make it nice and comfy." A few weeks later he delivered a full-sized prototype of *The Lean-Back*, and its companion angled computer stand. Nervous at first that I would tip the thing over, I leaned against *The Lean-Back*, feeling the stress in my back all but disappear. I was reclining yet standing at the same time. *Why hadn't anyone thought of this before!* Feeling good, I wrote Samir another check. The problem with *The Lean-Back*: my knees kept buckling, and the blood rushing to my head made me dizzy. Samir adjusted the angle of the incline, added knee supports and shoulder straps. But whatever he tried, just didn't work for me.

"What about writing longhand?" Samir asked. I always carried pens and notepads with me for scribbling ideas down and bits of overheard conversation, but ever since I was a teenager I'd composed my books using machines of one kind or another. "Shakespeare wrote longhand. So did your beloved Orwell," Samir said, pointing out that pens and pencils are writing machines too. I had become a careful letterer over the years sketching out my book covers, but that's very different from trying to keep pace with my racing thoughts, which usually end up being an illegible mess. I took out a notebook and showed Samir what I was talking about. He cringed. Moments later he had an idea. He'd met a whiz kid computer programmer (a recent grad from MIT) named Alberto Aguilar who he thought could be helpful. Several weeks later he and Alberto showed me the beginnings of a software program that could convert handwriting into typography. It looked promising so I wrote them each a check. The next time we met, Alberto was very excited. He'd converted his own handwriting into type with only a six percent character error rate.

Samir and Alberto ended up patenting their handwriting-to-type program, but, according to Alberto, my handwriting (he called it a scrawl not a handwriting) "had no predictable pattern to it whatsoever" and was therefore not translatable to type.

The time had come to face reality—*I was a full-time writer in a part-time body*. I dug out some books I had on Buddhism and Zen and started re-reading them.

The Second Noble Truth: *The arising of suffering, disharmony, and frustration comes from desire, craving, and clinging*.

The Third Noble Truth: *To achieve the cessation of suffering, disharmony, and frustration, one must let go of desire, craving, and clinging*.

From **The Eightfold Path To Cessation Of Suffering**: *Everything is impermanent and changes. Individual self is an illusion*.

From **The Sixth Path of The Eightfold Path**: *Effort should be properly balanced between trying and not trying*.

Siddhartha Gautama spent seven years lying on beds of nails and broken rocks, fasting, doing all kinds of extreme rituals until he gave up trying to attain enlightenment. Only then did a girl offer him a bowl of milk soup. Feeling truly relaxed for the first time in his adult life, he sat under a tree and felt his burden lift. He wasn't a self-obsessed seeker trapped in a bag of skin and bones—He was nothing! His ego was mere illusion. He was part of everything.

I put a piece of paper in my antique Olivetti typewriter and typed the words,

YES I CAN'T.

I took out the piece of paper, put in another one and typed, YES I CAN'T. Thought: *This should be my mantra*. YES I CAN'T.

YES I CAN'T. YES I CAN'T.

It wasn't a negative mantra. It was permission. Operative word, YES.

I put in another piece of paper, typed the word YES.

Took it out. Put in another piece. Typed, I.

Took it out. Put in another one. CAN'T.

YES I CAN'T gave me permission

to simply be with my thoughts without having to turn them into anything else.
YES I CAN'T gave me a license to offload the way of being that enables real estate developers to see a wild and beautiful wetland and think *condominiums*, or engineers to think they can correct every flaw of nature, or a king to look at a map and want to re-draw it to spell out his name. I typed out YES I CAN'T onto scores of pages. On some pages I described ways of thinking about *not doing*—techniques, suggestions, tricks.

A week later I called Monica and asked if she'd help me with the book I'd mentioned to her based on interviews I'd done with Gulf War veterans. She came over the next day and saw the piles of YES I CAN'T papers lying around.

"What's all this?" She asked, reading some of my prescriptions for not doing.

"It's a manifesto," I said. "The YES I CAN'T Manifesto."

"Really!"

"*No.* They're just notes to myself."

"This isn't a manifesto," Monica concluded after reading through one of the stacks. "It's self-help. This could make a fabulous book."

"Self-help! Give me a break."

"It's not *bad* self-help. It's the best kind because you wrote it to help yourself."

"And that's where it's staying. Here with myself."

"Alright. But this could be helpful to people in the same situation as you."

"And what is my situation?"

"Overachieving workaholic who got hit over the head by the big frying pan of life, and now you don't know what to do with yourself. You don't know who you are anymore."

"Look who's the wise professor all of a sudden."

"Sorry."

"No. You're right. You described my problem perfectly."

"It could be a book for workaholics."

"It's not just workaholics. It's the human condition."

"Even better. An antidote for the human condition!"

"What do you know about self-help books? Do you actually read that trash?"

"I've read a self-help book or two. Disappointed?"

"No. I just wouldn't have guessed you were the kind of…"

"You think I don't have problems?"

"I'm not saying that. I just don't see why you would seek advice on personal matters from someone who never even met you. Let alone *pay* for it."

"Would it be better I spend thousands of dollars on a shrink than fifteen dollars on a book? Aren't you the one always lamenting how people don't read like they used to? Would you rather they just watch Oprah Winfrey to learn how to improve their lives? Nobody teaches us about coping with life in *school*, that's for sure."

"*Hmm.*"

"Sometimes we, they, just can't find a way out of a hole. Whether it's a hole they dug for themselves or one they got thrown into. We look for help wherever we can find it. Seems to me, a bookstore is a better place to go for help than the corner drug dealer."

"Okay. But if it's *self*-help, how come it's always someone else giving the advice?"

"It's *self-help* because you seek it out yourself, then you pick and choose what you think might be worth trying, and ignore all the rest."

"What about these TV infomercials where the guy suckers you into buying his self help books and cassettes? Is that of your own free will too?"

"There are shysters in every field. What about all those books *you* have about birthing and child rearing. Didn't you tell me you found some of them very helpful?"

"Yeah, but I didn't know the first thing about pregnancy or having kids. I didn't even know how to hold a baby. I told you how I grew up. I was at a total loss for what to do."

"Exactly! And there are people who get to a place where they feel totally lost in their lives. *Anybody* can get to that point. You can look at them and think they have it together. But they don't. It's too easy to dismiss self-help books and the people who read them."

"And the people who write them."

"So use a pseudonym."

"I think I'd rather not."

"Use a pseudonym?"

"No, write the book."

"But that's what you do!"

"Not that kind of book. Not me."

"Yes. Not you. Someone else."

"Who?"

"Let's make up a name."

"For what purpose?"

"It could *help* people."

"I can't do this."

"Yes you can. Be positive, Bleu. Say, Yes I Can't! It can become a movement."

"No I Won't."

"Not just a movement—an antidote for the human condition. What could be more *right-livelihood* than that?"

"Okay."

"Okay what?"

"Okay, you want to help me come up with a pseudonym?"

In less than an hour Monica and I came up with a name. My grandfather Mordechai Jacobson turned himself into Jake Mobley. That's how I became a Mobley. Bring back Jacobson (I'd recently found out that my grandfather's father, Shlomo Jacobson, was a rabbi in Poland who helped many people with their personal problems.) Drop the son from Jacobson, you get *Jacobs*. Jewish-sounding, doctorly. Lying in a drawer someplace was a piece of paper conferring a PhD on me—put the *Dr.* title to use. Bleu is the color of the *Sky*— a place to look up to when you're not sure what to do.

Dr. Sky Jacobs.

Once we had the author's name, we developed his back story and finished writing the book in less than two weeks. To my astonishment, *Yes I Can't* became the subject of a bidding war, and eventually made it to number nine on the *New York Times* Bestseller list.

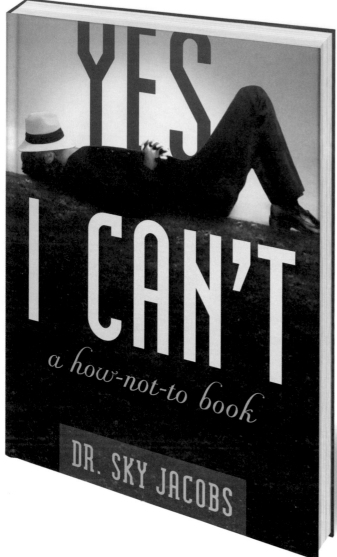

YES I CAN'T: a how-not-to book

SELF HELP

This 103-page guide to not accomplishing your full potential is written in a breezy, lackadaisical style by Dr. Sky Jacobs, a recovering workaholic and survivor of what he calls "The Never Say No Pandemic." Filled with non-obligatory exercises and visualizations, *Yes I Can't* is a slacker's manifesto—an upbeat procrastinator's license to not do very much of anything. Perfect for Type A personalities in need of lowering their blood pressure, or underachievers looking for a warm and fuzzy road map to oblivion. "Read this book from cover to cover and it may be the last thing you'll ever finish... Essential!" *High Times*

1995, Simon and Schuster, New York, NY

excerpt

REACHING THE NO-GOAL POST

Shortly after getting back on my feet, I set a new goal for myself: to have no goal at all. As contradictory as that may sound, it was necessary for me to make use of the addictive behavior (in this case, goal-setting) as a way of weaning myself *off* of the addictive behavior. How is this possible? Try this:

VISUALIZATION 17

Find a quiet place free of distractions. Close your eyes. Imagine you are about to play in a championship soccer tournament. The tournament means everything to you, but it's also the cause of a lot of stress and anxiety in your life and the lives of people closest to you. Now, in your mind's eye, picture the soccer field. Now take away the two goalposts and the two goalies. Take away the clock. You can keep the ball. Now go have fun. Picture yourself on the field having fun, free of goals. No winners. No losers. No ticking of the clock. Nobody in the stands to perform for. No stands! If you reach a point where you no longer want to play, just stop. Remember, it's your life. Your life is the field. Now picture yourself playing on the field with no goalposts and no clock. It's just you and people you really care about, running freely. If you don't want to run, walk. If you don't want to walk, put down a blanket, stick an umbrella into the field, lie down and relax. Now open your eyes.

Once your eyes are open, you can ask yourself if you've placed your life on the field you want to be on? Are there too many goalposts there? (Nine times out of ten the answer is YES.) Are there people and objects on your field who keep you from being happy? (Nine times out of ten the answer is YES.) This is how we utilize goals to get rid of goals. Once the goals are off the field, you can make the field any shape you want, and put whatever or whomever you want or don't want on the field.

LETTING THE RIVER FLOW

As I started eliminating goals and designing my own life field, I found it helpful to distinguish between goals I inherited (via parents, the culture, the media) from those goals I acquired on my own. In time, I yanked so many inherited and self-imposed goalposts off of my field, there were very few things left I felt I *had* to do. Certain activities that were supposed to be pleasurable, like reading, had become a marathon enterprise. Every wall in my apartment was covered with bookshelves. Each shelf was two, sometimes three books deep. Most surfaces (couches, chairs, tabletops, even my bed) were covered with piles of books. When it reached the point where there were more books in my home than air, I sat myself down and visualized a life not surrounded by books. I gave 95% of my books to the Salvation Army, a painful but necessary first step. Then I went three full weeks without picking up so much as a newspaper. This was very difficult, but I did it. Then I celebrated by not having to celebrate.

A week later I was over at a friend's house and saw a book about Buddhism lying on a table. Without thinking, I picked it up and opened to a random page. I read one sentence—something about not pushing the river, just letting it flow. I put down the book and walked away without writing down the title or the author's name or publisher. I didn't have to *own* the book or put it at the end of a long list of necessary acquisitions. I didn't have to do any of that. I also didn't have to feel guilty for picking up the book and reading a sentence or two. That one sentence gave me plenty to think about. The river doesn't need me! It doesn't need dam builders or bridge engineers or water purification systems or even Italian-made sandals to walk across its perfectly gushing flow.

Go to the nearest riverbank on a day that isn't too hot or too cold. Look down. There's a stone at your feet. Flat, oblong, about the size of your palm. *A perfect water-skimming stone!* If you're anything like me, your knee-jerk reaction is to pick up the stone, crouch, then fling the thing, counting out how many skips the stone makes as it skims across the surface of the river. Predictably, if you're any good at it, you take pride in this accomplishment just like you take pride in the number of children you have, the number of cars in your garage, or the number of framed diplomas collecting dust on the walls of your office.

Now, instead of taking the obvious route for once in your life, try letting the stone just be. Think of the stone for a second. Would you like someone picking *you* up and hurling you across a river? Enjoy noticing the stone at rest, noticing the river, noticing your feet, noticing your noticing. Close your eyes and listen to the wind rustling the unambitious leaves. Listen for a bird singing a song that will never make the pop charts. Then breathe a gloriously inconsequential breath, and move on. You're fine. The stone is fine. The river is fine. The day is fine. You needn't relocate a stone from over here to over there or move a mountain or write a symphony or discover a new way to blow up the world. Just move on to another day and another set of stones left peacefully unturned. Try this one day this year. Then next year try it once or twice more. After that, you needn't go to the river at all if you don't want to.

Soon after Frida was born, Aconsha and I gave away our television set as part of a plan to raise her with as little exposure to violence, materialism, and gender stereotypes as possible.

When Frida was one, Saddam Hussein invaded Kuwait and [the first] President Bush began beating the drums of war. As the buildup to invading Iraq intensified, so did my desire to watch the mainstream spin other Americans were consuming. After winning my own little war with Aconsha over the TV or no TV issue, I didn't only buy a television set— we got cable for the first time, which meant CNN.

It's terrible to admit, but much of the time I was watching the *Do We, Don't We, When Will We, Now We're In War* shows, Frida was right beside me, exposed to all that war talk and subversion of the English language. To her it was all flashing colors and men in funny costumes making incomprehensible noises. "The delivery of ordinances upon strategic assets was incontinent causing some collateral damage." Thankfully, a fifteen-month-old can't understand this kind of linguistic pornography. "Patriot missiles *penetrated* their targets... Saddam has *staying power*... You have to admire the *comingness* of the man... He just *shot his last wad*."

It's become commonplace to look back on what we now call Gulf War I, and think of it as a reasonable war. After all, Saddam Hussein did invade Kuwait, Bush [41] went to the UN and put together a genuine multi-lateral coalition that included other Gulf and Middle Eastern countries, the war itself was over in a little more than a month, and you could watch it on TV like a mini-series while eating dinner with the kids. It was a war of a thousand logos; precise, technological, faceless—from the first explosions over Baghdad lighting up the sky like an extravagant Fourth of July celebration, to the first satellite transmission of a laser-guided cruise missile heading down the shaft of an enemy building (followed by a fuzzy screen), to the daily briefings in Riyadh, B54s returning from their sorties doing stop-on-a-dime aircraft-carrier landings, to the video-game-like shots of the final "battle" on the road from Kuwait City to Basra.

When not-so-smart smart bombs careened into the Amariyah bomb shelter, killing a thousand women and children; it was hard to keep the horrifying reality of war from seeping onto American TV. For a day or two, the chorus of confident military experts was interrupted by soul-wrenching crics of weeping mothers, and bodies being whisked away in red-stained sheets. In the comfort of our living rooms, we shook our heads, distracted our children's gaze, and changed the channel.

Frida and I watched the victory parade—throngs of grateful patriots filling up Broadway, cheering newly minted war heroes in a blizzard of confetti. Frida clapped her hands to the rhythm of marching bands. Our brave new veterans had won back America's pride and they weren't going to be treated like Viet Nam vets were, commented most of the commentators. As soon as the war ended, it went from being named after an act of God—*Desert Storm*—to being named after the region. Good had triumphed over evil. No need to mention that Saddam had been a CIA-funded good guy only a decade earlier when he was fighting bad guy Ayatollah Khomeini in the war between Iran and Iraq. *That* Gulf War wasn't on TV. Neither were the other Gulf Wars: when Genghis Khan and his Mongol army invaded Baghdad; or when the Ottomans did; or when the Brits cobbled together their Arabian colonies and named them Iraq (severed from Kuwait); and then their puppet regime was toppled by a nationalist revolt; and that regime was toppled by a U.S.-backed coup, and that regime was toppled by Saddam Hussein and his Baathists. None of those Gulf Wars were televised, so they might as well have never happened. The important thing Americans needed to know—*we got our mojo back*.

Another war we didn't see much of on TV was the war against going to war during the months leading up to Desert Storm. Almost every night, hundreds—sometimes thousands—of people waged peaceful rallies in towns and cities across the U.S. and around the world, pleading for a non-violent solution. This movement, described dismissively in the mainstream media as peaceniks and fringe groups, filled the streets of Washington DC several times by the hundreds of thousands. At around the same time, the very same pundits were describing "democracy movements" spreading throughout Soviet block states. Two thousand people in the streets were signs of a democracy movement. Tens of thousands provoked questions about whether this or that government would topple.

Aconsha, Frida, and I were soldiers in the war against the war. We held up placards, stood and marched, three amongst many, as often as we could. Between breastfeedings, we taught Frida anti-war chants. "**No Bud Fa Erl!**" We spared her the details about the end of the Cold War, the president's dread of having to cash in on a peace dividend, his vision of a New World Order, or the nod our ambassador gave Saddam before he went into Kuwait— but she was old enough to understand the concept: *Make nice. Don't hit.*

Five years later, reclining on the living room couch, pressing my lips against the sweet-smelling forehead of our second baby, I penned the dedication to my 21st book:

"My deepest gratitude to all the Gulf War veterans who shared their stories of a war that was over quickly but may never end; to Monica Medollo, for her assistance and close attention; and to my two-year-old daughter Ella, who doesn't know yet about war."

Peace Is Just Another Word For Nothing Left To Kill *MINDSCAPES*
Back home after a triumphant victory, Gulf War veterans struggle with post-traumatic stress, bizarre physical ailments, unanswered questions, and a desire to move on with their lives. Inspired by conversations and interviews with Gulf War veterans, this collection of interior narratives by bestselling author Bleu Mobley portrays the not-so-glamorous realities faced by a new generation of war heroes.

1996, Velvet Hammer Books, Boulder, CO

Tiny particles of earth stick to my sweaty neck. Hands rule the shovel. A faint ray of light marks the way to the far end of the dark, damp cavern. No time to think of retreat or regret. Right place, wrong time. Wrong place, wrong time—or very very lucky. All you can do is thank your lucky stars and grope in a forward direction.

I'm digging a trench to hide the electrical under Mrs. Cahn's Englewood Cliffs, "set-into-nature," whoop-dee-doo house, while Harry and Raúl finish roofing her new art studio overlooking the Hudson River, the bridge, and Manhattan skyline. Wouldn't mind a view like that. Who the hell would?

I'm tunneling under the walkway to where the sunroom is, up the steep part of the yard, around the roots of the black cherry, to the retaining wall in the studio, down through a trench, across another stretch of yard, finally into the existing end-line power supply.

Harry's a good guy to work for. He sees a person for what they can do, not what kind of license they have. I can do plumbing, electrical, foundations, walls, ceilings, sprinkler systems. If you can see it, I do it. If you can't see it, I can do it. Harry calls me *The Mole*, not because I ever ratted on anyone, but from the stories I tell him about being in the Gulf War. He figures if I could tunnel ditches in the desert when it's 120-fucking-degrees out—guys urinating and defecating in there, sandflies and spidermites and every kind of dessert critter crawling over me (after dousing myself with insecticide), knowing any minute I could be sucking on a scud missile—I can put up with anything. Harry's right about that, except I don't know how much longer I can do this kind of work. My joints are killing me. My nerves are all screwed up. VA hospital says, what do you expect? You're not getting any younger. Here, take some more pills. The one for this kind of pain, take four. The one for that kind of pain, take three. The one for your eyes, take two. The one that cuts down the shaking. The one that makes you sleep. The one that wakes you up. I'm only thirty-two years old and I'm already a walking pharmacy. Even before I went overseas, had to hold out my arm and stick out my tongue for whatever they wanted to give me. No choice: You will swallow this or you will be court-martialed. One of my buddies popped the pills in his mouth and spit them out later. I figured, it's only a precaution—what the fuck. It's not like I hadn't popped pills before. Grew up in Greenwich Village for heaven's sake. Tried every street drug ever made. Even now I add some grass to my prescribed regiment when my stomach is bothering me or my eyes or I'm feeling suicidal. Whatever the pain happens to be, a little grass makes it not so bad. You're still in pain, but at least you can get some sleep. And sleep is important, especially if you have to go to work the next morning.

Harry's no dope. He's not going to put a half-blind crew member on a ladder or up on a roof. Hell, I prefer being on the ground, or under it, inside a wall, groveling through a crawl space. Anywhere you can't fall I prefer. Legally blind in the left eye. Right one, bracing for another operation. In the dark, I see with my hands. Back an heel, knees dug in, head forward. Measure by arm's length, squeeze through and dig.

Running through the desert,
Cause it's hot and it's dry.
Can't stop moving,
Cause I don't want to die.
Up jumped a snake,
Right out of its hole.
Hey there snakey
What do you know?
Point man stopped,
And pulled out his knife.
Cut that snake,
Within an inch of his life.

After two months setting up in the desert, we bomb the Iraqis back to the Stone Age. Ninety-seven hours later the ground war is over. Blink, they're signing a peace treaty under a Schwarzkopf grin. Only thing left to do is put the fires out in the sky from all the burning oil wells. Then I can go home.

Several guys in my brigade want to go pick up souvenirs at the Highway of Death—the place where the last battle was fought, if you call that a battle. Most everyone calls it a turkey shoot or a cockroach hunt. Once it was clear the Iraqis lost Kuwait, thousands of Republican Guard and other Iraqi units retreated in a panic down the six lane highway back toward Basra. As the convoy was fleeing, our fighter jets and mechanized artillery units bombed both ends of the highway and everything and everyone in-between.

It sounds like a bad idea to me—hunting for souvenirs in a desert steeped in anti-personnel mines. But we just won a friggin' war and everyone and their monkey's uncle is saying what heroes we are; they're gonna throw us parades for putting an end to the Viet-fucking-Nam syndrome. "We still got plenty of work ahead of us," I say looking up at the fiery hell in the sky. "C'mon wusshead, it's our day off. Let's celebrate!" There's no use fighting their unstoppable desire to pick up war trophies we can show our grandkids one day.

Our Filipino driver takes us in one of these oversized 1950s Mercedes trucks that the Saudis use as cabs. He drives us ninety miles an hour for three hundred miles until finally we see a graveyard of vehicles up ahead. The stench of gasoline and death permeate the desert air. We can't believe our eyes—all these burned-out trucks, busses, cars, and tanks spread out as far as the eye can see. I'm standing next to a dark skeleton of a bus, the front half of its roof blown off. Inside, between the incinerated seats and the exposed springs, are all these charred bodies. Everywhere I look, inside cars and vans or embedded into the sand are blackened, twisted bodies with gaping mouths, dumbfounded eyes, hands clenching vaporized steering wheels, barbecued in time.

We came looking for souvenirs. We left sick to our stomachs. Been sick ever since.

Some of my buddies have kids who are sick too. The ones born after we got back. Some of them never were born right to begin with. VA says they're running tests, but there's no way to prove nothing. You wonder, was it the oil well fires? Was it the air raids? Maybe we did get hit by poison gas that night. Or was there poison in one of the inoculations? Or in the dust we picked up collecting souvenirs on the Highway of Death—in the invisible spores from our own spent uranium-tipped missiles? Or have we all just gone mental? Nobody the fuck knows and nobody the fuck seems to care. My father says, "God's on our side," but I don't think God smiles every time we have a war. They'll have new wars to fight soon. New heroes to make. And the ones who survive will get shipped home, dropped on the streets like eggs in a frying pan.

I should be on lunch break, but I'm watching a colony of red ants raid a colony of black ants. When you're a mole, you get to watch other civilizations go about their business. It's interesting. Looks like the black ants just finished building a mound nest for their queen and now the red ants are taking it for themselves. The black ants are bigger, but they seem so tentative. Instead of defending the mound, they're running away from it. Some are going AWOL into tiny cracks. A line of reds stand guard at the entrance of their new hill as others run off with eggs, fifty, sixty paces to the entrance of a second hill. Soon there'll be a new generation of black ants growing up in a red world. Guess it doesn't matter whether you're stolen or adopted, it's how you're raised that makes the difference. Weird, this pillaging of eggs. Does the black queen make more eggs than the red queen? Is that what this whole occupation is all about? I never was good at figuring these things out till it was too late. "Follow the money," my friend Tony always says. I gotta tell him, in the ant world I think you gotta follow the eggs.

> *We're lean and mean*
> *And fit to fight.*
> *Send us anywhere*
> *Day or night.*
> *When bullets fly*
> *And rockets fall,*
> *We'll stand our ground,*
> *And give our all.*
> *We're on the move,*
> *We're on the march.*
> *We're diggin' ditches*
> *And breakin' starch.*

"Okay, but why?" Monica kept interrupting our character improv with questions, egging me on, trying to get me to talk about my motivation for writing a book about a genetically engineered hermaphrodite. This is a by-product of graduate school. It encourages students to analyze what they're going to do before they do it. They need a rationale, a theory, a thoroughly mapped out plan before blowing their noses. I resist this. I resisted it as a teacher and I resisted getting into it with my former student turned writing assistant.

I assured her, "There'll be plenty of time to analyze the book *after* we finish it." I continued improvising the character of the narrator in search of the music of her/his voice.

Ten minutes later, Monica interrupted. "Why is this Terry character so objective about all this? Shouldn't she/he be more emotional, more *enraged* after everything that's happened to her/him?"

I thought about this for a few seconds. "It's true, for at least half of Terry's life she/he experienced the worst kind of discrimination short of being murdered. But she/he also lived long enough to see remarkable changes in people's behavior toward third genders. You're right, there is anger brewing inside and we need to show it; there's also plenty of reasons for her/him to love life. After living so many years, she/he doesn't have to worry about who she/he is anymore. It's a perk of getting older—finally being content in your own skin."

"Are *you* content?"

"This isn't about me."

"Who is it about then?"

"It's about Terry, and..."

"But who is Terry? What is this book *really* about?"

"Why don't we write it first and then. . ."

"How can we write it if we don't know what we're writing?"

"This isn't an *opinion piece*. We're writing a novel, an interior..."

"Oh God. Quit with the interior narrative thing. WHAT - IS - THE - BOOK - ABOUT?"

"It's about kids. *Alright!* The way we raise them. It's about Frida and Ella and their whole generation coming up in a world that really hasn't changed all that much from when I was growing up, or from a hundred years ago. With all the advances we've made toward gender equality, we're still steeped in masculine/feminine."

"Tell me more about that."

"The molding and shaping starts long before a child is even born."

"What molding?"

"If it doesn't, why do people care so much?"

"So much about what?"

"The question. The all important question!"

"*What* question?"

"A boy or a girl? This is always the first question asked when you have a kid. Not, healthy or unhealthy? Attentive or dopey? Happy or too early to tell? It used to be the first question after a baby was born. Now it's after the first amnio. And it's expected that you'll share this all-defining piece of information with everyone. If it were up to me, I wouldn't tell anyone the gender of my kids till after they're five years old. Only the parents, the midwife, and pediatrician should know. Then we can see how much behavior is determined by genes, and how much is conditioned by society projecting all its baggage onto the child."

"Thank you. Now I know why you want to write this book."

"Huh?"

"To neutralize the effect of gender."

"Or the *affect* of gender. No! A book isn't going to change anything. That's not why I write books. I write to explore possibilities. That's what my books are about—putting characters into a framework and seeing what they think, what they do, how they interact."

"Don't you think the patterns of how we approach gender are breakable?"

"I think they're breakable *in a story*. With a story you can break any pattern."

"And don't stories help change the world?"

"You're way ahead of me. We haven't written the book yet, and you want it to change the world. Let's just say, I want to tell a story that imagines a different kind of world."

"Sounds like science fiction to me."

"Not science fiction. A parable, maybe."

"Is that what you want it to say on the cover? A Parable?"

"Good idea. *The Third Gender: a parable of blended chromosomes*."

"I have tremendous respect for you, Bleu, but in certain ways, you're very out of it."

"What are we talking about now?"

"There is no section in bookstores or libraries called *Parables*."

"Who cares!"

"Why do you think *Peace Is Just Another Word* isn't selling?"

"I guess there aren't that many people interested in reading about Gulf War veterans and the trauma they're going through."

"Wrong! It's because you *forced* the publisher to call it 'mindscapes.' A book of mindscapes. You sabotage your own chances at success."

"You're not the first person to accuse me of that."

"You think people should read whatever you produce just because it has literary value?

"I don't really care if anyone reads it."

"That's *such* bullshit! You're not just writing for yourself. There are reasons you tell the stories you tell. And in this case, I think it's because you're fed up with boys having to be boys and girls having to be girls…"

"And all the predictable… I mean, even the way we pick our leaders has outlived whatever usefulness it once had. We're trapped, responding to things like we're still living in caves."

"Well there you go. That's our brief. To write a book about gender roles that is nothing less than *evolutionary*."

"Jesus, Monica. Evolutionary?"

"If you don't want it to be revolutionary, it should at least be evolutionary. Something that can help us evolve our thinking about what is possible."

"Are you suggesting I call it *an evolutionary tale*?"

"No. I'm suggesting you call it science fiction."

"You know what I think of genre-writing."

"The world may have a gender problem, but you have a genre problem. And you know what? It's meaningless, this hang-up of yours. And self-defeating."

A little more of this tussling, and Monica got me to admit that I was jealous of Dr. Sky Jacobs because he knocked off a 103-page book that became a bestseller, while Bleu Mobley pours his heart and soul into books that few people buy (except if a filmmaker happens to make a movie out of it). Monica placated me, "Bleu Mobley is more important than Sky Jacobs will ever be. But Sky Jacobs has something Bleu Mobley can learn from."

"And what's that?"

"*Yes I Can't* filled a hole that had been on the self-help shelf for ages. And all these years Bleu Mobley has been filling holes in obscure unshelveable niches that nobody knows about: *Interior Narratives*; *Docu-Portraits*; *Bifurcated, trificated whatevers*."

"Gertrude Stein once said, 'The mind writes what it is.' That's all my mind can do—and my heart—is write what it is. Write what it sees."

"You don't have to change anything in your mind or your heart or in what you put down on the page. All I'm suggesting you do is re-title the aisles in your mind so they correlate more with the aisles in bookstores. You still get to choose your own subjects, compose your own books, all that good stuff!"

"Why are you asking me to do this?"

"I told you my dad is an entrepreneur—I was *weaned* on business plans. You should meet him one day. He's not a monster. If he had a little of your imagination and you had a little of his reality skills, you'd both be hugely successful."

"Fine. I'd like to meet him sometime. But what's it got to do with *The Third Gender*?"

"Because now we know that we're writing a work of science fiction. There's no shame in that. I hate to break it to you, but you've already written plenty of science fiction." Monica started counting off titles with her fingers. "*Boxland.*

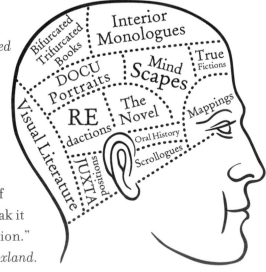

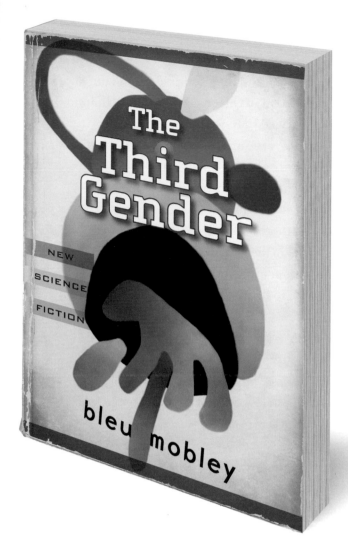

The Switch. Narcissistic Planet Disorder. . ."

"If you'd like, I can explain to you why I'm not a science fiction writer."

"It doesn't matter! Do you *not* go to the men's room because you don't feel accurately represented by the stiff little man symbol on the door? What's that look on your face? If your answer is yes you don't go, I don't want to know about it. Listen, the university press publishing my thesis is marketing it as a 'Women's Health' book. Does 'Women's Health' best describe a non-fiction novel about six women living with cancer whose husbands were used as nuclear guinea pigs by their own government? I don't think so. But it doesn't matter. If that's what it takes, so be it. I'm not letting them change my book. Not much anyway. The point is— I want people to read it. And even if *you* don't care, *I* care that people read your stuff. Millions of people should be breathless waiting for whatever the next Bleu Mobley book is. *Breathless!*"

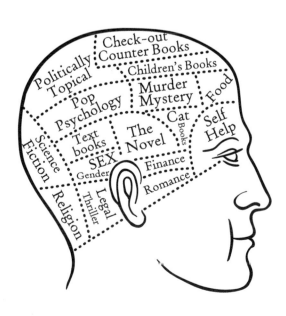

The Third Gender   *SCIENCE FICTION*

Bleu Mobley's science fiction debut chronicles the hard-fought, tender, funny, and triumphant personal history of a genetically engineered hermaphrodite. Looking back at the seventy-year legacy of the third gender (which by the year 2095 became the gender of choice for prospective parents), and ahead into the new genetic horizons at the cusp of the 22nd century (the prospect of a fourth gender), Mobley's narrator sheds light on today's debates over gender identity and rapidly advancing reproductive technologies.

1996, Del Rey Editions, New York, NY

In 1967, Aconsha's parents came to the United States with their four kids, and bought a three-bedroom house in a working-class neighborhood in Queens, known as Richmond Hill. They were part of a wave of South Asians who arrived in New York after the 1965 Immigration Act mandated an end to the discriminatory immigration policies that favored white Western Europeans. What the Lower East Side once was to Ellis Island, Queens was to the New York airports—the new ports of entry for immigrants from all over the globe.

By 1970, the first Hindu Temple in America opened in Flushing, Queens, and even though she had to take a subway and two buses to get there, Lakshmi Battacharjee was among its first and most loyal congregants. Once inside the unadorned Ganesha Temple (formerly a Russian Orthodox Church), Aconsha's mom forgot about her troubles and the troubles of the world, chanting and singing songs to the thousandfold manifestations of the divine. She wasn't always a devout Hindu. When she was a young woman, Lakshmi was quite the rebel. Her country had recently won its independence and she wanted her independence too—from her overbearing, religious parents. With the help of a full scholarship, she left her small farming village in Central India to attend the university in Bangalore, where she majored in sociology and fell in love with Manu, a star forward on the university soccer team, who proposed to her on their second date. Even though she was "marrying up" and there was no dowry being asked of them, Lakshmi's parents disapproved of their daughter marrying a *stranger* and becoming part of a secular lifestyle.

After graduating college, Manu couldn't make it as a professional soccer player and ended up getting a job as a pitchman for a textile company in Bombay. Once Aconsha and Prasad were born, the ice thawed with Lakshmi's parents, who visited their twin grandkids as often as they could while never officially retracting their boycott of the marriage. When Prasad died, Lakshmi turned to her parents for guidance and solace, and made a pact with God never to abandon Him or the Hindu faith again. Manu, on the other hand, blamed God for killing his eight-year-old son, and began to drink. Aconsha, suddenly an only child living in a house of desolation, felt ripped apart. Her twin brother was gone and so was the boundless sense of possibility that shaped her early childhood. She began to dream of a time and place beyond the stillness of a house where her parents slept a lot but couldn't really sleep and spoke but said nothing.

Within four years of Prasad's death, Aconsha had three more siblings. But all the kids in the world couldn't fill the void Prasad had left. Lakshmi became an ultra-protective mother, stricter with her children than her parents ever were with her. Faced with an ultimatum from his wife, Manu agreed to stop drinking, but he turned inward and lost much of the spunk that had attracted Lakshmi to him in the first place.

Coming to America wasn't anything Aconsha had ever dreamed of, but when Manu told her about the plan, she was excited by the prospect of a fresh start. Manu felt the same way. A little bit sad, somewhat nervous, and very much looking forward, the father and his oldest daughter held hands for most of the two days and a night it took to fly to JFK airport. But life in Richmond Hill turned out to be more of the same. Lakshmi's parents and grandmother came to live with them, there were three more babies in four years, and Lakshmi became almost more Indian, more zealously traditional in her ways than ever. She insisted that her children do as their father told them, even though in most cases she was the one telling Manu what to tell them. When Aconsha and her siblings pushed back on things like having to go to temple, wearing saris, being mother's helper in the kitchen, studying only practical subjects in school, and being told who to marry, Manu was deputized as the enforcer.

When she was little, Aconsha enjoyed singing in the temple, cooking dosas and chapati's with her mother, dressing up in lavish saris, and dancing in the Diwali and Deepavali festivals. But by the time she turned sixteen, Aconsha and her mother were fighting almost every day. When she was seventeen, her aunt and uncle moved into the house with their autistic son, and Aconsha could barely wait for high school to end so she could go away to college and escape the suffocating atmosphere of a house that only got smaller as an extra floor and two extensions were added to its modest frame.

The one free spirit of the family, her great-grandmother Medha, urged Aconsha to get away as soon as she could. Medha was the one who took Aconsha to see the Great Royal Circus of India when she was four years old, and told her she could be anything she wanted. When they moved to Queens, it was Medha who arranged for Aconsha to take dance lessons in the city, and instilled confidence in her that she would have a life beyond Richmond Hill one day with people she was yet to meet, people who were more like her.

On the eve of her eighteenth birthday, Aconsha took Medha's advice and left home, not for college but to join a traveling dance company.

Even though Lakshmi left *her* parents' home when she was a teenager, Aconsha's leavetaking was treated like a stabbing to her mother's heart, and she was banned from the house for years. By the time I entered the picture, the ban had been lifted and Aconsha was going home on holidays to see her siblings and her dear Parnaani Medha. But the vibe between her and her mother remained icy. Even while I was persona non grata with Lakshmi, I worked on getting Aconsha to give up the war with her mother. "You don't have to rehash the past," I suggested one time before she left for a family function. "Just bury the hatchet and move forward." As soon as I said this I realized it was a poor choice of words since Prasad's death still bled into everything between the two of them. Staring out our kitchen window, Aconsha said, "You know, I *could* love my mother, if only I didn't hate her." I thought that was a curious turn of phrase and wrote it down in my pad.

Once Frida was born, there was a rapprochement between Aconsha and her mom, and I was officially allowed into their Richmond Hill home which had expanded to include the house next door. After all those years of not acknowledging my existence, Aconsha's parents welcomed me into the fold as if there had never been a problem. I accepted their newfound acceptance, along with free babysitting, homecooked Indian food, and unrivaled insight into the world my wife had come from.

Whenever we visited Aconsha's family, we spent most of the time with Great-Grandma Medha, who lived to be 105. When Medha was 104, she moved into a nursing home, and nearly everyone in the family wrote her off as having lost her marbles. There's no doubt Medha had some form of dementia in those last few years, but her love of life and her philosophical musings (no matter how circular they became) were as revelatory and uplifting to Aconsha and me as ever. We'd find her in the courtyard talking to herself or any sentient being that came her way. She'd welcome us, and we'd bask in the clarity of her supposed incoherence. She'd think Aconsha was her mother, or call her *Doctor*, or by the name of a famous Hindi cinema star, and to each she'd tell a different story. Aconsha just went along with it. "Only with my Medha do I get to be so many people!"

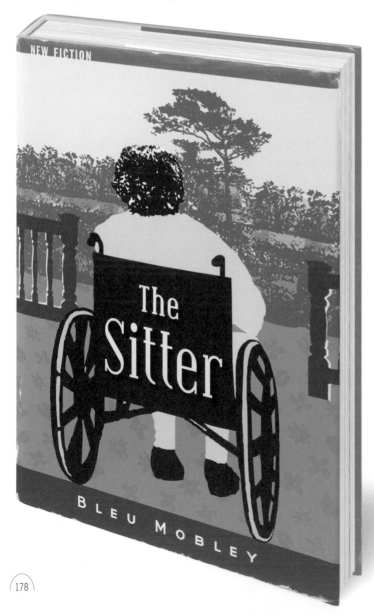

The Sitter *A NOVEL*

Mrs. Eunice Pinella is over 100 years old. Her daughter says she's 104. Her son is certain she's only 102. (He once had the papers to prove it, but at 81, he's having trouble keeping track of things himself.) Whatever her age, Bleu Mobley's front porch matriarch of 37 Franklin Street on Martha's Vineyard, turns out to be a sharp-witted, gregarious character who's not as out of it as most people think. "A non-believer to the bitter end, Mrs. Pinella has more soul than a congregation of holy men on judgment day." Desirée Morton *American Book Review*

1997, Harmony Splinter Books, Palo Alto, CA

Who's that? I can't tell if it's a he or a she. I don't even know if it's someone I know or a complete stranger. They wave, so I wave back. What harm can it do? I don't even know if they're a good person or a bad person. So what if it's a bad person and I lost a wave. I'm 104 years old. I still have plenty of waves left in me. I probably should be dead by now. My husband's dead. The bad man took him. The bad man tried to take me too just this morning. But I hid under the bed and Joanie chased him away by banging on the pots and pans. She said, "You can come out now, Ma." Joanie protects me. She says she's my daughter, but I think she's just a nice lady who felt sorry for an old lady and adopted me as her mother.

Look at the children on their bicycles. It's wonderful that so many children ride bikes today. I used to have a bike. Nellie Haverstram used to borrow it all the time. She wore a skirt with a slit down the middle, which was a good thing because otherwise she'd have to wear pants like I did. Papa always said, "You're not riding on that thing unless you put pants on." God forbid anyone should catch a glimpse of a girl's naked leg. Before I got this wheelchair I used to step on people's feet. I'd look down—my feet were a million miles away. I'd think, *Step left. Step right.* Before I knew it, the ground wasn't the ground but the top of someone else's shoe. I'd pretend like it wasn't me that stepped on them, like I had no idea what was going on, because by that time (maybe a year or two ago) I had already run out of excuses. That's why I finally agreed to the chair. Now I'm a sitter. (Maybe it was five years ago. Maybe it was twenty.) I don't know much about time anymore. I sneeze and it's a season later. Get dressed in the morning—a decade. What do you expect? I'm an old lady. I've been an old lady practically my whole life. First I was a kid for most of my life. Even when I wasn't, I was such a kid. Then one day—*poof*—I was an old lady.

Tell me, is Joanie my mother, or is she my daughter?
She's my daughter! Well that's good. She's not really my daughter, is she?
She is! Well that's nice. It's good to have family around.

Do you know why the bad man took away my husband? We used to have so much fun. When we were in Paris one time, we showed up to some friends. I'll always remember, they said, "Oh here are the Pinellas. We can have fun now!" When Sal died, it was like someone ripped out the other half of me and said, *"Oh well. You get to live. Ha ha ha!"* Had to re-introduce myself to myself. He was such a good man. He was a doctor. I was his favorite nurse. He was so faithful that after I died he refused to remarry, which doesn't make sense because he was lonely so much of the time.

Oh. I didn't die? He died! *Oh my goodness.* Why did he die? I think if he was a vegetarian like me, he'd still be alive. There's no reason at all to kill a beautiful cow for its meat. The milk is plenty enough to take from the poor cow. Actually, the cow *wants* you to take its milk. Otherwise it walks around feeling heavy all day.

Did you hear that? I think it's the grass. When the grass gets really tall it cries out, "Cut me. Cut me. I'm getting too close to the sun!" And boy, what a sun today. Even a breezy day like this. Even with this hat, the sun goes straight through me. Imagine what the grass feels or the cow. I'm no cow. I'm no grazer. I'm just a sitter. Wasn't always. Used to ride my bike whenever Nellie Haverstram wasn't using it. I'd ride from one end of town to the other, and then out of town. Nellie used to wear a dress with a slit down the middle. Otherwise she'd have to wear pants like I did.

It's nice Joanie comes to take care of me, and my son Henry comes to visit from time to time, but mostly I live alone with my thoughts. Usually, the more people come around, the more alone I am with my thoughts. Not because I don't like the company. I do. I like to see people having a good time, chattering about what's going on in the world and all the people they know in it. But ninety-nine times out of a hundred I don't have a *clue* what they're saying. So I put my face down on the straw, even if there's nothing left in my drink, or I send my head back on the end of my neck like I'm dozing off, but really I'm out somewhere on a sea of memories. Little bits of conversation spark off a memory wave or a thought that I know no one really wants to hear about. Because if they heard it, they'd look at me with their noses like, *That doesn't make very much sense at all, Mrs. Pinella.* Like the priest, Father Russo, or Rizzo, the way he looks at me when I ask him questions.

I keep my eyelids closed when people come and visit with me so they can sit around talking to each other. But not all the way closed, so a teeny bit of sun can peep through my eyelashes and keep me feeling cheery. I can tell if I have a little smile on my face because all through my life I often had a smile on my face when I was resting in the sun alone with my thoughts; like when I beg Joanie as if I'm a baby, to give a candy, and if she gives me one, I keep my eyes closed and suck on it ever so slightly like it's a beautiful new sailboat and my mouth is the ocean. It can float in there for a long long time before it capsizes. And if there's any sun at all, I'll open my mouth a little and sneak in some of its warmth. That's even more wonderful! And before I know it, the sailboat is just a little drop of colored sugar resting on the bay of my tongue. And then I savor it. I don't suck on it. And then it's gone. But like a good sunset, even after it's gone, you can still taste it. And if it starts to get dark and I don't get another piece of candy, I start to cry, *I want my Mama and Papa,* but Joanie won't tell me where they went or why the bad man came and took them.

I used to think the bad man just went around taking good people, but I just remembered he isn't so choosy. The bad man stands there sometimes in the doorway foaming at the mouth with niceness. Then he tries to comb my hair. He says, "I've got jars and jars of molasses. You love molasses, don't you? And a hot water bottle." Just this morning he tried pulling me in with one of his tricks. I told him, "You can't fool me. My son Henry is a lawyer and he says, 'Don't ever sign anything until you get it in writing.'" I spent a whole lifetime planting a garden. I'm not going to let some jerky bad man come and set fire to it in two seconds flat. He could give a damn about all the time I spent with my knees in the dirt, putting seeds in every spring with my bare fingers, row after row. Turning over the soil. Weeding. He has no imagination. Joanie says, "Maybe he's not so bad, Ma. Everybody's got a job to do."

Sal and I went to Africa one time. Those were good days. And to Asia and Italy. Even before we met, we went to Italy together. Before the second war. Before there even was an America. We went everywhere. Now I sit, and everywhere comes to me. I don't complain. If I could scream about all my aches and pains and that would make them go away, I'd do it. But all I'd end up with is a sore throat. So I keep quiet.

Joanie! There's a man here says he's looking for somebody with my name. Please, pull a chair up under yourself. Would you like something wet to drink? You know, you look a lot like my husband. *Sal! There's a man here looks just like you.*

Oh. Sal's not here. That's right, Sal went away. I'm all mixed up these days. *Joanie! There's a young fella out here without a drink in his hand.* She has no idea how exhausted I get sitting in this chair year after year. I'm sorry, would you like a candy or something? Such a wonderful breeze. Whenever there's a breeze like this, I pick up my face, just a little and let the wind dance across my cheeks. Even my fingers are a ballroom of activity. Like Sal and me doing the Charleston together when he was overseas between the wars. How we used to sweep everybody's feet right off the floor. Nobody could stop us.

Sometimes, I wish I believed in heaven or God or any of that malarkey. I never went for that father son holy ghost stuff. If there was a God I'd thank him for motion pictures though, because they certainly help pass the time. Always have. Nowadays I let Joanie take me to church. Not because I think God is in there. I just like seeing everybody all dressed up. Specially the kids. And I love the sound of the organ. I watch each chord rise up to the steeple, blend together with all the other chords. I always liked chords. When I used to play piano, there wasn't a chord I didn't like. It was single notes I never really cared for. Last Sunday after the service, the priest came over and thanked me for coming. I looked up, past his smile, and saw that beautiful old poplar tree as tall as the clouds. I asked the priest, "Do you think God made this tree, or is God the tree?" He laughed and went off shaking hands and hugging all the other customers.

Joanie says, "Ma. You know you were born in 1892. In four more years, you'll have seen three different centuries!" Just the thought of it makes me tired. I don't even know what it means—*a century.* All I want is candy or something sweet. Did I have my meal already? Who's that? Who's there? I can't tell if it's someone I know or a complete stranger.

4

ANY MEANS NECESSARY

At breakfast one morning, Frida mentioned something about *all the bruises.* Aconsha and I both thought she was talking about all the bruises she'd had in her seven years of life; from the time she fell off our bed and we decided she was ready to sleep in a crib (not something Frida has a memory of herself, just a story she's heard repeated so many times she's convinced she remembers it), to the various head bangs, bike falls, soccer and football bonks, eye pokes, knee scrapes; and the famous time she was staring at a woman in a wheelchair and crashed headfirst into a lamppost. Frida has always been accident prone, which I attribute to a healthy curiosity. She is athletic—*loves* playing sports—but most sports revolve around the movement of a ball: into a net or a glove, over a net or a line or a fence, or through a hoop. And the most important piece of advice in nearly every sport is— *keep your eye on the ball.* But if you're an insatiably curious child like Frida, there are so many other things besides the ball that can attract your attention, like a squirrel running across the field, or a flock of birds flying overhead, or some kid off to the side of the field being picked on by a bully, or another ball careening through the air from a game on an adjacent field. Those are the kinds of distractions that kept Frida from being a better athlete, and why bruises have always been part of the package with her. Aconsha, Frida, and I had a good laugh that morning retracing the history of Frida's bruises.

After breakfast I drove Frida to school, Ella to a play date, and Aconsha to the gym where she works out then runs back home the six miles to cap off her exercise routine. I dropped the car back at the house and walked to the local park with my lumbar cushion, a blanket, and a pad and pen (my writing machine of choice that week in April 1997).

Later in the day, Aconsha picked Frida up from school, and during the ride home Frida said something again about "all the bruises." Recalling the time Frida fell off our bed, Aconsha said, "It wasn't a bad fall, sweetie. You just went *plomp, thud,* and your father gave me this look like, *I told you so,* because he never thought you should be sleeping in the bed with us. Not at a year old anywa…" Frida interrupted. "No, Ma. I mean all the bruises I have right *now.*" She pulled her pants legs up to her knees. Both her legs were covered with black and blue marks. She rolled up her shirtsleeves to her elbows. There were little red blotches up and down her arms.

Aconsha nearly drove the car off the road.

"No," Frida answered in response to a barrage of questions. She didn't fall down a flight of stairs, didn't get hit by anything or anyone, wasn't in a fight, didn't eat something out of the ordinary that she could think of. She only first noticed any of the bruises and spots herself the night before.

Aconsha's heart was in her throat. She had no idea what she was looking at. *Had someone been beating up her daughter? Was Frida beating herself?*

The pediatrician agreed to see Frida, but she'd have to wait her turn. Aconsha felt like screaming: *It's an emergency. It cannot wait!* Then she looked around the waiting room at the other moms—saw them looking at her, like *my kid is just as sick and just as important as yours*—and decided not to press her luck. I was home by then, working with Monica on a novel about an unorthodox writing professor who takes her students on class trips to detention centers, public housing projects, and cemeteries. On my way to the bathroom I noticed the answering machine had a message. I pressed PLAY. It was Aconsha. "I'm at Dr. Hooper's office with Frida. Call me. Come here. Something's wrong. I NEED YOU!"

Half an hour later I'm at the pediatrician's. Dr. Hooper is examining Frida's bruised legs and spotted arms. It's hard for me to believe what I'm looking at. *If somebody beat up my kid, I'll kill them.* A lifetime of pacifism—wiped out in a second. Iris, the nurse is taking some of Frida's blood. She has a good way with her. They're giggling about something. Aconsha and I are terrified, but we're looking on confidently, smiling through panic. Dr. Hooper and her associate are pointing to spots on Frida's arms and legs like they're points on a map.

Behind the closed door of her office, Dr. Hooper tells Aconsha and me: "It could be Frida's immune system is depressed from the virus she had last month. It could be an anemia of some kind. It could be ITP." (I have no idea what ITP is.) "It could be any number of things. We'll know more when we get the blood results back tomorrow."

"What sorts of things are you looking for in the blood?" I ask, expecting her to say, *I'm sure it's nothing an antibiotic won't fix.*

"It's too early to even speculate. But just to be safe, we're checking for Lupus. Maybe Leukemia. Maybe Aplastic Anemia. I doubt she's got any of those. Her vital signs are good, and that's a good sign. All we know for sure is Frida's got some kind of bleeding going on under her skin."

It's the longest night of my life. Ella is acting out—her sister is getting all the attention over some bruises. Ella crashes her head into the refrigerator door. The blood and large bump on her noggin reestablish her as the center of gravity in the house. Ella has always been a force of nature. Perhaps being born at the precise moment the Northridge earthquake shook Southern California (January, 17th, 1994) was a sign of things to come. I'll never forget, one afternoon about a month after she was born, I laid Ella down on the changing table (in my zeal to be a more proactive parent, I was constantly checking to see if she needed to be changed); I balanced her on her back, undid her diaper, and lifted her legs apart. Suddenly, a projectile of shit shot out of her like a geyser onto the newly painted white wall. I looked down and saw her smiling for the first time. It looked to me like a smile of great accomplishment.

Even with a bruised and bloodied head, Ella is storming through the house with unrestrained frenzy. Aconsha comes to the rescue, and feeds her while I tell Frida a story about a family who miniaturizes themselves so they can live in their post office box. Frida and Ella fall asleep, but Aconsha and I are up most of the night imagining the worst.

The next day, Dr. Hooper explains to us that a platelet count in a healthy person is anywhere between 150,000 to 450,000 platelets per micro-liter of blood. Frida's platelet count as of the day before—which is just a snapshot in time—was only 6,000. "This is not good," she says matter of factly. "But there's no reason to assume the worst. There are over eighty autoimmune diseases and most of them are totally curable, transient conditions. It's in an acute state right now. That's all we know. We're going to put her in the hospital, get her platelet count back up to normal, and figure it out. We'll get through this."

I don't understand most of what I just heard. I know that AIDS is an autoimmune disease and so is mono, but that's about it. Aconsha knows more about these kinds of things, but we both need Dr. Hooper to break it down for us, slowly.

- Platelets are small, sticky components of blood that form in the bone marrow.

- The job of the platelets is to maintain the integrity of the blood vessels and seal small cuts and wounds by forming blood clots.

- If the blood doesn't have enough platelets, it can't clot successfully, resulting in excessive bruising and sometimes bleeding.

- The tiny red dots on Frida's arms are called petechiae (pronounced pe-TEEK-ee-ay).

- Frida's red and white blood cells look fine.

- At the hospital, they may or may not want to do a bone marrow biopsy.

Digging into each other's hands, Aconsha and I become one parental creature, our conjoined hearts beating insanely, our two heads spinning. The floor beneath our feet is no longer there. Everything in Dr. Hooper's office disappears. The only thing we can grab hold of is a crazy hope that we are dreaming.

Before going to speak with Frida, we dam up our tears and straighten ourselves out. Aconsha wishes she'd brought a make-up kit.

Over the next weeks and months, we learn more than we ever wanted to know about bone marrow, reading blood charts, interpreting daily platelet counts, the differences between a drug called Prednisone and its side effects, Danazol and its side effects, intrave-

nous platelet transfusions and their side effects. We learn that Frida *does* have the autoimmune disease ITP, and we quickly transition from disbelief to hoping that it's only an acute case and not a chronic one. We meet other people living with Idiopathic Thrombocytopenic Purpura autoimmune disease—young, old, in-between—and their family members. We hear stories of confusion, denial, cures, recurrences, remissions, misdiagnosis, self-empowerment, miracles, tragedy, and hope. We project ourselves into every story we hear. Our emotions are like putty, and some demonic entity we cannot see is stretching them—*us*—every which way. We hope that Frida doesn't ever need to get her spleen removed or have chemo or any of the other unthinkable procedures we hear about. We discover that Frida is a lot tougher than we thought. We watch Ella react by first getting jealous and then angry and scared, but once she realizes that her older sister's boo-boos are serious and not going away quickly, she takes on a mission to protect her from *ever* having to sleep over in the "teepee hospital" again. Ella brings Frida her bicycle helmet, checks her for red spots (which she calls teepees), and makes sure never to do anything that could bruise Frida, which takes a lot of self control since having a sister with a four-year head start on her in *everything* can be infuriating.

A few months after the onset of Frida's ITP, Samir calls to tell me that the real estate developer that bought the building on Fourth Street is winning the battle to convert our old bohemian/immigrant stomping grounds into a "luxury" condo complex. "They put in an elevator, shi-shi'd up the hallways with carpeting and mirrors and these putrid pastel-colored paintings that make me ill every time I look at them—the same painting on every floor. What kind of soulless painter paints the exact same painting over and over? This is like a military invasion going on here. First they occupied the major arteries of the building, then they infiltrated the apartments, one by one: painting, putting in ticky-tack kitchens, mostly cosmetic stuff. With every improvement they sock you with another rent increase, so Carla and I changed the locks on our apartment and refused to let them in. If you tell them you don't want to buy your apartment, they harass you, claim you don't have a lease, slip eviction notices under your door. You tell them you *do* have a lease. They say they can't find it. You show them your copy. They want you to prove you are who you say you are. You remind them that you were here before they were, and ask *them* to prove they are who *they* say they are. They wait until your lease runs out or they forget to send the renewal till after the expiration date. I'm telling you, these people are the scum of the earth."

"I thought you swore by the free market system?"

"There's nothing wrong with anyone making money, but there are rules for how to play the game, and they've broken every one of them."

"But the rent stabilization rules are a product of the liberal policies that you've been railing against since the day I met you."

"Rules are rules, Mobley. I never said anyone should cheat their way into making a buck. I believe in innovation and competition and that any person, black, white or orange, can make it in this country if they try hard enough. But these people bought the building telling everyone we could live here for as long as we want. Now they're using every trick in the book to force us out. So several of us got together, and we're *suing* the bastards. But Carla and I can't live here anymore. We're looking for another place, maybe in the boroughs. It's not been easy. Anyway, what's going on with you? How are the girls? How's your back doing?"

I tell Samir about Frida being in the hospital, what ITP is, that she's home now and going to school, how every day we check her platelets, and sometimes they're okay and sometimes they're not, how we're fiddling with the medications, not satisfied with anything yet. "We're scared, but Frida keeps us strong. You'd be proud of her; how gracefully she adapts to whatever comes her way." I tell Samir, "If I were seven years old and it was happening to me, I'd be freaking out all over the place."

Samir is mortified to hear about Frida. He wants to know why we didn't call. Before I have a chance to answer, he takes it back. "I understand. You're in the thick of it."

I tell him how sorry I am that we've been out of touch the last couple of years; how something like this gets you thinking about what's important. I don't tell him that I already know about the Fourth Street building—that Sidney Lewiston lost his place and moved into his ladyfriend's apartment in Riverdale, and Frances and Joey Jordon moved to Harlem, and almost everyone that lived there when I was there has either gotten priced out, bought out, or squeezed out.

He asks if there's anything he can do to help Frida.

I ask if there's anything I can do to help them find a place to live.

We both say "love you," before saying goodbye.

Aconsha and I talk it over. We'll offer Samir and Carla to come live with us while they look for another place. They can stay in the basement apartment, which has a bathroom and kitchenette, and use the garage as their workshop. If Samir agrees never to smoke in the house, they can live there as long as they need. Frida always had a lot of fun with her Uncle Samir and Aunt Carla, and it would be nice for us too to see them more regularly. They could babysit for Ella sometimes when we're at the doctors, and having battled her own serious illness and come out the other end, Carla could be something of a role model for Frida; though Aconsha and I agree, there's no reason to mention that to anyone.

I talk to Carla over the phone about them living with us on Long Island. Samir calls back the next day to say they can't accept our offer—*unless* we let them chip in for the rent.

"It isn't necessary," I said. "We'd be helping each other out."

"It *is* necessary," Samir countered. "We will not accept charity."

"It's not charity. The two of you can be a big help while we're figuring out the best way to get Frida's platelets back to. . ."

"We *insist* on paying something."

"Okay. Whatever. I'm sure we can work something out."

"No charity."

"Absolutely not."

"All right then, *landlord*."

"Please, Samir, don't start."

The Shotglass Gardener *YOUNG-ADULT FICTION*

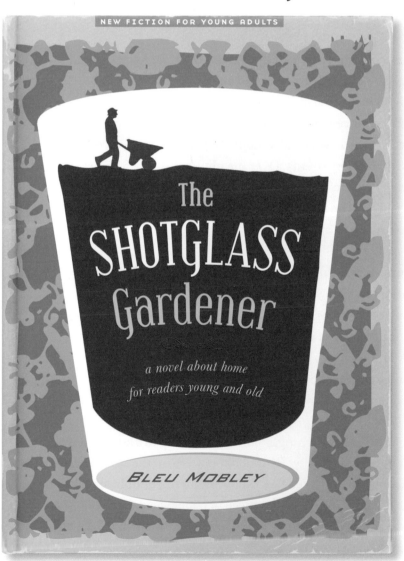

In his first novel written for young adults (and their parents), bestselling author Bleu Mobley tells a tale of three generations of an American family inhabiting small places in a very big town. Written in the form of a film treatment in 1001 scenes, *The Shotglass Gardener* begins with Schmeel and Ruchel's arrival to the Lower East Side after World War I, moving every three months with their young family in order to get the *First Month's Rent FREE*, and culminates sixty years later with their granddaughter, Esther, and her husband Phoenix, being forced out of their Lower East Side apartment due to a condo conversion; minaturizing themselves and their daughter so they can live in their much more affordable post office box. "A cinematic book about resilience and enduring love." **Library Journal**

1997, Little Brown and Company, Boston, MA

Frida's condition was like a roller coaster. As long as she was on the steroids her platelets were fine. As soon as she went off they'd drop back down. So the doctors put her on an intravenous antibody replacement therapy called Gamma Globulin. Frida called it the *Gamma Goblins* because of how sick they made her. But once she finished, her platelets were normal and they stayed normal. We thought, *That's it! Nightmare over.*

Six months later, Frida had a nosebleed and we couldn't get it to stop. We took her to the hospital and her platelet count was down to 7,000. The next day Aconsha told the hematologist, "Frida isn't doing the IV treatment again. That stuff was killing her. And she's not going to live on steroids. They make her blow up like a balloon and that makes her depressed." The doctor nodded sympathetically, then suggested a spleenectomy. "Ninety percent of the time in cases like this, the spleen comes out and the platelets are fine." On our way out of his office, Aconsha whispered, "If the pills don't work or the poison they stick in your veins, the only thing left they can think of is to grab a knife and cut out an organ or two."

We took Frida to another hematologist who suggested chemotherapy. A third hematologist wanted to put her through the much-loathed bone-marrow biopsy.

Aconsha wanted to take Frida to India to see a famous Ayurvedic doctor, the son of the doctor who had cured Medha of liver cancer. But then we heard about a homeopathic doctor in Patterson, New Jersey—Dr. Rahman—who had a reputation in the alternative health world for his high success rate with cancer patients. Over the phone, his receptionist (who I later found out was his wife) said she didn't know if he'd ever treated anyone with ITP. "But if it's a disease," she said, "I'm sure he knows what to do about it." I took the first available date. She said, "I have an opening at 2 a.m."

"You mean 2 p.m.?"

"No. Dr. Rahman's office hours start at midnight and he works through the night."

When I explained that the patient was a seven-and-a-half-year-old girl, and 2 a.m. was way past her bedtime, she said she was sorry but those are the hours the doctor sees patients. "During the daylight hours he works on his research."

"When does he sleep?" I asked.

"Dr. Rahman averages around four hours of sleep. When he was still in his seventies, he only needed two hours—not something you should try unless you live the kind of disciplined life Dr. Rahman does."

Three weeks later, at two o'clock in the morning, I pulled our car up to a small house on a poorly lit side street in Patterson, New Jersey. Four hookers were on the corner chewing gum, talking to each other. Two of them looked like they were men. I double-checked to see if the address matched the address scribbled on my piece of paper. Frida was asleep in the back seat. Before waking her, I shook my head, thinking, *This is craziness.* Reading my mind, Aconsha nodded, but said, "We've come this far."

Mrs. Rahman, a thin businesslike East Indian woman with white hair, buzzed us in and gave the three of us forms to fill out. The questions were about the foods you eat, how well you sleep, if you remember your dreams, if you fear death, if you enjoy life—nothing about health insurance ID numbers or if you have a secondary health plan. This was because Dr. Rahman didn't accept health insurance, or more to the point, no health insurance company in the United States accepted him.

Fifteen minutes later, a pencil-thin, bald-headed Dr. Rahman entered the waiting room wearing a white lab coat and a pleasant smile. He bowed three perfunctory mini-bows, one to each of us, a custom he probably grew weary of a long time ago but couldn't shake.

"This must be Frida. How are you feeling, Frida?"

"Tired. How are you?"

"I'm feeling hopeful that we can help you get better."

He turned to me and asked, "Did you bring the stools and hair?"

Mrs. Rahman had asked me to bring stool samples and hair clippings from everyone in our immediate family. I handed him a bag that contained eight labeled zip-lock bags of shit and hair. Dr. Rahman bowed again and left the room to analyze our specimens. I knew a little about system theory and the idea of the family being an organism, but everything I'd read about ITP said that it wasn't hereditary or contagious, so what my hair or Ella's or Aconsha's poops had to do with the spots on Frida's legs, I couldn't fathom.

I am not a man of faith. Yet during this whole period when we were doing battle with Frida's ITP, my faith was tested. I don't believe in God, but I found myself praying. Who was I praying to? When I hoped, who was I hoping to? I read everything I could find about ITP and every other malady Frida could possibly be suffering from. I deferred to science because I have a modicum of faith in the scientific process. But after a year of trials and errors and not much progress to show for it, I reached a point where there was nothing left to do but hope. I hoped to the forces of nature. To the celestial bodies. To the forgiving arc of time. I hoped to Goodness and the tendency of living things (especially young things, young creatures) to heal on their own. I hoped to Frida's strong constitution and the resiliency of the human body. And when none of that seemed to be working, I went ahead and hoped to God—for Her, Him, *It*—to listen up and pay attention to my sick little girl. I prayed to God, then I watched my prayers turn quickly into demands, threats, quid-pro-quos. *Spare her. Take me. If you take her, then take me too!* Next thing, I'm thinking, *Bad design.* *What kind of God puts a flaw like that in an otherwise exquisite creation? Into an angel like Frida? Is this a sadistic test of some kind? Are you a sadistic God?*

When I caught myself berating God, I panicked. What if there *is* an all-seeing, all-knowing God, and I just insulted Him—the one entity that could hear my prayers and do something to help Frida? Could I grab those thoughts out of the ether, hide them in a place where God couldn't hear them? *It was too late.* If He existed, He already made note of my insubordination.

Mrs. Rahman walked Frida into the doctor's office. We followed, not waiting to find out if we were invited. After a minimal physical examination, Dr. Rahman prescribed a suite of homeopathic remedies for Frida. "We're going to try some medicines—first one at a time, then in combination—to see what works and what doesn't work." I thought, *This guy wants to experiment on my daughter!* Aconsha read my mind. *It can't hurt*, her unspoken answer. *The steroids, the chemo, the spleenectomy can all do IRREPARABLE damage.*

I know, I know. But we're running out of time.

When we got home I looked up Lachesis-200 and Crotalus Horridus-30. *Horridus!* Turns out they're both derivatives of snake venom. It crossed my mind to call the cops. *People should know what this man is doing in Patterson, New Jersey in the middle of the night.* Meanwhile, Aconsha was already preparing the sunflower oil and the Chinese tea.

Our savings were nearly depleted. Whatever royalties were coming in weren't enough to cover our monthly expenses. The credit card companies didn't care that we were living beyond our means, and the health insurance company never even *pretended* to give a flying fuck about what we were going through. When I went off the state payroll, Aconsha and I decided to stick with the same health plan, but due to a several day gap during the switch-over from the state-subsidized plan to the one we paid for ourselves, the assessors determined that Frida's ITP was a "prior medical condition." This meant that Frida *was* covered by our plan, but any bills related to the treatment of her ITP were *not* covered. We fought this, appealing to reason, fairness, and compassion. When that got us nowhere, I hired a lawyer.

Through an ITP support grapevine we heard about a doctor in Australia who had cured dozens of chronic cases with a combination of Western and unconventional methods. After adding up what it would cost to fly to Australia, live there for six months to a year, and pay for the treatment, Aconsha decided she would teach dance lessons to kids at the local *Art Barn*, and I agreed to go back to teaching, get a commercial job as a copywriter or book jacket designer, rob a bank—*whatever* it took for us to have the wherewithal for Frida to get well. The first thing I promised to do was tell Monica that having an assistant was a luxury I could no longer afford.

When Monica came over, she was all upset—her parents were getting divorced *for the second time.* They split up the first time during her freshman year in college. She came home for Christmas after her first semester, and her parents told her that they'd both been miserable for years. Monica knew that the romance between her parents had dried up, but she was surprised to hear that they were so miserable, because they hardly ever fought. "That's part of the problem," her mother said. "If we had fought, there wouldn't be so much moldy crap under the rug. Everything's always fine according to your father. Well everything is *NOT FINE*, and it hasn't been for a long time." Monica's dad waited his turn. "I decided, if that's the way she feels, we better cut our losses now before it's too late for us to attract other fish in the sea."

After they divorced, Monica's mother was the one who right away dove into the sea looking for eligible fish, while her father fell into mourning over losing his first and only love, and for being such a fool. Monica's mother rebuked his apologetic advances, and moved in with a medical supply salesman ten years younger than her. After that relationship fell apart, Monica's parents started dating. Their courtship got hot and heavy real quick, and six months later they remarried, even had a ceremony, which some people thought was in bad taste, but they wanted to celebrate the resurrection of their love and make their vows to each other *publicly*. As far as Monica and her two brothers knew, three years into the remarriage, their folks were doing okay. Her father had become a lot more solicitous of his bride, and almost every time Monica visited she'd find a condom floating in the upstairs toilet, which she thought was a pretty good sign. But behind the calm façade, her parents were constantly hurling verbal daggers at each other about jealousies and resentments dating back to when they were high school sweethearts. If Monica's mother wanted a man who expressed his feelings, she ended up getting one who just couldn't stop.

Instead of telling Monica about the financial hole I was in, we got into a discussion about love/hate relationships. I told her about Aconsha's parents, the way Lakshmi has Manu on a leash and all the bickering about nothing that goes on between the two of them. "Wherever I go, I see a lot of anguish between loved ones," Monica said, questioning her own interest in ever settling into a long-term relationship. "I see husbands and wives haggling with each other over the most miniscule things—couples at each other's throats, sometimes quite literally. I just read in the paper that eighty percent of the murders in the United States last year were committed by people who knew each other. Eighty percent! And many of them were lovers, *so called*. We don't need locks on our doors to keep people out. We need escape hatches."

"No one should put up with abuse," I said. "But the answer doesn't always have to be escaping a relationship. You can free yourself from someone, then end up trapped in the same pattern with somebody else. The important thing, I think, is to *see* the pattern, and by seeing it and facing it, there's more of a chance you can break the cycle. I'm not just talking about couples: close friends, business partners, *any* kind of family relation—siblings, parents and their kids. It's so easy to say terrible things to the people we're closest to—without thinking. And then *Boom*, there's an accident or someone's stricken with a fatal disease, and just like that your child is gone forever, or your mother or your spouse, and the last thing you said to them was what an idiot they are or how miserable they make you. We shouldn't have to wait for something awful to happen before we figure out how to appreciate what we have."

"So is this what you wanted to talk to me about?"

"No, I. . . you. . . You're reminding me of something Aconsha said once about her mother. It was something like, 'I could love her, if only I didn't hate her.'"

"Sounds like a title for a Dr. Sky Jacobs book."

"Nuh uh. That guy's a one-book wonder."

"Or, how about, *I Love You, Therefore You Disgust Me?*"

"Very good! I like that."

"A book like that could make some serious money."

"You think so?"

"For sure. Think of all the people stuck in suffocating relationships. It's a *huge* market!"

Instead of laying Monica off, I made her an offer. Since I had no money left to pay her up front, we could write a book together about angst-ridden relationships under the Dr. Sky Jacobs name, and share whatever proceeds came of it.

"So, what. . . you're into making money now?"

"We *all* need money. There's no crime in making money."

"I agree. It's just, I never heard you talk about writing a book with money in mind. I mean as a goal."

"Look, Monica—my daughter is sick, and whether I like it or not, I live in a world where doctors and health insurance companies and lawyers and pharmacies and health food stores and airlines don't simply give you their services out of the goodness of their hearts."

"Hey, you don't have to convince me—I agree with you. So what would the split be?"

"The split?"

"The percentage split of the proceeds?"

"I don't know. . . sixty-forty?"

"Sixty-forty?"

"Yeah, and the satisfaction of helping people help themselves. We can share in that too. And we get to share in the anonymity."

"That's nice, but why not fifty-fifty?"

"Well, *there's* a question."

"Yeah. There is a question."

"I thought you'd consider sixty-forty a generous offer."

"I do."

"Then why are you asking for fifty-fifty?"

"I wasn't asking for fifty-fifty. I asked *why not* fifty-fifty."

"Huh?"

"I just wanted to see what you would say. Maybe I wanted to see you squirm a little?"

"Why would you want to do that?"

"Because I love you. All this talk about relationships, I thought I'd just come out and say it. I love you, Bleu Mobley. Therefore you disgust me."

"*Hmm.* I have a feeling we just started writing the book."

"Yeah. I have a feeling we did."

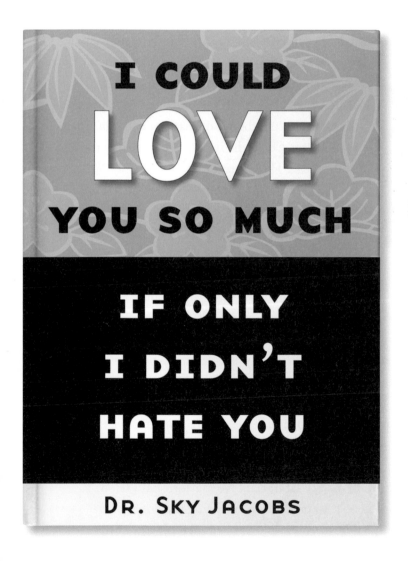

I Could Love You So Much If Only I Didn't Hate You *SELF HELP*

In his first book, *Yes I Can't*, Dr. Sky Jacobs guided the reader toward a less driven lifestyle. In *I Could Love You So Much If Only I Didn't Hate You,* he profiles an array of love/hate relationships and pairs them with useful insights and remedies. By casting light into the dark recesses of fatal attractions, family rivalries, and codependencies of all kinds, Jacobs unmasks the self-destructive behaviors and chronic cycles of negativity that keep us from sustaining healthy relationships. A perfect gift for the one you could love so much, if only. . .

1997, Random House, New York, NY

I Could Love You So Much If Only I Didn't Hate You was such a phenomenal success, particularly with married women, Monica and I wrote a sequel.

1997

After the second *I Could Love You* book proved to be as robust a seller as the first, the publisher offered Dr. Sky Jacobs a contract for an open-ended series. They would pay an advance for each title he delivered, keep the manuscripts on file, and publish them on whatever calendar the market could bear, be it one, two, possibly three titles a year. The contract acknowledged that Dr. Sky Jacobs was a pseudonym, required the publisher to comply with the author's desire for anonymity, but also stipulated that the author had to participate in promoting the books. Jacobs didn't have to do any television or live appearances; but whoever he or she was, would have to answer fan mail and do phone interviews for radio, print, and other media.

When asked why he never goes out on book tours or makes live appearances, he'd explain, "Because I made a pledge to my wife and kids that I wasn't going to be a slave to my work anymore." Dr. Sky Jacobs' ability to *not* chase the limelight served as a living example of a moderated approach to the *Yes I Can't* lifestyle. Phone interviews could be done from his home without having to get on airplanes or compromise his family's private lives. "I make no more excuses to my wife and kids," Jacobs would say. "I love them so much."

To disguise my voice, I practiced throwing it into lower and higher registers. I tried different accents: southern, midwestern, British, Rastafarian. No matter what I tried, I sounded like an overgrown kid from Queens. To pull off a convincing vocal mask I'd need the aid of technology. I asked Samir if he could help, but it was outside any of his areas of expertise. Under the pretense of working on a multimedia production of some kind, I asked the chair of the music department at the college if she knew of any voice altering devices. She introduced me to her electronic music tech, a guy named Nilo Zeigmeister, who hooked me up to a contraption called a *Pitch Shifter* that altered the register and timbre of my voice. It was natural sounding, and could give Dr. Sky Jacobs a voice that was bassier, smoother, and sexier than my own. I mail ordered one right away, and Nilo came to my home and rigged it to the phone line in such a way that I could talk into a microphone and hear the person on the other end through headphones. I paid Nilo well and thanked him in advance for keeping the work he did for me confidential.

I began doing phone interviews as Dr. Sky Jacobs with a fair amount of trepidation, but ended up getting an unexpected high out of playing the role, especially on radio programs that took listener phone calls. Bleu Mobley wouldn't have been any good at that sort of thing, but Sky Jacobs turned out to be so adept at interacting with callers, bringing out the particulars of their tortured relationships, and handling their questions, one radio station offered him a job hosting his own radio show. Jacobs politely turned it down, as he did the offer from *Cosmopolitan* to write an advice column.

To make the most of the open-ended offer to publish more *I Could Love You* books while the iron was still hot, I placed an ad in the *Village Voice*:

> Seeking excellent writers with interest in psychology for large book project. Send writing samples to: Box 9778.

From over a hundred replies, Monica and I narrowed the applicant pool down to fifteen. I interviewed each finalist, keeping an eye out for people who were able to write in different styles, showed some understanding of the vagaries of human relationships, and seemed trustworthy. Josiah (24), Najela (26), and Gil (31) all accepted the job. They each were paid a weekly salary plus an eight-percent profit-share of any book they worked on. Monica was back on salary, plus she got forty-five percent of whatever Sky Jacobs books she and I wrote together, and a fifteen-percent share of all other Sky Jacobs books.

I rented a second-floor office space (near to where I lived) in downtown Port Jefferson, with a large window that looked out onto the marina and the Long Island Sound. I equipped the office with desks, computers, comfortable chairs, a marker board, a water cooler, and a treadmill. On the first Monday in December 1997, I gathered my team of writing assistants for an initial meeting.

I COULD LOVE YOU SO MUCH IF ONLY YOU DIDN'T HATE ME

DR. SKY JACOBS

1998

195

I COULD
LOVE
YOU SO MUCH

IF ONLY YOU
WERE WHO YOU
SAID YOU WERE

DR. SKY JACOBS

1998

I COULD
LOVE
YOU SO MUCH

IF ONLY I
WAS WHO I
THOUGHT I WAS

DR. SKY JACOBS

1998

After a round of introductions, I talked about working as a team, and expanded my film animator analogy to other professions. "Boat builders don't build their boats all by themselves. Choreographers need their dancers, bandleaders need their band members, architects need draftsmen and engineers and construction workers, even visual artists through the ages have had assistants helping them make their art. Within the universe of creative practitioners, it's pretty much only writers of books who are still expected to sit alone typing every comma, participle and preposition of their manuscripts, which is exactly what I did for fifteen years. And I wouldn't have wanted it any other way. Then three years ago I thought my life as a writer was over."

"Five years ago," Monica corrected me.

"Wow. It's been five years? Okay, *five* years ago I thought my life as a writer was finished when some herniated discs made it impossible for me to sit in a chair for any length of time. If it weren't for my wife and kids I would have considered myself of no value whatsoever. Instead of blowing my brains out, I swallowed my pride and called Monica and asked if she could help me. You can imagine how difficult it was to make that call, and how difficult it's been letting go of the ingrained images of the solitary writer toiling alone at a desk, communing with his muse. But Monica has made it as painless as possible for me. I owe a lot to her for helping me shed all kinds of unnecessary baggage. What have we done, six, seven books together now?"

"Nine," Monica said with a bemused smile.

"Nine books. *Really*? Alright then. And now we have an opportunity to be even more productive." I leaned into the circle of chairs and held my hands out toward my assistants. "Together we have fifty fingers, ten eyes, ten ears, five noses, a mix of cultural, ethnic, and geographical backgrounds, both genders, and countless experiences to draw upon. I may be the one steering this book-composing machine, but the end results will be different than if I was doing the work all by myself. When I write with a pen, what comes out of me is different than when I type on a typewriter or recite into a tape recorder, and I expect there'll be differences when I develop a book with each of you.

No matter how precise a plan I give you, know that I want you to take chances. Writing a book alone is a mysterious process. Writing one with another person can be equally mysterious. Together, hopefully, we'll come out with some good books, and if we're lucky, we'll make some money too. Which brings me to the project at hand. *Project Sky*."

I took a few sips of tea.

"I call it *Project Sky* because it's about lifting people up—from the ordinary dregs of their ordinary lives, out of their ruts, their impossible-to-live-up-to expectations or their too-low expectations, maybe even out of some dangerous situations. I also call this *Project Sky* because Dr. Sky Jacobs is the name we'll be writing under."

When I mentioned Sky Jacobs' name, I saw a look of *aha!*, a look of shock, and no recognition at all, respectively, from my three new assistants. "I won't ask if you know of Dr. Sky Jacobs or read either of his books, but I *do* need you to read them now. We have copies for each of you."

I went on to explain the importance of anonymity to this project. "Like any pseudonym or anonymous author, the true identity of Dr. Sky Jacobs is not to be revealed. Essentially, this is a small business, and Sky Jacobs' identity is one of our trade secrets. I won't ask you to sign a confidentiality agreement or have you tell me a secret of yours so I can keep it as ransom. I just need to know that I can trust each of you to keep quiet about our working methods here. That means you tell *no one*. It's fine to say that you work for Bleu Mobley, assisting him with research, copy-editing, scheduling, promotion, and helping him deal with his messed-up back. Ultimately, I am responsible for Dr. Sky Jacobs, but he is not me. He isn't Monica. He is none of us. His name goes on the cover of his books just like Uncle Ben's name is on boxes of rice, and the Pillsbury Dough Boy brands his pop-up rolls. Does anyone have a problem with any of this?"

"Excellent!"

"For the rest of the morning, I thought we'd watch a favorite film of mine, one that I think sheds light on what Dr. Sky Jacobs is getting at in these *I Could Love You* books."

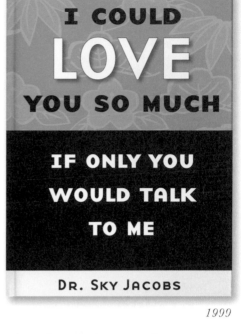

1999

1999

2000

2000

I handed out boxes of popcorn, turned out the lights, and for two hours we sat in darkness watching Hiroshi Teshigahara's 1964 black-and-white masterpiece *Woman in The Dunes* based on Abe Kobo's novel about a man whose goal in life is to discover an insect and have it named after him.

The film begins with the amateur entomologist wandering alone in a barren desert searching for bugs. By evening he loses track of time, misses the last bus back to Tokyo, and stumbles across a seaside village where he hopes to find a room for the night. A few townspeople help him out by lowering him into a giant sandpit, the home of a young widow who the villagers (he later finds out) have condemned to a life of shoveling sand that they sell on the black market for construction materials.

When the man wakes up the next morning he's horrified to see that the rope ladder he used to climb into the pit has disappeared. He is stuck in a pit with a woman he considers a barbarian and part of a conspiracy to imprison him. Cut off from his life in the city and the wider world, he's forced to carry out the endlessly repetitive physical labor of shoveling the sand that every day threatens to engulf the woman's (and now his) ramshackle home. At one point he asks her, "Are you shoveling to survive, or surviving to shovel?" He tries trapping a crow that he could use to send SOS messages. This effort and his countless attempts to climb up the sand dune to freedom prove futile. While trying to catch the crow he accidentally discovers a way to extract water from sand. He wonders if this discovery may be the one tangible accomplishment of his life. Everything else, he says in the voice-over narration "is contracts, licenses, deeds, ID cards." In time, he gives up trying to escape and begins to accept his new life. His anger toward the woman subsides, and their sex shows signs of tenderness. By the end of the movie, the villagers throw the ladder back into the pit. He is free to go back to his life in the city, but he chooses instead to stay in the pit with the woman who is now pregnant with their child.

At first, all four of my assistants said they enjoyed the film, especially the black-and-white cinematography with its sensuous close-ups of sand, skin, and sweat. Then Gil admitted he found it far too slow. "They could have cut the movie in half and added more action." Najela thought the soundtrack was too melodramatic. Josiah said it was a *perfect* film in every way and he couldn't wait to read the

2001

2002

book. It reminded Monica of the Sisyphus myth. "A man condemned by the gods to spend eternity rolling a boulder up a mountain, only to have it roll back down."

"So is this a tale about the meaninglessness of life?" I asked.

"The *endless toil* of everyday living," Gil singsonged, mockingly.

"You get that message from the very beginning," Najela chimed in. "When the man, what's his name? *Niki*, is worrying that his life will turn out to be pointless, or just ordinary."

"Like another grain of sand," Josiah added. "I loved that sequence of shots when he's searching for bugs and the camera closes in on a single grain of sand making it look as big as a boulder, then it zooms out to a wide shot of the rippling desert sands, and you can't help but compare the specialness of the individual with the insignificance of being just one out of millions."

"So are you left with hope by the end of the film?" I asked. "Or did it leave you feeling hollow and despairing?"

"Pretty despairing," Gil said without hesitation.

"Oh, lots of hope," Josiah affirmed.

"Why?"

2003

"Because the man comes to accept his life, finally, his here and now. Instead of waiting to find some stupid bug he can put his name on."

"The guy ends up living in a hole in the ground, digging sand. What kind of life is that?" Gil asked, slicing the air with his hand.

"He discovered a way to make water from sand." Josiah rebounded. "That could be very useful where he is."

"What about his relationship with the woman?" I asked, trying to steer the discussion to the subject they'd soon be writing about. "Did you see any love there?"

"I don't see how they could love each other," Najela said. "They barely talk. They have nothing in common except for the random condition of their circumstances."

"But it's so moving to me that after this guy's valiant struggle to get out of the pit, after feeling so trapped and so repulsed by this woman, once he's able to leave, he chooses to stay!" said Monica. "I think by the end he *does* love the woman. At the very least he comes to admire her."

"I think the message of the movie," Gil said, after giving it a little more thought, "is to make the best of whatever hole we find ourselves in, do the work that comes our way without complaint, and be decent to whoever else is down in the hole with us."

2004

"You make it sound like life is something you have to resign yourself to," Monica said, standing up. "I come away from the film with more of a feeling of revelation than resignation. That we're each more alike than different from each other, and our relationships can be a lot simpler than we make them out to be with all our modern, complicated expectations. I could love you if only you lived in a bigger hole. I could love you if only I could get you to a hairdresser and buy you some nice clothes. I could maybe have loved you if only you were from the city or had a graduate degree like me and we could talk about the same kinds of things. None of those *if onlys* seem relevant by the end of the film. We're left in a very elemental place, identifying with these two people. We live in a pit. We work hard. We sleep. We cook. We eat. We fuck. What else is there, really? That's the transformation the viewer goes through. For most of the movie, I felt trapped, helpless. By the end, I almost envied these people. It made me want to go somewhere far away, look for a man in a dune. Just a little less physical stress to the work, a few more amenities, and I could be happy in a place like that." She sat back down.

"I find it strange," Najela said incredulously, "that no one is bothered by the fact that *this Niki* fellow has a wife back in Tokyo. He mentions in the narration at the beginning that he's married, but then we never hear about his wife again. What kind of bullshit is that? First he goes off on his vacation *without her*, chasing a bug dream. And okay, when he's held captive he loses control of his life. But once he has the ability to leave, he decides to stay with this other woman. It's such a common male fantasy. I'd rather see a movie about what happened to his wife back in Tokyo."

At this point I was thinking, *Now we're getting somewhere. What a fabulous group!* I decided to add a personal story to make more of a link between the movie and the books we were going to write. "My wife is originally from India. Her mother broke with her family's tradition of arranged marriages and married a man she met in college. They call it *a love marriage*. But I wouldn't call it a happy marriage. They fight all the time and one of them holds all the power in the relationship. My mother-in-law's sister and her husband live in the house next door to them. They were an arranged marriage. They met each other only once before their wedding. She was pointed out to him across a room. He gave his approval and several months later they were married. By everything I can see, and my wife can corroborate this, these two people have grown to adore each other. There's great affection between them and mutual respect. From my observations of the arranged marriages and the so-called love marriages in my wife's family, I can tell you that it's hit or miss which have ended in divorce, which seem happy, and which seem utterly miserable, leading me to think that the traditional criteria for sustaining long-term relationships in healthy ways are not all they're cracked up to be. Something else must be at play."

Najela looked at me like she was having second thoughts about the job. "You're exoticizing arranged marriages. You have no idea what kind of relationship your wife's aunt and uncle have. You say that *he* got to check *her* out before they were married. Did anyone ask *her* what she thought? No! I am Afghan-American, and there are many arranged marriages in my family, and I can tell you as sure as there is blood running through my veins, that you have NO IDEA what takes place behind closed doors. My mother was fourteen when they made her marry my father. He was twenty-six. On their wedding night, his parents held my mother down on the bed. Sure, you look at my parents today, you can say they are happy. Like a broken horse inside a corral, my mother is happy, or like an indentured servant who laughs at her master's stupid jokes. To an outsider, everything

2006

seems fine. That said, I wouldn't want any of you criticizing my parents or the practice of arranged marriage or women covering their heads with chadors. You're not in a position to judge."

"So, what do *you* think, Najela? Are the couples you know who are the product of 'love marriages' clearly better off than the couples whose marriages were arranged?"

"No, I can't say that. I just don't think you should romanticize this notion of random couple selection. Truth is, most arranged marriages are not all that random. They're usually matched up by caste, by education, by looks, certainly by tribe. If you want to test out your theory of random cohabitation, you might have to look somewhere else."

Our conversation continued along these lines for a while. After a lunch break, I handed out briefs to each assistant. "Our goal with these books is to tell the truth," I said as they looked inside their envelopes. "The truth about soured, hard-to-stomach, passionate-one-second, at-each-other's-throats-the-next relationships. How do two people start out so happy together and become so wretched? When do they begin to lose sight of each other? Why do they get like that? How can the cycle be broken? If *you've* had trying relationships, begin by writing about them. After drawing on your own experiences, I want you to go outside, to laundromats, poolrooms, bus depots, senior centers, nursing homes—go to wherever people are, and talk to them. I'm not paying you to sit here in front of computers all day. I want you to talk to people about their relationships with their husbands and wives, with their lovers and ex-lovers, siblings, kids, parents, closest friends. Talk to people nearing the end of their lives when they have nothing to lose by being brutally honest. Listen carefully to what they tell you, and write it down. Then we'll look for patterns in what we've gathered, trends, demographics. But our focus will be on stories. That's what's at the heart of these *I Could Love You* books. Stories and any lessons to be learned from them. If nothing else, we can make ourselves and our readers a little more aware of how we interact with the people closest to us. Are we going to stop the batterers or the pedophiles or the double-crossing cheats from doing what they do? Probably not. They won't be reading these books anyway. So let's write to satisfy our own curiosities. If the book you work on ends up making money, that's great, but don't concern yourselves too much with that. I've been licked in the face a few times by the gods of mass appeal, and I can tell you they're an unpredictable lot."

2006

Each brief included a title, an outline, and a draft introduction of an *I Could Love You* book in need of writing. "Please read these, then let yourself run with the theme, and don't be afraid to ask questions. There are no stupid questions, thoughts or ideas around here." I took a few questions and then gave everyone the rest of the day off.

After the others left, Monica asked me why I didn't mention Frida. "I thought you were going to tell them about her disease, how much money it's costing you, and how you have to find a cure for her before she starts getting her period..."

"I planned on telling them. I even thought of calling this *The Frida Project*. But I didn't want any of them to ever look at Frida with pity in their eyes. She's a sensitive kid. The last thing she'd want is to be seen as a charity case. You know, one of *Jerry's Kids*. I figured, if they're going to have pity, let them have pity on me."

After three years—going to scores of doctors, dozens of labs, too many clinics, treatment centers, and hospitals—Frida, Aconsha, and I became experts at waiting.

Bringing your own stuff is key, whether it's reading or writing materials; headphones, needles and thread; or in Frida's case, drawing pads and pencils. A majority of Frida's drawings were of other people waiting: dozed off, sprawled out, hands folded, bodies with magazine heads, mothers braiding their daughters' hair, daughters braiding their mothers' hair, faces cupped between hands, legs and feet intermingled with the legs and feet of chairs and the spaces between. She also drew waiting room tables sprewn with magazines, goofy statues of doctors holding gigantic stethoscopes, coatracks overflowing with winter coats, wall clocks branded with the names of pharmaceutical companies. She drew the stuff of examination rooms: jars full of cotton balls, boxes of gauze, tube racks, instruments of injection neatly lined up according to size, examining tables, blood pressure monitors—and in hospitals: RADIOACTIVE and DO NOT ENTER signs, folded cloth and paper gowns, IV lines hanging from half-filled plastic bags, and bandages adhered to her own arms, legs, and belly. By the time she was nine Frida was so experienced at drawing—a habit born of anxiety and boredom—people called it a God-given talent.

However patient she became at waiting her turn, that's how impatient she got when being bullshitted or condescended to. A shy person by nature, the more Frida became a part of what Carla coined, "the club that no one wants to belong to, of people in need of help but who are not helpless," the more her inhibitions receded. With Carla's encouragement, Frida would brazenly tell doctors and nurses to stop beating around the bush and tell her the truth. This frankness was a quality shared by many of the long-term patients she met in pediatric wards and clinics. Her closest friends were battling afflictions like cancer, HIV, Lyme Disease, and Chronic Fatigue Syndrome, and though they all were kids at heart, full of gossip, silliness, and soaring dreams, many of them possessed a maturity that transcended their age. And with Frida, the more serious her condition became, the more focused she was on how the other kids were doing.

When the idea of going to the blood disease clinic in Australia came up, Frida refused to go. She'd gotten used to not being a hundred percent healthy; didn't see any reason to leave home and everyone she knew to go get poked and pricked and experimented on in a foreign country. Carla openly defended Frida's right to make this decision, which caused a good deal of tension in the house, since Aconsha and I were the parents, and Carla the houseguest. It didn't matter to Carla that Frida was only a child. She insisted that Frida was old enough to know what was right for her. "It's not as if she's refused to cooperate with any of the treatments she's been put through. On the *contrary*, she's been an amazing patient!" The bottom line, according to Carla: "It's Frida's body, *Frida's life*, and if she doesn't want to go to some faraway place chasing a miracle cure, that's her decision to make."

Carla was in her mid-twenties when she was diagnosed with breast cancer, and she went along with the doctors' and her parents' recommendations. "I had the mastectomy, the chemo, the radiation, the whole toxic roast; now I'm considered a survivor, and I have few regrets. But *I* made the choice." When Aconsha asked if she could acknowledge the difference between a nine-year-old and a twenty-five-year-old, Carla said, "Frida isn't just a nine-year-old. She's a smart girl who knows her own mind. Don't force this on her. She'll make the right decision if you get her to think that it's *her* decision. Why don't you give me the weekend with her?"

We took a chance and let Carla take Frida up to the Berkshire Mountains for the weekend. I'm not sure what they did up there, but when they came back, Frida informed us of her decision to give Australia a try. Two months later, Aconsha and Frida flew to Melbourne and stayed at the clinic for five-and-a-half months.

When they came back, I had a big surprise for Frida—a new house with her very own bedroom. I say *new* house; it's actually an old farmhouse on a parcel of land, a little further east on Long Island, that once was part of a large potato farm. Aconsha was in on buying the farmhouse, which came with a caving-in barn and two-and-a-half acres of land abutting a vineyard, but she didn't know that I hired an architect and contractors, got all the permits, and pushed for an accelerated schedule to renovate the barn into a dance studio for her, build a stand-alone studio space for me and my crew of writers and a small two-story house/art studio for my mother.

My fantasy was to have the whole compound completed by the time they came back, but no matter how much I was willing to pay or how hard I pushed the crew, the place was still a construction site when I drove Aconsha, the girls, Einstein, and my mother down the long driveway that rainy November afternoon.

Frida couldn't contain her excitement about having a bedroom all to herself on a floor that was just for her and Ella and all their little critters, a piano downstairs, and so much outdoor space to run around in and explore! She had no idea that her dad (a lifelong renter and not the greatest gift-giver in the world besides his handmade cards which were often his entire gift) was capable of pulling off such a "totally awesome" surprise. Ella was looking forward to living there too, but more than anything she was relieved to no longer have to keep such a huge secret. My mother was surprised, also confused, and not exactly overjoyed by the sight of the place I was calling her new home. "It's very nice, but why would I want to leave my apartment?" Aconsha was shocked, favorably, to see the old barn with a new roof, and on its way to becoming both a dance studio and performance space. But when we were alone she expressed mixed feelings about living in such close proximity to my mother. Yes, we had *discussed* the idea, but it was never agreed upon, officially.

Perhaps I did overreach. In my newly minted position as a person with money, I thought I could please the people I loved the most by being their Santa Claus, inventing wish lists on their behalf, and making them come true with great panache. Now that I had a six-figure bank account, I found myself saying things like, "I'm renovating a barn for my wife's studio and building a carriage house for my mother." This is what a little money can do to a person. It can make him think that he built what he paid for, without once lifting a hammer. It can help him emancipate his mother from public housing even though she didn't ask to be emancipated. It can help create an environment for his wife that would entice her back into dance, and a workspace for himself where he could compose books at a rate he never thought possible. Most importantly, it enabled him to send his daughter to the other side of the world to get the best medical care money could buy. And sure enough, Frida was drug free, bruise free and blotch free, her platelets were normal, and she seemed healthier and happier than ever.

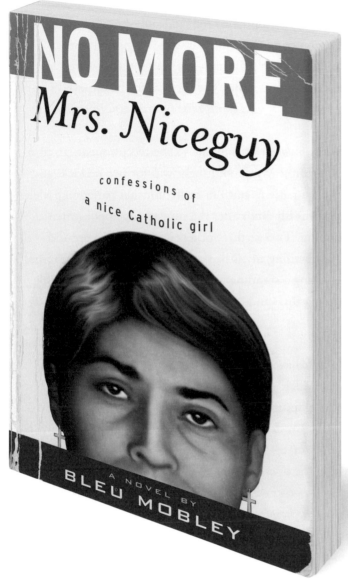

No More Mrs. Niceguy: confessions of a nice Catholic girl

A NOVEL

Paula Martinez was a dutiful, God-fearing daughter, wife, mother, church member, citizen—known for putting everyone else's needs before her own. Then she got cancer. Within a few months she educated herself about her disease, discovered who her real friends were, and found a voice she never knew she had. "Bleu Mobley's disturbing and hilarious novel skewers the medical profession, the self-help industry and the cult of positive thinking, as it celebrates the transformative power of hard-earned rage." *Rolling Stone*

1998, W.W. Norton, New York, NY

excerpt

NO MORE MRS. NICEGUY

I'm reading this bestseller by this famous psychologist guy about the power of forgiveness. He's pounding his thesis like a twelve-inch nail into my head, same point over and over. The really annoying thing is, he's leaving out a tremendous amount of information and his reasoning is fuzzy. I could write his whole book in a single paragraph. In one sentence! *Why even bother?* I put the book back in my bag and pick up a three-month-old magazine. The cover article is written by the same famous psychologist guy. I toss the magazine back onto the table and check my watch. I've been waiting forty-five minutes. I walk up to the receptionist and say, "I understand Dr. Crenshaw is a very important man, and his time is extremely valuable and mine is worth nothing, but can you give me *a clue* how much more of it I have to waste before I get called in to wait in yet another room and have to sit there half-naked, feeling vulnerable and humiliated for God-only-knows how long?"

I don't really say that. I don't even get up from the way-too-soft brown leather couch. I just sit there staring at the waiting room paintings—the large sunset watercolor, the lighthouse painting with the whitecaps lapping onto the rocks, and the big-eyed puppy dog prints. *If this doctor is as good in medicine as he is in his taste in art, I am in serious, serious trouble.*

After waiting thirty more minutes, I *do* get up and talk to the receptionist. "Excuse me, Ma'am. How much longer do you think? My appointment was for two o'clock, and it's a quarter past three. I realize I'm just a patient, but I'm really not that patient a patient when it comes to waiting in waiting rooms for *hours* after the time of my appointment."

Someone behind me starts clapping. Two or three others join in. I turn around—all nine people in the waiting room are applauding my little tirade. Two of them are standing! Three more stand to join them. I'm getting a standing ovation for being a pushy asshole. I'm not sure it's a good thing, reinforcing this kind of behavior. Less than a minute later, I get called in to see the doctor.

Prior to six months ago, I wouldn't have *dared* speak to anyone like that. I would have simply waited for however long, and felt grateful that my name was called at all. Then I'd have rushed myself with the doctor, skipping over many of the symptom details and questions I'd written out on a list, a list I would have felt embarrassed to take out of my bag because the doctor might think, *What's with this woman, she can't remember what's wrong with her?* Always worried about wasting the doctor's valuable time, I'd think things like: *He's got five or six other patients waiting in other exam rooms, plus all those people in the waiting room, then he probably has to rush to the hospital to save the lives of patients with far more serious problems than I. If I keep him any longer he'll get home from work later than normal and be all the more exhausted and probably miss having dinner with his wonderful family.*

I've lived most of my life like a quiet little mouse. Sister Lucia always told us not to complain. "Life is hard," she'd often say with the grim expression of a life filled with joyless obligations. "Have patience in this life and you'll reap the benefits in Heaven." Father Michael, Sister Henrietta, and Sister Agnus had cheerier dispositions, though they all praised the virtues of keeping quiet, especially if you were a girl. But Sister Doherty—the most open-minded teacher at St. Mary's—taught us in her seventh-grade theology class how important it was to question things. She unleashed a tidal wave of probes and challenges from me. I'll always be grateful to her for that, though I soon found out that she wasn't talking about questioning our Lord Jesus Christ or the tenets of the Catholic Church. I wrote a report for her class about the possibility of making a test-tube baby.

"If they can pull it off," I speculated, "it would call into question the whole Catholic idea of the soul." It might even be the end of the Catholic Church because God was supposed to bestow the soul into the microscopic baby at the moment of conception. "But with a test-tube baby," I wrote, "there wouldn't be a conception, and if there isn't a conception, where is the soul going to come from?"

After I summarized my paper to the class, Sister Doherty said, "Very interesting theory, Paula, but scientists will *never* be able to make a test-tube baby." (Five years later when I saw the healthy looking blue-eyed, blonde-haired "test-tube baby" on TV, I knew that I was Catholic only in name. But I kept it to myself since my father, a stringent enforcer of church doctrine, was sitting across the room from me.) After handing in my paper, Sister Doherty talked to me privately about the difference between being curious and being "perfidious." A week later she lost her temper with me for suggesting that Jesus being the Son of God might be a metaphor. She made me write an essay on John 3:17, which explains precisely why God sent his son into the world. For the next quarter century, I pretty much kept my thoughts private.

Then six months ago I found a lump under my arm. Waiting became a matter of life and death; waiting for my name to be called, waiting for interminable weekends to turn into Monday when the doctor could look at the lab results, waiting for the phone to ring, Tuesday, Wednesday, Thursday, till finally I am told to come into the office. I come in. My primary care doctor asks me which I would like to hear first, the good news or the bad news. I say, "I'm not a child. Just tell me." I can't believe I said anything like that to a doctor! He tells me, "Okay. The bad news is you have cancer. The good news is it's stage one and we have an excellent record eradicating this particular cancer when we catch it early in the game." A week later a different doctor, about to inject me with a very large needle, says, "Would you prefer I sing to you or tell you a joke?" I snapped at him. "Just give me the god-damn needle and get it over with." Was that a sane thing to say to a man with a needle in his hands? You wouldn't think so, but it was a painless shot and that doctor has treated me with the utmost respect ever since. No songs. No jokes. No talking to me like I'm a child.

Now that I am violating every rule I ever learned about being a nice Catholic girl, my life is taking a turn for the better. After I told my boss he could take his lousy executive assistant position and shove it up his flat, greedy ass, he offered to give me a raise. I quit anyway. I tried the same thing with my husband, but he's being so nice to me now, I'm not about to give up the special treatment. We'll see how long it lasts.

Just yesterday I went to my father's grave and talked to him. I said, "Hi Daddy. It's Paula, your prodigal daughter. The one you always wished was never born. The one that was supposed to be Paul, but ended up a girl, so you pinned an "a" at the end of my name and raised me like a son anyway. I used to think Mom prayed for boys to make you happy, and that's how she ended up with six out of seven, but I recently read an article about procreation in a science magazine, and having a boy or a girl (it turns out) has nothing to do with what you *want*. It's about how fast sperm swims. You were slow at most things, Dad, but your sperms must have been little Jesse Owenses. How the hell are you, Daddy? They got enough cocktails down there for you? You know when people ask if I'm a survivor of an alcoholic father, I tell them no, I'm a survivor of Alcho-Catholicism. They ask, 'What's that?' I tell them, 'My father was such a religious man, he even drank religiously.' I tell them, 'Before three in the afternoon, you always knew where you stood in his black and white world. But by nighttime his eyes would be bloodshot, his face purple, and if you were his wife or kids, you'd have *no idea* what might tick him off.' I'm thinking of starting an Alcho-Catholicism support group. Naming it Anthony's Group, after you. Won't ask for your blessing, Dad. Don't need that anymore.

"You know, for forty-one years I've felt this beam of rejection coming from you to me, like *b*zzzzzzzzzzzzz *b*zzzzzzzzzzzzzz.

Even after you died I felt it coming right under my arm.
But you know what, Dad?
They just irradiated the receiver.
Zapped it down to nothing,
so there's no use even trying to put me down anymore.
You know, after you died I asked Christopher if he felt bad that you and he never had a chance to reconcile? He said, 'What was to reconcile? We totally saw eye to eye. We both didn't ever want to see each other or talk to each other for the rest of our lives.' I asked him, 'Didn't you once in sixteen years ever want to pick up the phone and say, 'Hi Dad. It's your long lost son, Chris. How you doing?' He shook his head and laughed. I could never be that way. I've always come crawling back to you like a dutiful daughter. And here I am again. But from now on, everything's going to be on *my* terms. Any fits of anger, they'll be coming out of me, and there isn't anything you can do about it. You're just going to have to lie here and listen."

After I said my peace, I had a good cry. I kissed his plot and whispered, "That's it for now, Daddy. That's my gift to you this month—*the truth.*
That's my reconciliation, like it or not."

When Aconsha and Frida first landed in Australia, Monica and I were just starting the second draft of a novel that (as outlined in my brief) was supposed to be about an unorthodox writing professor. I chose Monica to be my assistant for this book so she could help me with the student perspective. By the time we completed the first draft, the student perspective was *so* fleshed out, the teacher had been expelled from the book (except for flashbacks), and the student (who turned out to be the central character) graduates from college by the end of the Prologue. But Monica's involvement most likely wasn't the only thing working its influence on the storyline of *A Damn Good Plot*.

A week after Aconsha and Frida arrived in Melbourne, I got a phone call from Aconsha; she was in hysterics. "Frida's very sick. She has a high fever and has been throwing up for the past day and a half. Dr. Kondracki says this kind of reaction is not unusual. *'By definition'*—that's how he talks," Aconsha said, imitating Kondracki's doctorly Australian accent. "'*By definition, the detoxification program releases toxins from the body, and when that's occurring the patient appears to be getting sicker even though they're actually taking the first baby steps towards wellness.*' Arrrgghh! The man grates on my nerves. Frida's not a human being to him. She's a specimen! So if he *loses* one specimen, no big deal. Right? It could be very interesting data."

"Aconsha, sweetie, Frida's not going to die," I said, as reassuringly as I could considering I had no basis for knowing what was actually going on. Intellectually, Aconsha understood that detoxification can make you sicker before you start feeling better.

"But I'm petrified," she said through tears, "that our baby is dying, and I can't have that. I can't survive that again."

I wondered if she had lost a child—had an abortion or a miscarriage with someone else—and never told me. Then I realized she was talking about her twin brother. All I knew was, Prasad had died in an accident when they were eight. Whenever I broached the subject in the past, Aconsha didn't want to talk about it. No one in her family did. So I didn't push it.

"Can't they give Frida some medication to reduce the fever and stop the vomiting?"

"They won't! Kondracki says all that will do is add to her toxicity."

"Do you think this guy knows what he's doing?"

"I don't know. It's just... one second the person is alive. The next second, you turn around and they're *gone*."

"Nobody's gone. Nobody's going anywhere."

"I know. I mean, that's the thing. We weren't going anywhere, and just like that, he was gone."

"*Who* was gone?"

"We were at our summer cottage in Roha. It was a scorcher that day. Prasad and I went to cool ourselves off in the Kundalika River, like we always did. It's not like New York. Parents don't escort their kids everywhere. Least they didn't back then. That's why my parents bought a place in the country. So they could get away from Bombay and all the worries of city living. Today Roha is suburban, but it was rural back then, and totally normal for eight-year-olds to play on their own.

"Our cottage was in the woods, not far from the river. We weren't afraid of nature. We *should* have been more afraid, more respectful of it, but we weren't. We weren't good swimmers, Prasad and I. We stayed in the shallows, got our feet wet, dunked and splashed, kind of like what you did with fire hydrants.

"But that day, I . . . I *still* don't understand what happened. We must have wandered farther out than usual. Or the tide was in. I don't recall it being a tidal part of the river. Maybe it was the dam. We didn't know about tides or dam schedules. It was just the river to us, and the river was always shallow. We'd walk through the woods, through some bramble and grass onto the rocks, into the water. The moment our feet touched the cold water was the most wonderful feeling. If we stayed close to the riverbank, the water only came up to our ankles, the most to our knees, and we could cool ourselves down. That was something Mom ingrained in us—*stay close to the shore.*

But somehow, that day. . .

Prasad had gotten farther out into the water.

I saw him up ahead of me, so I followed.

The next thing I knew, the water was up to my chin. I turned around

and the riverbank was farther away than I realized. I turned around again and

Prasad was gone. I thought he was playing a game. I went to where I'd last seen him, then I dove under the water with my eyes open, but it was too muddy to see anything. I don't know if the river was polluted then like it is today, but it was murky. I started screaming, Prasad! Prasad! as I felt myself getting pulled farther out into the river. I couldn't get to where I thought I'd last seen him, and I couldn't get back to shore or to someplace where I could stand. I knew how to pretend swim, how to splash around, but I didn't know how to breathe in the water, or tread, or float. Prasad was the better swimmer. (He was better at almost everything.) I started screaming, swallowing water, and freaking out about Prasad. *If he didn't make it, there was no way I would.* That's when I knew I was going to die. I'd never thought about dying before. I assumed I'd live to be an old lady. I was choking on the salty water—the river was overpowering me, dragging me out, pulling me down. I could see people standing on the shore. . . I must have been just a speck on the horizon to them.

"But someone *did* hear me. A fisherman. And before I drowned. . .

When I think about it now. . . I. . . I was going down, Bleu.

I was getting sucked down to where my brother was. . .

"I was leaving the. . . together with my brother, we were leaving the world just like we came into it, surrounded by fluid, pulled by forces beyond our control. But then I heard a voice yelling at me, telling me to tread. 'Just keep treading,' he yelled. I can't remember what happened after that. The next thing I remember, I was on the shore throwing up, a fisherman slapping my back, his shirt wrapped around me. I started screaming again, 'MY BROTHER! HE'S OUT THERE. YOU'VE GOT TO GET MY BROTHER!' The fisherman dove back into the water. I clambered to my feet, directing him to the spot where I'd seen him last. I'm howling, 'PRASAD! PRASAD!'

"An hour later, a rescue team was scouring the river with powerboats, searchlights, megaphones. But Prasad's body was never found.

"My parents blamed themselves for letting us roam around unsupervised. After Prasad died it was all rules and restrictions. We never talked about him, but he was there when we woke up, when we went to sleep, at every meal he was there with us.

"Prasad's presence has faded, but he's still. . . Almost every day I think of my other. . . my shinier half. And I lost that. *I was there.* I was with him. One second he was his glorious self, alive and glistening and full of adventure. The next second he was gone. That's what's shadowed me my whole life—the suddenness, the sneakiness of death. And whenever I start thinking that there was something I could have done to prevent it, I feel like I'm Death's little partner. No matter how many shrinks tell me I'm not to blame, I shouldn't feel guilty for enjoying life—I can't help but feel cursed.

"Please, Bleu, I need you to call Dr. Kondracki. He thinks I'm a crazy American. He thinks I think Frida is his only patient. He thinks I don't trust him. Maybe accusing him of trying to kill our daughter has something to do with it. I shouldn't have said that. Apologize for me. He doesn't respect women. Do the man-to-man thing. Use your Dr. Sky Jacobs voice, *doctor to doctor.*"

"I'll call him right now."

"We can't let Frida die because someone's feelings might be hurt."

"Nobody's dying."

"We're all dying."

"I mean nobody's dying *now.*"

"You don't think. . ."

"What?"

"You don't think I'm a curse, do you?"

"A curse? You're a blessing! Nothing but a blessing to me and the girls."

"Thank you, my darling."

"Thank *you*, my darling."

"For what? For *being hysterical*?"

"For telling me... about Prasad."

"You should be here, Bleu."

"I wish I was."

"Now call Kondracki!"

Dr. Kondracki didn't appreciate getting a phone call in the middle of the night, though he assured me that Frida was not dying, and he agreed to give her some medication to alleviate the symptoms.

After one more adverse reaction, Frida started getting better. She responded well to the second stage of the treatment, and magnificently to the last. Aconsha changed her mind about Kondracki. He wasn't a jerk after all, or a misogynist, or charlatan, and before leaving Melbourne she put on a fundraiser for his clinic.

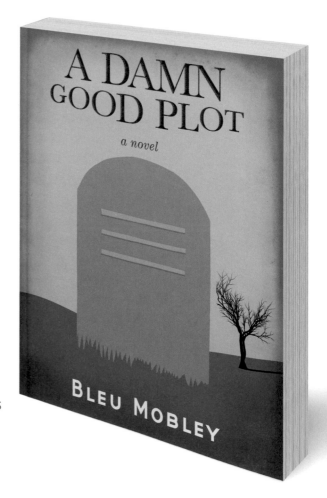

A Damn Good Plot *A NOVEL*

Ever since she was a little girl, Min Yen Sung dreamed of being a writer. Then she became obsessed with the life and premature death of a girl who died a century earlier at the age of six. This preoccupation became Min's first case in what would turn out to be an illustrious career as a forensic detective specializing in long-unsolved mysteries. "Bleu Mobley's debut mystery thriller is a richly layered tale that spans three centuries; the plot is serpentine, the solution ingenious!" *U.S.A. Today*

1998, St. Martin's Press, New York, NY

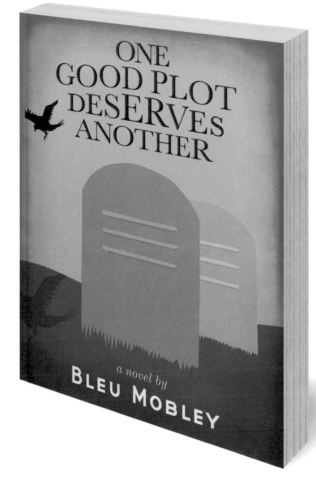

1999, 2000
(A three-volume boxed set came out in June 2001 bundled with a DVD of *The Making of The Damn Good Plot Movies*.)

BEST SELLER

excerpt [from the Prologue]

Each student in Juliette Valesquez' class was required to find a "resident" of the cemetery to write about.

No one in the class knew where they were heading as they boarded the bus. Valesquez had already taken the class on day trips to a nursing home, a shopping mall, a forest (with no discernible paths), and Harlem. The Harlem trip raised some eyebrows. When they got to 125th Street and Amsterdam Avenue, Valesquez said, "Okay, listen up. I'm going to visit my mother in Spanish Harlem. You all have a good day. I'll pick you up at 4:30 on this corner. Nobody be late." From the driver's seat, Valesquez closed the bus door, then sped down Amsterdam leaving her mostly white and Asian suburban students to fend for themselves in a place known to them less for its historic renaissance of black American literature and art than for its crime and poverty.

Everyone lived to write about the hustle and bustle of the Avenue and the encounters and emotions they had during their five hours in Harlem. Most students understood when they signed up for *Writing From Life* that they weren't going to sit in a classroom listening to lectures on grammar and syntax. But there was always the occasional student who got bent out of shape by something their famous and infamous teacher did or said. Several parents complained to the dean about the Harlem drop-off, as parents complained the year before about the whorehouse, and before that about the AIDS Hospice. Yet Valesquez was never told to change her ways. She was a world-renowned poet and novelist (one of few faculty stars), and her name was too valuable to the university's fundraising to worry about a handful of disgruntled parents.

Professor Valesquez must have a method to her madness, Min Yen Sung kept telling herself as she scanned tombstones for one that "spoke" to her. Min had never heard of Valesquez before enrolling in *Writing From Life* and was often shocked by the things she asked students to do. Nothing in Hong Kong could have prepared her for a teacher like Valesquez, who was such an enigma to Min (at least in the beginning), she saw no good reason to even mention the strange class to her insufferably square parents. But by the fifth week, Min's unease gave way to respect. She no longer had to *understand* the purpose of every assignment. Valesquez was unquestionably a master teacher, and it wasn't the student's job to second-guess her methodology.

Once a student found a tombstone, Valesquez recommended they sit on the plot and face the stone, like a mirror or a lover. "Then consider that life, that human being who lived on this earth and died. Begin with evidence you find at the plot." Min sat cross-legged in front of a tiny old stone, notebook at the ready. She pulled off the cap of her ballpoint pen, and made a note that the tombstone was very small. "It is a rudimentary design for its vintage. A granite rectangular slab with a rounded top. Its weathered inscription is covered with a thin layer of moss. There are no angel's wings, no cupids, crosses, scalloping orna-ments, or balustrades. It's just a simple stone with three lines of text engraved in cursive letterforms. The name *Allison Hagadorn.* Below that, an engraved divider line tapered at each end, followed by *1895 - 1902.* Under that, *Beloved Daughter.*"

There was something about this stunted stone tilted in the ground like a runt tooth in an old mouth that triggered Min's curiosity. The other stones in the Hagadorn family plot—the three other sisters, a brother, father and mother—were all equidistant. Allison's stone was set behind the rest near a stone wall a good distance from the nearest stone— her father's. Allison was the last born and first to die.

"Scattered around the same grove of this sprawling cemetery are other Hagadorn family clusters, including several spelled with two Gs, and another with an E at the end. A small dynasty—the HAGADORNS, HAGGADORNS, and HAGGADORNES," Min noted as she considered Valesquez' next questions: "Who was this person, really? What were the conditions of their life? Their relationship to others and the world they lived in?" Valesquez asked her class to open their hearts to the life of their deceased subject, but remain skeptical of all inscriptions and epitaphs. "Ask yourself, who were the authors of these chiseled texts? Was the woman *truly* a devoted wife and mother? Does the cross above the man's name *necessarily* indicate the faith he did or didn't have? Should the person *really* be remembered for all eternity as a soldier or was he or she really more of a dreamer or a dope or an incredibly dear friend?" Min closed her eyes and tried to picture this Hagadorn girl who died when she was only six years old, two years into a new century. *Who was this little girl, really? How did she die? Why did she die?*

Before letting them off the bus, Valesquez told the class that whatever plot they found that day would serve as the seed for their final project. It was up to each student to choose between fictionalizing or writing historical accounts. Min opted to pursue the "real" story of the short-lived Allison Hagadorn. With dogged determination she searched for every public document she could lay her hands on. She pored over newspapers, tracked down a coroner's report, and foraged for medical and school records. She interviewed family members, relatives of the priest who administered the funeral, and great-grandchildren of several people who could have been Allison's Brooklyn neighbors. She corresponded with Hagadorns in Cork, Ireland and traveled to Massachusetts, where the family lived before they moved to New York. Min's efforts to find out all she could about the life and death of Allison Hagadorn extended beyond the semester by nine years and included exhuming the dead girl's remains.

Min didn't complete her paper for *Writing From Life*, but Valesquez gave her an A anyway, saying, "I trust that whatever you do with your life, Min, you're going to do it with your entire heart and soul." Valesquez wished her the best with a big hug, which Min wasn't used to from anyone, let alone a teacher.

Min never became a novelist, but she did author thousands of masterfully thought-out, well-written reports as a leading forensic archeologist famous for cracking murder mysteries that were considered closed cases if not ancient history. Her work could fill volumes, but this book chronicles only one good plot—Min's youthful, tenacious hunt for Allison Hagadorn's true story.

After *A Damn Good Plot* became a bestseller, the story transformed again when it was turned into a motion picture. Then Monica and I wrote a sequel, and a movie sequel followed that. Then we wrote a third book loosely based on a sequence of scenes in the second movie. Then someone wanted to option *Good Plot* for a TV series, and that's when I said *enough is enough*, and put an end to it.

5

THE FACTORY

It took me two days to make Ella a card for her fourth birthday. On the front, I hand-lettered **HEY ELLA!** in a rainbow of colors. Inside, there were four numbered pull-tabs scattered throughout a landscape of grass and sky. Pull the first tab and rain poured down from a few clouds. Pull tab two, the sun came out from behind a cloud and purple tulips opened from stem tops. Three, a flock of birds flew across the card. Four, out popped

HAPPY
BIRTHDAY
SWEETIE!

It was the best card I ever made—but it was still only a card, so I needed to get a few presents to go with it.

Since the one independent bookstore near us had gone out of business, I succumbed to driving to the big box bookstore twenty minutes away. I loathed the very idea of these book-stores and had promised myself never to step foot into one. But I'd recently done some book signings in a few of them and they weren't as bad as I'd imagined.

I entered the five-story mega-bookstore ready to sprint to the children's section, and get out as fast as I could. The sheer size of the place was disorienting, the quantity of books and number of sections overwhelming. As I escalatored up to the fourth floor, I was pleas-antly surprised to see how crowded the place was and felt encouraged to see so many people interested in books.

Snaking my way through the maze of the fourth floor, I noticed people sprawled on the floor, leaning against walls, sitting in chairs—quietly reading, taking notes, even dozing off. One middle-aged man was snoring loudly—his head propped against a rolled-up sweatshirt—an unpaid-for book face down on his wheezy chest, and nobody was bothering to wake him. Once I found my way to the children's section, I headed for the pop-up books (Ella's passion at the time).

Several parents sat on the carpeted floor reading to their kids. I found this impressive—that a store would let customers read entire books to their kids, let the kids get their peanut-butter-and-jellied paws all over the pages, and not pressure them to buy the books or purchase anything at all. This laissez-faire policy struck me as extremely civilized, and probably a brilliant business decision.

No longer feeling an urgent need to head for the exit, I took a handful of books and settled myself into an armchair on the periphery of the children's section. While fingering my way through a technically intricate pop-up book about a mischievous dodo bird, I dozed off. When I woke up, I had a fully realized idea for a children's book on the history of capital punishment. I stood up, collected the books I decided to buy Ella, turned around and noticed, right behind where I'd fallen asleep was a section called *Criminology*.

I escalatored down, ordered a cappuccino and a seven-grain muffin in the bookstore café, and began writing on a stack of logo-emblazoned napkins. Two cappuccinos and two hours later, I was done. I had never felt compelled to write a children's book. I love my daughters and I'd do anything for them, but having kids does not a good children's book author make. I felt strongly about this. Then again, I'd felt strongly about never wanting to write self-help books or murder mysteries.

How Bad People Go Bye-Bye *JUVENILE*

This pop-up, pull-out book by bestselling author Bleu Mobley tells the story of capital punishment from the earliest days of stoning up through today's sophisticated lethal injection techniques. *How Bad People Go Bye-Bye* is written and designed to provide parents with a family-friendly way to introduce children to the age-old consequences of being very, very bad. Suitable for ages 4 to 104. Full color.

1998, Callahan Editions, New York, NY

"What's *wrong* with you?" Aconsha asked after I showed her my napkin sketches for *How Bad People Go Bye-Bye*. "This is completely inappropriate for children!" I reminded her that Frida had recently written a school report on the death penalty, and when Ella asked her what she was writing, Frida had no idea what to say. There was nothing she could point to that could help her explain why or how a government commits premeditated murder.

"How do you know about this paper? I never heard about it "

"Frida told me."

"When was this?"

"One night last week when I put her to bed."

Ever since Frida stopped breastfeeding, I was the one who put her to sleep. In the early years I'd either read to her or we'd invent stories, but as she got older we spent more time reviewing her day. I asked Frida what she told Ella.

"I pretended like I didn't hear her question." Fortunately, Ella just shrugged and continued playing with her monkey puppet, Zeda.

"What are parents supposed to do when their kid hears about an execution on TV?" I asked Aconsha. "It wasn't a problem in the seventies when the Supreme Court banned capital punishment. But now there's an execution almost every week in this country. Don't blame me, honey. Blame the Reagan and Bush Court."

"Is absolutely everything political with you, Bleu? Good parents try to *shield* their kids from the cruel world that awaits them when they grow up, not *shove* it in their faces before they have any idea what you're talking about. This is one project I can't get behind. Don't do it. I'm telling you, it'll be a huge mistake."

We agreed to disagree.

sample pages

in early times
when a man did wrong

pull tab

There wasn't much of a reaction to *How Bad People Go Bye-Bye* when it first came out. In a mostly favorable review in the *Library Journal*, one paragraph addressed the question of

age appropriateness, but the reviewer concluded that it was up to the parent to decide when and if to expose a book like this to their child. In a surprisingly positive review in *Parents Magazine*, Dr. Candice Kroessler wrote, Whether a parent is for or against capital punishment, they need to be honest with their children, should the subject come up. An interactive, illustrated book like this could help them answer many of the youngster's questions. Pro-death penalty parents could conceivably use *How Bad People Go Bye-Bye* to instill the fear of God and State in their children. Anti-death penalty parents could instill outrage and a sense of injustice in their children. More enlightened parents could use the book to actually allow children to reach *their own* conclusions. And parents of all persuasions could learn a thing or two about the history of capital punishment in America, as I did reading this lyric survey."

Other than those reviews, few people paid attention to my wayward kinderbuch until a first-grade teacher in El Paso, Texas read it to her class, and a parent complained to the principal, and a local TV news program covered the story and fed it to their national network. Within two days, the story about the Texas teacher who was suspended for reading a book on capital punishment to her first-grade class was in every newspaper in America. By the end of the week it was an international story. Within two months, *How Bad People Go Bye-Bye* was banned in public schools in every state of the union (except Massachusetts).

HOW BAD PEOPLE GO BYE BYE

we threw some stones
till he was gone

I appeared on dozens of network and cable television programs—the bespectacled author—wedged between pro- and anti-death-penalty advocates. Child psychologists, educators, clergy, and "experts" on the criminal justice system and First Amendment law

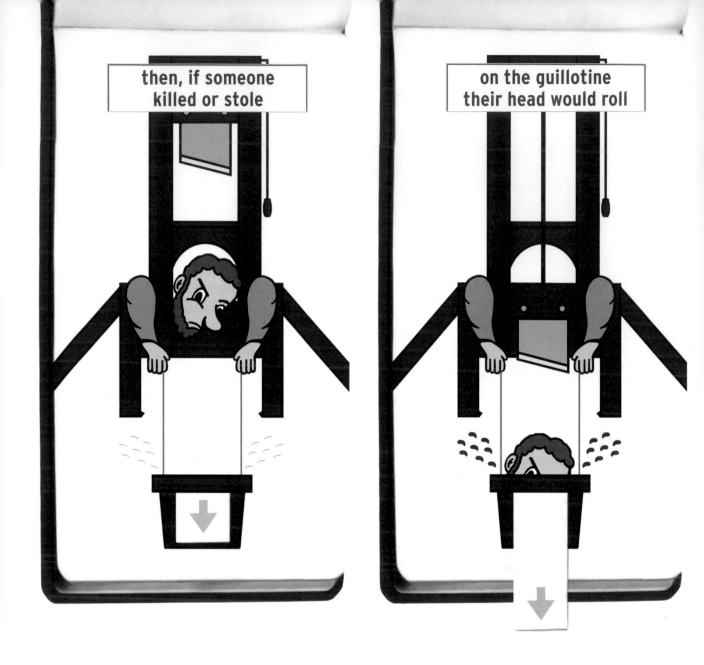

were empaneled to weigh in. Even Dr. Sky Jacobs was asked to comment on whether it was healthy "to subject five-year-olds to this kind of subject matter." Jacobs agreed to one radio interview on the subject, in which he came down in favor of the school bans, but also for reinstating the first-grade teacher if she apologized to the offended parties.

During this time, I was accused of being a pornographer, a propagandist (for *both* sides of the issue), a child hater, a sly manipulator of the media, the devil's accomplice, as well as a truth teller, a lone voice in the wilderness, and God's accomplice. Thanks to all the controversy, *How Bad People Go Bye-Bye* became the top-grossing children's book of 1998, and my first number-one bestseller.

The first daytime talk show I was on, the producer came into the Green Room, shook hands with all the guests and welcomed us to Chicago. Then he got down to business. "All right. This is the thing about what we're doing here. I know you all have very strong feelings about this issue, each of you for different reasons. We want to *know* what you're feeling. We didn't bring you all this way to have you sit on your hands and be polite. I'm counting on you to speak your mind. If somebody's saying something that makes you mad, let him have it! *Be real.* This is just like reality, only a little bit faster and a little bit brighter."

He also prepped the audience. "This is an exciting topic we have for you today, so let's show the viewers at home what excitement is. You see this big sign above my head? When it says `STAND UP`, I want you all up on your feet. If it says `SCREAM`, and you feel like screaming, scream. Whatever the sign says— `LAUGH`, `APPLAUD`, `CHEER`—that's what we want you to do. If you have a question to ask, or an opinion you'd like to share, fill out a card with Darcy or Shakira, and maybe your friends and relatives will get to see you on TV."

The audience was in such a frenzy by the time they brought me on   *the man who wrote a children's book on capital punishment*—and sat me next to a woman whose son had been murdered (and the convicted murderer was due to be executed the following week), I felt like a slab of tenderloin being thrown to the wolves. The audience welcomed me:

Kill *Him!*
Kill *Him!*
Kill *Him!*

Thankfully, there were only six minutes left in the show.

The hatred directed toward me on the first four or five programs caught me so off guard—I barely got a word in. Then Samir started coaching me.

He and Carla took over the lease on the rental house in Port Jefferson after we left, and kept the cable service. Samir is one of these people who never had a TV, but once there was one in his house, he couldn't control himself. He became a cable-news junkie and an aficionado of out-punditing the pundits.

- "If the question you really want to answer never gets asked, as soon as you see an opening, just blurt out what you want to say and see what happens.

- If someone interrupts you, don't wait for them to finish. Interrupt back.

- Don't talk in paragraphs, not even sentences if you can help it. Think and talk *nuggets* of information. Remember: the people watching at home are probably eating. That's why you have to give them sound bites."

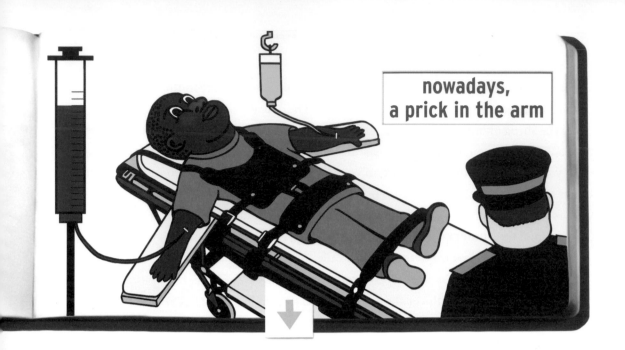

nowadays,
a prick in the arm

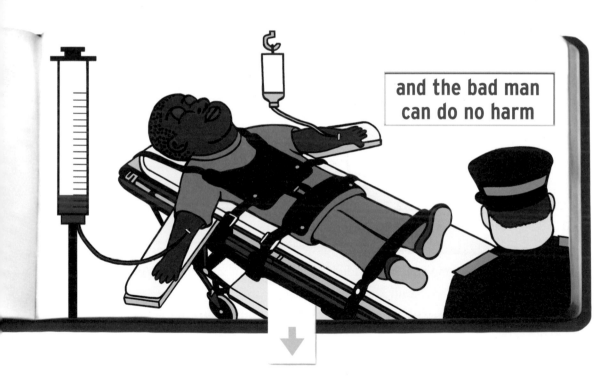

and the bad man
can do no harm

My appearances as controversial author improved. I always tried to keep calm and steer the conversation away from name-calling, back to the substance of what I wrote and why. Maybe you saw me on some of those shows with the words **WROTE CHILDREN'S BOOK ON CAPITAL PUNISHMENT** written across my chest or under my chin. One show captioned me as **THINKS NO CHILD IS TOO YOUNG TO COMPREHEND ANYTHING**. (Like I ever said that!) I accepted the invitations—I told myself—because it opened up a national conversation about the death penalty. It also was opening something inside me.

When I was growing up, my mother used to get called all kinds of names by kids in the neighborhood—*retard*, *psycho*, *loony tune*. I did what I could to defend her. When I couldn't, I assured her that those assholes didn't know her from Eve. She swore it didn't bother her, but a lot of decisions she made sprouted from fear and retreat. Thirty-five years later, similar names were being hurled at me in a very public way. Instead of hiding, I fought back. And once I got going, there was no stopping me, especially with Frida watching at home, cheerleading me to knock 'em out with the best arguments I could deliver.

I caught the bug of being *on the air*, and having an influence (however small) over the public discourse, though I didn't care for the crowds or the sparrings that came with being a talk show guest. If I wanted to feel that rush of broadcasting my ideas over the airwaves, I'd have to get my own show. Next best thing—when the offer presented itself again, Dr. Sky Jacobs accepted the invitation to host his own radio program.

Jacobs broadcasted from home (with the help of a digital radio line Nilo rigged up). His weekly Friday afternoon program, *Radio Sky*, enabled him to test out, revise, and refine his ideas through a mixture of monologues and listener phone calls. After a few months, the show picked up national syndication, and people from all over the country wrote and called in to share their stories. Jacobs was humbled by the way people opened themselves up to him and his listeners about the most personal matters. Over time, Sky Jacobs and his assistants saw the hundreds (and then thousands) of testimonials as an archive of the human experience and a primary source for new theories, commentaries, and books.

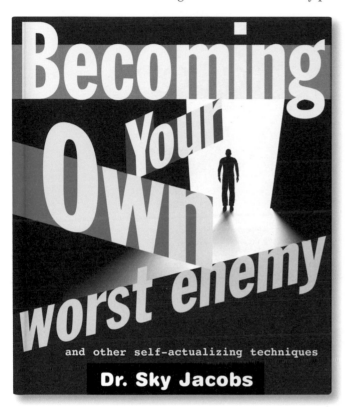

Becoming Your Own Worst Enemy

POPULAR PSYCHOLOGY

"Only after you embrace your own loathsome, rock-bottom, mean, hypocritical, lowlife self, can you deny others the opportunity of bringing you down. Once you've come face to face with the absolute worst in yourself, you can become your own best friend, advocate and hero." In his provocative new book of stories and advice, the bestselling author of the *I Could Love You* series turns everything you ever thought you knew about self-reliance on its head.

1998, Avery Books, New York, NY

There Never Was a Good Old Days

POPULAR PSYCHOLOGY

In his new book, Dr. Sky Jacobs makes the case that nostalgia—in anything but its mildest form—is a manifestation of delusional thinking capable of causing long lasting harm to individuals and societies. How else, he asks, could millions of people harken back to the days when black men hung from trees, women had few rights, workers worked seventy hours a week in dangerous conditions, the poor and the old died of starvation in the streets. After establishing the link between nostalgia and delusion, Jacobs presents a forty-nine-point program designed to help individuals and societies detach from hallucinatory images of the past in order to live more fully in the present.

1998, Avery Books, New York, NY

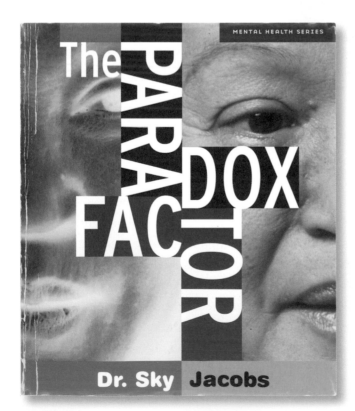

The Paradox Factor

POPULAR PSYCHOLOGY

According to Dr. Sky Jacobs, as many as three out of ten adults become who they are as a way of counterbalancing a perceived weakness manifested during childhood. By virtue of *The Paradox Factor*, these weaknesses—whether they are a result of nature, nurture, or some combination of both—are contradicted in the individual's personality and life choices. In the first half of the book, Jacobs lays out his theory in an easy-to-read, jargon-free style. The second half features 101 profiles that illustrate how *The Paradox Factor* influences biography.

1998, Avery Books, New York, NY

I'm not sure what kept pulling me back to that big box bookstore, but I kept going there two or three times a week, aimlessly strolling the aisles as if they were the streets of Amsterdam or Venice. I could walk for hours exploring every lane, nook, and cranny till I finally grew tired and settled on a spot to rest. One day, I lost all sense of time, having sauntered for hours through HORROR, ROMANCE, POETRY, SCIENCE FICTION, AND FANTASY. By the time I got to THRILLERS I was exhausted. I sat down on the floor and looked up at all the erect spines lined up like cadets in tight-fitting jackets. The completeness of it all made me dizzy. *What could anyone possibly add to this orderly inventory of twisty-turny plots, lawyerly labyrinths, murder and mayhem? A sentence maybe.*

I lay down on the industrial carpet, taking in one bank of shelves with one eye, then the other bank with the other eye, alternating at varying speeds until my eyelids grew heavy. In the darkness, I heard voices of other customers and bookstore employees. Footsteps. Shuffling of pant legs. Sounds faded to silence. Shadows stilled. The darkness grew darker. For a few minutes, maybe more, I slept in a canyon of words, and dreamt about a man who was on such a litigation rampage, he ends up suing himself. I snapped awake, then closed my eyes to recapture the expression of the judge's face trying to focus over his bifocals at the odd-looking fellow at the litigant's table. I could hear the judge's gravelly voice.

> "It appears to me, Mr. Krupova, that you are asking to sue yourself. Am I correct in my reading of your motion?"

With my eyes shut, I could picture Alex Krupova precisely as he appeared in my dream. He reminded me of a slavic version of Samir, springing out of his seat, facing the judge with bloodshot exuberance. Krupova's socks didn't match, a shirt-tail stuck out from below the hem of his jacket, but he addressed the judge with the confidence of an experienced legal mind. "Not exactly, Your Honor. While it's true that my client did *start* the corporation in question, and is its sole owner, please understand that the corporation got away from him and took on a life of its own."

Judge Fairnéz interrupted. "Excuse me. Are you referring to yourself as your client? Or am I missing something here?"

"Yes, Your Honor. I've taken myself on as my client in this case. I'm not a lawyer, by training, Your Honor, but I'm fully conversant with the relevant case law. I think you'll be pleasantly surprised by my knowledge of the law, Your Honor. I wasn't born in this country, but I have the greatest respect for its Constitution and laws, perhaps more than many people who were born here and take their liberties and rights for granted. So if it's all right with you, Your Honor, I will continue to address myself as my client."

"Let me ask you, are you charging yourself a fee, or have you taken this case on *pro bono?*"

"*Pro bono*, Your Honor, except for supplies and expenses."

"Very generous. Please continue."

"Thank you, Your Honor."

"Oh, one more thing. I appreciate the deference you show when you address me as Your Honor, but don't put it in every sentence. Like mustard, the *Your Honor* thing can be unappetizing when you lay it on too thick."

"Yes, uh, *sir*—I understand. So, respectfully, sir, the answer to your first question is *no*, it would not be correct to say that I am suing myself."

"You *are* filing to sue a corporation that you are the sole proprietor of. Correct?"

"Technically, yes, that is true, but what I was saying, Your Honor, *sir*, is that the corporation is conducting its business as a completely independent entity."

"How can that be?"

"Oh, because it has a personality of its own, sir. I mean, it's a small corporation, just a few people, but it's on a runaway course. I will prove to you that the corporation acted in ways not in the best interest of its owner. It has sullied his reputation as a man of unimpeachable values, a hard thing to earn back. I can't tell you, sir, how shocked he was when he first discovered the kinds of transactions being done in his name."

"By he, do you mean you, *you* were shocked?"

"Yes, Your Honor. I was shocked, my client was shocked and disgusted to find certain products and certain *services* being sold under the name of his corporation. The second he caught wind of this, he went to the employees responsible for sales and inventory, but they said there was nothing they could do about it, especially as those items and services were amongst the most profitable in the online catalogue. The corporation, they said, wouldn't allow the removal of those items."

"Didn't you hire these people yourself? Don't they report to you?"

"Yes, Your Honor, my client hired them—but they're no longer answerable to him. They're only answerable to the corporation. All these young people and their *World Wide Webs*. I tried firing them, but the corporation wouldn't allow it."

"What does that mean? Isn't it *your* corporation?"

"That's what I'm trying to tell you, sir, the thing has a will of its own. You can blame it on the 1886 Supreme Court ruling in *Santa Clara County vs. Southern Pacific Railroad;* which, as I'm sure you know, defined corporations as 'persons.' I have no choice but to accept *Santa Clara* as the law of the land (though I'm positive Thomas Jefferson would not go along with this reading of the Constitution). No matter. I am a law-abiding person, Your Honor, *sir*, so I treat my incorporated business as if it were a person. I respect its rights and privileges and its personality quirks, but for every right there is a responsibility. Parents have responsibilities to their children, spouses have responsibilities to each other, every citizen has responsibilities to their country, and corporations are responsible to their shareholders. In this case, my client—being the sole shareholder—was *wronged* by the corporation that should have been beholden to him and no one else! And now he is asking for justice, Your Honor. In my brief, you can see that he. . . that I am asking for a legal separation from the corporation and 2.3 million worth of damages."

"Excuse me for not memorizing your tome, but these damages are for *what?*"

"It's there on page two. Misuse of corporate assets, defamation, and emotional duress, sir. But like I said, this is mostly about sullying my client's reputation."

"It's not about the money?"

"No, Your Honor, this has nothing to do with money."

"And the 2.3 million? What do you call that?"

"Your Honor, I am standing here on principle, not only on behalf of my client…

I was able to recall every word and action of the dream—from the bizarre hallway encounter with the Russian sex trafficker, to the judge granting Alex the right to sue himself, but not allowing him to also be his corporation's defense lawyer. The dream seeded my first legal thriller, just like other dreams in other aisles spawned ideas for books about cats, globalization, spammers, and megalomaniacs.

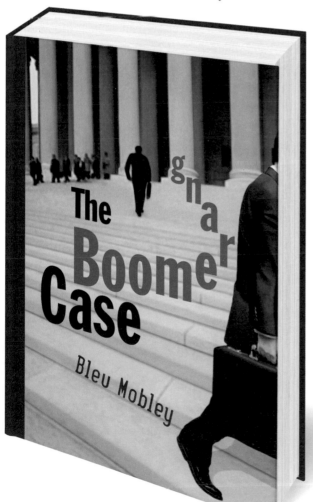

The Boomerang Case *A NOVEL*

Over the course of six years, Alex Krupova has sued his landlord, two former business partners, an ex-wife, a restaurant, a vitamin company, the City of New York, the Bulgarian government, the Vatican (for perpetuating falsehoods), and his father's estate. Running out of opponents to litigate, and seeking a means to retire, Alex decides to sue himself. He hires a private investigator to dig up dirt on his own midsized import/export company, only to discover that the company that bears his name is entangled in a network of international sex traffickers.

1998, Putnam, New York, NY

Outsourcing Grandma *A NOVEL*

Take a few dozen countries on a handful of continents, some rich, some poor. Add a few "free trade" agreements with little or no provision for labor or safety regulations. Replace manufacturing with clever branding campaigns in the richer countries. Seize control of the natural and human resources in the poorer countries. *Shake well.* You've concocted a world where Made in America could be Made in the Philippines or China. Grandma could be a twelve-year-old girl with knitting needles. A happy father and successful CEO could be a ticking time-bomb plagued by child-labor-law activists. In *Outsourcing Grandma*, Bleu Mobley follows the path of one "crocheted" cell phone pouch and the people it encounters along its global path: from inception to production, shipping, distribution, marketing, sale, use, resale, and disposal.

1999, Basic Books, New York, NY

abyssinia estop dystrophy:
a spam play   *THEATER SCRIPT*

While most of us greet spam emails with disdain, bestselling author Bleu Mobley has been studying them with great curiosity since the filter-busting non-sequiturs started filling up his inbox. The result is Mobley's first full-length play, which received its premiere in an intercontinental performance simulcast live over the world wide web. In *abyssinia estop dystrophy*, elected officials speak in spam, as do news reporters, clergy, parents and their teenage kids. Within the spamified language of the play, audience members and now readers discover coded truths about what we've become (dream discordant doppler droolers) and where we may be headed (cobwebs of gristmill missives). "As evaluable a spectra artifact as a Rosetta inkwell!" **Wired Magazine**

1999, Samuel French, New York, NY

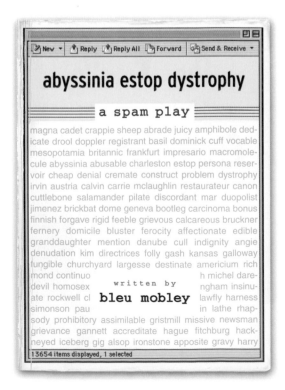

The Megalomaniac *A NOVEL*

The lead singer of a once-popular local rock band runs an auto repair shop named after himself in the upstate New York town where he's lived his entire life. Employees and other hangers-on are charmed by Cody's charisma, big ideas, and seeming encyclopedic knowledge of everything. But not everyone has good things to say about the man who thinks he's God's gift to the universe. Bleu Mobley's new novel weaves together the testimonials of twenty-four first-person accounts of *The Megalomaniac*. Whether you end up loving or hating Mobley's complicated protagonist, you'll never forget him.

1999, Grove, New York, NY

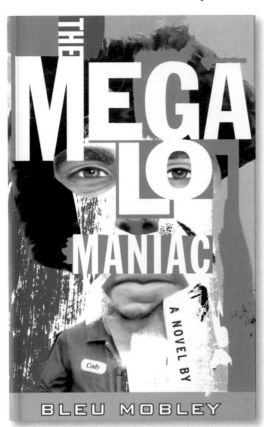

The clear-cut division of labor among my team began breaking down. Before long, all four assistants were helping with Bleu Mobley and Dr. Sky Jacobs books and were privy to all projects. I still assigned books to assistants based on their strengths—Josiah's natural feel for the dramatic and his ability to see the goodness in most characters; Najela's skepticism, keen sense of voice, and first-hand experience living on three continents; Gil's fascination with death, his training as a screenwriter, and grasp of things technological; Monica's versatility and developing business acumen—but our group meetings turned out to be so useful, we ended up working together as a team on nearly every project.

My assistants were all younger than me, had graduate degrees (in one thing or another), and had been trained in brainstorming, mind-mapping and lateral thinking techniques. They drew diagrams and logic trees on our marker board, mapping possible trajectories of character, theme, and plot. If we were working on a series, they would chart out the connections between each book in advance. They used words like *intentionality*, *intertextuality*, *agency*, and *simulacrum*, and referred to semiotic and deconstructionist theories like they were air and water. I was resistant to all this gabble-gammon, but over time I had to admit that some of their methods were useful, especially for working as a group. They made fun of my intuitive approach. I made fun of their over-intellectualization. Somehow, together, we found a middle way. I introduced theater games and playacting to their problem solving repertoire. They called me a Luddite and forced me to use the internet. I insisted they get off of their media-saturated perches and go interact with flesh and blood. They spoke without compunction about marketing plans, peripheral merchandising, synergies, serialization, and subsidiary rights, and advised me on everything from changing literary agents to what clothes I should wear. After a while, almost everything I did in my creative and professional life was the result of groupthink. My problems became the group's problems. My obsessions, group obsessions. My former self would have felt like he had lost control of his work and his identity, let alone the sanctity of his gut. But my new self—captain of a team of five—felt liberated to pursue almost anything I could think of, and accepted the whole as greater than its parts.

Puss Dude: and other curiously adorable [and disturbing] cat stories
PET LITERATURE

Bleu Mobley hates cat books, but he doesn't hate cats. In *Puss Dude and other curiously adorable [and disturbing] cat stories*, he attempts to bridge the gap between the two. This collection is based on stories Mobley told his own cat-loving daughters. Bertha the Burmese Beauty, Gritty Kitty, Russian Rex, Cat O. Tonic, Tabby G., Catman Du, and Puss Dude himself provide unique insights into the secret lives of cats.

1999, Chronicle Books, San Francisco, CA

By the waning months of 1999, the utopian visions and dystopian nightmares having to do with all those nines turning into zeroes had permeated popular culture with an inescapable contagion of end time babble. If on the other side of the millennium, the earth did not explode, it was certain to never be the same. History, science, commerce, art, and personal relationships as we knew them were surely coming to an end. Even the Democratic president of the United States declared "the end of big government as we know it."

As the producer of *Radio Sky*, I decided it was time to have Sky Jacobs do a show that shed some perspective on feelings that can bubble up at the end of a millennium. A few days prior to that show I went to my local big box bookstore, which had become my go-to place for doing research. I started out in the History section, read about some of the wacky things people did toward the end of other centuries and millennia, then worked my way down to Science Fiction, then across to Psychology, finally to Religion where I found dozens of new releases on the coming armageddon. I took a pile of books over to an armchair and started skimming through *Last Days of Sin, First Days of Tribulation*. Somewhere between sin and tribulation I fell asleep. A half hour later I woke up with an idea for a Bleu Mobley novel about a sex addict turned evangelical fanatic. I scribbled a few notes to myself, then I stood up and noticed that right behind the Religion section was Human Sexuality. The two categories must have conflated in my sleep, planting the idea for my second hybrid-genre book.

I drove back to the writing studio and described the dream to my crew, and the changes the protagonist would need to go through in a novel. "It would have to be both sexually explicit and devoutly evangelistic. Like when you see an old rock'n roller talking to young people about drug abuse and sexual misconduct. He's supposed to be motivating kids to live a clean lifestyle, but he's having a little too much fun telling stories about screwing anything that moved and taking every kind of drug ever created. At the same time there's an earnestness about his redemptive journey that keeps you from dismissing him as a total asshole."

"I get it," Najela said. "But your guy sounds like a detestable creature before *and* after his transformation. Why even bother writing him?" I understood her question. I'd written lead characters who were morally ambiguous before, but never anyone quite so unappealing. "We don't have to *like* every character we write, as long as we *love* them," I said, sounding somewhat evangelical myself. "It's natural to want to write about people we admire, or to write villains in ways that make them come off as villainous or farcical. The greater challenge is to find humanity in characters we're inclined to despise."

"It would be hard enough for me to write about someone who treats women solely as sexual objects," Najela said, "but to portray him being born-again into a doomsday cult as the triumphant means to his redemption—I don't think I can do that."

"I wouldn't exactly call evangelical Christianity a doomsday cult," Josiah said, throwing in the fact that his father is an evangelical preacher. "Nothing against your dad," Najela said, softening her tone, "but a lot of these people aren't just peaceably practicing their religion. They've infiltrated the political system in this country so they can roll back the freedoms that make me and a lot of other people want live here. My family already left one country after religious fanatics took over. I don't want to have to move again because of the same kind of medieval thinking. I'm sure your dad is different, Josiah, but I can't stand these preachers who froth at the mouth in anticipation of a nuclear war in the Middle East, so their flock of born-againers can rise to heaven and reunite with Jesus, while the rest of us fry in an armageddon. If that's the kind of transformative thinking that enables this Markus character to get control of his pecker, I don't want anything to do with him."

The group grilled me. "What is it you want to say with this book? Do you have a sex addiction problem? Are you becoming religious? What's the cultural critique you want us to make?" I told them that this character had nothing to do with me, and I had no ulterior motive. I simply had a vivid dream and was curious to know more about the character.

This was unacceptable to my crew. They kept prodding me to define my intentions till I came up with a redeemable reason for the book's existence. Backed into a corner, I blurted out, "because it's my *Project*."

"Oh, good. And what *is* your project?" Josiah asked.

"To paint a panoramic portrait of America—of humanity—one person at a time. Sort of like how Bruegel painted vast village landscapes populated by everyone in a village, and each person, no matter who they were, had a story. Only with my work, I suppose, the panorama won't be complete till I write my last book. Even then it won't be complete, but a reader could still go through all the books, zooming into the individual stories and out to see the bigger picture. So to ask me why I paint this person and not that one, or what it has to do with me, is sort of meaningless."

excerpt

Those were god-awful times. Every morning waking up to the smell of a different woman. The sun's rays exposing my sin to another empty shell of a day. Whether the lady was still lying next to me or not, I was alone. Alone and godless. In the evenings I fooled myself into thinking I was happy. Days were harder. In the afternoon I'd go down to a bar and get some drinks. Once it was dark, I'd find any kind of drug I could smoke, swallow, or snort, then go looking for a good time. Dancing with strangers till morning. Groping frantically past buttons and zippers. In search of something—perhaps the unconditional love I never had and couldn't imagine was waiting for me in Jesus Christ. *Praise be his name.*

I used to be like: hungry/eat, horny/look at porn, sleep/have terrible dreams, wake up feeling sick/eat some more, nearly out of money/spend what's left on a prostitute. When I depleted the money my grandfather left me and couldn't afford real women, I got hooked

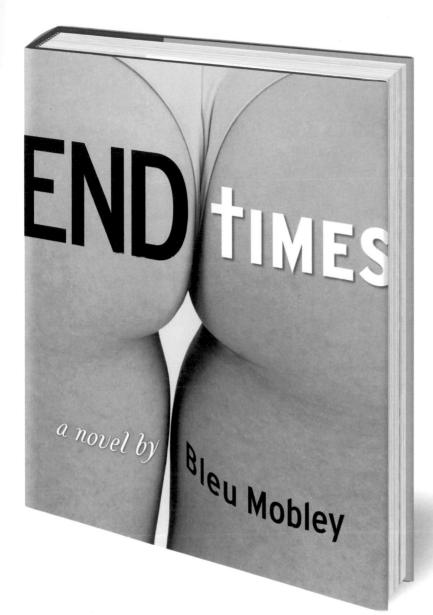

End Times *A NOVEL*
Published originally as one of the first serialized online novels, Bleu Mobley's saucy opus tells the story of Markus Hammerton, a sex addict turned evangelical zealot. Written in the form of a confessional memoir/course in Bible study, Hammerton chronicles his descent into debauchery and despair, followed by his discovery of true love, discipline, and purpose through the teachings of Jesus Christ. Since its online publication, *End Times* has been credited as a spawning a new literary genre—*Religious Porn*.

2000, Papyrus Books, Tulsa, OK

on porn. Before I knew it, I sold my car and was going to food pantries to keep from starving.

The day I got rid of my porno, it took four trips to the dump. What a sticky business. Before I chucked it, I thought maybe I should give it to my friend Rusty. Dialing his number I thought, *Hold on. If this stuff is poison to me, why give it to someone I even halfway like?* I hung up the phone and headed to the dump. Five boxes of magazines and a few dozen videos is probably worth a thousand dollars. But I wouldn't have felt right making money off of that crap. The right thing to do was getting it OUT of circulation. Then it struck me, somebody at the dump could find the boxes and *their* life could spiral into ruin. So I took everything out of the dumpster and dragged it to where they burn stuff, slipped the guy two dollars and watched my collection become an inferno. I cried watching it go up in flames. *Having therefore these promises, dearly beloved, let us cleanse ourselves from all filthiness of the flesh and spirit, perfecting holiness in the fear of God.* (2 Corinthians 7:1)

Within an hour of coming home from the dump I was digging through my closet looking for the *Hustler* magazine and the two videos I had stashed away. My whole body was shaking. Disgusted, I went out behind my building and burned them. Luckily, no one saw me.

Several weeks earlier, two well dressed people came to my door asking if I believed in God. I told them, "I was brought up Catholic. That's why I'm an atheist." Then I shut the door. They knocked again and asked, "If you died today, would you be ready to meet your maker?" I had no answer. They left me a flyer for a singles Bible study group that met Friday nights. Out of curiosity I went that Friday and noticed Bethany right away: a flower in a field of weeds. I went every Friday till I built up the strength to say something to her. During that month I got rid of every dirty picture, picture card, and flip book.

Once my apartment was as pure as my mind was trying to be, I asked Bethany if she'd like to have dinner at my place, maybe watch a movie on my VCR. She said she'd like that. The second I gave up porno I started renting regular movies—old classics based on books like *Gone With The Wind* and *To Kill a Mockingbird*. After the movie I'd mention that I read the book (which usually was a lie since lying was one of my sinning ways I hadn't yet overcome). I'd say something like the movie focused too much on the action instead of the interior lives. As far as the movie—*as a movie*—I usually agreed with Bethany that it was excellent. With regular movies, you see aspects of your own life. Sometimes you take on the personality traits of the lead characters. For a while I acted like Jimmy Stewart in *It's A Wonderful Life*. And Bethany was Donna Reed. I could look into her eyes and see what her life would be like if I had never been born. I got teary-eyed at the thought, but I couldn't show those kinds of emotions. I was afraid if I showed her what I was feeling it would lead to having sex and that could ruin the basis of our relationship. *For I say unto you, I will not drink of the fruit of the vine, until the kingdom of God shall come.* (Luke 22: 18)

I never felt the way I do toward Bethany with anyone else, or about the Bible with any other book. My sister calls me a Jesus freak (like it's an insult). She says I scare her more now than when I was stoned all the time. She asked if I'd be interested in the Bible if I hadn't been interested in Bethany. I told her it's not for me to question how God works. "Let's just say I think of Bethany as heaven-sent." Then I told her I loved her and hung up. My sister and I have disliked each other forever, but with the Lord's help, I was able to tell her I loved her. Why was it taking me so long to tell Bethany what I felt about her?

The first time I said the word love to Bethany, I said, "I love your legs." She thinks her legs are huge. "I think your legs are beautiful. They're muscular and strong, and I love that." Then I heard crying from the other end of the phone. That's when I said, "I *love* your legs," because I *do* love her legs, not because I love her *legs*, but because they're *her* legs. Then I panicked that she'd take it the wrong way. She knew about my history because in Bible study we tell stories about our lives. Finally she spoke. "I think it's time for you to come to my place for dinner. And don't get jealous that I have a male apartment-mate, because you're the only man I really care for." She called me a man.

I was thirty years old and the last time I had feelings for a female, other than wanting to bang the _____ out of her, was when I was fourteen. The way I've lived my life since then turned me into an emotional retard. That's what the interpersonal advisor on my favorite Christian radio station told me. He said, "You emotionally retarded yourself from all those years of not relating to women as human beings. So when this woman called you a man, it didn't match your sense of yourself, because developmentally you're still going through puberty." Then he thanked Jesus for entering my life. "And should the Lord want you and this fine Christian woman to get married, you can end your celibacy on your wedding night. And enjoy yourself." *For all have sinned and come short of the glory of God. (Romans 3:23)*

You can't go from being a fourteen-year-old to a thirty-year-old in a month expecting everything to be peaches'n cream. After six months, Bethany and I started fighting because I wouldn't go all the way. (She'd been married once before.) "We're no spring chickens," she'd say, pinching my belly flab. "Jesus wouldn't mind if we did it from a place of fidelity to Him." Unable to explain my fears, I quoted scripture. *Blessed is he that waiteth. (Daniel 12:12)*

I was alone in my apartment watching *Great Expectations* when the phone rang. It was Bethany. I put the VCR on pause. It didn't take long before we got into a fight. A half hour later Bethany called back saying she was sorry for saying I was *emotionally unavailable.* She admitted it was a "poor choice of words." I asked, "Are you talking poor word choice or are you sorry you had the thought?" She hung up on me for asking rhetorical questions. I called her back. Her phone was ringing and ringing, so I undid the pause button. Pip and Estella were at some highbrow London party. I desperately wanted Estella to give up her high-falutinness and tell Pip he's the one. Then Bethany picked up the phone, saying, "What!" I said, "What happened to—*You're the only man I really care for?*" That's when it came out that one of her friends told her she was asking for trouble going out with a man who was a sex addict. "Once you're an addict, you're always an addict." There was silence on both ends of the phone. *Be careful for nothing; but in every thing by prayer and supplication with thanksgiving let your requests be made known unto God." (Philippians 4:6)*

In a matter of months I'd grown up like in a time-lapse movie—fifteen years old, seventeen, twenty-four, twenty-eight—and the conversations Bethany and I were having (about the Bible, Judgment Day, movies) just kept getting better and better. The closer we got, the more we fooled around. The more we fooled around, the more scared I got. The more scared I got, the more we bickered. One night, I decided to pop the question. We'd been stuck on second base for months and I didn't know what to do. We were sitting on my couch eating Ritz crackers and low-fat cottage cheese. I put my arm around her, but instead of popping the question, I popped a copy of *Wuthering Heights* into the VCR. Ten minutes into the movie, Bethany's blouse was completely unbuttoned. My shirt was on the floor. At the point where I usually tried to stop things from escalating, Bethany unzipped my pants. I started to panic. Something was telling me, *It's going to get jinxed.* I pushed her hand away. "Let's not ruin the beautiful thing we have." Bethany said, "What we have is beyond flesh. What we have is knowing the real inside of the person. Why not add the flesh to it?" *Let us be glad and rejoice, and give honour to him: for the marriage of the Lamb is come, and his wife hath made herself ready." (Revelations 19:7)*

I released her hand. She reached inside my pants. I said, "Wait. Let me touch you first." I placed my hand between her legs, on top of her underwear, and started to rub. "Let's kiss," I said, very conscious of not turning what was happening into a pretend-she's-a-porn-star mind-flip where I'm not really with this person I love but with a 2-D centerfold. Sex is about letting go, but I'd been holding on—until that night. I'm not sure what I did, but it worked. I didn't once lose sight of who I was with, and it worked because being so self-conscious made me less excited which kept me from being too fast—another problem I have. Jesus led me to a righteous love and re-opened the gates of pleasure. *Let thy fountain rejoice with the wife of thy youth. Let her be as the loving hind and pleasant roe; let her breasts satisfy thee at all times; and be thou ravished always with her love. (Proverbs 5:18-19)*

Even though we didn't watch it, I brought *Wuthering Heights* back to the video store the next day to avoid another late fee. (I'm afraid that when I die I won't be allowed into heaven, not from being a sex addict, but because of all the videos I've returned late.) Somehow I ended up in the triple-X section. The skin of the stars on the boxes looked either too red or too pink, and the leather and lace, too shiny. My stomach felt like a dryer on spin down. A familiar voice inside my head was saying, "What's the big deal? Have some fun." Another voice was saying, "Are you out of your f__ing mind? You don't need this!" I put whatever I had in my hand back on the shelf. A minute later I put the *Little Women* box on the front desk. The woman behind the counter said, "$3.50" in the same nasty voice she used when I used to take out porn. I thought, *What's wrong with Louisa May Alcott all of a sudden!* I got back to my apartment feeling proud that I rented *Little Women* instead of *Little Women With Big* whatevers. Every choice at that time in my life seemed like a test.

Now I run a Bible study group every night of the week except Sunday. Sunday Bethany and I go to church with the kids. I have a steady job too. *Praise the Lord.* And every night I do my exercises, zealously. *That the man of God may be perfect, thoroughly furnished unto all good works. (2 Timothy 3:16-17).* I'm up to 300 sit-ups a day and pressing 150-pound weights. I praise the Lord all day long: for giving me a second chance; for giving me Bethany, our son and daughter and a third on the way; for finding me the job at the power plant; and for sweeping me of all my addictions. *And God said unto them, Be fruitful, and multiply, and replenish the earth, and subdue it: and have dominion over the fish of the sea, and over the fowl of the air, and over every living thing that moveth upon the earth. (Genesis 1:28)*

"Dinner on me dinner tonight, just the two of us," Samir proposed over the phone. "And we can celebrate." He wouldn't tell me what we'd be celebrating. I asked if it could wait a day or two because of the Nor' Easter predicted for later that night. We agreed to have an early dinner at the Japanese restaurant off the Nesconset Highway, and keep it short.

Samir poured two cups of hot saké and offered up a toast. "To you! For having the courage to become what you once railed against. You've grown up. I'm proud of you."

I asked what he was talking about.

"Would you like to know what happened to me yesterday?" he asked.

"Sure." We hadn't seen each other in months.

"Carla and I were waiting on the checkout line at the Barnes and Noble on Eighth Street. The line was endless because of the holidays, coiling around the front of the store like

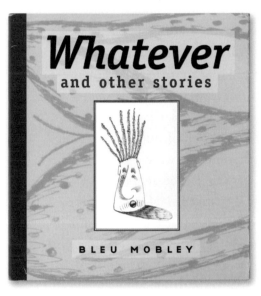

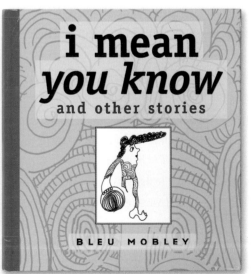

an enormous intestine. We didn't care—we were engrossed in conversation. Before I knew it, someone was tugging at my coat. 'You're next.' As we walked to the checkout counter—I guess I wasn't watching where I was going—I collided into one of those self-standing cardboard what-do-you-callits… *point of purchase displays* that have multiple copies of the same book. Luckily, I caught the thing before it completely toppled over. I had no idea what I'd bumped into. Then it came into focus and I saw at the top of the display it said *Check It Out Series* in big letters. I picked up one of the books that had fallen to the floor, and read the title: *Whatever: and other stories.* When I saw your name on the bottom, I exploded with laughter."

"Sorry about that," I said laughing along with him, picturing the scene. "You didn't get hurt, did you?"

"They're not exactly made of steel, those things. But what a display! And pretty ironic," he said, recalling how I used to make fun of all those "cutesy little books" sold by the cash register. "You were Mr. Idealist back then. Now look at you—writing pocket books for the masses, in the language of the masses. *Congratulations!*" He lifted his cup for another toast.

"I don't think I've changed that much. I'm still writing about everyday people. I just caught some luck."

"Everyday people? Is that why you wrote a book about me, because you think I'm an *everyday* person?"

The Check It Out Series

SHORT-SHORT STORIES

whatever, i mean you know, awesome

This series of pocket-sized short-short story books by bestselling author Bleu Mobley features teenage characters grappling with identity, loneliness, friendship, love, loss, technology, and coming of age at the tail end of the 20th century. "Written for teens and the people who love them, these heartfelt and surprising stories go by so quickly, you don't even notice that you're reading." *Seventeen Magazine*

2000, Bantam, New York, NY

"No, I don't mean everyday in that way."

"That's okay. What matters is, you've made it to the front of the store, baby."

"I don't have anything to do with that."

"Wasn't making them *pocket-sized* your decision?"

"Yes, but that's nothing new for me. The very first books I ever made were miniatures. You could just as easily say that I'm returning to my roots."

"So you're not being strategic in any way?"

"A lot has changed since the eighteen-hundreds when there wasn't much to do at night but turn up your oil lamp and read three-inch-thick books. There's a lot more competition for our attention today. I know I read less than I used to, and that gets me wondering how other people are reading books. Are they on the subway? In a car waiting for their kids to get out of school? On line at a coffee bar? Reading during TV commercials? I never used to think about how people read. I only knew that I wanted to write."

"It's called catering to the needs of the market-place. Like I said, you've changed and I'm proud of you."

"Call it catering to the market if you like. I think of it more like learning from my readers. *That's* how I've changed. I've become aware of the other side of the equation. It's not about market. It's about dialogue."

Samir glanced at me, skeptically. An analogy sprung to my mind. "Say I'm a comedian, and I come up with a joke about... I don't know, a recent Supreme Court ruling. I think it's a very funny bit and timely, and then I tell it to an audience and nobody laughs except for one nerdy-looking guy in the back. Shouldn't I pay attention to that? If I was simply concerned with feeding the marketplace, I'd replace the Supreme Court joke with a joke about farting or something sexual. But if I think the point behind the joke is important, I'll keep reworking it till I get audiences to laugh, or at least get them scratching their heads enough to go home and find out what I was referring to."

"So you think of yourself as a comedian?"

"Jesus, Samir! Okay. Think of an architect who for twenty years designed very unusual, intriguing-looking buildings that won awards and critical acclaim, but for the people who live and work inside them, his buildings are too dark, they have too many peculiar angles that jut into heads and funny bones, the air doesn't circulate well, and they're too expensive to maintain. Wouldn't it make sense for the architect to change his approach?"

"So you see yourself as an architect?"

"No. But I *have* made adjustments to my work through the years. My sentences are a little shorter, my books don't have as many pages, and it doesn't hurt that people can actually find them in bookstores (even if it's only by crashing into them). Other than that, I'm doing what I've always done."

Samir looked unconvinced. "I have only one thing to say—*Whatever*. Whatever you want to call it. I think it's great you're a capitalist now." He raised his cup. "Welcome to the club!"

Anxious to change the topic, I asked Samir what was new with him and Carla. He told me he had really exciting news—another cause for celebration—and related to that, he had a favor to ask.

During the previous five months, he and Carla made a good deal of money selling off two of their inventions: the latest version of the handwriting-to-type software that they co-patented with Alberto Aguilar, they sold to Oracle; and their designs for a robotic seeing-eye dog, they sold to a company that makes products for the blind. He wouldn't say how much money they made. However much it was, I was happy for him. I knew that making it rich in America (without any help from his father) was a goal of his. I also knew that he was proudest of the inventions that helped people live better lives. I raised my cup to make a toast. Samir waved it down. "I haven't told you the *really* exciting news yet."

He and Carla had reinvested their recent earnings into a project that was going to "revolutionize the paper industry." The project, which first got started in a media technology lab at MIT, was the invention and eventual manufacture of electronic paper. "It will be soft to the touch and malleable like regular paper, but made of synthetic materials."

The *e-paper*, as he described it, would contain an imperceptible matrix of holes that release *e-ink* to form whatever text or images are programmed into it. "The same sheet of e-paper," he said, "could be used again and again, and would cause none of the eyestrain associated with looking at computer screens for long periods of time." Eventually, all newspapers and books will be "delivered" on this electronic paper. Alberto (who had been hired by his alma mater as a research professor) came to Samir and Carla looking for private sector partners, and now they were the project's top investors. "Once it's all figured out and in common use, e-paper will save millions of trees and cut the garbage problem in half."

Since, according to Samir, even *everyday* people like him are becoming familar with the name Bleu Mobley, it would be great (very helpful to "the cause of progress") if I would give them an author endorsement. "All you have to do is write a few sentences about how much you look forward to using it, and then you can become one of the beta-testers and take advantage of e-paper's mutable characteristics."

"Mutable characteristics?"

"You know, like hyperlinks and embedded animations and other things that allow the user to interact."

I admitted to Samir that the whole idea of electronic paper was anathema to me. He reminded me that I'm often slow to embrace new technologies, but I always do come around, and "brilliantly so." He asked me to think it over as a favor to him and Carla, and to get in on the ground floor of what will unquestionably become a "game changer" in the way people read and write. Once it becomes an actual product, I could get a lifetime supply.

"Why would I want a lifetime supply if all I need is one sheet?"

"Just because you *can* use the same sheet again and again doesn't mean you'd always *want* to. The developers expect people to use different e-papers for different purposes. What do you say, Bleu? Can we count on you?"

"To endorse something that doesn't exist yet?"

"To endorse the idea."

I agreed to think about it.

By the time we left the restaurant the storm was descending on the north shore of Long Island—very strong gusty winds and starting to snow. Samir and I hugged good night and got into our cars. As I recalled the dinner conversation on my drive home—being hailed as a capitalist, Samir crashing into a display of my books, robotic seeing eye dogs, mutable e-paper that will forever replace paper as we know it—I could feel my Honda Civic fighting the mounting winds that rattled its chassis and whistled through its closed windows. Once I got off the highway and onto the side roads, I saw trees bowing to the wind, streetlamps teetering at precarious angles, and snow spirals whirling across the road like flattened mini-twisters. Closer to my neighborhood, garbage cans rolled across streets and onto lawns, their contents littering the road. Two blocks from home, a large tree branch snapped from an old sugar maple and torpedoed through the front windshield of the car in front of me, which skidded to the right, then plowed into a tree trunk, preventing the car from driving into the illuminated baby Jesus in the manger scene and the Christmas-lighted house behind it. Instinctively, I swerved my steering wheel to the left and slammed my foot on the brake, causing my car to jump a curb and plunge into a looming privet hedge.

Within minutes, someone was breaking their way through the boxwood branches to get to me. A crowd of people appeared through the disappearing hedge asking me how I was (except for the guy threatening to sue me). "I'm alright," I said, even though there was broken glass everywhere, blood dripping onto my hands, and a sharp pain in my back.

"You're very lucky."

That's what everyone said to me in the hospital. I could have been dead like Mr. Chin, the man in the car in front of me. Besides the black and blue marks, the lacerations on my face, neck, arms and hands, and the shattered disk in my back, I was fine. I wasn't disfigured, and I wasn't going to be a paraplegic. The orthopedic surgeon even thought that after he performed the surgery—the *only* way to clear out the shards of disk matter from the nerve canal—I might feel better than I had in years. "In a way," he said, "you could see the accident as a gift. No one ever *wants* to have elective surgery, but since we're cutting into you anyway, we're going to do what probably should have been done years ago and fuse your fourth and fifth lumbars. You're a lucky man," he said patting my blanketed ankle. On his way out, he reminded me that all I had to do was press the yellow button if I needed more pain relief "See you tomorrow." He and I had a date for surgery the next day, but I cancelled it a few hours after he left when I found out Mr. Chin's funeral was scheduled for the same time.

I'd never met Mr. Chin, but I felt inextricably linked to him. If he hadn't been driving in front of me, *I'd* be the one having a funeral. Why, in an accident which the insurance company calls *an act of God*, does one person live and another die? Aconsha understood this question all too well, and she never could find a satisfactory answer to it either. "At least you didn't know the other person," she said, rubbing my arm, staring into that far away place she sometimes goes. Whatever I was feeling, I knew it couldn't compare to the loss of a twin brother, so I kept my grief over Mr. Chin's death, and the intensifying connection I felt toward him, to myself.

Canceling a five-hour surgery on such short notice turned out to be an expensive impulse. I told the doctor I had a funeral to go to that I couldn't miss. He was sorry for my loss (I didn't tell him who it was that died), "but rescheduling," he said, "will cost you an extra seven thousand, *minimum*, and there's nothing I can do to make it any less." I didn't tell Aconsha about the seven grand, but I couldn't think of a way to disappear from the hospital for a day without saying something to her and the girls. I thought of different excuses, but decided to tell them the truth, that I needed to go to this man's funeral.

Joseph Chin was born Jiang Li Chin in the city of Nanking. After his parents were killed by the Japanese in the "Nanking Massacre," Jiang Li was taken into an orphanage run by American missionaries. It was during that time that he became a Catholic and was given the name Joseph. When the communists took over the Mainland after the war, fifteen-year-old Joseph Jiang Li Chin built a raft out of discarded materials, which he and eight others used to cross the strait to Taiwan. I know this story because the man at the funeral service who told it was one of the nine people on the raft. "It was probably Joe's first work of engineering," he speculated, "or at least his first to save lives."

Joseph Chin went on to study engineering in Taiwan and eventually came to the United States where he married, had two sons, and worked for thirty-one years as a mechanical engineer for a medical supply company. "Joe never took personal credit for any of his designs," a colleague of his at Medco Supply Corp told the bereaved crowd. "Instead, he would always give credit to the team, even if we had little to do with it."

Mr. Chin was a remarkable man. Though unknown to the world at large, he enlarged the worlds of the people who knew him. According to his wife, Joe considered his two sons his greatest achievements. "Not because he took credit for the fine men they turned out to be, but because they loved him despite his imperfections, and they continued to call or visit at least once a week even after they were married and had kids of their own."

Whatever denominational turf wars had taken place behind the scenes, the funeral came off as a model of ecumenical harmony, presided over by a Catholic priest and a Buddhist monk. Mr. Chin's wife was the Buddhist, and deferring to her wishes, their two boys were raised as Buddhists. The older son held a piece of paper in his slender hands that had been typed out by his father years earlier and left with his will. Kevin Chin read portions of the letter with a mix of tears and laughter: "Upon the occasion of my death... Please, none of you get into fight over what to do with my dead body. After many years using this expression, I can now say with utmost seriousness—Not over my dead body! Ha ha ha. Buddhist tradition will have my body cremated, my ash placed above ground and xi bo ignited to attract the gods and ensure my passage to reincarnation or nirvana. Catholic law says to bury me intact so I can reunite with the soul when Jesus comes again. Both religions assume the deceased person has attain high level of goodness in his life, which I have not yet attain, though I have try. Either way, I know that I will reunite with God one day, so it does not matter to me what you do with my body. Since those of you burden with having to deal with my funeral and my remains most likely are used to Buddhist way, please feel free to cremate. To do otherwise on my account makes no sense since funerals really for sake of the survivors. Whatever you do, please, don't cry. Sing, eat, drink wine, light firework, and don't make the kids sit still in their seat. What do they know about death? And make certain to thank everyone for showing up, and on my behalf, for the privilege of knowing them."

The letter of instruction, though telling them to cremate, made it clear to the sons that their father would prefer to be buried. So they bought a casket and buried him whole, but they also built boats of folded spirit money and burned them at the grave. Prayers in Latin, English, and Chinese were sung, spoken, and chanted. The priest sprinkled holy water on the body. The monk poured a cup of wine and placed it on the casket. Friends and family ignited firecrackers and left plates of food by the gravesite. After the burial there was a gathering at Mrs. Chin's house where family members talked about Joe's devotion to his sons. Neighbors talked about him being the block's Mr. Fixit. Churchgoers talked about his volunteer work reading scripture to people in hospice care. And almost everyone considered it a good omen that he died in front of a nativity scene, and they all hoped that the last thing he saw was the face of the baby Jesus.

When Mrs. Chin asked me how I knew her husband, I told her. I must have been quite a sight: this scraped-up, shell-shocked stranger with a circumstantial but grave connection to her husband, leaning on a pair of crutches in her crowded living room. "I'm so sorry for your loss," I said, unsure what else to say. Mrs. Chin looked over at Aconsha (who insisted on coming with me). They embraced each other. Out of politeness I put some fish on a plate and sat down at a table where people continued telling stories about the saintly Mr. Chin.

On the drive back to the hospital, I thanked Aconsha for putting up with me. She shook her head and said, "No, I'm glad we came."

A little while later, as I gazed out the car window in silence, Aconsha said, "I know what you're thinking, and you should stop."

"What am I thinking?" I asked, acting as though I wasn't thinking anything.

"That the tree branch snuffed out the better man."

"Didn't it though?"

"Please, Bleu. Try not to go there."

"Actually, I was looking at the lines."

"The lines?"

"All the lines connecting everyone in the houses along the highway and down the side streets, and the people in all the cars. It's dizzying how many lines there are."

No response.

"We think we're independent agents. We're not. They're running between everything."

"What are you talking about?

"Can't you see them?"

"See what?"

"The lines. There are *millions* of them."

No response.

"I know what you're thinking," I said, reacting to Aconsha's silence.

"What am I thinking?"

"You're wondering whether or not the pain medication is causing me to hallucinate."

"Well, do you think it is?"

"I think it's allowing me to see what I normally can't."

"That's a good sign then."

"Why is that?"

"Because if you were in a lot of pain, the medication would just be working to fight the pain, not helping you see what you normally can't."

"I think everyone in the hospital should get to go outside for a day, if they can."

"But you just got there."

"It could be a new cure. The one-day-out cure."

"Not only to attend funerals I hope."

"No. They could go to the park or see a ball game."

"Or go see a dance performance."

"Dance for sure. Or just to see the lines in the clear light of day."

"Ah yes, the lines are always nice to see when the sun is out."

"So you *do* see them!"

"Yes I see them."

"Can you see the ones running back and forth between you and me right now."

"Of course."

"Do you really?"

"Definitely. They're all aglow."

"You know, I *am* a lucky man."

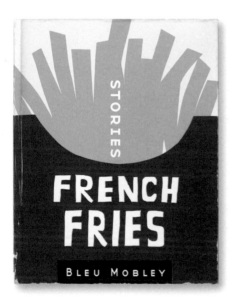

For Here Or T'Go Series

SHORT-SHORT STORIES

French Fries stories

Cheeseburger stories

Diet Coke stories

Ice Cream stories

Bleu Mobley's second series of pocket-sized books feature easy to read, harder to digest stories that take place in and around fast-food restaurants. You may not have time to read many full-length novels these days, but once you take the first bite of a *For Here Or T'Go* book, gobble up any of the salty and compelling short-short stories, you'll soon discover (as many people already have) that you can't read just one. "A multi-culti, quick-service circus of fast-reading stories about life in the fast food lane." ***New York Magazine***

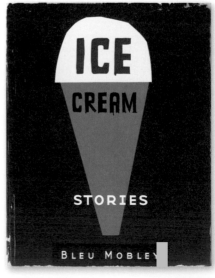

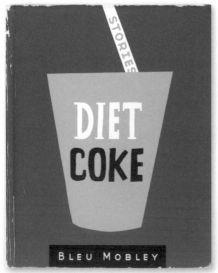

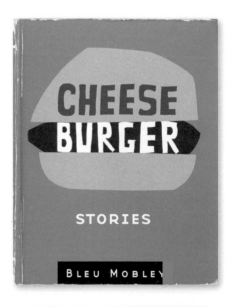

2000-2001, Bantam, New York, NY

My name is *Phor*, but today I guess you can call me Lucky. Lucky Phor. That's P.H.O.R., pronounced like the number. My real name is *Saleeb*. When I came to this country, kids in my fifth-grade class didn't want to call me Saleeb. They called me *Raghead, Towelhead, Taj, Sambo*. When I switched to just wearing a white net over my hair knot, they called me *Snowball*. When I wore a red net, I was *Redball*. Saleeb became *Leeby, Sally-Boy*, and *Beelass*, which is Saleeb pronounced backwards (extra emphasis on the *ass*). For a while, kids called me *Sale* (I think because I was always selling knickknacks for pocket change: french fry fridge magnets, key chains, flashlight pens). Then they started calling me *For Sale*, which I didn't appreciate—being For Sale—so I dropped the Sale and kept the For, only I changed the spelling to make it more unique. And for some reason that stuck.

I'm a Sikh by birth. That's spelled S.I.K.H. In India, we say Sik*h*, but in English-speaking countries people can't say the *kh* sound for some reason. They pronounce the *k* too hard and make the *h* silent, so it sounds like *Sick* which is not a good thing because sick means *ill* in English. The way my father tells it, after the Brits colonized us, we said, No, we can't have you associating us with being ill. Please say *Seek*, like a person who seeks (which is close to what Sikh actually means. The exact translation is more like disciple or student, meaning someone who is supposed to keep learning throughout their life). That's the only part of my religion I believe in—to keep learning throughout my life. And one of the things I keep learning is: religion puts limits on your brain. In India, religion is infused into every-thing. They live for religion over there. They kill for it, die for it, eat for it. They even have sex for it. As mortified as I was about having to leave my friends in Punjab, I looked forward to coming to a modern culture like America. Imagine how surprised I was when I discov-ered what a big deal religion is here too. The only difference—in America they don't live and die for religion so much as they talk about it a lot.

By ninth grade I quit going to temple with my parents. I was sick of hearing about samsara, karma, reincarnation. I wanted to make *this* life my heaven. I stopped wearing any kind of headdress and repeating the name of God. I still believe in being a good person because that has nothing to do with religion, and I still don't cut my hair, only now I put it in a pony tail instead of pinning it up into a patka, and I'm still a vegetarian, not because it's part of my religion (Guru Nanek didn't care whether you ate meat or not), but because I was raised as a vegetarian and the taste of cooked meat makes me physically ill.

I'm nineteen now and my plan is to become an astrophysicist, but until my Green Card comes through I work as a day laborer. You know, I'm one of those guys you see lining up under the elevated subway tracks on Roosevelt Avenue waiting for a van to pull up looking for workers. Some jobs are a one-day thing, like the title, *day labor*. Some jobs, they need you for a week or a month or however long the job takes. Some jobs you just lift and load or sweep and shovel. Some jobs are more like skilled labor. I've put up dry wall, poured cement floors, run electrical lines, put in toilets and sinks, and pruned exotic trees. Some jobs, you have to dress up like a cookie or a rabbit. Some jobs you're all wrist, handing out flyers. Some jobs the boss is decent to you. Some jobs you never see the boss.

The thing about day labor is: the pay is shit because you most likely don't have papers and it's understood you are willing to do the crap work no one else will, and for a whole lot less. Most guys I work with are from Mexico or Central America, but to a Chinese or just about any white person who pulls up in a van, they can't see the difference between me and the rest. We're all Mexicans to them. Black-haired bronze boys. "Yo, hombre. Trabajar. Dineros." I say, "Si Señor." What do I care who they think I am? Dinero is dinero.

Today, me and seven other guys got picked for a job clearing a site that used to be a medical center and is going to be a large video arcade. The medical center had already been demolished, and it was our job to clear the debris. It's a good thing I brought my working gloves because they had us lifting broken glass and chunks of steel; some guys were doing it with their bare hands. They're supposed to supply us with gloves for work like that, and headgear, but nothing about this job was by the book. At the same time that we're clearing, another crew was putting up the new structure at the back end of the lot, which is unusual because you're supposed to clear everything off of a site before you start to build on it again. That's like, the *first thing* you learn in Construction 101. A year ago I would have said something, but I've learned to keep my mouth shut. One day, when I'm the head of an astrophysics team, I'm going to listen to what the people working for me have to say.

Anyway. A half hour before lunchtime—so as not to lose a minute of work out of us—the boss, a Greek guy named Mr. Petracca, takes orders for a *Burger Dream* run. I ask if I can place an order from somewhere else because I'm a vegetarian. He gives me the sourest of looks and says, "No. The *Burger Dream* is just down the block and they got everything there—salads, chicken sandwiches." I decide not to put up a fight and order a salad and a coke. But then I change my mind because I was hungry for some bread. I tell him, "Make it a cheeseburger, no meat," figuring that would be like a grilled cheese sandwich. Petracca says, "*What?*" Like he didn't understand me. I say, "Order me a cheeseburger, and tell them to hold the meat. *Please.* Also a side of fries and a coke." He writes it down, collects the rest of the orders, and grabs one of the guys from our crew to go with him.

Twenty minutes later, Petracca is back, handing out lunches. "Your coke. Your fries. Your cheeseburger, no meat."

I thank him and sit down with some of the other guys around a large cable spool somebody turned on its side to use as a table. I put a few fries in my mouth and unwrap the burger. I lift up the top bun and *sure enough*, underneath the tomato, lettuce and cheese, there's a burger inside. I call over to Petracca. "Excuse me, Sir. This has meat in it!"

He yells back, "That's what they gave me. I *said* to the girl, 'Cheeseburger, no meat.' And she said, 'Cheeseburger, hold the meat,' *right* into her microphone. Hey José!" (The guy's name is Juan Carlos, but Mr. Petracca calls everyone José.) "Didn't you hear the girl say 'Cheeseburger, hold the meat?' *You see!* He heard it too. They even wrote NO MEAT on it. Don't it say CB NO MEAT on the wrapper?"

"Yeah, okay," I say waving at him to forget about it. Under my breath I say, "and you're the greatest humanitarian the earth has ever seen." What am I going to do, start a war over this? My dad told me, "We're *guests* in this country. Don't pick fights."

So I take a plastic knife and do my best to separate the cheese from the greasy slab of meat. I toss the meat into the wrapper, put the top half of the bun back on and take a bite of my now meatless cheeseburger. The second it's in my mouth, I realize I cannot swallow this. The taste of the meat has permeated the cheese, the bun, my mouth, *my entire being.* I spit everything out into the wrapper. The other four guys around the cable table go, "*Yeeuuck!* Gross, man." One of them asks if there was a mouse in the burger. I'm thinking to myself, *Maybe right now is the time for me to begin my semi-annual fast.*

I get up off my bucket and walk to the nearest trash can to throw out the remains of the burger. I don't feel like eating the fries either. As I'm trashing my uneaten lunch, I hear somebody say, "*Oh Fuck!*" I look up and see this enormous steel I-beam wobbling in the air like a stoned whirling dervish. The crane operator is trying to regain control of his machine. He looks like a little boy trying to reel in a whale with a fishing pole. As he's screaming at the I-beam—**COME BACK, BABY, COME BACK**—one of two wire slings snaps, leaving only one side of the beam secured to the choke. The beam swings in our direction, and what was supposed to be horizontal is fast becoming vertical. That's when the second sling snaps and the 10,000-pound I-beam comes crashing to the ground like a thunderbolt, shaking the earth with a deafening BANG, sending a plume of dust and shards of metal and all kinds of crap into the air. The beam is sticking out of the ground at an angle like the Leaning Tower of Pisa. Once the dust and debris settles, I can see that this massive beam landed right on top of where I had just been sitting, plunging the cable table along with all four of my fellow lunchmates into the ground. The whole episode couldn't have taken ten seconds from the *Oh Fuck* to the time the beam crashed into the ground.

When the ambulances came, right away the paramedics started working on people with shrapnel injuries and on the crane operator who was in a state of shock. Once the beam got hoisted out of its crater, you could see the four day laborers squashed totally flat, like a tablecloth print of figures eating around a table; two of them looking up, the other two, happily biting into their burgers. They never had a chance. And now they will never breathe fresh air or get to hold their wives and kids again. It was the most horrifying sight I've seen in a long time. And if it wasn't for that greasy hamburger, I'd be part of that dead meat print too, connected forever and ever with four other Josés on a spool to nowhere.

A crowd of people gathered around my car asking if I was all right.

"Yes. I'm fine."

"But are you *happy*?" asked Mr. Chin as he helped me out of my car. I recognized him from photographs I saw at his house after the funeral.

Normally, I'd think, *What does happiness have to do with anything?* Out of deference to the dead, I said, "Oh, happy enough, all things considered."

"I didn't *ask* if you were happy," Chin said, revising his question. "I asked what you've done today to serve God?"

"I'm not sure I believe in God," I replied. "At least not in the way that you put it."

"Don't get tangled up in semantics," Chin said leading me down an unfamiliar street. "What have you done today to help someone other than yourself?"

As I thought about his question, he handed me a fortune cookie. I cracked it and the fortune floated up to the sky before I could read it. Then a teenage girl stepped off a school bus and asked me for directions. She looked a lot like Ella, only older. I told her I'm not good with directions. "I don't even know what's up and what's down anymore."

"Oh," she said, "do you have topographical disorientation?"

"What's that?" I asked.

"A fancy name for bad sense of direction. I read it in a book about benign maladies."

"Well yeah," I said, looking around to see where Mr. Chin had gone. "I guess I do have topographical. . . *whateveryoucallit*. Thank you for the information."

"No problem," she said, still looking around for a direction to go in.

I woke up before I could help the girl find her way. Aconsha was sitting beside me in a post-op room at the hospital. "Everything went perfect," she said, "even though the surgery took seven hours instead of five." She kissed my forehead and whispered, "You're adorable when you're unconscious."

Two days later I was released from the hospital. "I've done *my* job," Dr. Schmerler said, satisfied that he'd performed a flawless discectomy and fuse job combo. "Now it's *your* turn to do the work."

"Do I have to lie in bed for three months?"

"Oh no. The protocol has changed 180 degrees. We now know the most important thing to do after surgery is exercise. In your case, since you're not a swimmer, I need you to walk an hour a day for the rest of your life. Don't think of this as rehab. Think—change of lifestyle."

As soon as I got home I went for a walk, and nearly got run over by a truck. This is one of the drawbacks of living in suburbia—there are very few sidewalks! I started taking the train into Manhattan several times a week. Once I was at Penn Station, I'd go outside and walk; it didn't matter in what direction—east, west, uptown, downtown. After walking my required hour, I'd stop and talk to people.

There is nothing like walking amongst the kaleidoscopic throngs of New York City, especially when you're not in a rush to be somewhere. But the thing that really brings the city to life is sitting across from another person—on a park bench, a stoop, at a table in a café—and you reach that point in the conversation when you're barely saying anything yourself, except, *Oh my God. . . Then what happened?* And the park, the stoop, the cafe, your own troubles melt away—and all that exists is that person's face, their voice, their eyes leading you down the alleyways, valleys and peaks of their story. For an hour or two you feel like the luckiest person in the world—you got to meet this person. They feel lucky too, someone cared to ask, to listen. And then it's time to go. It's gotten dark out. Surroundings come back into focus. The city reappears.

On the train ride back to Long Island I'd write about whoever I met that day. Sometimes I'd tire myself out from all the walking and talking, and end up staying the night at a friend's place or a hotel. After a few months, I decided to rent a studio apartment on the Lower East Side not far from where we used to live. Aconsha liked the idea of our having a crash pad in the city, as long as I promised not to stay more than two nights a week.

During this period, I came to realize that my *Project* wasn't only about chronicling people's stories. There was something more I was searching for, some kind of unified field theory of personality and behavior. Perhaps, not having a religious faith created a need in me—to find my own (un)holy grail of modern-day truths that I could refer to at moments of crisis or when either of my daughters looked to me for answers.

LifeMaps *LIFESTYLES*

We all use maps when we visit a new place. But have you ever used a map to help find a way into and around the next phase of your life? Mostly we stumble through the challenges and opportunities in life as if we were running an obstacle course in the dark. In *LifeMaps*, radio host and bestselling author Dr. Sky Jacobs serves up 101 maps and diagrams that help you figure out where you're going, where you've been, how you got there, and if necessary, how to change direction.

2000, Harmony Books, New York, NY

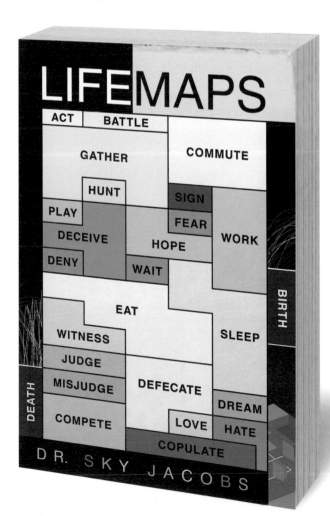

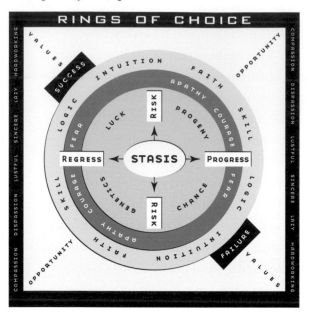

In a dream, I'm sailing through the air, kind of like skydiving, looking down at the earth. I'm not scared, which is odd because I am someone who never would skydive, even in a dream. As I look closer, what I thought were mountains, rivers and villages are actually the terrain of people's lives—a topography of choices and chances, opportunities and accidents, forks that lead to easy or hard roads, tributaries of regrets and satisfactions. I'm making drawings of all this in one of my pads. After filling every page, I come in for a smooth bellylanding—hands in front of me, fingers combing the grass, feet gently breaking—on a field of equanimity. For a novice, I have pretty good landing technique. As I'm dusting myself off, a young woman in a checkerboard dress walks up to me and asks for directions. Instead of telling her that I'm new to the area myself, or giving her the topographical disorientation line, I hand her my notepad. She flips through it quickly, then hands it back.

"Can't you just tell me where I'm at?"

I say, "Do you want to know where you *are* or where you're *going*?"

She says, "Tell you the truth, Mister, I don't even have a clue where I've been."

I say, "That's the thing; it's all inter-twined and very personal in the end—the past, where you'd like to be tomorrow, let alone this second. As much as I'd like to, I can't give you the answers. I'm only a cartographer. But take this." I hand her my notebook again. "Please, it's a gift."

When all was said and published, Dr. Sky Jacobs and I were only able to offer up puzzles and enigmas. For every rule, there was always an exception. And when I/he/we tried making the exception the rule, we'd come upon an exception to the exception.

250

Follow your bliss,
unless your bliss
is hurting other people.

Mind your own business.

A few years later, realize something
horrible has happened because
you and a lot of other people never
said a word or lifted a finger
to do anything to prevent it.

Birds of a feather flock together,
and often suffer from problems
associated with inbreeding
as well as terribly wrongheaded
perceptions of others.

Don't bite the hand that feeds you,
unless it's feeding you poison.

If you don't have
something good to say,
don't say anything,
unless you have a good reason to
say something critical, in which case
you should say it nicely,
unless it's a matter of great urgency,
in which case you may have little
choice but to curse and scream.

Business is business.
In other words:
we have no choice
but to fuck you over.

A Treasury of UnCommon Knowledge

SPIRIT AND WISDOM

So many of the homilies and aphorisms we learned
as kids are excellent thoughts to live by, except for
when they don't apply, which is quite often. In this
pocket-sized lifesaver of a book, bestselling author
and radio host Dr. Sky Jacobs serves up 101 common
wisdoms turned upside down and inside out. "For
those unbookish moments in life, this anti-handbook
handbook is a must—especially for skeptics of
age-old or new-age adages." *Tricycle Magazine*

2001, Beacon, Boston, MA

All good things
must come to an end.
But don't feel bad because
bad things come to an end too.

6

WITH US OR AGAINST US

It doesn't seem to matter that a sizeable majority of the candidates and issues I've voted for over the years have lost—I continue to cling to a faith in the system, and never once missed a chance to exercise the right to vote.

The first year we moved to Long Island I missed the registration deadline to vote in the general election, so when election day came around, I drove into Manhattan—to the polling place on the Lower East Side where I was already registered—double parked, ran inside, waited on line, voted, snatched the parking ticket off my windshield (cursing the price of democracy), and drove back to the Island.

Ever since that election, going into New York City to cast my meager but ever-hopeful vote became a once-, sometimes twice-a-year ritual. I usually came in alone (since Aconsha never became a U.S. citizen), and was back home the same day. After we started renting the Ninth Street apartment, I made sure to overlap my junkets into the city with Election Day, like I did for the 2001 New York primaries.

I took the train in the night before, got up early the next morning and went outside to take my first walk of the day. It was one of those perfect late summer days when nature graces the city with a crystal clear sky, temperatures in the seventies, a gentle breeze, and not a trace of smog, humidity, or the coming Autumn chill. After my walk, I came back to the apartment, flipped on the radio and the local news anchor was talking about a fire in one of the Twin Towers. He described a smoldering gash in the North Tower and mentioned the possibility that a plane had crashed into it. Not having a TV or a view of the Towers from my apartment, I ran up five flights of stairs to the roof where several of my neighbors were already watching the smoke rising out of the left Tower, some twenty blocks to the southwest.

"Do they know what happened?" I asked a frizzy-haired woman with headphones on.

"A plane flew into it," she said, shaking her head in disbelief.

The guy standing next to her said, "It's a wonder it doesn't happen more often."

"Shut up," said the woman, jamming her elbow into his ribs with the familiarity of an intimate. "People are *dying* up there!"

Police cars, fire engines, and ambulances raced through the veins of the city, sirens at full screech. People poured out of buildings and subway stations onto the streets looking up at the smoke, running in all directions. I thought of joining the herds sprinting toward the accident, but I couldn't run like I did when I was a young reporter rushing to be first on the scene. Instead of going out, I ran down to our apartment to call Aconsha. The line was busy. After a few more tries I double-stepped up to the roof. Dozens of people were up there by then with binoculars, cameras, radios. One guy had a telescope—almost everyone had cell phones pressed to their ears. Same scene on every rooftop.

I shuddered at the thought of sitting in an office, looking out the window, seeing a plane flying toward me, and hoped that the people on the upper floors could get down before the plane exploded. Surely, a plane couldn't fester in there forever.

Another plane flew into sight. I figured it was a Special Ops crew or National Guard, and wondered what they could do: *Send men down on ladders? Use hoses? Drop flame retardant?* The closer the plane got, the more apparent it became that it was too large, making too much noise, flying too low and too fast, and heading straight for the other tower.

Screams rippled across rooftops.

This was *not* an accident. Not a Hindenburg. More Pearl Harbor, a day of infamy. There was a fireball in the sky, orange flames, the smell of jet fuel. A plane in each tower. I ran downstairs. The phone was dead. Back to the roof. A woman was screaming at her teenage son to come down. "**This is a war, Ronnie! We should be down in a shelter, not up on the roof.**" She had a point. The fellow next to me pulled a headphone away from one ear to report that some radio stations were off the air.

That's right. Most of the radio and television transmitters are on those towers!

Two years earlier, U.S. fighter jets bombed a television broadcast tower in Belgrade where many civilians worked. NATO called it a "dual-use" target of vital importance to the enemy. *Fucking cocksure men and their justifiable targets.*

I asked a young man lighting a cigarette if I could look in his binoculars. Searching the sky, I found smoke, then focused on the combed steel façade of one of the towers. People were waving towels out windows. I saw a body falling through the air.

"Oh my God, they're jumping out windows!"

"I know," said the guy who loaned me the binoculars. "I just saw a man with a make-shift parachute. It slowed him down for a couple of seconds. Then the sheet fell apart and he was gone." I handed the binoculars back and dropped to my knees.

It's happened.

The bubble burst.

The winds of blowback are upon us.

I'd seen warfare against civilians before, in Beirut and Port-au-Prince. But whose work was this? When the federal building in Oklahoma blew, everyone thought for sure it was Muslim terrorists. It turned out to be a white guy—ex-Marine.

Will more planes come flying out of the sky into other dual-use targets?

Bridges? Government buildings? Power plants? Refineries?

A little while later the South Tower tilted, and then each floor collapsed onto the floor below a hundred-something times over, crushing everyone and everything in its wake. Just like that, a mile-high tower was swallowed up in a mushroom cloud of mothers, fathers, lovers, children, rescuers, a small city's worth of steel, paper, concrete, silicone, lead, asbestos, who knew what else. Then the North Tower flattened like a plastic toy under the boot of a drunken father. An avalanche of debris, soot, and ash enveloped lower Manhattan, surging down streets, chasing tens of thousands of dust-covered survivors and spectators over bridges to Brooklyn and New Jersey, onto boats, into the arms of strangers, into ambulances, and anywhere uptown enough to breathe.

In the hours and days that followed, I wasn't sure what to do. I could sit in a neighbor's apartment as I did for a while, with other neighbors I hadn't known till then—gaping at the TV, watching replays of the horrifying and spectacular images, listening to experts spin instant speculations wrapped in certainty, based on scant evidence, laying down a drumbeat to the retaliatory wars that were sure to come—or I could go out and try to be of some help.

After giving blood—which ended up being of little use since there were few survivors—what could I do? I had no emergency medical experience, no fire-fighting skills, my back disabled me from lifting anything or anyone. Unable to get close to "ground zero" or go home to Long Island to be with my family, I walked around the gray mist and inextinguishable odor—under the sound of F16s (a little late, fellas!), over singed interoffice memos that carpeted the streets—along with thousands of other nerve-rattled New Yorkers, each of us looking at the other with an unguarded recognition rarely experienced in the city.

A middle-aged woman with a hollowed-out look lit up at the sight of me. She approached with outstretched arms. Just before wrapping herself around me, she realized I wasn't who she thought I was. The man she mistook me for had been in the South Tower the morning before, and hadn't been heard from since. I felt terrible being the cause of this mirage. She felt doubly terrible. We embraced anyway and cried into each other's confusion and heartache. Delia told me about the missing man, Anthony Karush, a lawyer who worked for Cantor Fitzgerald. She'd become friends with his wife through the PTA. Tony was no angel, but a decent, loving father. Delia was a freelance graphic designer, so she put together a flyer with Tony's photo and contact information, and was plastering copies all over the city. I took a flyer, noticed a vague resemblance, and promised Delia that I'd keep an eye out for him. We hugged again and wished each other good luck.

Instead of triple-locking themselves inside their apartments, New Yorkers from all over the city opened their homes and offices to tens of thousands of temporary refugees who couldn't get to their homes on the lower tip of Manhattan. In the weeks following 9/11, the crime rate plummeted to levels not seen in a hundred years. Men and women came out of retirement to help in any way they could. Friends like Delia became family to survivors of the missing. Neighbors who'd never spoken were becoming friends for life, and 'strangers' came together in places like Union Square Park to share experiences, erect spontaneous memorials, and cover makeshift walls with photographs and descriptions of the missing. Union Square became a people's shrine that no politician or law enforcer dared try to regulate or shut down; and it was in that park—after reading a seven-year-old girl's letter to her missing mother—that I realized there *was* something I could do to help.

With Aconsha's permission—as long I agreed to buy a cell phone (finally), and talk to Frida and Ella and my mother every night—I stayed in the city volunteering as an intake person with an organization called New York Cares, writing down descriptions and bearing witness to the stories of missing loved ones, holding hands, dispensing tissues.

Six days later, Aconsha called me up on my second cell phone (having lost the first), saying, "You have to come home now."

"I can't," I said. "There are too many people who need. . ."

"I know you want to help the *Family of Man*, and that's honorable. But *your* family needs you now. This hasn't been a lovefest out here on the Island. It's different for us, Bleu. Maybe you never noticed, but the girls and I are not white. In the eyes of some people, we're not American."

"Why? What happened?"

"Lots of little things that I haven't bothered you with, but today Ella got into a fight with a boy at school after he called her *Osama Girl*. She told him to shut up, but he wouldn't, so she gave him a bloody nose."

I spent the next seven months in hibernation with my family, relishing the time being a dad, husband, son, walker of dog, raker of leaves, carver of pumpkins, groomer of hair, cutter of toenails, shoveler of snow, builder of snowmen, scraper of cars, watcher of snowboarders, lacer of ice skates, rinser-slicer-dicer of vegetables, handwasher and dryer of dishes, cleaner of any surface, tidier of rooms, corrector of homework, syncopational banger of pots and pans, page turner of piano music, sing-a-longer of songs, dancer of devil-may-care improvs, player of board games and card games and word games, reciter of books, kicker of soccer balls, spotter of birds and birdsongs, drawer of baths, dropper-offer and picker-upper of teammates and cast members and sleep-overs, tucker-inner, savorer of soft cheeks and just-washed hair, queller of fears, sultan of safe, purveyor of normal.

Other than doing the *Radio Sky* program on Fridays, I didn't bother going into the studio. I suspended all book projects until further notice but continued paying a salary to my assistants who were all wrestling with their own 9/11 repercussions: Josiah—beside himself with grief over a close friend, an artist, who had just started a studio residency in an unoccupied office on the 104th floor of the North Tower and spent his first all-nighter up there on September 10th; Najela—devastated that the three years she spent filling out paperwork so her uncle could come to the U.S. was undone in an instant because the INS wasn't about to let a bearded, fifty-year-old Muslim man from Afghanistan into the country anytime soon; Monica—bummed out because her second nonfiction novel (a book based on her grandmother's secret love affair with a priest) came out the week of 9/11, causing it to join the ranks of many worthy projects swept into oblivion by "the day the world changed forever."

The release of my own trio of culinary murder mysteries, scheduled for September 21st, was put off indefinitely. The publisher and I both agreed—in the redefining light of 9/11— *The Prickly Pear Murders*, *The Night Crustaceans Screamed*, and *A Bell Tolls For Mr. Frosty* were too morbid to release. Close to 100,000 copies stood on skids in a New Jersey warehouse wrapped in thick plastic. As far as I was concerned, they could stay there forever.

Five months later, I got a call from the editor, saying she wanted to release *The Last Bites* books. She had re-read all three the night before and "saw them in an entirely new light."

"Let's face it, Aurora," I said on my third cell phone, "those are the wrong books at the wrong time. Maybe they're the wrong books for *any* time."

"Read them now, with the perspective of all that's happened in the last months. That's what I did, and you know, they're not gory. There are very few graphic depictions of violence in any of them. You want to know what I think those books of yours are really about?"

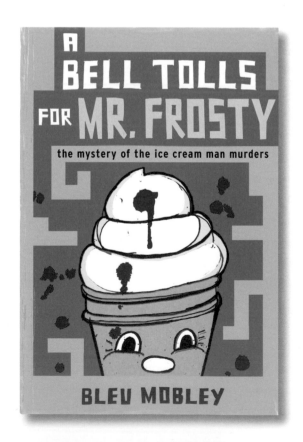

"Sure."

"They're about people coming together after unthinkable tragedies befall their communities. They're about the human potential to overcome catastrophe and short-sightedness. They're *exactly* what readers are yearning for right now."

"It doesn't matter how you spin it. The public doesn't have the stomach yet for a series of books that equates what they eat with murder, and does it with a sense of humor."

"Listen, Bleu," Aurora groused, not used to arguing with authors who *don't* want their work published. "It's not up to you. People are laughing at jokes again, they're coming into town, they're even buying books. We're releasing *Last Bites* with or without your blessing."

Immediately after 9/11, the consumer confidence index was in the toilet. The only consumables that were doing well were alcohol, canned goods, flashlights, and cell phones. Then the president of the United States and the mayor of New York (two names I'd rather not sully my story with) urged people to show their patriotism by shopping. "Otherwise," they both said (independently of the other) "the terrorists will have won." Americans responded to the call of their leaders, and the 2001 Christmas shopping season yielded better returns than anyone predicted. America was indeed on the mend. Despite my objections, *The Last Bites* books were published, and as I predicted, they were unmitigated flops.

Last Bites Trilogy

MURDER MYSTERIES

A Bell Tolls For Mr. Frosty

The Night Crustaceans Screamed

The Prickly Pear Murders

What if lobsters screamed bloody murder while Grandpa boiled them alive in his beach house kitchen? What if a handful of the millions of wishes to disappear the Mr. Frosty ice cream man and his blasted bells came true? What if a couple of migrant field workers from south of the border were accused of a series of gruesome prickly pear murders they didn't commit? These are some of the scenarios that come to life (and death) in Bleu Mobley's deliciously unsettling culinary murder mysteries. Once you've read them, eating may never be the same.

2002, Houghton Mifflin, New York, NY

Every summer for nearly half a century, the sappy, trying-to-be-happy, bell-like melody of the Mr. Frosty ice cream truck stimulated the sweet tooth of a small but profitable fraction of the city. Like Pavlov's dogs, children and their parents, people of all shapes, colors and sizes zombied down elevators and staircases into the grimy sauna streets salivating for their fix of frozen sugar. While some New Yorkers simply tuned out the persistent chimes like they do ambulance and fire sirens, car alarms, shrieking children, and desperate calls for help, many others felt nothing less than molar-gnashing fury when the wobbly jack-in-the-box-like tune rang for hours at a time outside their high-rise apartment complex. Even the most peace-loving city dwellers succumbed to exclamations of

I'M
GONNA
SHOOT
THAT BASTARD

at the sound of the unrelenting bells.

Like the mugger, the tow trucker, the repo man, the umpire, and the meter maid, the Mr. Frosty man (and his four-wheel bell tower) was one of those perennially reviled figures most New Yorkers loved to hate.

And yet, when the tabloids screamed their bloody murder headlines and filled page after photo-illustrated page with one slaughtered Mr. Frosty story after the next, almost every one of the city's nine million inhabitants reacted with horror, sorrow, and outrage. The mass condemnation and spontaneous outpouring of support for the victims' families hadn't been seen since Son of Sam terrified the city with his senseless killings twenty-five years earlier. Thousands of New Yorkers showed up to memorial services, and many more volunteered to do whatever they could to track down *the savages* who had turned ice cream and summer into a living nightmare. Was it surprising that so many residents of the city came together around the murder of these ice cream pumpers after they had been the object of so much vituperation? Not really. Who were these young men and women after all, but the city's own children coming of age, earning their way through college, or just trying to make ends meet with a job that didn't require a tie, and put smiles on the faces of the overheated and sugar-craved. Even the most rabidly outspoken Mr. Frosty detesters never really wanted anything bad to happen to the actual Mr. Frosty guy and gal operators. The million-fold fantasies—of dynamiting the truck, suing the ice cream company into bankruptcy, or castrating the bells out of the blasted vehicles—never were intended to cause any real harm to the grunts who drove the trucks and lactated ice cream for fifty cents above minimum wage.

Clouds of guilt hovered over the city that summer, which an essayist from *The New Yorker* called, "psychic condensation from all those who had wished death upon the jinglers of cool relief." Some of the most guilt-ridden were the first to call for the death penalty. They swore whoever the serial killer was should rot in hell for an eternity. As if the mass psychology of this tragic episode wasn't already bizarre enough, when the Mr. Frosty Corporation indefinitely muzzled its fleet of urban carillons, there was an unexpected wave of nostalgia and revisionist affection for the silenced bells. On the first anniversary of the killing spree, one of the city's most famous composers premiered a post-minimalist opera that elevated the Mr. Frosty murder episode to epic lore. Commissioned by the city's Department of Cultural Affairs, the opera, performed at the Brooklyn Academy of Music's Next Wave Festival, spun the once-detested melody a hundred different ways into contemporary arias sung by six slain Mr. Frosty men and women with spiraling ice cream-heads, a porchload of terrified children, and a Greek chorus of mass regret crooning through oversized wafer cones.

Even after several years without any ice cream man assassinations, Mr. Frosty's parent company (on the advice of their lawyers and branding experts) was reluctant to bring back its sonic logo. Their trucks continued to park at the same locations, but they waited quietly for customers to notice them—making no sounds other than the rumble of idling diesel engines, the tinkling of soft ice cream rolling in sprinkles, and the clinkety clink of making change. By the third anniversary, a critical mass of New Yorkers had shaken off their grief and shame, and begged for the "song of summer" to return. One citizens' group, calling themselves New York Is Back, collected 14,000 signatures pleading with the company to reconsider its no bell policy. Psychologists and social workers chimed in on different sides of the issue, but they all assured city dwellers that only the murderer (wherever he was) had blood on his hands. Nobody else was to blame. Vicious and violent thoughts are not the same as vicious, violent actions. One TV psychologist admitted, "Every one of us has fleeting thoughts of wanting to kill or rape somebody. But that doesn't make us murderers or rapists unless we act on those thoughts." That comment lost the psychologist his job as a television shrink, but the message to the city's beleaguered psyche was clear: it's time to get on with life, eat ice cream, and let the bells ring again!

My story and the story of the entire detective unit that worked on this case really begins three summers after the harrowing ice cream murders. The Mr. Frosty assassin was still out there, somewhere, on the loose, but the city had not been subject to any more ice cream or other serial killings. Its inhabitants played and worked and loved and laughed, yet in the back of their minds they were always a little bit wary of their new sense of normal. By popular demand, Mr. Frosty's 'bells of summer' were back. When the familiar tones reverberated through the steaming asphalt neighborhoods, parents remembered simpler times that may or may not have ever been, and their kids looked up at them for a reassuring smile, a pat on the head, and a handoff of a couple of dollars and change.

It didn't take my mother very long to get used to living in her own little house in a countrified setting, or to put her own stamp on the place. But it took more than three years for her to go up one flight of stairs to the floor I called her *studio*. "What do you want me to do up there, Bleu, paint masterpieces?"

The idea of going to a studio to work on her art was an alien concept to Rose Mobley. She knew there were pre-stretched canvases, boxes full of paints and brushes, and flat-files stocked with art papers waiting for her upstairs, but she still lay around in a bed full of pads and pencils, sat by the kitchen window with a dollar-store notebook and a ballpoint pen, even drew on the walls from time to time. I could have built her a mansion and she would have holed herself up in two rooms like she was used to. I know she preferred seeing spruce trees and sumac bushes out the window to all those brown brick buildings, and waking up to the songs of finches and wood thrushes instead of police sirens and the demented cooing of pigeons, yet a part of her also missed watching the swarms of people going to and fro at all hours of the day and night, knowing she was part of a city that mattered and was never at rest. Sadly, she didn't leave any real friends behind when she left Queensbridge. Many of her neighbors were fond of her, but she never took the extra steps that make it possible for acquaintances to become full-fledged friends. A neighbor of hers from across the hall once told me, "Your mother and I can have a truly marvelous conversation. Then the next time I see her it's like she barely recognizes me." I knew what her neighbor was talking about. When I was growing up, I never could tell if it was something *I* did that caused my mother's mood to suddenly sour. I didn't say anything like that to the woman—better she think of Rose as distant or fickle than pathological. As long as one or two trustworthy people from the building knew her history and kept an eye on her, there was no reason to broadcast her medical record to every Tom, Dick or Harriet.

Aside from her dependence on medication and government assistance, my mother was remarkably self-reliant. Like many artists, she spent much of her life preoccupied with her own thoughts and creative process. But unlike most artists, she didn't aggrandize herself or her creations. Making pictures was like breathing. "It's no big deal," she'd often say when I'd compliment a drawing or sneak a peek at a notebook. Once a picture was made or a notebook filled, she showed no interest in it. Her art was completely integrated into her life. The bathroom, the porch, leaning against a lamppost or tree was studio enough for her.

Fortunately, she ran out of paper one day and wandered up the stairs to find something to draw on. She grabbed the first pad of paper she saw and in her rush to get back downstairs, she accidentally knocked over one of the blank canvases. She picked it up and placed it back on its easel. As she lowered the top clamp to keep the canvas from falling again, sunlight streamed in from the window illuminating a scuff mark on the surface of the primed cotton duck. She took a pencil out of her pocket to erase the damage, but in her haste she used the wrong end and accidentally added a pencil mark on top of the scuff. Suddenly, the canvas wasn't so threateningly pristine. One mark begot another and two hours later the canvas was covered with pencil marks. By the end of that week she had covered all seven pre-stretched canvases with wistful lines and amorphic shapes.

I brought her more canvases of different sizes. Using only pencils and pens, she covered their whiteness with hieroglyphic-like markings, fanciful figures, fields of dots and cross-hatchings. Over the next months and years, I gingerly suggested she try using the oil paints or acrylics since they were designed to work on canvas and could make her process less painstaking. She thanked me for my suggestions, but kept working with pencils and pens and occasionally with a watercolor kit and the thin sable brush that came with it. When the storage racks in her studio were filled to capacity with finished canvases, she asked me to have them reprimed—not to waste any more canvas or money on her dabblings. Instead of bringing someone in to Gesso over her canvases, I brought in an art dealer to come take a look at them. Donald Price flipped at the sight of her densely packed, obsessively rendered labors of necessity. On the spot, he offered her a solo show in his Soho gallery.

Markings

canvases, notebooks, envelopes

Rose Mobley

DONALD PRICE GALLERY

Donald curated an elegant exhibit consisting of twenty-six pencil-laden and ball-point-penned canvases, and four vitrines full of graphite and ink-saturated notebooks and assorted scraps of paper. The opening reception was well attended by art-opening regulars, many of my and Aconsha's friends, and a dozen or so former neighbors from Queensbridge who we car-serviced in with the promise of free food and drink. Instead of appearing awkward or anxious, or making a scene like I had feared, Rose Mobley looked ravishing and relaxed. Her long silver hair, her black and white patchwork dress that she'd sewn herself, and her soft round face whose age lines contradicted her youthful expressions harmonized perfectly with the work in the show. Like the artist, the art was seasoned yet childlike, exuberant yet melancholic, abstract yet earthy. She laughed, told stories, fielded questions like an old pro, and gracefully soaked up the attention. It was a tremendous relief and one of the most rewarding nights of my life.

Three weeks after the opening, a favorable review came out in *The New York Times* with a large reproduction of one of mom's canvases. By the end of that week, nearly every piece in the show had a red dot next to it. When I first heard that a critic from the *Times* came to see the show, I panicked. *What if he pans her work and it turns out that I disrupted my mother's anonymous life only to get her massacred by the soul-destroying words of some vampire art critic?*

The article in the *Times* only briefly mentioned Rose Mobley being the mother of "the bestselling author Bleu Mobley" (thankfully), but it devoted three paragraphs to her mental health and to the "long tradition of madness and art." I was furious when I read it, and couldn't decide whether or not to show it to my mother. By the time I brought her the paper that afternoon, she already knew about it. Donald Price had called all excited and read it to her over the phone. I asked what she thought. She put on a smile for me, looked at the paper, then asked if I would leave her alone for a while. "Should I leave the paper with you?" I asked, unsure of what she was feeling. She shrugged, which I took to be more of a *why not* than a *no*. The next day, she wouldn't talk about the article, but I sensed that reading about herself described in that way tapped her deepest feelings of insecurity and shame. There she was, a seventy-three-year-old overnight success, feeling exposed—*contextualized*—by an art critic's brilliant psycho-socio-historic point.

I called up the *Times* critic and asked him how he got a hold of my mother's mental health record. He sounded surprised to hear that her "condition" was something we wanted kept private. He recommended I talk with my mother's gallery director. I called Donald. "Well yeah," he said in that up-speak intonation that Frida and all her twelve-year-old friends had been infected with. "I had something to do with it. I was sitting here with all this amazing work on my walls, and nobody was writing about it. Out of the thousands of exhibits opening this month in New York, how do you get people to notice one more unknown artist having her first solo show? I sent out a second press release playing up the age angle, and that reeled in a kid reporter from an NYU student newspaper—not the kind of ink that attracts people with anything other than a debit card. I wasn't gonna sit on my ass till the exhibit closed, praying that a one-inch review shows up seven months from now in an art magazine. Your mom's stuff is too good for that! So I pitched the mental illness angle, and it worked. Now you're gonna bust my balls because her show is completely sold out and I've got collectors from Hollywood to Hamburg calling me up? By the way, I just got an email from a curator at the Tate who's putting together an exhibition on manic depression and genius." I thanked Donald for his efforts, then I hollered at him for violating my mother's privacy. But it was too late. Every article about her show that came out after the *Times* piece contained the mental health issue, and there was nothing anyone could do to stop it.

Mom was down in the dumps for a week or two, but there wasn't much of an ego there to crush. Before long she was making pictures again in notebooks, on shoeboxes, across the pages of newspapers and sales catalogues, as well as on the canvases her part-time studio assistant stretched and primed for her. A different art dealer—a woman with a gallery in Chelsea—respectful of our concerns about how to represent Rose Mobley, came around

I Am Not An Issue *POETRY*

In his first epic rant, Bleu Mobley is a gay man, a battered wife, an African-American, a Muslim, a Jew, a homeless person, an undocumented worker, a crack baby, a refugee, a cancer patient, in foster care, on welfare, hungry, alone, schizophrenic, anorexic, bulimic, divorced, HIV-positive—a diversely abled, multi-cultured chorus of individuals who collectively proclaim their independence from the issues and symbols used to signify their plights.

2001, New Rivers Press, Moorhead, MN

twice a year, took whatever pieces she liked, put them into group shows at her gallery and entered them in national and international exhibitions with titles like: *Journals and Notebooks*, *Notations*, and *Drawing on Canvas*.

I'd been the subject of newspaper articles myself, experienced the unpleasantness that can come with being on the other side of the printed word, but for some reason, watching my mother become subject matter—an exemplar of *Art Brut* and *graphomania*—was much harder for me to accept. However loving my intentions may have been, there is no doubt that I set her up for a kind of scrutiny she never asked for or wanted.

Did I project my own desire to be recognized and understood onto my mother? I think so. And what of *my* work? How many times did I write about people or create fictional characters in order to peddle an agenda?

The release of *I Am Not An Issue* got me invited to read at the Nuyorican Poets Café, birthplace of the live poetry scene that had caught fire around the country, reviving the traditions of oral and lyric poetry for a new generation. To my surprise, the crush of young people that showed up to the café that night went wild for my defiant rant. Other invitations to appear at live poetry clubs led to getting a hip-hop band to back me up, releasing my first audio CD, and starting a fledgling career as a "performance poet."

if i am attacked,

> brutally beaten, or not so brutally,
>
> but repeatedly, or even just once,
>
> attacked, physically, verbally, eye-glancingly

attacked

> because i am gay,
>
> because someone *thought* i was gay,
>
> because i am black,
>
> because i am a muslim, or a sikh mistaken for a muslim,
>
> because i am a jew or an asian or south asian,
>
> or from south of the border,
>
> because i am alone,
>
> because i was thought to be any of the above,

if i am attacked

> in a thousand small ways and not so small ways
>
> because i am a woman,
>
> attacked by the man i cooked for and comforted,
>
> by the man i confided in, trusted and adored,
>
> if he forces himself on me,
>
> this man whose children i gave birth to and raised, then blackens my
> eyes and threatens to kill me, and you come to my aid, you shelter me,
> advise me, defend me, argue on my behalf,
>
> EVEN if you write an article or a book about me,
>
> or pass a law named after me,

remember,

> i am not an issue

if i am HIV-positive

> or have full-blown AIDS,
>
> if i have cancer, be it from negligence, genetics, bad luck, or my own stupidity,
>
> if i was doused with daily dosages of synthetic medications when i was a fetus,
> and have endured medical calamities because the pharmaceutical companies
> chose to bury their research in order to skyrocket their profits,
>
> if i am overweight, even obese by national, state or city standards,
>
> if i binge and barf or take diuretics because i think i'm fat even though i'm
> twenty-three years old and only weigh a hundred and ten pounds
>
> if i'm diagnosed schizophrenic or manicly depressed,
>
> if i am hungry, on welfare, or just became eligible for food stamps,

if i have good debt or bad debt or i'm so poor i couldn't possibly afford debt,

if i am homeless, living in a shelter, with a relative, or on the street,

and you see me and walk past me like i don't exist,

or you look at me with guilt in your eyes, or you pass me by

and then you turn around, reach into your pocket and give me change, or even a five spot, remember,

i am not an issue

if i was downsized,

right-sized, sized up and spit out,

if i am a single mother, work in a sweat shop,

am a limo driver or a refuse collector or a carpenter or teacher

and i belong to a union that my employer refuses to meet with,

if i have *no* union and no health insurance and no doctor to speak of,

if i bring my kids to the hospital emergency room when they get sick,

if i can't find a job in my field and i'm working as a cashier at the

supermarket handing you a credit card receipt for your signature,

if you know me only from

a picture you saw on tv or on the side of a milk carton,

if you heard talk of me on talk radio,

if i am the child of a broken family,

if i am an interracial child or of so much

mixed blood you can't even begin to define who or what i am,

if i was abused by a parent or a teacher or a priest,

if i had to foreclose on my home or my building was condemned,

if i once was in a gang,

if i was convicted falsely of a crime

or i did the deed and am paying for it,

if i got caught in the crosshairs of the war on drugs

or the war on terror or the war on crime,

if i'm serving fifteen to life,

if i am on death row in a state that does the deed,

if i am on death row in a state that hasn't done

the deed in a long time, but might at any time,

if i am in a juvenile detention center,

if i'm on parole

and you take a chance on me, give me a job, despite my having a record, remember,

i am not an issue

i am not your three-dimensional, walking-talking poster child,
though i thank you very much,

            i am not your issue

if i am dyslexic,

            or have ADD or HDD, or am "special ed material"
            if i am under- or over-achieving,
            if i'm in a failing or a sought-after school,
            if i was never able to go to college,
if i wrote my doctoral thesis on an issue of interest only to my thesis advisor,
            if i suffer from post-traumatic stress or some other "syndrome"
            if i had a family member killed on 9/11 or on flight 800
            or in oklahoma or afghanistan or lebanon or sudan or the gulf war,
            if i was shot by a gun that was purchased legally, or illegally,
            if my program was cut back then cut altogether,
            if my elected representative is charged with extortion or having sex with
            the wrong partner and you are running for his seat and a tape recording
            of your voice calls me up and asks for my vote,
      remember,
            i am not an issue

if i am an alien,

            that is to say, born on this planet but in another country,
            if the name of my country is known to you mostly as the name of a war,
            if i walked across deserts and mountains with all my belongings
            and my baby strapped to me,
            if english is my second, third or seventh language,
            if i'm applying for political asylum and placed in what they call
            "indefinite detention" without recourse to a lawyer,
      if my demographic category, ethnic designation or voting block is on a pie chart,
      if i changed careers eight times in my life like i'm supposed to,
      if i am diagrammed, cause and effected or double blind studied,
      if my name or number is printed in the report,
      if i am on the agenda of your meeting—or not,
even if i'm a sociological, anthropological, psychological, pharmacological phenomenon,
            remember,
                  i am not an issue

if i choose to have an abortion
or not
if i marry my same sex partner
or not
if i pray to a god you never even heard of
or not
if my children are required to learn 'creationism' side by side with evolution
or not
if i get a social security check when i retire
or not
if i vote this way or that
or not,
remember,
i am not an issue

if i am abducted, inducted, deducted, mandated, pro-rated, excoriated
or just plain fucking agitated, please
try to remember,
i am not an issue

if you visualize me into a set of data points, fund or de-fund, praise or dissect me,
remember,
i am not an issue
i'm not your issue
not your NGO's issue
not your auxiliary committee's issue
not your enemy's issue

i am a human being

if you'd like to get to know me,
or understand me
come over sometime and we can talk,
i can read you a poem i wrote,
or two

Rose Mobley was coming out of her shell in ways I never could have imagined. Friends visited her and took her on outings. Mail trucks came in and out of her driveway picking up and dropping off packages. She bought a cell phone, and on her own hired someone to design a website showcasing her art. She became so independent, she didn't mention *a word* to me when the Whitney Museum of Art bought one of her drawings. She also neglected to tell me that she was seeing a man she met at an art opening, or that she was applying for a passport so the two of them could fly to London together to attend an exhibition she was in.

Perhaps the biggest shocker was when I discovered that she'd stopped taking her meds. I called her doctor in a panic. "Sorry," he said, "I can't talk to you about a patient's treatment."

"She's my mother for God's sake!"

"That's right. She's your *mother*, not your child. Unless you become her legal guardian or she says it's okay, I am required by law not to share details of her case with anyone."

Soon as I started screaming, the guy caved. "Okay, Mr. Mobley. I hope I don't regret this. The answer is Yes, I *am* aware that your mother isn't taking her medications. I've been easing her down from them slowly, testing the waters, and then, without my say so, she just stopped taking them. And she seems fine. She is fine. I've had her blood levels checked and given her a complete…"

"How could she be fine?" I asked, confounded by his anwer. For years I'd been taking my mother for consultations with holistic shrinks who believe in treating mental illness with diet and herbs and the talking cure, and even *they* told me she would have to be on lithium and three or four other drugs for the rest of her life. And here was this run-of-the-mill *Medicaid* psychiatrist telling me it was fine that she wasn't taking her pills. I accused him of not caring about my mother, not knowing her like I did, and not having a scientific explanation for her recovery. All he could give me was a *theory*—that her metabolism might have changed and her disease simply ran its course.

I came to my own theory: my mother's cure, if that's what it was, had to do with her finally being accepted for who she was and for her art—by people other than her family. Whatever the reason, for the first time in over a half century, Rose Mobley wasn't a pharmaceutical conduit. She was thinking clearly, was more present and alive than ever, and feeling the joys and pains of life without them pushing her to the edge, or over it.

When she started spending weekends at her boyfriend Alvy's Upper West Side apartment, I was nervous. When they started traveling together, I thought, *Who the hell is this guy?* I found out later, Alvy wasn't the first man my mother had gone out with since my father.

For most of my life, my mother wasn't a reader. She knew how to read, but she couldn't concentrate on more than a page or two of text. I don't know whether Alvy got her interested in the news of the day (he was addicted to current affairs), or if she naturally became more inquisitive about the world as her fog lifted. All I know is, at seventy-four, she was subscribing to eight magazines and newspapers—and actually reading them. She'd never read my books, not cover to cover, but through the years she would read the reviews just to see if people were saying nice things about her son. Yet there she was—reading entire newspapers and engaging in conversations about national and international affairs.

The only downside to my mother's awakening was that it occurred at a time when the world was reeling out of control. In 1999, nearly everyone was talking about Y2K, the prospect of global infrastructure meltdowns, and—*the end of* just about everything. Adding fuel to this millennial fever were floods and storms the likes of which hadn't been seen in centuries. Then came 9/11, and the anthrax threats, and color-coded national security warnings; and everybody in New York waiting for the next shoe to drop, especially with the president trumpeting *War On Terror* with no end, disbanding civil liberties, enacting a foreign policy of preemptive war... The things my Rip Van Winkled mother was waking up to were enough to make anybody question their sanity. My mother's reaction to all of this was perfectly sane—she was saddened and scared, and then she started getting angry. And when she found out that Aconsha's brother Dilip had been detained for no good reason, and he wasn't allowed to see his family or talk to a lawyer or find out on what grounds he was being imprisoned, she was livid. *"We can't stand by and let them do this to him!"* she said, eyes bulging. *"You have to get him out of there, Bleu."* As if I could call up my good friends in the Justice Department or go on TV like Edward R. Murrow and shame the country out of its misguided witch hunts.

The End Of The End of Books Book *A NOVEL*

After twenty years in a psychiatric hospital, Claus Bauer is given a clean bill of health. His release comes at the cusp of a new millennium, at the height of the Y2K scare. Certifiably sane in a cracking-up world, he begins reading newspapers again and book reviews. Many of the books he reads about have titles like *The End of History and The Last Man, The End of Nature, The End of the Nation State, The End of Print*. There seems to be no end to these "End of" books. Filled with appreciation for his second chance in life, Claus starts typing sentences on his old manual typewriter. Over the course of a year he types enough sentences to comprise an entire book.

2002, Farrar, Straus, and Giroux, New York, NY

Dilip had been running late for a big show at the Javitz Convention Center when two police officers pulled him over at a security checkpoint on the Jersey side of the George Washington Bridge. Dilip knew the scene. He'd grown accustomed to the special treatment that came along with being a South Asian man in post-9/11 America. He'd learned to tuck in his anger, compliantly hand over his ID, describe his destination, put his hands up, and if he was driving to or from a job—open the trunk of his car and explain that he runs a business mounting multi-media presentations. But that morning, there was nothing he could say or do to satisfy the macho police officer who, according to Dilip, was "showing off in front of his rookie female partner." Dilip had recently traded in his van for a station wagon with big windows to avoid just these kinds of situations. Anyone could see that he had a car full of audiovisual equipment, but this cop made him take each item out of its case for inspection. After five minutes of this, Dilip made a mistake he would regret for a long time to come. He let a snide remark slip off the end of his tongue: *"And would you like me to bend over for an anal search, or do you suppose I've got the bomb strapped to my chest?"*

It took more than a week before Dilip's wife was informed that her husband was being imprisoned and interrogated in a privately-run detention center in Elizabeth, New Jersey. It took four months before he was finally released, with no charges. Inside "Wackenhut," Dilip heard the stories of Arabs, Muslims, and other South Asians who'd been picked up for overdue inspection stickers, expired visas, not exhibiting proper deference, or simply looking like the wrong kind of foreign on an Orange Alert day. Dilip explained to his interrogators that he felt as attacked on 9/11 as they did, that he was neither a Muslim nor an Arab, and Hinduism—the faith he was born into but didn't practice—is considered an ancient enemy of Muslims, though he held no animosity toward anyone of *any* creed. His interrogators (he never was sure if they were FBI, Homeland Security, or private contractors) threatened to charge him with any number of crimes; but it was the taunts about deportation that got him to confess his opposition to the U.S. bombing of Afghanistan, and to having some Muslim friends from Northern India and Pakistan.

A few months after Dilip was released, the president signed an Executive Order mandating the registration of all adult male foreign nationals from countries considered Arab, Muslim or South Asian. Hundreds of thousands of men were fingerprinted, photographed, and "interviewed" about their beliefs and associations. Not since the "relocation camps" that interned Japanese and Japanese-Americans during World War II, had the United States corralled so many foreign-born suspects within its own borders.

Even though India wasn't on the list of suspicious countries, and my pacifist brother-in-law (a permanent resident of the U.S.) had already been cleared of any evil-doing, he was called in for another round of questions. Someone had named him as a customer of a Jersey City record shop where many South Asians go to buy imported music and discuss politics. Dilip could see his interrogators referring to his previous round of interrogations, from a file that wasn't supposed to exist any longer (according to his lawyer) since an agreement had been reached to expunge any record of his (non-)detention in exchange for his not suing the government. After a two-hour interview, Dilip was released, but he never again felt like he was a part of this country. He moved his wife and kids out of New Jersey, back to India where he started what turned out to be a very successful digital imaging business

Before Dilip left, my mother urged him to tell people about his experience. "If ordinary Americans HEARD that this was happening in their country, they wouldn't stand for it." What they did to Dilip for saying something stupid and having associations with the "wrong kind of people," reminded her of the McCarthy era. "Only now, instead of commies, it's Muslims and Arabs we're supposed to be frightened of."

When her favorite cabdriver—a Sikh named Harjit, who occasionally drove her shopping, and to and from the train station—was badly beaten by two teenagers because they thought he was a Muslim, she implored me to write a book about the stupidity of Islamophobia. I told her I had something in the works, but it would come out under the name Dr. Sky Jacobs, an identity that had to remain a secret. "Oh, you don't have to worry about me spilling the beans," she said with an impish smile. "I've known you were Sky Jacobs for years."

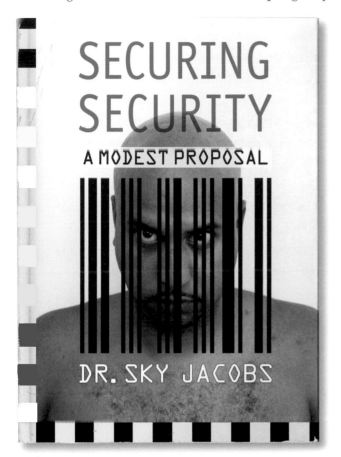

Securing Security *A MODEST PROPOSAL*

Following the 9/11 attacks, the federal government mounted a registration and interrogation program of all men residing in the U.S. from twenty-five mostly Arab and Muslim nations. While Dr. Sky Jacobs does sleep better at night knowing that these files exist, he worries that the Department of Homeland Security is getting complacent. In *Securing Security*, Jacobs lays out a plan that if enacted would surely secure America's sense of security once and for all. The final point of his 101 point proposal involves rounding up and penning in ALL men. "After all, if you took all the men off the streets, the world would be a safer place."

2002, Common Courage Press, Monroe, ME

My contract with U.S. Home Paper Corp—the world's third largest manufacturer of toilet tissue—stipulated that *The Poetry Roll* would be sold exclusively in supermarkets and grocery stores. This meant that an unimaginable number of people would be exposed to poetry on a daily basis. Even people who normally didn't read books could make their way through a seven or ten word poem as they sat on the toilet doing what they came to do.

With the help of a thirty-second TV ad that ran in major markets, and on-the-ground sales reps pushing their "exciting new line of toilet tissue," many of the large supermarket chains in the lower forty-eight, Canada, and the Philippines ordered *Poetry Rolls* for their stores. No book publisher on the planet could have managed that kind of distribution for a book of poetry.

As news of this unusual deal spread within the publishing industry, a number of literary connoisseurs accused me of being a sellout. I didn't let it bother me since I felt certain that this was the most revolutionary act of my life. They could keep their ivory towers— I had infiltrated the culture right where it sat; much credit due to Monica for seeing the potential in *The Poetry Roll*. One of the first things she did after I promoted her from Chief Writing Assistant to Director of Entrepreneurial Projects, was to look through my notebooks. I couldn't help but smile when she asked to see them, because I used to look through my students' notebooks hoping to unearth their overlooked diamonds in the rough. Fishing through boxes and boxes of

The Poetry Roll *TOILET PAPER POEMS*
When nature calls, you needn't sit there mindlessly staring at the wall or bathroom tiles. With *The Poetry Roll* you can read one or two very short poems, reflect on the words, then wipe and flush! Guaranteed non-toxic and biodegradable. Stripped to their bare essentials, these quick-reading poems—written by bestselling author Bleu Mobley—are perfect for people whose lives are so overflowing with things to do, they don't have time to enjoy the poetry of life.

2003, U.S. Home Paper Corp, Stamford, CT

old stuff, Monica came across a pad (at least twenty-years-old) that had a sketch I'd made of someone sitting on the toilet reading a roll of toilet paper. Under it I'd written, *The Poetry Scroll*. She pointed out the sketch to me and said, "Let's do this." I had no recollection of making the drawing but thought it would be a good format for these very short poems I'd been writing through the years.

Out of thousands of mini-poems, we selected fifty for a prototype, which we made using iron-on photocopy transfers. I wasn't sure whether we should publish the *Poetry Rolls* ourselves or look for a publisher of limited-edition poetry books. Monica admonished me

sample leaves   THE POETRY ROLL

wipe

sitting here
reading,
lost for a moment
in eternity

pre-emptive strike

war begets democracy
like a blowtorch
waters the lawn

new-age therapist

replaces pills
with megadoses
of compassion

one man show

corey faces reality,
draws many
dark conclusions

for thinking small, and convinced me that we should send proposals to the major toilet paper companies. "What have we got to lose?" she said confidently describing her vision of *Poetry Rolls* being sold in every grocery store across America. I liked her thinking and felt reassured that I'd made the right choice promoting her.

After getting turned down by the two largest toilet paper companies, I was ready to print up twenty rolls to give away as presents, but then we got the call from U.S. Home Paper Corp. Our first meeting with the CEO, Raymond Maxwell, was very promising. It got trickier when we started meeting with his "people" since most of them equated poetry with Hallmark greeting cards. Luckily, Maxwell knew a little about haikus from his wife who had taken a class on Basho and Rumi when she was at Smith College and considered herself an expert on "Eastern poetry." She explained to her husband that the best short poems "stimulate the reader's imagination to fill in the gaps for themselves."

We found out later that Maxwell's wife just happened to find our prototype lying around his office, read the poems, and convinced her husband to "grab this thing" before one of his competitors did. She'd recently caught him in bed with another woman, and he was desperate to get back in his wife's good graces. By the time he contacted us, Maxwell was touting *The Poetry Roll* as a way of re-branding U.S. Home Paper Corp as the company who brought together the act of sitting on the toilet with the act of reading—something people had been doing for ages, but hadn't capitalized on.

Once the major hurdles were cleared within the company, there still was the matter of the poems themselves, many of which (though short) were not sweet. The poems we used as examples in the prototype were relatively mild. When it came time to choose the final selection for the first printing, I saw no reason to hold back. After all, we had a thousand and one squares to fill! So we front-ended the roll with pastorals and unsexy love poems, but by the 200th sheet, we started putting in more provocative poems that touched on things like greed, preemptive war, incest, obesity... Since they weren't book publishers, U.S. Home Paper Corp didn't have editors for the content of their products. (The only editors they had were in their marketing and packaging divisions.) They trusted me to make sure the poems were catchy and spelled correctly, just like they trusted the people who designed their floral rolls to make sure all the flowers had petals and looked pretty. And we trusted U.S. Home Paper Corp to make sure their paper was soft to the touch, had perforations between each sheet, and millions of rolls got shipped out to tens of thousands of stores.

Unfortunately, there was a tremendous uproar as soon as customers in the Midwest and down South started reading the leaves of their new toilet paper. This reaction came as a total surprise to the mucky-mucks at U.S. Home Paper Corp who never bothered to read past the first thirty poems. As soon as complaints started coming in, Maxwell and his people rolled out a *Poetry Roll* onto their conference table and started reading. By the end of that day, all *Poetry Rolls* were recalled. Lawyers on both sides claimed breach of contract, and our dreams of a resurgent appreciation of poetry infused into every day experience were flushed down the toilet.

at the conference

inside:
academicians pontificated

outside:
pigeons encircled
the square

nature

something as lovely
as a tree
can only be seen
on *public* t.v.

urban removal

your renovation,
my eviction—
a neighborhood booms

clemency

a horsehoe
lands in a prison cell
sprouts golden wings

over the summer

politicians
legislated the universe
out of the university

girlie men

wage sensitive
bored soldiers
write poetry

When I was a kid, I used to walk along the East River, just a few blocks from Queens-bridge Housing, inhaling the odors of a big old paint factory, wondering if the different smells on different days were the smells of different colors. Since I couldn't see through the factory's soot-encrusted windows, I imagined huge vats of color that the workers would swim in when their bosses weren't looking. As I got older, my fantasies about the place matured. Instead of swimming in the paint, the workers would throw the dismembered body parts of despised bosses into vats of crimson and ruby red. In all my imaginings, it never entered my mind that I might return one day and become the owner of that paint factory.

Aconsha needed a rehearsal space somewhere in the city for her dance company; I needed a place to store 600,000 *Poetry Rolls* (thanks to my lawyer who worked out a settlement with U.S. Home Paper Corp); and our accountant had been urging us to invest in real estate. When I saw that the former paint factory on Vernon Boulevard was for sale, I was curious and went to take a look.

It turns out, the old factory was more than one building; it's a square block complex of four buildings with an inner courtyard—far more space than Aconsha and I needed. Many of the soot-drenched windows now were covered in ivy. Others were boarded up. Doors were graffitied, bricks needed pointing, gutters had all but disintegrated—yet, standing on the roof, looking out at the East River and the Manhattan skyline, I couldn't contain the fireworks going off inside me at the prospect of owning this place.

I decided I would buy the property, renovate it, and rent out most of the spaces at affordable rates to non-profit organizations, small businesses, artists and craftspeople with the hope of turning this otherwise dead part of town into a thriving, creative community.

But there was a hitch. The realtor neglected to tell me that people were squatting inside those buildings; entire families had been living there for years! When I had asked about the beds that were there and the tables and chairs and refrigerators, she told me that the buildings had been used as shooting galleries and clubhouses, "but that was a long time ago." The truth is, the listing agent was engaged in an all-out war against the squatters—*seventeen of them*—who had been evacuated several times by the police, had gotten themselves a volunteer lawyer, and were asserting their rights of occupation on the grounds of having fixed up the buildings with their own sweat equity and rescued the block away from drug users and rats.

The night before I was scheduled to close on the property, the squatters retook two of the four buildings, barricaded the doors, and held a *Let It Be*-style rooftop concert with rap groups and hip-hop poets spouting revolutionary messages to the ever-expanding crowd on the streets below. Alerted to the "action" in advance, the New York news media was there in full force. Headlines on the evening news and in the morning papers decried:

Bleeding Heart Author Swats Squatters

Bleu Mobley In Battle Royale With Homeless Families

HOMETOWN BOY RETURNS TO QUEENS WITH VENGEANCE

BLEU MOBLEY TO HOMELESS FAMILIES: GET OUT!

I cancelled the closing and had a meeting with the squatters, prepared to settle the problem with reason and cash.

My sense of entitlement as the legitimate owner-in-waiting crumbled at the sight of the squatters sitting across the table from me: the waitress/songwriter and her adorable twin toddlers, the gay couple who once owned a clothing store but ran into hard times when one of them contracted AIDS, the Rastafarian gardener, the collective of found-object artists, and the anarchist ringleader who calls herself Zora (not, she said, after Zora Neal Hurston, but after Zorro, feminized). Once everybody introduced themselves, I felt completely disarmed. What hat was I going to wear in this meeting? My champion of the underdog hat wasn't going to hold any sway with these people. My peacemaker hat was of little use. I'm sure all Zora and her compatriots saw was a middle-aged man in a robber-baron top hat.

"Under the legal principle known as *Adverse Possession*," explained their lawyer, a well known advocate for radical causes, "my clients' decade-long occupation make them the effective owners of the property. In any case, they can't be forced out of their common-law homes without going through eviction proceedings in housing court." My lawyer made the case that I was purchasing the property from the title holder, fair and square, and besides that I had plans to rent out three of the buildings and was open to renting to any of them at a good rate. Zora waited till my lawyer was through, then launched into an impassioned monologue about the human right to shelter as described in the *Universal Declaration of Human Rights* adopted by the UN in 1948. She took out her wallet and showed me a photograph of her Navajo grandfather, quoting him saying something about the fallacy of land ownership. For the first time in my life I was speechless. My lawyer scuttled an effort to set up another meeting, hoping she could get me to stop empathizing with the opposition.

"Do you *want* the place or not?"

"I thought I wanted it, but I need time to think all this through."

The listing agent didn't wait for me to get back in the game. He had the squatters removed again and continued showing the property. After discussing the situation with Aconsha, I met with representatives of the squatter group without any lawyers and offered to let them have one of the buildings. Zora asked what I meant by *have*.

"Live there rent free. You'd only have to pay utilities."

"Why can't you just deed the building to us?"

"I thought you don't believe in owning property?"

"In a perfect world, we don't. But this isn't a perfect world. On paper we will own it, but in our hearts we'll simply be grateful to the earth for the use of the space."

"I don't even know if I'm allowed to subdivide the property, but if I can, I will."

We shook hands and went to our lawyers with the outlines of an agreement. Somehow, those outlines showed up in the local news the next day. The Department of Buildings

Author Brokers Deal With Squatters

weighed in objecting to any such agreement because "those buildings are zoned for commercial use only." We could apply for a zoning change, but approval could take years.

All the news reports describing the tug of war over the 17,000-square-foot complex across from the East River stirred up new interest in the property. Suddenly two other bidders were jacking up the price. I matched the new bids and raised them. My bids were met and raised, then met and raised again by me with a price that was equal to what I could have paid for a property in Manhattan. That's when I came to my senses and pulled out.

Aconsha and I ended up buying a building in the South Bronx, in a neighborhood the realtor kept calling *Mott Haven*. From time to time we got together with Zora, who became a friend and was still squatting with her cabal in the old paint factory. Several people almost bought the place after I backed out, but the Power Authority gave itself the authority to build a "temporary" power plant directly across the street, spoiling the view of the river and the Manhattan skyline, insuring that nobody of any financial wherewithal would ever want to live there. When we asked Zora about the rumors that she actively lobbied *for* the power plant and *against* the locals opposing it, she laughed. "Now why would I go and do a thing like that?"

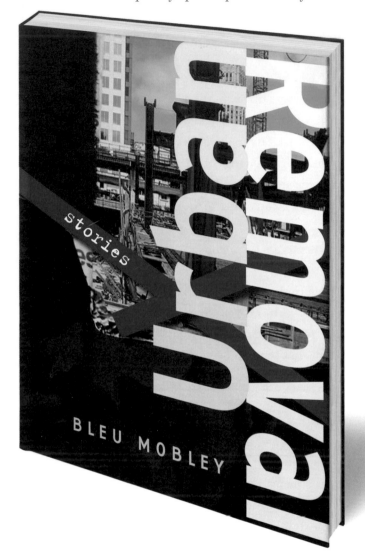

Urban Removal   SHORT STORIES

Immigrants, artists, and other outpost residents transform "undesirable" neighborhoods into thriving, picturesque communities. Once the real estate agents and land speculators find out, property values escalate, new people move in, others are forced out. Old story. End of story. Or is it? In *Urban Removal*, Bleu Mobley tells uncommon tales of individuals and communities fighting back against development and displacement.

2003, Grove, New York, NY

excerpt [from the story *The UnBeautification Campaign*]

Already gentrified out of two neighborhoods, the sculptor Celia Bigwater was dead set on not having to relocate again.

In the early seventies, with a year-and-a-half of art school behind her, and dreams of being an artist in the art capital of the world, Celia moved from Sante Fe to New York City, where she rented the ground floor of an abandoned textile factory in SoHo [South of Houston Street] for $175 a month. She exterminated the rats, fixed the windows, put up walls, sanded the floors, installed kitchen and bathroom fixtures, planted trees out front, mosaicked the front door, and opened her studio to the public for salons, studio visits, and performances. Over the course of fifteen years, Celia—along with other artists, bohemians and homosexuals—transformed this once industrial district into a vibrant village. Once the hard work was done, real estate people descended, galleries morphed into boutiques, and limousines crept into the SoHo night depositing the chic to nouveau restaurants.

Skyrocketing rents forced Celia to move out of Manhattan to Brooklyn, where she and other dislodged artists helped alchemize other neighborhoods into desirable meccas. In less than half the time it took to turn SoHo *around*, Celia's Brooklyn neighborhood gentrified beyond her means. Once again, she found herself looking for abandoned buildings, this time in Queens. Living in the perennially unhip borough wasn't her first choice, but Celia found a deal on an old bread factory in an industrial part of a mostly Guyanese neighborhood known as Richmond Hill. At first, Celia couldn't figure out why these people from Guyana—which she thought was a country in the Caribbean—looked, sounded and cooked food like people from India. It didn't take long before she found out that her Guyanese neighbors were indeed of East Indian ancestry. According to Gupta Subramanium, the corner grocer and neighborhood historian, back in 1838, two hundred Indians got shipped out of Calcutta as indentured laborers to work on British sugar plantations in what was then British Guyana. It took eighty years of unspeakable subjugation and fierce rebellions before indentureship was finally abolished in Guyana. "But it wasn't until 1966 that we won our independence from Britain. Imagine that!" Gupta exclaimed to Celia, his hands raised in front of a poster of the wild-eyed, four-armed Kali, the fearsome goddess known for destroying ignorance. "The United States won its independence from the Brits in 1776, but Guyana didn't unshackle itself from the imperial dragon till the U.S. was heading to the moon! That's why so many of us decided to come here. We wanted a piece of that moonglow for ourselves. You know, there are 40,000 of us Indo-Guyanese living in this one neighborhood, and after all these years we are still connected to our customs back in India. I've never set foot on Indian soil, but the blood, the spirit, the stories—*it's all in here*," Gupta said pointing to the center of his chest.

After years as a renter, Celia became part of the ownership society. Her ancestors, Navajos from the Rio Grande Valley, never even had words in their vocabulary for landowner or real estate. They saw themselves as custodians of a sacred land marked by vast deserts bordered by thickly forested mountains. But then the Anglos arrived in the 16th century and took possession of "Nuevo Mexico" in the name of the Spanish crown. Celia's ancestors didn't understand they could lose something they never had the right to possess. By 1848, the northern part of Mexico (what later became New Mexico, Arizona, California and parts of Colorado, Utah, and Nevada) was annexed by the United States after a bloody war. A little less than a hundred years later, Celia was born on a reservation in Central New Mexico to a weaver and a woodworker. Though she picked up a few skills during her stint in art school, Celia learned most of what she needed to know from her parents about functioning in the world and making things with her hands that were beautiful and solid. By the time she was 56, she learned other things about surviving in a big city that ran counter to the lessons she'd learned from her parents:

- - Don't make the outside of your home look too pretty.
- - Buy a little something for yourself or forever be moving to the next outpost.
- - Sometimes you must follow the path of the trickster.

Just as the appeal of *ethnic Queens* was leaching its way into feature articles in the real estate sections of the New York papers, Celia bought her building on a "bad street" on the "wrong side" of a "problematic" neighborhood. On either side of her place were condemned buildings, and across the street—an empty lot with a trailer that functioned as a clubhouse for a teen gang. Nearer to the center of town, many of the Guyanese families had already spruced up the outsides of their small homes with ornate iron gates made of intricate interlacing patterns crowned with white and gold Ganeshes (potbellied elephant deities known for destroying obstacles and paving the way for success). Despite her love of natural light, Celia kept the windows on the street side of her building boarded up. She added graffiti to the front door. Inside, she built an incredible sculpture studio (her best yet), and a very comfortable living space with a lush indoor garden and a Japanese-style pebble fountain.

Within ten months of Celia's move to Richmond Hill, a large real-estate developer "discovered" the area and started buying up properties. Then the Housing Authority approved a plan from another developer to build a high-rise luxury condo complex. The developer's vision encompassed a four block area with six high rises, a three-story parking garage, indoor tennis courts, and a shopping center. All they had left to do was find investors, buy out all the current residents of the four-block area, hold one or two public hearings, and fast-track an environmental impact plan.

Once a fairly low-keyed basset hound of a person, Celia turned pit-bull almost overnight. As the real estate people started bringing around potential buyers, Celia started putting up signs. The first sign was about Richmond Hill and its proximity to JFK airport:

> **WELCOME TO RICHMOND HILL**
> **WHERE AIRPLANES CONSTANTLY FLY OVERHEAD**
> **MAKING UNBEARABLE NOISE**
> **DROPPING PEE AND POOP ON OUR HEADS**

When the real estate ladies came around with important-looking people, if there wasn't a plane flying over at the time, Celia would supply an auditory illustration with the help of two powerful speakers and an old sound effects record. The real-estate ladies would be standing there talking to some suits, pointing into the air toward the future high-rises, and suddenly they'd be drowned out by the deafening sound of a supersonic jet coming in for a landing. Celia got such a kick out of spoiling their deals. One time she started screaming, "A rat! A rat!" Fleeing from the supposed rodent, she just happened to run into a tour in progress. "We've got a mayor who fired the people who control the pests. He is a mouse, our mayor. A *cartoon!* But that's okay because he's *our* cartoon. Put a suit on Mickey Mouse, he looks just like the mayor. Don't you think?"

Everyone looked at Celia like she was insane. That gave her an idea for her next sign:

> **HALFWAY HOUSE COMING SOON.**
> **MENTAL HEALTH PATIENTS MAY NOW APPLY.**

The battleground was not just in Celia's neighborhood. Much of the borough had to be saved from the real-estate vultures. Someone had recently written a bestselling book about all the new immigrants in Queens, and now everyone was coming there to eat in the ethnic restaurants, shop for bargain imports, and deep pockets from Manhattan were buying up houses, jacking up the prices. Celia put copies of her next sign all around the borough:

> **QUEENS IS A RAT-INFESTED PLACE**
> **WITH CUTTHROAT CRACK-HEADS**
> **WHO DON'T SPEAK ENGLISH**

As Celia's scheme caught on, other residents of the borough began putting up signs:

> **WASTE TRANSFER STATION COMING SOON**

> **METHADONE CLINIC**
> **NEXT RIGHT →**

A lot of Queens' homeowners—no matter how small their property—keep up proud little gardens. But many of these people, taxpayers all, were more terrified by the prospect of their houses getting reassessed and their neighborhoods changing than they were attached to their gardens. Neighbors reached out to Celia for guidance. She started conducting *Unbeautification* workshops. She taught brick scarring, weed proliferation, stoop decrepitation, and indoor gardening techniques. Within a few months, *The UnBeautification Campaign* spread throughout the borough as thousands of Queenszites made their pretty little dwellings as unkempt as they could possibly live with. On the one hand it was an awful shame making a mess of such quaint neighborhoods. On the other hand—*it was working*. The borough's reputation began to sink back to its former maligned status, and tens of thousands of inhabitants, including Celia and her neighbors, were able to breathe a sigh of working-class relief.

7

SEMIOTIC OCTOPUS

Mom stroked my hair.

I wanted to comfort her, but she was comforting me. "There's nothing wrong with letting her see you cry," said Darlene, the hospice volunteer who had become the indispensable member of my mother's caretaking team.

Ever since I was a kid I tried to be strong for my mother. As I got older, being strong meant not expecting her to be anyone other than who she is, which necessitated steering clear of certain subjects. But I sensed she was ready, before she died, to tell about my father. If she had anything to tell.

Then it was too late, and all I could do by that point was allow myself to cry into her soft shoulder. The cerebral aneurysm made it impossible for her to talk, and the emphysema made her extremely weak. She smiled a lot, though, frail as she was, wafer-thin, her head peering out from the covers. She could smile with her eyes almost till the end, and hum tunes. Some tunes were recognizable. Others rose up like deep chanting from some primordial well. When she couldn't draw anymore, she sang. When she couldn't sing, she hummed. When she no longer could hum, she looked at me and the girls and Aconsha and Alby with reassurances—*It's okay, sweeties.*

Before she was bedridden, I would dance Mom to the bathroom. It could take a half hour to go ten feet. Micro-step by micro-step, we'd dance the entire round trip, me singing, her humming any song either of us could think of. It took a while before I could let go of needing to talk with her, and of needing her to keep on living. Darlene Santos was my guide. She never wrote a book or had a school of thought named after her, but she was a genius when it came to helping people die in a dignified way; helping the family as much or more than the person dying.

"Hold your mother, Mr. Mobley," Darlene said to me one afternoon when the absence of words seemed unbearable.

"Please, call me Bleu."

"Hold your mother, Bleu. There's nothing to be afraid of. This is the other end of life. A lot of babies come popping out who don't look so great either. The minute a baby comes out of the womb, everybody wants to hold her and cradle her. When she's going out the other way, why don't we do the same thing? She doesn't need to talk back. A baby doesn't talk back. Just say, You did good, Ma."

"You did good, Mom," I'd say after she swallowed a spoonful of pureed vegetables or smashed bananas. Feeding could take hours. She'd want to feed me back. We giggled together like parent and child. I'd turn on the news to see what the news was saying about the war in Iraq, thinking that would get her fired up. She went with us on several marches against the war. The first time, we got penned in with tens of thousands of protesters, cordoned off on Second Avenue by police barricades preventing us from joining the rally on First Avenue, where I was scheduled to speak. Mom started a chant. *"Let Us Through! Let Us Through!"* It rippled out in all directions until thousands were roaring her matter-of-fact demand. Ella proudly carried the sign that her grandma had painted:

A few weeks later we marched on the nation's capital. It was her and Ella's first march on Washington. Mom couldn't get over the endless sea of people peaceably insisting on peace. She felt so connected that day, so filled with hope knowing she was one of millions of people around the world marching against starting a war. On her last protest march, after the war started, she power-wheelchaired through the streets of the capital and down the mall, incensed that the drunk frat boy and his puppeteers didn't listen to us. A little more than a year later, after the artery in her brain ruptured, the war—the war against the war, and the other stories the TV and newspapers deemed important—didn't have much meaning for her anymore. She could process what was going on, but it became noise to her.

Darlene explained: "When you get near the end, life really narrows. There comes a time you're not interested in what's going on in the world anymore. Some people's lives are pretty narrow to begin with and it just gets narrower and narrower till it gets to the point all you care about is when you last pooped, getting something wet inside your mouth, loosening the elastic on your oxygen mask—and with your mother, she loves kisses, which is nice. It doesn't get sweet like that with everybody. Dying can bring out the worst in some people."

I told Darlene about Sidney Lewiston, how lucid he was before he died.

"Some people are lucky. Before they narrow down, they can go through a life review."

"Exactly! Sidney got to do that with his kids, his girlfriend, even with me. He made amends and started a new chapter."

"They were lucky. But you and your mother are lucky too. You're communicating in other ways."

"I know."

"Can I ask you something, Bleu?"

"Sure. Anything."

"Did you ever fight your mom? I'm sure when you were a teenager, you rebelled."

"I fought the rest of the world, but not her so much. Even with all her problems, she was a sanctuary. She rarely ever judged me."

Two nights before she died, a little past 3 a.m., my mother sat up in bed. I know because Frida was with her. She called us on the phone to hurry over.

"Grandma gestured for me to get her something to draw with," Frida said when we got there. "I brought her a pad and pen but she shook her head and made a brushing motion with her hand." Somehow Frida had known that her grandmother wanted the paints she'd started using before the aneurysm. Frida had gone upstairs and grabbed some oil paints and brushes. "Grandma slid the brushes and her blanket to the side, took a tube of yellow and squeezed out a large circle onto the bed sheet. I don't know where she got the strength. It happened so quickly, I wasn't sure what to do except help her by keeping the sheet flat."

By the time Aconsha and I got there, the bed was already a blazing sun—of ochres, golds, and siennas. Mom sat propped against the bedboard with her knees to her chest, smiling mischievously, exhausted. I ran back to our house to grab a camera. By the time I made it back, the sheets were already changed and she was asleep.

After Mom died, I continued to visit her house.

I would lie on the floor of her bedroom looking through the pages of her notebooks, trying to know this unknowable person who I'd known all my life. I could feel her presence in that room, and when I slept, sometimes she would come to me in my dreams, which is probably why I slept a lot after she died. When I wasn't sleeping or pretend sleeping, I made sure to go into work, show face at least once a day. I showered, brushed my teeth and hair, got dressed as normal, and tried my best not to brood openly in front of the girls who were grieving too. I didn't want to burden Aconsha either with my dyspeptic meditations—the what ifs, and if onlys, the might've, should've beens—and the daydreams of slitting,

       swallowing,

           jumping,

               shooting,

                   dangling,

                       running out into the middle of. . .

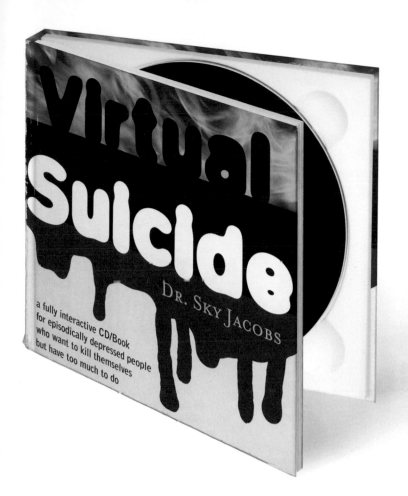

Virtual Suicide *INTERACTIVE CD ROM*
A fully interactive electronic book/CD-Rom for episodically depressed people who dream about killing themselves but have too much to do. Choose from dozens of traditional and unconventional ways of committing suicide, then select a method or invent your own, and *virtually* experience your own death. Choose from sample templates to write your suicide note. Witness reactions to your death and attend your own virtual funeral. Go to virtual heaven. Meet your virtual maker. "When I first tried Dr. Sky Jacobs' *Virtual Suicide*, I was skeptical. Then the day after I virtually killed myself, I got up and went to work feeling better than I have in years!"
New Age Journal

2004, Voyager, New York, NY

Having finished her homework for the night, Ella walked into the living room where I was watching television, a book face down on my lap. I put the book on the floor to make room for her. A gallery of disturbing images flashed across our widescreen TV, settling in on one of naked men piled on top of each other, circles of digital fog covering their private parts. Behind the mound of light brown- skinned bodies stood a white man and a white woman in U.S. military fatigues, smiling, thumbs in the air. Another photograph showed a naked man on his hands and knees, a leash around his neck. Ella asked what I was watching. I grabbed the remote control and pressed OFF. My ten-year-old daughter had caught me watching the pornography of the evening news.

"*Nothing*, sweetheart. Just the news."

"From the war in Iraq?"

"Yeah, the war of terror."

"What?"

"Never mind."

"Were those pictures of the terrorists, Daddy?"

"Um. Well, it's complicated, honey."

"But what were those pictures?"

"Just bad things that happen in war."

"Bad people doing bad things?"

"Probably good people doing bad things."

"Can you still be a good person if you do bad things?"

"That's an excellent question, pumpkin."

sample pages

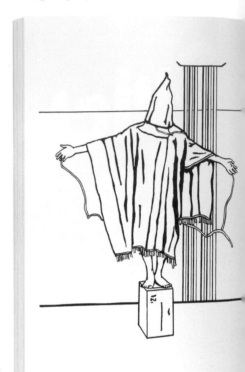

BEST SELLER

U.S. versus Them

COLORING BOOK

Bestselling author Bleu Mobley and Cuban-American illustrator Marianna Loyola have created a coloring book celebrating U.S. military interventions since World War II. Filled with bold compositions based on real events, *U.S. versus Them* presents the user with iconic history lessons, while it challenges the necessity of always having to stay within the lines (such as those established by the Geneva and other Human Rights Conventions). It may not always make a pretty picture, but it's time Americans faced the on-ground sacrifices so many people have made in order to bring democracy and freedom to all parts of the globe.

2004, Graphic Language Press, Aquebogue, NY

I would have made *U.S. versus Them* a Dr. Sky Jacobs book, but after the firestorm *Virtual Suicide* ignited (with parenting and mental health groups going apeshit, the publisher

recalling the product, and the sudden cancellation of the *Radio Sky* syndication), I decided to suspend the good doctor's writing and radio career indefinitely. No more hiding behind pseudonyms. Whatever I had to say, I'd say it as myself. With Monica's encouragement, I decided to take control of the publication and distribution of all new projects. No more conditional contracts. No more getting my work pulled from shelves without consent. Everyone in my team agreed, in the age of e-entrepreneurship, we were better off going directly to the people.

Chrysalis (my new interactive media person) put up a website for *U.S. versus Them*. It just sat there for months, getting the occasional sale. *So much for e-entrepreneurship*, I thought. Eight months later, a very popular Italian blogger put up a post describing *U.S. versus Them* as a "must-have work of visual agit-prop lit." He put a link to our website and in one day we were bombarded with sales from Italy. The online buzz spread through Europe, then the Middle East and Latin America. Eventually (with the lion's share of sales coming from overseas), *U.S. versus Them* became *the* bestselling coloring book of all times.

From a transcript of an interview on a top-rated right-wing cable TV news program. BO = The Host. BM = Bleu Mobley.

BO: Welcome to the show, sir.

BM: Thank you for having me.

BO: So, Mr. Mobley. I understand you grew up in the projects in New York City. Your mother was an immigrant. And she raised you herself.

BM: That's right.

BO: And you learned how to print books in public school. And now you're a bestselling author. Won lots of awards, the whole nine yards. You've obviously been able to express yourself freely, pursue your dreams. I understand you have a wife and two kids and a very nice house on Long Island. I presume you have a car. Maybe you have several cars. I'm not saying I know everything about you, sir, but it seems to me like you've been able to acquire the American Dream. So let me ask you one question: Given all that it's given you, why do *hate* this country so much?

BM: I wouldn't say I hate this country at all.

BO: Well, would you say you love it?

BM: It's hard for me to say I *love* a country. I do love a lot of what this country stands for though. And I—*Marianna Loyola* and I—wanted to clear up some of the misunderstandings about the United States that are becoming all too prevalent around the world these days.

BO: Oh, like what kind of misunderstandings?

BM: Like the perception that the United States is a selfish nation. I think that's not at all true.

BO: You're whetting my curiosity. Tell me more.

BM: After the attack on the World Trade Towers and the Pentagon, many Americans asked, "Why do they hate us?" Of course the answer is: Because we *love* them so much.

BO: Continue.

BM: As the sole superpower and the richest country in the world. We could simply stay home and enjoy our wealth, our freedom and democracy. But we're not that kind of country. We *love* our way of life and we're confident it's the best way to live. If we were a selfish nation, the story would end there.

BO: I can't disagree with that.

BM: Since we are, by nature, a generous nation, we are compelled to spread our way of life to those less fortunate than us. For instance, a country might be in danger of getting toppled by its communist neighbors. Or a country might have a military dictator ruling over it, or it might have a democratically elected president who is not friendly toward free enterprise, or it might be a breeding ground for drug traffickers or terrorists. Whatever scourge has befallen a foreign country, particularly a weaker, strategically situated foreign country, the United States—depending on its mood and political will at the time—has often been poised to liberate it. While other large nations may talk the talk, the U.S. takes action.

BO: You baffle me, sir. I had you for a left-wing peacenik!

BM: I'm not left wing or right wing. I am but a wingless writer with two left feet.

BO: But this book of yours, *U.S. versus Them*, doesn't have any *writing* in it at all.

BM: You're right about that. In this book, my collaborator Marianna Loyola (an amazing illustrator) and I wanted to make visible—through pictures—the proud history of United States foreign interventions after World War II, be they overt, covert, infamous, or forgotten.

BO: Hmmm.

BM: After the United States pre-emptively invaded Iraq, and then it was found to be torturing its war prisoners and engaging in all kinds of gruesome activities, we heard so many people here and abroad say—*This is not the United States of America that we know. The United States doesn't start wars. The United States doesn't lie. The United States doesn't deliberately kill innocents or kidnap them to countries that torture.* The fact of the matter is: the United States has a long tradition of getting down and dirty, of sacrificing its sons and daughters and its laws and moral codes of conduct, in order to save another country from its darker self.

BO: Okay, Mr. Mobley. You had me going there for a while, but now I *know* you're a traitor.

BM: And we wanted to allow readers everywhere to retrace the courageous acts of . . .

BO: That's it! Get the hell out of my studio right now, you filthy son of . . .

 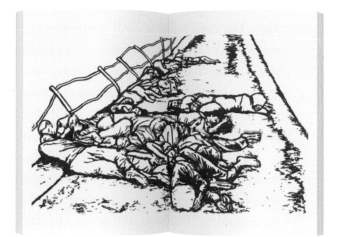

"Why do you call them 'pamphlets,' Daddy?" Frida asked, eyes rolling. "You're BLOGGING! You and Al Gore might have *invented* the internet, but it's like, so far ahead of you guys now."

My sixteen-year-old daughter had a MySpace page and a blog, and I didn't even know about it. I understood that she'd reached the age where she needed to separate her identity from her parents', but it still was painful finding out that I wasn't one of her 83 *Friends*. Regardless of my out-of-network status, she took time out of her busy schedule to show me how easy it was to create a blog. "Anything you see or hear that you want to share, any thought that pops into your head, you just put it up there."

The next day I asked Chrysalis to put up a blog page for me on my pamphlet series website **whenidiotsrule.com**. Months passed before I entered anything on it. Then the 43rd president of the United States was elected for a second term—despite his crimes against humanity, the truth, the Constitution, international law, and the English language. Within minutes of posting my first short commentary, a reader posted a response. I posted a response to the response. Somebody else responded to my response, and something she said inspired me to write another entry.

Before long I was blogging every day, not only on my own blog but as a contributor to other blogs. I blogged on matters global, national, state, city, town, block, kitchen sink, dew drop. In less than six months, I was hooked on a medium that requires none of the patience book projects require, is free of gatekeepers, and provides instantaneous feedback, 24/7. The more worried I became—about the world my kids were growing up in, and about my country devolving into a proto-fascist empire—the more my blog entries took on a kind of breathlessness, of someone trying to come from behind in the last laps of a do-or-die race. The race was between humankind's reptilian self (slithering toward extinction) and our more evolved self (capable of learning from failures and changing course). It was also *loads of fun* firing off intercontinental word missiles and watching responses roll in. The more outrageous my blog entries and essays became, the more fodder they provided for the chattering punditocracy—that shrill choir I would soon join myself when I accepted a salaried position as an in-house crank on one of the major cable news networks.

The head honcho at the network seduced me into accepting the job. "You can really make a difference," he said, proceeding to count off however many millions of viewers they have, scores of countries they broadcast to, and number of figures there would be in my salary. "I want you to be your provocative self, no holds barred. As long you are entertaining, and mindful of FCC regulations, you can say whatever's on your mind."

I accepted the job on the condition that I wouldn't have to commute into the city and could do the live feeds from an affiliate station ten miles from my home on Long Island. Maybe you saw me during that period of time, any of three nights a week on either of two shows, a disembodied head in a floating rectangular screen, trying to inject my two cents into the polarized fray.

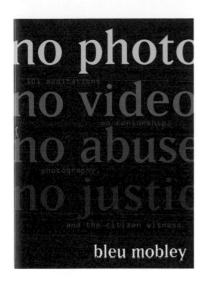

When Idiots Rule Series PAMPHLETS
In the tradition of Thomas Paine, bestselling author and social critic Bleu Mobley presents a series of common-sense pamphlets with essays and meditations on the current state of leadership and democracy in the United States and an ever-shrinking global village. Readers can add their own comments and download each pamphlet absolutely FREE at **www.whenidiotsrule.com**. For hard copies send $5 per pamphlet (for postage) to: Graphic Language, PO Box 186, Aquebogue, NY, 11777.

2004-2005, Graphic Language Press, Aquebogue, NY

excerpt   NO PHOTO

MEDITATION 31

Materials recovered from raids on Al-Qaeda compounds included photographs of buildings and other potential targets such as bridges, waterways, power plants, and subways. Soon after the recovery of these materials, the mayor of New York announced a *No Photo* policy—no photography allowed in subways, by waterways and bridges, and of government or landmark buildings. Photographers complained, but the policy held. Then the tourism industry complained, and the mayor retracted the policy. Several years after the policy was retracted, the retraction was retracted, and the *No Photo* policy was reinstated.

A few years later, after it became known that terrorists also utilize drawing as a means of preparing for attacks, the mayor of New York outlawed drawing in subways, by waterways and bridges, and of government or landmark buildings. As would be expected in a city that considers itself the center of the art world, there was a loud (if small) hue and cry. But the policy held.

Several years passed, and the mayor of New York was made aware of terrorist writings— in journals, letters, manuals—used to develop and spread terrorist ideas. Despite some disagreement amongst his cabinet, the mayor announced a *No Writing* policy—no writing allowed in subways, by waterways, bridges, around government or landmark buildings. As would be expected in a city that considers itself the epicenter of publishing, there was strong reaction against the edict. But the editorials, ads, protest rallies, debates and public hearings did nothing to prevent the policy from being enacted.

Despite the ongoing War On Terror, the banning of public photography, videotaping, cell phoning, hand gesturing, drawing, and writing in the nation's big cities—acts of terrorism continued taking place with greater frequency, not less. When the mayor of New York realized that talking was another important tool of the terrorists, he banned all talking in subways, by waterways, highways, bridges, around schools, stadiums, theaters, government and landmark buildings. You can imagine the outcry that resulted from a mayor trying to shut the mouths of

New Yorkers. Columnists complained: if they wanted to live a monastic life they wouldn't have moved to the Big Apple. Illegal images of protest marches showing thousands of people with their mouths duct-taped shut made front-page news around the globe. But the policy stood. For the first time in centuries, the city was hushed. The eerily silent crowds were chilling to almost everyone except the terrorists who felt more and more victorious as each successive freedom was eliminated.

Over the decades, it became obvious that the real threat to security was thought itself. In spite of her "liberal" orientation and her campaign pledges to *loosen* restrictions on expression, the mayor (the fourth since the original *No Photo* edict), became convinced that it was time to get at the root of the problem. With little fanfare, on a Saturday afternoon, she announced her *No Thinking* policy—no thinking allowed in parks, subways, buses, by waterways, highways, on streets, bridges, walkways, in or around schools, stadiums, stores, hospitals, theaters, museums, and government, private, public or landmark buildings.

Once considered the intellectual capital of the western world, New York City became an official thought-free zone. While most law-abiding New Yorkers tried their best not to think, criminals and terrorists didn't care about the rules and ended up occupying a lot of the emptied-out thought space. This policy would have probably dealt the final blow to the once great city, if it wasn't for the ingenuity of New Yorkers who were not going to let not-thinking stop them from thinking up a new, untraceable means of thought and communication now known throughout the world as #/★>;x°<!

"Hey, could you slow it down? I'm not in any rush," I yelled, pressing my face against the bulletproof plexiglas separating me from the cab driver. That's when I noticed he was talking very quietly on one of those phones that look like a miniature jet ski docked to an ear. Even if he was speaking English I wouldn't have been able to make out his conversation. The cabbie finally noticed me vying for attention. *"You want something?"* he asked, averting his eyes from the road. "No. Nothing," I said, "Just watch where you're going." He resumed his phone conversation, probably quipping about his fidgety fare.

After failing to get anything going with the cab driver, I took out my laptop and continued writing the true story of a couple who met and fell in love online. Never before had either of them felt so understood, so intimate with another person. The only problem—the man lived in New Jersey, and the woman in Auckland, New Zealand. When they finally met in person, fourteen months into their relationship, it was awkward. Physically. They were strangers, yet they knew each other so well. Having met online, all the superficial things like fashion, body type, and social skills meant very little, allowing them to get to know the *real* person. Two weeks together in the flesh, and they both agreed it wasn't meant to be. She went back to New Zealand. He stayed in New Jersey. Months passed. The two of them kept in touch, emailing on holidays and birthdays. Within a year they were at it again, fulfilling each other's fantasies over the internet. They decided to get married, but each remained living in their respective country. They've been married six years now; they get together once a year and are very content in what they describe as a "profoundly spiritual relationship based on total honesty and communication."

I finished writing up the story, which was part of an essay called, *The Art of Conversation: Lost or Found.* I put my laptop back in its case, and looked out the window at an animation of Chuck E. Cheese chasing a $6.99 Special across an electronic billboard in a darkening sky. I pulled out a pill case from my pocket and popped two Go-pills to keep from falling asleep.

Aconsha had been on the road for several months with her dance company touring *Hotel Terra Firma*, a large multimedia work that equated different parts of the body with different strata of society. I was so happy that she was getting the recognition she deserved, from audiences *and* critics; but her absence meant I was sleeping alone for long stretches of time, and when I sleep alone I don't sleep much. I'd go to bed with my laptop, tapping out emails, trolling the internet, channel-surfing the radio and TV (sometimes simultaneously), making notes for my next pundit appearance, and writing blog entries till it was time to get breakfast ready for the girls. I sustained this pattern of near-round-the-clock news junkiness with the help of pills that somatized me into a few hours sleep, pills that pried me awake, and pills that kept me from feeling the aches and pains of my barely exercised body.

The cabbie, still on the phone, dropped me off at the television station. Inside, the make-up guy put more gunk on me than usual. The tech woman wired me for sound and seated me, alone as usual, in front of the large photographic wall of books meant to look like my study. *Five, four, three, two. . .*

On the way home (in a cab whose driver was also on the phone the entire ride), I had trouble recalling the round table shout-down I'd just participated in. I felt a hollowness in my gut and wondered if it was a side effect of the pills I was taking, if there was a pill I could take to make the hollowness go away, or if the daily phone call from my wife wasn't doing it for me anymore and I actually needed to see her and hold her to feel whole. I wanted to open the window, but it was electronic—only the driver had the controls. I knocked on the plexiglas. He pulled a no-see-um headphone out of his right ear. I asked if he could open my window. My window opened all the way. A few minutes later I was feeling a chill and wanted to ask the cabbie to raise the window *halfway*, but it wasn't worth the effort.

Looking out the backseat window, taking in the sea breeze mixed with the smell of car exhaust and fried food, I thought about how my audience had grown to unthinkable proportions as my connection to the actual world was shrinking. Within the field of blogging and TV talking-head craft, it didn't matter whether you had any direct experience with whatever it was you were mouthing off about. The crucial thing in the loopular galaxy I'd gotten sucked into, was devouring the news of the day, mostly from online sources, then processing strong opinions and expressing them with more passion, wit, and speed than most of your fellow opinionators.

When I entered my house, there was a note on the kitchen table from Samir and Carla. "The girls were great. Aconsha left a message to call. Email us if you need anything else. xxoo. S&C." I felt thankful for my old friends, that they live close by, although I hadn't actually seen them in, I couldn't remember how long.

The next morning, while stirring oatmeal, I silently composed the finishing touches of my *Art of Conversation* blog entry. I could do this while cooking breakfast with hardly any guilt that I was ignoring my daughters since they were busily typing away at their own intensely-focused communications around a kitchen table that once was the gathering place of a family that actually looked into each other's eyes and talked.

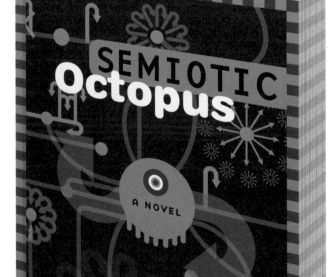

Semiotic Octopus *A NOVEL*

A woman wearing headphones walks through an intersection—oblivious to the DON'T WALK sign—checking her email on a hand-held wireless device. A cab almost hits her. The cabbie (unaware of the near accident) talks into a headset to his girlfriend from his home country, while the rider in the backseat types out a blog entry on his laptop. On the 23rd floor of the apartment building on the north side of the street, three members of one family, each on their own computer, interact with different global communities. In the apartment next to them, a thirteen-year-old boy is threatening to kill himself if he can't marry an online robot he's been chatting with for the past two years. Bleu Mobley's slice-of-life novel takes place over the course of one hour of one day on one city block. It is a multi-tendriled portrait of a digitalized world bursting with signs, information, and communication—deprived of knowledge, wisdom, and community.

2005, Graphic Language Press, Aquebogue, NY

It was one of those restless nights. Even after swallowing a couple of reds, the pull of the semiotic octopus enveloping my bed kept me from sleep. I thought of lowering the shades and searching for my blindfold when the orange-purple dawn started rising from the darkness—too beautiful a scene to miss. I turned off the TV and the radio, eyeballed my laptop one last time for messages, threw on a pair of sweatpants and a t-shirt, tiptoed down to the kitchen, made a cup of coffee, and went out to the writing studio to get some work done before my employees started showing up.

If someone had told me back when I was a starting out as a writer, that in the year 2005 I'd have a staff of eleven people working for me—a project manager, four writing assistants, a development person, a webmaster, a 3D designer, an illustrator, a marketing person, and a bookkeeper—I would have told them to get their crystal ball examined. In many respects, the people saying that I had become an entrepreneur were correct. I didn't take issue with that. But it was inaccurate to call me a *capitalist*. I never even had a business plan! What I had was an obscenely good-paying TV gig and several royalty checks coming in that were bankrolling my little publishing venture, which was in red ink since the day I incorporated it and functioned more like an experimental laboratory than a business. Very few of the products we brought to market hit what business people call "a sweet spot," and we priced everything too low to make a profit. If there was a marketplace we were targeting, it was the marketplace of ideas.

It wasn't even 7 a.m. and Monica's car was already in the studio parking area. I'd recently promoted her to Project Manager, which was one part Office Manager, one part Brand Overseer, one part Vice President. She seemed to like her

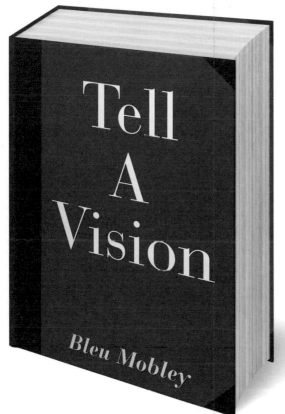

Tell A Vision *BOOK PRODUCT*

Finally, a book for people who can't stand reading but have an image to maintain. You're the head of a family. You're a teacher. Maybe you're the principal of a school or the president of a corporation or country. You don't only hate reading, you're addicted to TV. Don't despair. Now you can pull out a copy of *Tell A Vision*, a handsomely produced, respectable-looking hardcover book written by bestselling author Bleu Mobley. Crack open the cover and pretend to read while watching your favorite television programs on the wireless TV conveniently camouflaged inside the pages of your *Tell A Vision* book.

2005, Graphic Language Press, Aquebogue, NY

new role, but I was surprised to see her at work so early. I opened the door. She wasn't at her desk. I walked to the back room and saw her crouched down taking photographs with her cell phone of an open file cabinet where we kept manuscript revisions. She let out a yelp when she saw me standing behind her. I apologized for startling her. She slipped the phone in her shirt pocket, her face beet red. Before I could ask what she was doing, she told me that she'd been keeping a diary ever since she was kid. It was a personal diary "that NO ONE has ever seen." In addition to her written entries, she pastes in photographs and other keepsakes from her life. She promised me she had no plans to publish her diaries or write a memoir. I asked her if she kept a blog. Yes, she kept a blog, but she never divulged any of our trade secrets. She understood my desire for confidentiality on those matters. Then she gave me a reassuring hug and whispered in my ear, as if the walls could hear, that I could trust her, *always.* I whispered, "I know," but didn't withdraw myself from the hug after the normal amount of time one allows for a hug of reassurance between friends or a longtime employer and employee. Still wrapped around each other, our heads straightened, our eyes locked. We could feel the beating of each other's hearts, and I'm pretty sure she felt me hardening down below.

The hardening was involuntary, but the penetration of our tongues in each other's mouth, was, I suppose, a matter of choice. So too was my pulling away after a minute of passionate tongue kissing. I apologized. Monica said there was nothing to apologize for.

"This isn't me," I said.

She said it wasn't her either. She had a spouse herself, whom she loved.

"But maybe," she said, drawing closer to me again, "it's good to *not* be ourselves every once in a while."

---

sample pages

If it wasn't for that book I'd be a dead man right now. It was a fluke thing really. The drug store three blocks away (the one I'd just been to a few hours earlier to pick up my asthma medication) got stuck up by a couple of thugs with stockings on their heads. It's a small drug store owned by a Jamaican pharmacist—nice enough guy and obviously no idiot. He tells the cashier (who happens to be his daughter) to hand over everything from the cash register. After she does that (from what I read in the paper), the crooks demand to see the safe. Soon as the pharmacist tells them he has no safe, one of the robbers shoots his gun at the floor to show he's not kidding around. The pharmacist takes his framed license off the wall and opens the safe. When the robbers leave, he calls 911 and to their credit the cops are on the scene within minutes chasing these two guys around the neighborhood till they're right across the street from my little house having a shootout like it's *Lethal Weapon 3*. I thought I heard some kind of commotion going on outside, but I didn't pay much attention to it because I was way deep into watching one of my favorite TV programs, which happens to be a cop show, and there were guns going off in the show too, and innocent people getting caught up in it. The program has been off the air six years now, but in my opinion the re-runs hold up better than when the show first aired, and the episode that night happened to be one of my *all-time* favorites. Anyway, I must have dozed off on the couch because of the medication—with the book I wasn't reading lying on my chest—when the bullet came through my bay window. It must have come in at an angle, ricocheted off the south wall of the living room and head straight for my chest. Luckily, the bullet penetrated the book (which is more than I could do) and lodged itself between two ribs right below my heart. I woke up in the ambulance and the medic was telling me what a lucky man I am. "You're gonna be all right, sir. That book you were reading saved your life."

242

I didn't know what to say to this.

"Like Dr. Sky Jacobs. Is he you or someone else?"

"Jacobs is gone. Out to pasture."

"I mention him only as an example of how you can be yourself *and* somebody else."

"I'm not into hiding behind masks anymore."

"Well then, would it be all right if I wrote in my blog about all that we do here? And posted pictures?"

"No. I'd rather you didn't."

"Then I won't. But that's hiding, isn't it? What've you got to hide, Bleu? So a few people help you write your books. I really don't think there'll be as big a stink over it as you fear. They're still *your* books."

"You could be right, but I'd prefer we kept the precise details to ourselves."

"It's your call. You can trust me. You know that."

"Yes, I know that. And I do."

"And you can trust me that *this* didn't happen either."

"Yes. This didn't happen."

"All right then."

TELL A VISION

The front-page headline in *The Daily News* the next day screamed BROOKLYN MAN SAVED BY BOOK IN SHOOTOUT. I told the reporters I was reading the book when it happened, but the truth is I wasn't reading it. The truth is I *hate* reading, but I often try to have a book in my hands when the kids are around because I'm their father and I need to set a good example. That's a small little pretense I have going between me and my two daughters. My wife plays along with it, bless her soul. We both figured, what's the harm in pretending daddy loves to read. But now I'm like *the most famous reader in the world.* FOX TV, CNN, even a crew from the BBC are doing interviews, asking me about the book I was reading, and what my favorite books of all time are. I don't feel good lying to millions of people, but what am I going to say, that I never really liked reading? That ever since I was a kid I've moved my lips when I read  and it takes me so freaking long just to make it through a single page? Should I tell them I am addicted to TV? That I think you *can* tell a book by its movie, get the visuals and the story, all the sounds in three hours or less? That television today is like a million libraries rolled into one? You got Public TV. The History Channel. The Discovery Channel, and all you good people at the 24-hour news channels keeping us informed about what's going on in the world. Of course I haven't told that to anyone. I just change the subject. Tell them how lucky I feel and how grateful I am for the police who captured the gunmen, and for the EMS woman who took such good care of me, for my wife and daughters who gave me a reason to live, for the Good Lord giving me a second chance, and for the person who invented hardcover books. Then I wink into the camera. Must be charming the pants off a lot of people. Got a call yesterday from a woman who works for a *literacy campaign* wanting me to do a public service ad for TV. All I have to say is, "Reading saved my life. It could save yours too." I'm not sure what to tell her. Just got another call from a man interested in manufacturing books for self-protection.

243

Walls: stories of enclosure was my first book in years to receive near unanimous critical praise.

Without a doubt, *Walls* is Bleu Mobley's best work in over a decade. / *Time Magazine*

In *Walls,* Mobley combines the thoroughness of a scholar with the approachability of a seasoned playwright. / *Newsweek*

The Village Voice

Soon after the pre-publication raves came out, biblicalists of all kind began waging a holy war against me. One group of fundamentalist Christians sent thousands of posts to my blog accusing me of sacrilege.

Mr. Mobley.
Many of the words you ascribe in your book "Walls" to people like Rahab and Nehemiah and the Lord Jesus Christ Himself are nowhere to be found in the Bible. What proof do you have that they said these things? Were you there? If you were there, you must be thousands of years old, which means it's high time for you to expire! If you're not that old, then you're nothing but a LIAR!

Evangelical Christian Zionists accused me of twisting the word of God and chastised me for equating Israel with *any* other country. There IS NO equivalency! One self-described Christian Zionist wrote, Do you have any idea who you're dealing with? Clearly a threat, it was less clear if the person meant that I was dealing with a tough guy like him (capable of God knows what), or that I was dealing with (the one-and-only, often vengeful) God Himself?

The most vociferous attacks came from Jewish Zionists. They mocked my sympathetic portrayal of a Palestinian family living in the West Bank and the contemporary Israeli character in the same story who describes her fear that "Israel is becoming the very thing it was created to provide sanctuary from." First they defined me as a Jew. Once defined, I became a *self-hating* Jew. Then they disowned me as no longer Jewish.

These accusations were fiercely rebutted by Jews who said that I criticized Israeli policy because I (like they) love Israel and want to insure its survival. This debate triggered a protracted "discussion" about my genealogy, the worst of which devolved into unseemly characterizations of my mother and all kinds of speculation about who my father was.

Things I said or was purported to have said in obscure interviews were taken out of context and hurled back at me in twisted ways. One person, claiming to have known my mother in the late forties, said that she had a reputation back then as `an easy lay.` Like most of the really mean-spirited commenters to the blog, this person hid behind the name *Anonymous*. He (or she) went on to accuse me of being a prostitute (like my mother).

> You obviously will write any kind of book you think will make
> money, and in this case, at the expense of your own people.

Another Anonymous coward posted this comment:

> If you're such a good historian that you were able to find the
> EXACT words people uttered thousands of years ago, then you
> should have been able to find out who your own father is by now.

Other Anonymous postings claimed to know who my father was. The list included: the Jewish mobster Meyer Lansky, Yasser Arafat, and a slew of anti-Semites from Charles Lindburgh to Henry Ford, and (I kid you not) Albert Spear. *My Dastardly Fathers.*

When I instituted a No Anonymous policy on my blog, it was as if I had declared martial law. People accused me of being a hypocrite and violating their First Amendment rights. Up to that point I'd kept out of the flame wars, but I broke my silence with a post explaining that my blog was *my* blog, and I could make, break and change the rules as I saw fit.

The attacks against me I could take, but once my wife's and daughters' names were invoked, and someone posted our address overlayed on a target, I blackened the site. Right away an anti-fan blog popped up in its place posing as my site, with photos of Frida and Ella. Aconsha and I thought hard about who to contact. We didn't feel like inviting the FBI to rummage through all our correspondences, so we went to the local police. The detective assigned to the case respected our request not to go to the press or get into a drawn out investigation. Instead, he assigned two officers to keep an eye on us and watch our house for a week.

Aconsha and I talked all through the first night of the cops keeping watch. As we watched them through the blinds watching us, Aconsha told me how hard touring had been for her over the past year-and-a-half. She used to love being on the road, always moving, barely having time alone to think about anything other than dance. "But it's different now," she said. "I really have something to lose now. I felt scared much of the time we were touring, that something terrible was going to happen to one of the girls, or to you. Except during performances. I mean, when I wasn't freaking out, it was *heaven*. And seeing people respond so positively to the work and to the company felt great. But I don't need to... I don't *want* to be away from home for that long again."

"You put up a very good front. You should have said something."

"You should have told me what was going on with the blog and the threats. I knew something was wrong. I just didn't know what."

"How could you tell?"

"I was in my hotel room in LA one night, and I turned on the TV and saw you, and my heart sank. I could see in your eyes how lost you looked. It was a valiant effort, trying to reframe the popular narrative, but somehow I could tell it was backfiring on you."

"You could see that?"

"Look at the tapes. You looked like you were sitting on nails. I wanted desperately to be there for you, but I had my own shows to put on. There was nothing I could do but promise myself to come home as soon as I could. *Now look at us.* We're like prisoners here." Aconsha began to cry.

"I'm sorry, Bleu."

"*You're* sorry? I'm sorry!"

"I want to be strong, but I'm just a wreck of a human being."

"You're not a wreck."

"*I am!* Let me be a wreck, okay?"

"Sure, you can be a wreck. We can be wrecks together."

I told Aconsha that I'd become "a little bit hooked on pills."

"What kind of pills?"

"Different kinds, you know."

"I *don't* know. How little bit hooked are we talking about?"

"You know, in the morning, at night. In the afternoon, sometimes."

We held each other for a long time—two leaking wrecks—and agreed never to keep secrets again. "We are buffers for each other's pain, but if we don't tell each other what's going on, no buffering can take place."

"You need professional help for the pills. Promise me you'll see a doctor."

"I *am* seeing a doctor. How do you think I get the pills? Three doctors, three different pills."

"Then you need to see a *different* doctor."

"As long as I don't have to join any twelve-step programs."

"Maybe you will. Whatever it takes, right?"

"Sure. Whatever it takes."

Two weeks later, Marty, the guy who hired me at the cable network, took me to lunch and explained "the fickle ways of television." He got his current job, he said, only because he was let go from his previous job at another network. I didn't want to wait for Marty to start saying that it wasn't the right fit anymore. Before he could say it, I told him I was tired of showbiz. He said he understood perfectly. We spent the rest of our lunch talking about jazz; all the while I was thinking that my run-ins with the Zionists must have been the last straw. Marty probably fought for me, at least for two minutes, but he had his own neck to watch out for.

Instead of being upset on the train ride home, it felt like an elephant had been lifted off my shoulders.

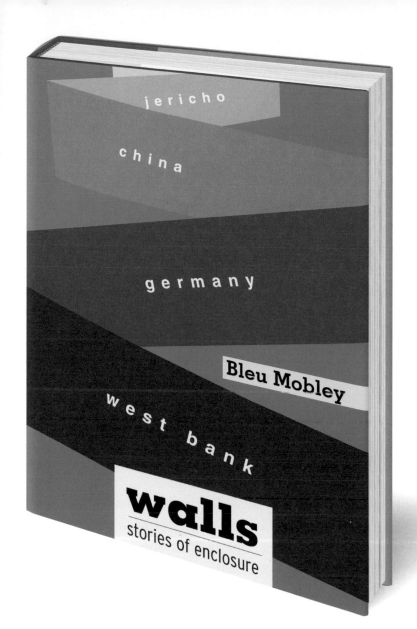

Walls: stories of enclosure

HISTORICAL FICTION

Throughout history, human beings have constructed large-scale walls designed to enclose a city, country or occupied territory. Whether intended to keep people out, keep people in, or both, these great barrier walls—ordered into existence by heads of state, built by slaves and manual laborers, and guarded by soldiers—stand as monuments of hubris and fear. In this work of historical fiction, controversial author and cultural critic Bleu Mobley looks beyond bricks and mortar as he brings to life the stories of people who dreamed up these walls, those who built them, those who lived in their shadows, and the brave souls who dared to fight against them.

2005, Graphic Language Press, Aquebogue, NY

excerpt [from the chapter on Jericho]

Rahab had grown weary of the war hysteria the king stirred up every few years. She'd heard the call to remain vigilant plenty of times before—*beware of foreigners, report on neighbors who might be collaborating with the enemy, keep an eye out for suspicious satchels, stock up on water and food supplies in case of a siege, don't venture out beyond the walls of the city*, and no matter who was fighting the King's army at the time, there was always talk of *the villainous Israelites* coming to get us, a warning Rahab never took seriously since the Jews were slaves and former slaves with no army of their own or wherewithal to threaten a mighty city like Jericho.

As for the latest round of stories about the Israelites, Rahab found them laughable. To her, the fantastic tales were a sign that the king was feeling vulnerable and would say anything to keep the people scared and In need of his dominion. The stories   *of first borns dying, of wrathful hailstones falling from the sky, of the Red Sea parting and the Israelites escaping the*

Egyptian army—lacked all credulity. Some of Rahab's customers were high-ranking nobles prone to exaggeration and fits of paranoia. Other customers, from every rung of Jericho society, spewed conspiracy theories like spiders spin webs. Rahab tuned most of it out. Over time she became deaf to politics. "I'm not a political person," she would tell customers who tried drawing her into partisan debates. "All I know is, I enjoy people."

One night, soon after the Red Alert went out about the Israelites, Rahab heard some kind of demonstration going on outside Jericho. She was in a good position to hear since her house was attached to the inside of the outer mud-brick wall of the city. It was hard for her to believe that Joshua and his Jews were the ones making the racket. Even if it *was* them, she figured they were harmless. She had occasion to know a few Israelites, and they were the least-macho men she'd ever met. And once their clothes were off, they were like most other men: sad little boys looking for love and attention. *And if the Israelites did take control of Jericho, so what,* she thought. *Maybe things would improve for working slobs like me.*

A few hours after the sun set, she heard a knock at the door. *What am I supposed to do, stay locked inside all night?* she asked herself. *I am a working woman, and customers are calling.* For Rahab, answering a knock at the door wasn't a matter of patriotism or Kingdom Security. Rahab was a prostitute and she needed to answer the door if she wanted to put food on the table and continue helping her parents who were old and had no savings.

The two young men at the door stared at her with overanxious eyes. "How can I help you two tonight?" she asked in the sultry voice she put on for customers. The taller of the two strangers said, "Well, we um, were wondering if you knew of a place we could stay the night?" Rahab had regular customers amongst the townsmen of her poor mud-hut village, but she depended on clientele that came from beyond their walled-in slum. Amongst her specialties, Rahab was known for de-virginizing young men in sensitive yet fun-loving ways. Often, these youngsters would fall in love with her and become steady customers, imagining themselves to be the one true love of Rahab's life.

She ushered the two visitors inside her modest hut, assuming they'd heard about her from satisfied customers. One of them tripped over the cuff of his pants, landing flat on Rahab's floor. The other looked at her like he'd never laid eyes on a woman before. Once inside, Rahab could see that they were mere pubescents, fourteen, fifteen years old at most. They dressed like they were from the desert, and though young, they had the haggard look of bookish men forced to do more physical exercise than they were cut out for. As the boys drank tea and chatted about the inclement weather, Rahab detected a dialect that wasn't exactly Canaanite. She picked up a large candle from the table and held it in front of their faces. "You're Jews, aren't you!" The boys said nothing, but their stunned expressions confirmed that she was right. Rahab rushed to the windows to shutter the room from prying eyes. What if they had been spotted and she was found cavorting with the enemy? The king had given strict orders to execute all collaborators. These were ugly times.

The Israelite boys sat at the table, barely blinking, mesmerized by Rahab—the way she walked and talked, very much like a woman but with the confidence of a man. They were smitten by the scent of her sandalwood incense, the sounds of her mysterious beaded doorways, and the multi-colored fabrics that lined the walls of her one-woman brothel. After an hour of small talk, they neither asked for sex nor threatened her in any way. The boys may have been virgins, they may have even been horny, but Rahab sensed the smell of a different mission on them. Using her powers to elicit nearly anything out of the opposite sex, she got the duo to admit that Joshua had sent them to investigate the military readiness of Jericho. But why, Rahab wondered, did they come to her? Was it because (like many spies and soldiers) they wanted to get laid after putting in a full day's work, or did they think she possessed secrets told to her by Jericho's mightiest men? Whatever it was, Rahab felt no reason to fear these boys. If they didn't want to screw, she would answer their questions.

But they weren't asking any questions, so Rahab asked them a question. "I heard a wild story that your God parted the Red Sea on your way out of Egypt, and two million Jews walked across the floor of the sea by foot. There isn't any truth to this, is there?"

"Yes, Yahweh did that for us, after he pointed us to the Promised Land, which is where we're heading now."

"That's what you call this God of yours, Yahweh?"

"Yes, Moses instructed us to call Him Yahweh, Ma'am. In Hebrew, Yahweh means 'I Am Who I Am.' He's very firm about things."

"Sounds like a mighty powerful God, this Yahweh."

"He is the one and only Lord of heaven and earth."

"Could it be true then, that Yahweh brought ten plagues to Egypt in order to prove to the Pharaohs that He is the one and only God of Creation?"

"Yes, it's true. Water turned to blood, frogs multiplied, gnats tormented people and animals, flies spread diseases. Uh, what am I leaving out?" one boy soldier asked the other.

"There was a festering of boils…"

"Oh yeah."

"And hailstorms that destroyed the crops," the other boy continued. "And locusts devoured everything that survived the hailstorms, and then there was darkness over the land for three days, and first-borns died."

"Many of us thought it was overkill, but that's what it took for the Pharaohs to believe our God was their God too, and He was seriously upset that they questioned His Word."

"And is it true then, that after you all left Egypt, Yahweh helped your people defeat two kingdoms east of the Jordan?"

"Yes, we were victorious over Ammon and Bashan."

"And after you crossed the Jordan, is it true that Yahweh ordered Joshua to circumcise all the Israelite men?"

"Yes, we made flint knives and cut away the disgrace of Egypt from our penises," they said, wincing at the memory of "the hill of the foreskins."

"Even the old men were circumcised?" Rahab asked, squeamishly.

"I still hear the screams. I'm telling you, this exodus thing hasn't been easy for *anyone*."

"And now you have come to Jericho..."

"Now we are following Yahweh's orders to circle Jericho for six days."

"And on the seventh day, you will rest, right?"

"Well, *normally* we would rest on the seventh day, but for some reason Yahweh told us to circle the city once a day for six days, and on the seventh, we're to circle the city seven more times, while seven rabbis blow seven ram's horns. (Yahweh is big on sevens. Seven and forty are His favorite numbers.) Not sure what's supposed to happen after that. If Jericho fares like the other kingdoms we've passed through, there won't be much left of it."

Rahab sat in a chair with her head in her hands, looked across the table at the Israelite boys, shook her head, and said, "All this murder and mayhem. What comes of it? Kings sacrifice the children of their kingdoms. Walls crumble and a kingdom burns. The king is given amnesty in a nearby land while grieving mothers throw themselves on their sons' empty graves. One empire falls, another rises in its place. The slaves become the masters and the masters the slaves. The tortured become the torturers. One brutal God is replaced by another, and His name is prayed to through the lips of the people. Then one day another God, as ill-tempered and jealous as the men who claim Him as their Holy Father, will be conjured up. And another incomprehensible war will be waged in the name of Justice. And thousands of other children will be sacrificed in the name of Life.

Who is going to stop this wheel of death? I'm asking you, who?

"Please, go back to your people and tell them that we are simple commoners here in Jericho. *Look at this village.* It's nothing more than a ghetto! Tell Joshua we are scared, just like the Jews have been under the Pharaohs. Tell him we are trembling with fear behind our walls and our locked doors. Tell him we heard all the things Yahweh has done already for his Chosen People, and our hearts are melted and everyone's courage has vanished because we know your God is the one God in heaven above and earth below. Tell Joshua to skip Jericho, because we have already succumbed. We are like tamed house-pets here. Tell him to go around Jericho and go straight to Jerusalem from the west. Everyone there will have heard of your Yahweh and what He can do. They will surrender their streets to you. *I'm sure of it.* You needn't harm the people there either. They will be your slaves. They will care for your children and build your homes and temples and tend to your crops. Just tell them to put down their..."

Rahab's fervent plea was interrupted by a loud rapping at the front door.

"Open up in the name of the King. We know you have Israelites in there. Open this instant or we'll break down the door."

Rahab whisked the two boys out the back door, pointing them to the bundles of flax drying on her flat roof. She returned to the front door and opened it. Three of the king's soldiers stormed inside and began searching the house. "Yes, two boys came to me," Rahab admitted, "but I didn't know they were Israelites till I saw their... till I gave them what they wanted," Rahab said, winking at the lead soldier. "Then they took off ☞ in that direction. You better run, or you'll never catch them."

Rahab knew how to look sincere. Her reputation had a lot to do with making men believe that she loved the work she did. But it was not true. She was not born to be a harlot. As a little girl Rahab dreamed of becoming a surgeon, but there was no place for professional women in her society other than prostitute. It was either that or become a wife and mother. Rahab did what she did as best she could, and that meant she had to lie and conceal as a matter of course. She never told the wives of her customers about their cheating husbands unless she had reason to believe that a wife or a child was in danger. Now *she* was in danger. She lied to the two Israelites about fearing their God, and now she was lying to the soldiers about the Israelites. If her plan worked, a battle could be avoided; word would spread throughout Jericho that she had convinced the Israelites to leave them alone; she would be free to pursue her textile venture marketing flax for clothing and paper goods; women all over the Canaanite world would get work as peacemakers and be able to pursue their own businesses; and the Jews would live in their promised land peaceably with their neighbors.

After the king's soldier's left, Rahab climbed onto her roof, into the flax bundles to talk with the two Jewish boys. They couldn't promise that Joshua would spare all of Jericho, but they made her a pledge. If Rahab agreed not to tell a soul about their whereabouts or the imminent invasion, they would make sure to spare her house and everyone she was able to pack inside it. All she had to do was move the red rope—the signpost of her profession—from the door to her window, and her house would be spared.

The rest, of course, is history (or at least Bible study). The rabbis blew a mighty roar with their shofars, a million-and-a-half Israelites shouted, the walls crumbled, Joshua and his men stormed the city, set it on fire and burned Jericho to a crisp. The only thing left standing was Rahab's house and the people in it—her extended family, several musicians, dancers and artists, a few thieves and saboteurs, a midwife, a pagan sorcerer, and a flax farmer. Rahab went on to marry a prince named Salmon from the tribe of Judah. They settled in Bethlehem, had a son named Boaz who married a woman named Ruth, and they had a son named Obed who had a son named Jesse who had a son named David who became the King of Israel. According to one Jewish tradition, Rahab married Joshua and they spawned a lineage that included the prophets Jeremiah and Ezekiel. Whichever prominent Jew she married, it is written in the Old and New Testaments that Rahab lived out her days as a loyal, righteous Jewish wife and mother, eternally grateful to Yahweh for saving her and her family and friends. But Rahab's secret diaries paint a different picture—

of a broken woman who never recovered from the loss of her city and her feelings of having betrayed her own people. She knew how to put on a happy face for public consumption. *"If there's one thing I do well, it's deceive."* She prayed in Hebrew with her family. She observed the Sabbath. She loved her son and raised him with little help from servants. She stood by her husband's side, slept with him every night, and acted like an adoring wife. Her true feelings she kept walled up inside for four decades. Shortly before she died, she scratched out this poem:

At What Cost, Life

Life is a battle waged between a woman's weary legs
Reprieved by day to scrub a floor or poach some eggs
Spears of love, a nightly duty—caught
Walls of stone and hardened mud, her heart

Freedom comes with death, she hopes it's kind
Her exchange with Ishtar flashes back to mind
'I'll conceal the scarlet rope, the bribe is fraught'
'Too late fair Lady, your soul's already bought'

Once you encounter the field of scholarship known as bible science, you discover there's no end to the stuff, but it exists in a million little pieces: in hundreds of books, thousands of articles and speeches, and untold numbers of footnotes. *The New New Testament*, published under the imprint *theword.com*, was an attempt to compile a comprehensive anthology on the subject and let people decide for themselves what kind of science they were looking at.

After receiving his complimentary copy, one very influential televangelist with ties to the Republican party came up with a strategy for using *The New New Testament* as a weapon in the ongoing battle against secular society. He deputized an army of literalist Christians armed with the methods of science as a way of backing up their religious beliefs. In a matter of days, the trade edition sold out and we had to order a large second printing.

For better or worse, the science cited in *The New New Testament* did not hold up to scrutiny. Truth be told, the well-meaning believers—who used our book to debate neighbors, teachers, archaeologists, evolutionary biologists, historians, television pundits, and secular humanists of all kinds—ended up looking pretty ridiculous. Within a year,

The New *New Testament* had zero credibility, and all those righteous people who thought they finally possessed proof that the word was *The Word* had to go back to old-time ways of practicing religion, like relying on faith and praying to God for forgiveness.

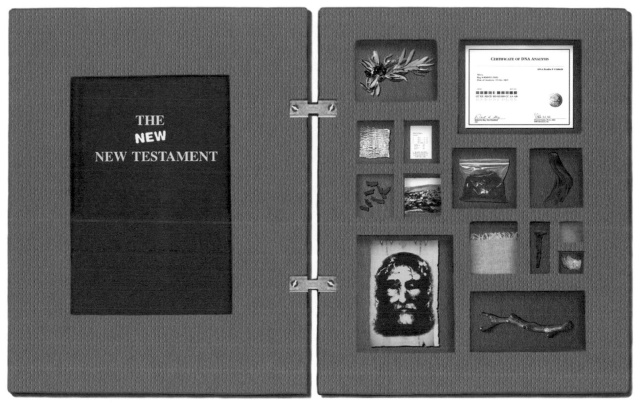

Matters of Fact: Deluxe Edition

The New New Testament *BIBLE SCIENCE*

By annotating *The New Testament* with the latest scientific, historical, and prophetic evidence, this long overdue edition provides irrefutable proof of the facts of Christ's conception, birth, life, prophesies, resurrection, and much more. For believers and skeptics with a little extra money to spend, *Matters of Fact* is a one-time only, limited boxed edition that combines a gilded copy of *The* New *New Testament* with objects that include: notarized DNA certificate; actual soil from Bethlehem; and facsimiles of holy bone, shroud, nails—and other sacred artifacts.

2005, theword.com

The trip to India was Aconsha's last chance to take the girls to see the Motherland before Frida went off to college and India completely lost its soul and became "just another corporate park." Frida had been there once when she was younger, but only as a patient. Most of what she saw then was the inside of an Ayurvedic clinic. For Ella, the trip was not only her first to her mother's home country, but her first time flying over an ocean. Promised a window seat, she was abuzz with anticipation. I was looking forward too, to taking a family vacation with no project in mind or book to peddle. It was also a demon-slayer trip for me since I got terribly sick the first time Aconsha and I went to India. Before we had even set foot on Indian soil, I was doubled over in pain. To this day I'm not sure whether it was a reaction to the inoculations or something I ate on the flight over. All I know is, when we landed, I had to be taken off the plane on a stretcher. Aconsha's relatives looked at me with such disappointment, then they nursed me back to health. By the time I recovered, it was time for us to leave. Through a haze of fever and nausea, I could see that India was the most beautiful, mysterious, extreme, and infinitely complex country I'd ever been to—the nearest thing to visiting another planet.

When I was a young reporter, I didn't give much thought to flying off to war zones any-where in the world. Like most young people, I acted as if I were invincible. As I got older, I became less inclined to travel or put my body on the line. Most of the risks I took were within my work—sitting (more often, reclining) inside my home studio, or speaking truth to power in a TV studio (with the aid of pharmaceuticals). Then my wife spoke truth to me, and I agreed to go for help. She came with me to the drug counselor, Dr. Leonard Michaels, for the first session. After that, I was on my own—a common pill-popping addict going to therapy three times a week, discovering demons I didn't know I had, living a day at a time. I'd have to do India one day at a time too, with no recourse to my therapist—*for fourteen days!*

At the curbside check-in at JFK Airport, the baggage handler, an old-timer with a Jamaican accent, was tagging our luggage, printing out our boarding passes, when his expression stiffened. "I'm sorry," he said, "but you have to go inside to check in." I looked through the window at the long lines, reached into my wallet and took out a twenty. He shook me off. "I'm *sorry*, but I can't process you here. Your name is on a list, sir."

"What do you mean, a list?"

"The No Fly list. You know, the Terrorist Watch List."

"That's ridiculous! There must be a mistake."

"I'm sure there is, sir, but there's nothing I can do about it. You need to wait on the inside line and speak to any one of those Air India clerks." I pulled a fifty out of my wallet and pressed it into his hand. "You can give me a *million* dollars, sir, and there would still be nothing I could do for you."

We got on the end of a roped-off line, four lanes deep with travelers. Twenty-five minutes later, the airline clerk asked for our reservation numbers, collected our passports, and began preparing our boarding passes. Then she asked if I had any other forms of ID—something with my address on it, anything with a middle name or initial? I handed over my car registration and told her I don't have a middle name. She whispered something in the ear of the clerk next to her. He looked at her computer screen. They conferred. She turned toward me. "I'm sorry, sir. I can't issue you a boarding pass right now because your name is showing up on a list."

I played dumb. "What kind of list?"

"I'm not at liberty to say. Do you mind if I show your proof of identity to a TSA officer?"

Frida asked, "What's TSA stand for?"

"Transportation Security Administration."

"Go ahead," I said, mindful that the time of our flight was drawing closer.

Several minutes later, the Air India clerk returned with a starched looking man in a blue uniform.

"Are you Mr. Mobley?"

"Yes."

"Can you come with me?"

Ella asked, "All of us?"

"No, just him."

The TSA man lifted a retractable part of the counter and took me to a back room with a metal desk, two chairs, and a bench. "Take off your jacket, your shoes, your belt, and empty all your pockets."

"What's this about?"

"Just doing my job, making sure the public is protected."

"Aren't I part of the public?"

"Yes sir. This is for your protection too, sir."

"You're protecting me from myself?"

"Your name is on a list of people who pose a possible threat to national security."

"If I pose a threat to national security, then why don't you arrest me? On *what grounds* am I on this list?"

"I don't make the list, sir. It's quite possible you're a false positive."

"A false positive?"

"That's when your name is the same or similar to someone who *is* on the terrorist watch list. It happens all the time. One in four male Arabs is named Mohammed. One in ten has the last name Hussein. Spread your legs, please."

He wanded between my legs.

"Hold out your arms."

"Shouldn't you check to see if I'm a false positive before scanning me?"

"Just following procedure, sir. You can put your hands down."

"It's *possible* there's another Bleu Mobley, but I never heard of one. It would be a drag if I had a namesake who was a terrorist. What is the name you have on the list?"

"*I'll* ask the questions, sir. Have you always spelled your name B L E U?"

"Why, is there a B L U E Mobley?"

"Please, don't answer my question with another question."

"All right. My mother has some French in her background, and I was born with a blue complexion. She was a visual artist, so she named me Bleu."

I glimpsed my name on his printout. There was also a Blue Mobley, a B. Mobley, a Sky Mobley, a Dr. Sky Mobley. These motherfuckers were all over me!

"Do you have a criminal record, sir?"

"No. I mean, well… I was arrested once for being in an anti-war demonstration. Someone set a papier-mâché dragon on fire. I had nothing to do with it. I was part of the group with the dragon, but no one knew these two jerks were planning to set it on fire."

"So you've participated in political rallies."

"Yes. I consider it part of my patriotic duty."

"Just so you know, they ban people from flying who've done a lot of that kind of thing."

"You're saying that I'm a threat to national security because I've marched for peace?"

"Sir. After 9/11, every t needs to be crossed and every i dotted. Do you have a middle name that could differentiate you from another Bleu Mobley?"

"No. My mother was a person of few words. I'm the word person in the family."

"Are you a writer?"

"Yes."

"Of books and articles and stuff like that?"

"Lots of stuff like that."

"Well *that* could get you on the list right there."

"Wouldn't that be a violation of my First Amendment rights?"

"I'm not going to engage in a debate with you. All I can say is there are thousands of reasons a person can be put on the list. Even a bad credit check. Is this your *only* address?" he asked, studying my car registration.

"My wife and I also have a tiny apartment in downtown Manhattan."

"On Ninth Street?"

"Yes. 337 Ninth Street."

"That matches the address of the person on the list."

"Does that mean I'm *not* a false positive?"

"You still could be a false positive, or you could very easily be an erroneous positive."

"An erroneous positive?"

"That's when you *are* the person on the No Fly list, but you're on the list erroneously."

"I flew a few months ago and nobody stopped me then."

"The list is continuously being updated. One day I came in and the list went from 44,000 names down to 24,000 overnight. Like the deck of a battleship, they're constantly scrubbing it. Now it's up to 31,000 names."

"Is this the same list that Ted Kennedy and Nelson Mandela were on?"

"I believe so, sir."

"So, *anybody* could be on this list—erroneously, false-positively?"

"As I said, I'm not going to engage in hypotheticals, but I'm sure even when mistakes are made, the people tasked to put names on the list have their reasons."

"So how do I get my name off this frigging list?"

"There's a Redress Inquiry Application for travelers who think they're on the list either as a false positive or erroneously. Do you have a computer at home?"

"Yes, I have a computer."

"Excellent! When you get home, go to the Homeland Security website. Do a search for the DHS RIA page, print and sign the application, and attach several identifying documents. Here's an instruction sheet."

"How does this help me now?"

"I have good news and bad news for you. The good news is, your wife and daughters have been cleared to board the flight to India. The bad news is you won't be joining them for this trip. If you come with me, I'll introduce you to Inspector McClousky who has a few other questions he'd like to ask you."

"Are you fucking kidding me!?"

"I don't kid on this job, sir. I mean exactly what I say."

"You're not even going to let me say goodbye to my family?"

"Just come with me, Mr. Mobley."

"Take your hands OFF me!"

"Hey! Step away from the door and put your hands in the air. [*I need back-up in 4B. We have a situation here with a No Fly.*] Sir, *Sir!* I said, PUT YOUR HANDS IN THE AIR! You see this little thing above my head? That's a camera. And that thing in the corner there? And the thing up there? There are cameras all over this room. So don't try anything you wouldn't want a jury to see. Hands in the air. *That's* a good boy. Now step away from the door. Now put your hands behind your back. You see how much easier this is when you cooperate?"

TRACE: a surveilled novel

Bleu Mobley asserts that his new novel is not written, but culled from the vast oceans of public, private, commercial, and governmental records that monitor Americans every second of every day. *TRACE* describes—in chillingly intimate detail—the activities of its protagonists using currently functioning surveillance mechanisms that scan and sift through: cell phone conversations; internet transactions; consumer, bank, and credit profiles; surveillance camera tapes; RFID and GPS trackings; bar code, biometric, iris, voice, fingerprint, and face recognition scans; IRS, INS, FBI, CIA, Homeland Security intelligence files; and library, bank, and health insurance records including mental health, substance abuse, and reproductive histories.

2005, Graphic Language Press, Aquebogue, NY

©: a novel came bundled for free with every online purchase of TRACE: a surveilled novel

©: a novel

A teenage girl downloads a song onto her portable MP3 device at no cost. A week later she writes a poem reminiscent of the song and posts it on her blog. A hotel guest stares at a framed silkscreen print of the teenage girl curled up on a carpet writing the poem. The guest lies down on the hotel bed, turns on the TV and watches a news program that informs him that he has no legal rights to his own genetic code... In *©: a novel*, Bleu Mobley takes a roving-lens view of the creation, duplication, permutation, marketing, and consumption of human artifacts in a digital age.

2005, Graphic Language Press, Aquebogue, NY

7:26 a.m. Subject 121.48.7036 (Dinsmore, Jonathan), Caucasian, American citizen, Irish descent, male, 46 years old, 163 lbs, 5 feet, 10 inches, darting cornflower blue eyes, birthmark the shape of Croatia below left ear, drives vehicle 638114698670 (Subaru Legacy) through yellow traffic light at intersection of Tuckahoe Rd and 3rd St, Yonkers, NY. Photo of car taken, saved, flagged [penalty points on Subject's license already above probationary limit]. **7:34 a.m.** Subject parks vehicle on Tuckahoe and 9th, inserts quarter into parking meter, locks car, enters Tuckahoe Bodega, inserts Debit Card 671194 9375 in ATM machine 389184, attempts $80 withdrawal. INSUFFICIENT FUNDS. Attempts $60 withdrawal. INSUFFICIENT FUNDS. Withdraws $40. Waits on [seven customer] line. Purchases one large coffee [three sugars], one muffin [chocolate chip], one pack Carlton Menthols [note: brand infidelity—Subject purchased Marlboro Lights previous six times]. Total: $37.23. Pays cash. Iris scan matches repeat costumer ID. Yellow Security Alert downgraded to Green since no recent incidents linked to Subject other than erratic credit history related to unpaid dental and audiology bills (gum disease and ringing in ears), and seven unreturned library books. *Warning: one overdue library book titled, *Religions of the World: Introduction to Islam*. **7:49 a.m.** Subject returns to vehicle, removes $65 meter expiration violation from windshield. Subject re-enters vehicle, slams driver seat door @ equivalent of 88 m.p.h. causing coffee to spill onto pants. Subject screams, removes napkin from plastic bag, wipes pants, lights cigarette with car lighter, drinks whatever coffee is left in cup. From cell phone 917.734.6248, dials 203.949.3281. After four rings, 131.63.8491 (Halabi, Nadimah), Lebanese, Muslim [secular], Green Card holder, female, 27 years old, 5 feet 5 inches, short black hair, vine-like tattoo running from below belly button down toward crotch, in excellent health but with genetic marker for colon cancer, answers, "Hello" [sleepily]. Fuming, the Subject complains to her about the [expletive-expletive] parking summons, [expletive] meter maid, [expletive] burn on thigh. Halabi, Nadimah employs calming tactics. "It's not like you get points on your license for a parking ticket. . . Don't worry, Jonathan. You come here, I'll kiss the boo boo on your thigh. Make it go away." Subject says, "You're too good to me. I don't deserve you." They discuss meeting later in the evening, 7:30 p.m., location [undecipherable] something something Service Road Motel. No time for him to drive all the way to Connecticut. Subject and Halabi, Nadimah whisper [undecipherable] utterances, make puckering noises. Signal interrupted mid-pucker. Subject looks down at coffee-stained pants, shakes head. Looks left toward Bodega. Looks inside his wallet. Looks at the parking enforcer down block. Looks in rear view mirror. Subject lowers himself in driver's seat, screws top off small bottle of nasal spray, grabs a pinch of white powder from 35mm film canister, places it into bottle, remounts spray top, shakes vigorously, squirts deeply into each nostril once, then again. Wipes nose with jacket sleeve. **8:03 a.m.** Subject turns car ignition on, starts vehicle, enters Parkway, North, tunes radio past news about war casualties, past news about flood casualties, to talk-radio (shock-jock) program; host complaining about taxes and tits, one too high, the other too small on previous guest. Subject's vehicle averaging 8-13 mph over speed limit. No police pursuit triggered. **8:17 a.m.** Subject's vehicle takes wide turn off Exit 27, scrapes back fender against railing, turns right at traffic light, drives into unmonitored zone. Reappears at parking lot D of *Tots 'N Toys* Corporate Headquarters. Vehicle Parking tag ID—Match. Subject enters building D. Nods to security guard. Employee tag ID—Match. In elevator, alone from floors four to seven, Subject blows nose into [used] tissue, rubs tip of index finger inside upper lip, across gums, glances up at camera, grins, straightens face, straightens tie, straightens attitude, exits elevator, enters Accounts Receivable Department. **8:29 a.m.** Subject sits at one of 24 partitioned cubicles, logs onto computer using password [date of daughter's birthdate plus her name plus the date she died]. Password ID—Match. Subject receives automatic online news headlines: war casualties, flood casualties, sex scandals, sports scores. Subject checks email: 36 spam messages [offers for zero-down home mortgages, penis enlargement, university diplomas, horny housewives, Nigerian bank transfers], 19 work related messages [8 from superiors, 7 from account customers, 3 from peers, 1 from personnel office], and 2 personal messages. Subject opens first personal message from Subject's mother: "Dearest Jonathan, I thought you'd like to know that your father's latest angioplasty was not successful. Dr. Yamaguchi is trying to reschedule, but the O.R. is as clogged as your father's artery. Your father claims he's not worried, but I can tell by the way he's eating non-stop (since he can't drink alcohol anymore) that he's scared. I know the two of you haven't spoken since Nora's funeral, but please consider paying him a visit before it's too late. I know you're waiting for him to apologize, but that day may never come. He didn't really mean the things you say he said. If he dies and you guys didn't reconcile, I think it will eat away at you for the rest of your life. He'll be dead, and you'll be miserable. Also, your 79-year-old mother has a significant birthday coming up and she wouldn't mind seeing you either. Luvya, Mom." From his office phone, Subject dials 305.450.3690, leaves message on answering machine: "Sorry Ma, about being out of touch. I've had a lot going on at work and on my mind. Tell Dad I'm sorry he needs a new balloon job. I'll call later." **9:12 a.m.** From office phone, Subject dials 718.295.8924. Subject's wife [Dinsmore, Lindsey], Caucasian, American citizen, female, European descent [blend], 47 years old, 5 feet 9 inches, pretty face creased by despair [three days late on filing quarterly tax returns for her social worker practice], answers phone, "What's up? I'm with a client." Subject says, "Nothing. I just felt like saying hi." He apologizes for being distant lately, says he has been worried about his Dad who has to have another heart operation. Subject corrects himself, heart *procedure*. Dinsmore, Lindsey says, "That's too bad about your father. You should go to South Carolina and visit them." He says, "Lindsey. I've been thinking about what's happened to us since Nora died, remembering how it used to be. How close we…" She interrupts. "Can't talk right now, Jonathan. Let's talk about it tonight." Click, dial tone. Subject shakes head, stares out floor-to-ceiling window onto the manicured landscaping for 93 seconds, sits up straight, reads seven more emails, picks up office phone, dials interoffice extension 2914, hangs up in middle of first ring, starts new email message, addresses same office colleague he just phoned. Types: "Hi Martin, Sorry about what I said Friday. I don't really think this place is a fucking toxic garbage dump or that you're the dump-master. It's not. You're not. I have a lot on my mind these days, things at home, and my Dad has to have another heart operation. Lots of stuff that just needed to release itself, like when there's too much pressure in a pipe, and the pipe finally bursts. Well my pipes burst Friday, and you just happened to be standing there. I hope you can accept my apology. Respectfully, Jonathan." Subject starts to send email, hesitates, starts to send email, hesitates, saves email, but does not send it. Subject bites down on bottom lip, looks up at ceiling, pensively. From cell phone, Subject dials 203.949.3281. After nine rings, Halabi, Nadimah answers. "Hello" [out of breath]. Subject says, "It's me…" "Oh hi, I'm doing my exercises. What's up?" "I can't really talk right now, but I, well, something came up and I don't think, I mean, I *won't* be able to make it tonight…" Long silence… "What came up?" "Gotta go to a meeting right now. Sorry, but I…" "I don't believe *anything* came up, other than your guilt. That's what's coming up. This is the third time in a month something has *come up.* I think you're going to have to make a decision some time very soon, Jonathan. That's what I think." Click, dial tone. **9:32 a.m.** Subject walks to north wing Men's room, 7th floor. Enters toilet stall, pulls down pants, leaves underwear on, sits. Stares blankly at floor. Eyes well up. Subject sobs, silently, takes out nasal spray, inhales deeply into each nostril, once, twice, wipes eyes with sleeve, nose with toilet tissue. Subject pulls up pants, stands. Toilet flushes automatically. Subject looks back at toilet, suspiciously. Subject does not wash hands, flashes a look in mirror, avoiding eye contact with self, runs fingers through hair [no discernible effect]. Subject returns to desk. Note: **9:46 a.m.** and Subject has not completed one job-related task since signing into work. Subject reopens email to Martin from Drafts folder. Begins to send, hesitates, then sends the email, displays expressions of relief and anxiety. **10:07 a.m.** Subject's office phone rings. His supervisor wants to see him, *now.* Subject takes out hand-held digital device, logs note to self: "i'm fucked." Subject returns device into jacket pocket, bites down on fingernail of left thumb, then straightens tie, clears throat, blows nose into tissue, puts on unconvincing smile. Walks down hallway, past sensor-activated sliding glass doors into reception area. Employee tag ID—Match. Face recognition ID—Match. Iris ID—Match. **10:07 a.m.**, Supervisor's male executive secretary tells Subject, "Have a seat. She'll be with you in a minute."

Enraged as I was—about being forcibly separated from my family, finding my name on a terrorist watch list, being handcuffed and kept from going on a long-needed vacation—a part of me was glad to know that the government was in charge of securing the airports from *real* terrorists. It wasn't always in charge. Two months after the 9/11 attacks, Congress passed a bill transferring control of airport security from private companies to the federal government. The shocker was watching the forty-third president of the United States sign the bill, since one of his core goals was to privatize as much of the public sector as he possibly could—not the other way around.

We elected a president who doesn't believe in government. He believes in Jesus Christ and the inherent goodness of the free market. He gave us:

- *The Faith Based Initiative*, so churches and religious organizations could administer social services with public funds.
- *The Benefits Sharing Program*, opening the national parks to commercial use.
- *The Clear Skies Initiative*, loosening pollution regulations on private industry.
- *No Child Left Behind,* another pleasant sounding program that actually withdraws federal funding from public schools whose students don't score well on standardized tests.

The idea behind all these anti-government government programs is to "starve the beast" so people say, *Oh man, government sucks! The public railways suck. Public schools suck. The Post Office sucks. A public health care system would suck! Just give us tax incentives and let us invest in the stock market before Social Security goes broke.* He even tried to privatize Social Security.

I couldn't help but wonder what world these people raiding the protections and benefits of the public sector live in. *Don't they have children and parents who need air to breathe and roads to drive on and medicines to take? Is there any line these free market ideologues won't cross?* To try to understand this mindset, I started writing a novel about a right-wing think-tanker who espoused the privatization of just about everything, and also happened to be a very loving family man. Halfway through the first draft, the voice of the protagonist—Blane Masters—became so palpable to me, I decided to scrap the novel and make Masters the author of his own book. When I told Monica my idea, she asked, "What happened to your

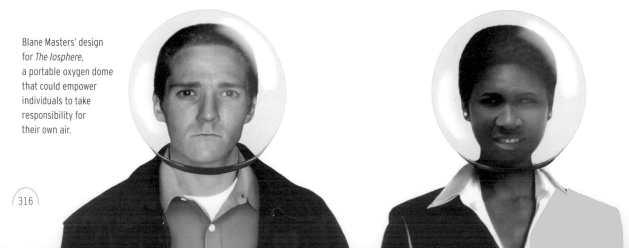

Blane Masters' design for *The Iosphere,* a portable oxygen dome that could empower individuals to take responsibility for their own air.

not wanting to hide behind pseudonyms or masks?"

"This is different," I explained. "Blane Masters isn't an alter ego. He's a counter-ego. I couldn't pretend to be Blane Masters—he's too different from me. I want to hire an actor to play him. Have him go on a book tour, do interviews and debates. It could be an experiment in *living fiction*. Instead of writing characters and trapping them in a book, what if we play them out in three dimensions, see how they react to different situations? Let's face it, Monica, the old-fashioned novel is an endangered species. Creating fictional characters who speak for themselves and interact with others might be the novel of the future."

Monica and I auditioned dozens of actors before Bobby Goode showed up. Bobby had moved to New York several years earlier to start his acting career; landed a few non-paying roles in Off-Off-Off Broadway plays, and joined a comedy improv group that played for tips. After two years, the starving actor scene began taking a toll on his spirit. Even the improv comedy gig, which was so much fun at first, started getting old. Bobby is a history buff and voracious reader, and his improvised references to Greek myths, ancient history, Russian literature and the news of the day never went over as well as the crotch-centered punch lines that rolled so easily off the tongues of his fellow improvisers.

For his audition, Bobby had memorized entire passages from the galleys I sent him of *Privatizing Air*, and his improvised answers to my mock interview questions were, well... I couldn't have written what was coming out of him any better. Bobby *became* the smooth-talking, far-right wonk. The only thing that kept me from offering him the job on the spot was his race.

I hadn't conceived of Blane Masters as a black man. But the more I thought about it, the more it made sense. Ninety-five percent of African-

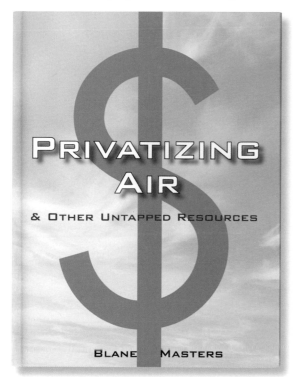

Privatize Now! Series

ECONOMICS/LIFESTYLE

Now that so many of America's social services are becoming privatized, it's time for the most elemental staples of life to follow suit. In this revolutionary series, Blane Masters lays out a comprehensive privatization plan for the last outposts of the public sphere. His visionary insights empower the individual consumer to take ownership of those remaining sacred cows that the public sector has taken for granted and despoiled. "Together—as individuals and entrepreneurial owners of the air we breathe, the roads we ride, and the beauty we enjoy—we can fix and preserve these precious resources for generations to come."

2005/06 Privatize Now Institute, New York, NY

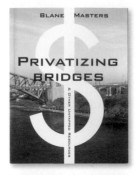

Americans consider themselves Democrats. The remaining five percent (as far as I can tell) are conservative TV pundits. Why does the right wing love having all these great looking, well-spoken black people making their case for them? Not because it's done them any good attracting people of color to their camp, but because liberals can't accuse black conservatives of being racist when they speak against social programs while referencing their pre-bootstraps-lifted hardscrabble beginnings.

Like all the actors who tried out for the role, Bobby assumed he was auditioning for a part in a play. When I explained to him during the 'call-back' what the job really entailed, he didn't blink an eye. He would cut his hair, wear the suits I bought him, study the Blane Masters ideology, and work on embodying the character, his ticks, his charm, his autograph, his back-story, his sense of humor and boiling points.

I paid Bobby Goode a full-time salary for a year to *be* Blane Masters at conferences and readings and on radio and television. I even got to debate him once on national TV. Masters' prescriptions for curing society's ills were totally preposterous to me, but *Privatizing Air* was taken seriously by some prominent conservatives who invited him to explain his ideas to their think tanks and on their talk shows. Bobby Goode as Blane Masters did a masterful job arguing the case for a completely unregulated society (even though in real life Bobby was a left-winger who used to hand out *Free Mumia* flyers at street fairs and demonstrations).

Privatizing Air did so well, I re-upped with Bobby for another year and included him in the writing team that wrote the sequels. Blane Masters—the writer, thinker, personality—extended the goalposts of the libertarian dream far beyond what any social Darwinian had ever dared suggest before. Some say his bold plans infuriated progressives so much, it inspired them to mount a much more organized fight against the privatization of everything.

Blane Masters' design for *The Roadcar*, a tank-like vehicle that comes with its own road. If adopted broadly, *The Roadcar* could eliminate the need to collect taxes in order to pave and re-pave roads.

8

Samir wanted Carla to wage an all-out war on her re-emergent cancer, even if
that meant enrolling in an experimental drug trial or trying the kinds of non Western
medicines he'd been a longtime skeptic of. But Carla didn't want to be a guinea pig or
a warrior. She just wanted to live a quality life, one day at a time.

When she was diagnosed with breast cancer thirty years earlier, Carla chose the most
aggressive option: a mastectomy and six months of radiation and chemo. It was a terrifying
and degrading time for her, but she survived it, she says, thanks to the one activity she had
the energy for—reading. She must have read a hundred books that year, and the one that
had the most long-lasting effect on her was E.F. Schumacher's *Small Is Beautiful*.

After she finished the treatments, and the doctors declared her cancer-free, she told
Samir that things needed to change if the two of them were going to continue working
together *and* remain married. She confessed to not liking the way he always talked about
pulverizing the competition and being the *biggest* and *best* at whatever it was they were
undertaking. All his bravado hadn't gotten them very far with their entrepreneurial
pursuits. If indeed she was a survivor, she was determined to live more humbly and
frugally, and she needed her partner to do the same.

At first Samir didn't know what to make of Carla's pronouncements. How could he
have known that his soft-spoken wife was leapfrogging out of the shadow of his immense
personality? He was proud of her newfound gutsiness with the doctors, but he was her
husband, not her doctor. She had been sick. Now she was better, and it was time for
everything to go back to the way it was.

But it didn't go back. Once he understood that her plea for him to change was really
an ultimatum, he did his best to stop the conquest talk and take on goals that were more
doable in scale. The last thing he wanted to be was his wife's oppressor, like his father was
to his mother. Within three months of working together again, they hit upon a project that
would turn out to be their first real money maker. They started enjoying their time together
more too. Samir thought he liked his women a few notches down from him in the power
department, but it wasn't until Carla came out of her shell and reordered the priorities in
their lives that he realized just how much he loved her. (He still wanted to pulverize the
competition and become a multi-millionaire, but he didn't talk that kind of talk around

Carla. He once told me that he wanted to be the humblest man in America. I asked him, "Why not the humblest man on earth?" He said, "America is the greatest nation on earth, so that goes without saying.")

After thirty years of annual check-ups and clean bills of health, Carla's cancer not only re-emerged, but spread to her bones. She had imagined getting bad news like that from her doctor many times throughout the years. "Oddly enough," she said to Aconsha and me soon after she was diagnosed, "knowing that I had a potential time bomb ticking away inside helped me live each day to the fullest. Now that I know that the fuse has been lit, I'm not about to change the way I live." Samir saw this as a false choice. "You still can live to the fullest while fighting the fight of your life. The odds the doctors gave you," he argued defiantly, "are nothing more than the limited thinking of small minds."

After a round of radiation the doctors started her on chemo, but after one six hour session on "the toxic drip," Carla refused to subject herself to anymore treatments. "They say it's not curative—it's about quality of life. But it's making me sick! This is *my* body, *my* life, and I say no more." Samir had little choice but to accept her wishes.

The last ten months of Carla's life were as inspirational as they were heartbreaking. Samir wanted to take her to faraway places—make her last wish fantasies come true. But Carla's wishes were to stay close to home and do the things she was already doing. "Don't you see what a gift you've given me? I already have the life I wish for." She and Samir continued to go sailing, she went to work, gardened in her garden, and spent as much time as she could with Frida and Ella.

Nobody ever said it out loud, but it was obvious that Carla treated Frida and Ella as though they were the kids she never had. By example she showed them how to stick up for themselves and how to have fun without computers or store-bought stuff. The daughter of Chilean émigrés, Carla passed on to our daughters many of the things she learned growing up in a family that sang songs for almost every occasion, danced, fished, boated, gardened, and in so many ways knew how to live off the land and enjoy themselves with barely any money. When Carla reached the point where she could no longer do much of anything physical, she sang songs she learned as a kid, and when Frida and Ella were around, they sang with her. She also loved listening to Frida play the piano.

Frida was becoming an accomplished piano player, but for some reason she suffered from a severe case of stage fright. When she came to me and Aconsha one day saying she didn't want to perform at recitals or school events anymore, we said, *Okay, fine*. She was relieved by our reaction. Also surprised. I suppose she expected us to put up a stink about the money we spent on lessons, and how you shouldn't be a quitter. She continued learning new pieces and playing piano for the sheer pleasure of it. As long as there was just family around she was fine. And Carla was family. Whenever she came to visit, especially after she became ill, Frida played piano with a kind of passion I'd never seen from her before. Almost every Sunday for several months, Samir drove Carla to our house for lunch and a private recital, and Frida would play her heart out. After one of these Sunday recitals, Aconsha told Carla, "You know, if it wasn't for you, Frida might have stopped playing piano altogether." That gave Carla an idea about how Frida might overcome her stage fright. "One Sunday, Samir and I will come over, and a whole bunch of other people will *just happen* to pop by too. Frida will already be in her comfort zone, prepared to play, there'll be no expectations of performing at a concert or being judged, and we'll see what happens."

Two Sundays later, Carla and Samir came over, as did twenty-some-odd friends and neighbors. Frida asked what was going on. I whispered, "We thought it would be nice for Carla to have some company. Didn't we tell you? Look, it's getting late, honey. Will you play something for her?"

Frida had Carla in her line of vision as she performed a difficult but gorgeous Edvard Grieg sonata she had just finished memorizing. When it was over, instead of getting up and excusing herself, she went on to play two Schubert Impromptus, Brubeck's *Rondo a la Turk*, and a couple of Joplin Rags. We had asked everyone to take it easy with the applause, but by the time Frida was through, nobody could restrain themselves. Frida barely noticed the ovation. For her, Carla was the only one in the room.

Frida's performance that Sunday turned out to be a breakthrough on the stage fright front. It didn't lead to her entering piano competitions (thankfully), or to her becoming a concert pianist, but she is currently minoring in music at college, and is happiest (she told me the last time she visited) when she's playing with her all-girl Caribbean-jazz-hip-hop band.

That Sunday was the last time Carla made it over to our house. She sent out an email asking anyone coming to visit her to please bring their favorite book with them. "I always loved being read to as a child. What a privilege it would be to be read to again." Instead of having all these people read to her from the same book, Carla got to hear bits and pieces of many books—the favorites of her favorite people. As she grew weaker and life narrowed, she shook off the readings and asked whoever was still coming to visit to tell her what was going on with them. You'd come to Carla wanting to be of help to her, and after two or three hours you'd walk away feeling like she had helped you just by asking a few questions and insisting that you be honest. Truthfully answering very fundamental questions like, *how are you? what are you doing these days? are you happy?* while looking into the eyes of a woman who literally has no time or interest in bullshit can really get you thinking.

A few days before she died, Carla had Aconsha give her a haircut and put some makeup on her, mostly I think so her caregivers and survivors wouldn't feel so bad. Carla's body had withered away, but her presence of mind and heart—and her ability to draw pleasure from a piece of fruit, a melody, or the face of a friend—left everyone who witnessed it with the knowledge that death didn't have to be as gruesome or as lonely as feared.

As Carla was dying, I decided I no longer wanted to play God in my work: creating characters; choosing who wins, who loses, who lives and who dies. I'd written over ninety books whose characters were struggling with everything from alienation to xenophobia. I felt neither regretful nor proud of the books I'd written and all the years I'd spent obsessing over the darker aspects of the human experience, chasing slivers of light. It had been a decent run, but it wasn't the only thing I wanted to do with my life.

Carla died at the end of May 2005. In the weeks that followed, Samir was sinking further and further into inconsolable sadness. Before she died, Carla asked me to keep an eye on him, and to "keep loving him, even if he makes it difficult sometimes." When July came around, Frida and Ella went off to sleep-away camps, and with Aconsha's blessing, Samir and I went to Vermont for a two-week camping trip. We hiked to as many summits in the Green Mountains as our out-of-shape bodies could manage. Looking out at the great expanses seemed to only accentuate the immensity of Samir's loss. He wept on and off, like a faucet, and I wept with him. Anyone walking past us probably assumed we were a couple. People had often thought we were lovers the way we used to carry on with each other—walking arm in arm, arguing or in hysterics. We didn't laugh much on the Vermont trip, but we talked a good deal. Life without Carla made no sense to Samir. He wasn't sure whether to take a sabbatical, try to lose himself in his work, or jump off a bridge.

"It's hard enough Frida and Ella lost their favorite aunt," I said. "To lose their Uncle Samir too, I don't think they could handle that. *I* couldn't handle that. Promise me—killing yourself is not an option."

"I don't want to make promises I can't keep."

"You kill yourself and I'll murder you."

"That sounds fair."

Samir deflected the focus off of him by asking me about my life, and like Carla, he insisted I be honest. I told him it was time for me to simplify—"make more time for my family and friends." *That* made him laugh. "You know how many times I've heard you make that resolution? Face facts—you're a workaholic!"

I told him I was working on addiction with my therapist.

"That's because you're seeing *an addiction therapist.* If you were seeing a sex therapist, you'd be working on your impotence."

"I'm not impotent."

"Okay, your sexual inertia."

"I'm not sexually inert."

"Therapists assume addiction is bad for you. Sure, if you're addicted to the wrong thing, it can kill you, but addictions also keep us alive. Like being addicted to work. Why do you think so many people die soon after they retire?"

"You asked me, so I'm telling you that I'm ready to shed a lot of things. As far as work is concerned, I want to be less like a grasshopper and more like a turtle. Less Paul Klee, more Jasper Johns." Samir knew of Paul Klee but he didn't know who Jasper Johns was. I described how Johns figured out a solution to the problem of subject matter in his paintings. "For years at a time he painted nothing but American flags or targets or numbers."

"What was his problem with subject matter?"

"His work was about the *act* of painting. *What* Johns painted didn't matter much to him."

"So he painted the same painting over and over?"

"No, the paintings are all different. Only the compositions are the same."

"Sounds like a con job to me."

"When we get back, I'll take you to the Museum of Modern Art and show you my favorite Jasper Johns paintings. Then maybe we'll go see some live music together. Like we used to."

"Don't start getting nostalgic on me, Mobley. You do that, I'll throw *you* off a bridge."

We got back on a Sunday night. The next morning I convened my team's usual beginning-of-the-week pow wow with an announcement. "I'm not sure how many of you could tell, but I've been going through a hard time lately. No reason to get into the gory details except to say that I was having trouble sleeping, so I started taking pills, and before I knew it I was hooked on the little buggers. I've acknowledged the problem, sought professional help, and am making changes in the right direction. But I need to make changes in my work too—in the work we do here—which has also fallen into some habit-forming ruts.

"My friend Carla died recently, and over the last weeks I've had time to think about what's important to me and what's not, and I've decided not to keep plodding along with what I'm *used* to doing, but to pursue what's in my heart. And what's in my heart at this point in my life is not writing. I've decided to retire from writing."

There was a collective gasp in the room.

"*No no. It's a good thing!* There are tons of people writing books, and I've contributed more than my share to the glut." Eleven very concerned-looking faces were staring at me with stunned expressions. "Don't worry. I'm not shutting down the studio. No one is losing their jobs. We're just going to change the focus. Instead of creating new content, we're going to zero in on the form."

"What are you talking about?" Josiah asked, impatiently.

"I'm talking about *the book*."

"The book? Which book? I thought we're not writing any more books."

"We're not. But our work here is not over. What we're going to focus on as of today is the *book* itself."

"Huh?"

"The legacy and future of the book—the very *idea* of the book as a vehicle for stories. I want us to consider the book as a 'spiritual instrument' (as Mallarmé put it a century ago), the book as a body, a body of letters, as a dear old friend, even as a lover (we've all cradled books in bed), and the book as a historical continuum that happens to be at a point of crisis. Like a beached whale that finds itself on an unfamiliar shore, discombobulated, longing for water, struggling to survive, the book has at least one thing going for it (besides its inherently remarkable qualities)—adoring fans gathering at the shore. That's who *we* are. We're the adoring fans, the hug-a-whale people, standing at the shore ready to do whatever it takes to keep the creature alive, to shepherd it back into deep waters. Even if there's nothing we can do, we stand poised to try our best. That will be the mission of our studio from this point on.

"I have no idea how the story of the book will end. It could be extinction, transformation, some kind of retro appreciation, or something else I can't even imagine. All I know for sure is: whatever we do, as book lovers, we can't just stand at the water's edge, watching. We need to be proactive. And we can't simply cling to the past either, mournful and whining. Everything changes. It's unfair to the object of our love to keep it from changing. If the book is morphing into a new form, so be it! Then again we can't just stand there like overfed tourists passively watching the object of our adoration get swept aside by short-term waves and idiot winds. Whatever happens, whether we're heading to a funeral or a resurrection, let's do it with our chins up and our eyes on what's important."

"I have NO IDEA what it is you're asking us to do," Josiah persisted. "You don't want us to write, but are we supposed to be *making* something? Composing books of some kind? Books with no words in them? With other people's words in them? Or are you going to pay us just to sit around and contemplate?"

"Yeah," Monica agreed. "I don't understand what you want from us."

"Me neither," echoed Najeela.

"Well, that's because I haven't said what I'm looking for, yet. Frankly, I don't exactly know what I'm looking for. If I knew, I wouldn't be asking for your help. But that's what I'm doing. I'm asking you to help me imagine what life would be like *without* books. That's one scenario. Another scenario: what would life be like if there *were* books but nobody read them. We have them around, we refer to them as symbols of this way of thinking or that story, but we don't have the time, interest, or patience to actually *read* them. Or, what if books evolve into something indistinguishable from movies? Or indistinguishable from websites? Or what if books exist only as antiques? Like you go to a restaurant and instead of old-time musical instruments nailed to the walls as decoration, or twelve-inch vinyl LPs and their record jackets, there are yellowing, leather-bound books patterning the walls.

I don't know what the future is bringing, so help me out here."

I grabbed a black marker, and in the middle of our dry-erase board I sketched a book.

From the top of the book I drew a line up toward the top edge of the board and wrote:

THE FUTURE WITH BOOKS.

I drew a line toward the bottom and wrote:

THE FUTURE WITHOUT BOOKS.

I made a circle around the drawing of the book,

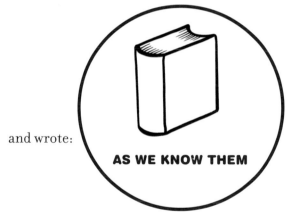

and wrote:

AS WE KNOW THEM

on the inside of the circle.

Outside the circle I wrote:

AS WE DON'T YET KNOW THEM

Across the middle, to the left and right of the book, I wrote:

THE HISTORY   **OF BOOKS**.

To the left of that:

CAVE PAINTINGS,   and all the way on the right, I drew a big

Two hours later the board was covered with ideas branching out from other ideas, in four different colors. Here is some of what we came up with that day:

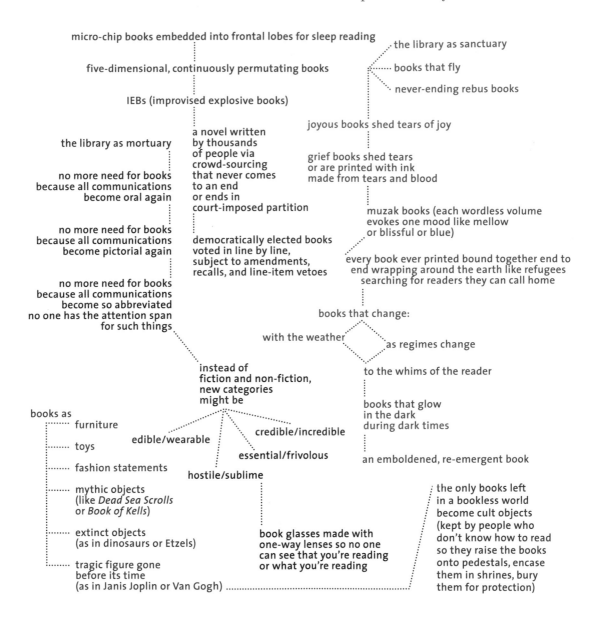

micro-chip books embedded into frontal lobes for sleep reading

the library as sanctuary

five-dimensional, continuously permutating books

books that fly

never-ending rebus books

IEBs (improvised explosive books)

joyous books shed tears of joy

the library as mortuary

a novel written
by thousands
of people via
crowd-sourcing
that never comes
to an end
or ends in
court-imposed partition

grief books shed tears
or are printed with ink
made from tears and blood

no more need for books
because all communications
become oral again

no more need for books
because all communications
become pictorial again

democratically elected books
voted in line by line,
subject to amendments,
recalls, and line-item vetoes

muzak books (each wordless volume
evokes one mood like mellow
or blissful or blue)

every book ever printed bound together end to
end wrapping around the earth like refugees
searching for readers they can call home

no more need for books
because all communications
become so abbreviated
no one has the attention span
for such things

books that change:

with the weather

as regimes change

to the whims of the reader

instead of
fiction and non-fiction,
new categories
might be

books that glow
in the dark
during dark times

books as

furniture

toys

fashion statements

edible/wearable

credible/incredible

essential/frivolous

hostile/sublime

an emboldened, re-emergent book

mythic objects
(like *Dead Sea Scrolls*
or *Book of Kells*)

extinct objects
(as in dinosaurs or Etzels)

tragic figure gone
before its time
(as in Janis Joplin or Van Gogh)

book glasses made with
one-way lenses so no one
can see that you're reading
or what you're reading

the only books left
in a bookless world
become cult objects
(kept by people who
don't know how to read
so they raise the books
onto pedestals, encase
them in shrines, bury
them for protection)

On another dry-erase board we resolved to:

make book vessels that infuriate, enthrall, incite, delight, provoke, cajole.

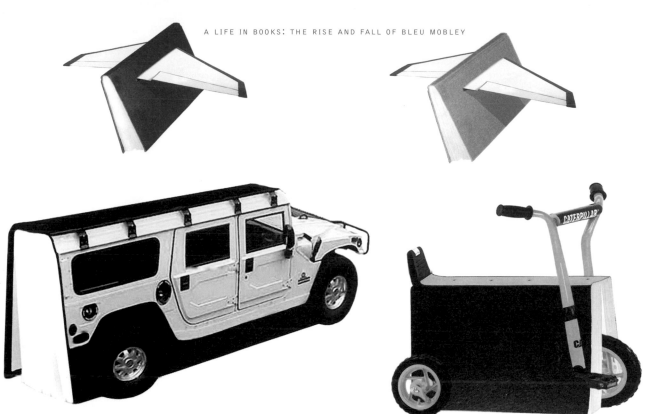

Books For Boys *TOY BOOKS*

With so many distractions competing for their attention, it's almost impossible to get boys interested in books these days. One solution: a line of toy books that drive, chug-a-lug, roll, wade, and fly. With the advent of *Books for Boys*, our sons may not be reading, but at least parents can rest assured that they are playing with books. Available at independent toy stores and through www.bookobjects.com. Winner of the Interactive Juvenile Consumer Product Award. "Ever since I brought these into the house, I can't get my sons to put down their books for a second!" *Sharon Stone*

2006, bookobjects.com

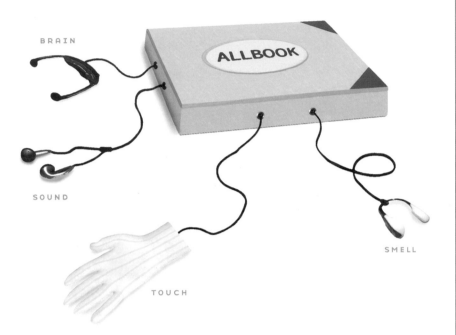

ALLBOOK® *MULTI-SENSORAL ELECTRONIC READER*

Unlike other electronic reading devices, *ALLBOOK*'s direct-to-brain image stimulator, surround-sound headphones, nostril sensors, and the patented electronic glove, leave no page unturned in delivering a complete sensory experience to the user. Hear the cries and whispers of the characters in a book. Smell their smells. Take hold of what they are holding. Take hold of them! Attach the brain sensors and nothing at all need be left to the [reader's] imagination. With a capacity of storing up to 10,000 books at one time, the *ALLBOOK* may soon be the only book you'll ever need. Should the user feel uneasy about any character, plot point, or ending, they can revise and edit to their heart's content using the voice-activated *My Way* feature.

2006, bookobjects.com

sampling of the collection

Totem Headdress / Thesaurus Earrings

Gertrude Stein Vest / Album Skirt

Codex Mask

Researcher's Hat

Marinetti Jacket

Book Pants with Chaps

Dostoevsky Slippers (Notes from Underground)

Dada Recycle Bag

Page Turner Toupée

Datebook Hairclip / Pablo Neruda Earrings

Book Stylings: The Rose Collection

WEARABLE BOOKS

Inspired by Bleu Mobley's mother, the fashion designer and artist Rose Mobley, this collection of unisex apparel and accessories will keep you looking language-savvy from head to toe. Wrap yourself in a book jacket, put on a pair of book boots or book earrings, don a book hat or headdress, and you will surely be one of the most well-read people at work, at a party, or on your block. Whether or not you've read any of Bleu Mobley's books, *The Rose Collection* gives you the opportunity to wear books created by the bestselling author and his award-winning book object team. Available exclusively through www.bookobjects.com.

2006, bookobjects.com

TRANSCENDENCE ↑

TELL ME A STORY ↓

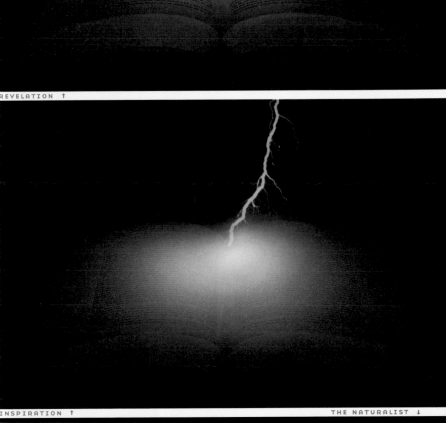

REVELATION ↑

Illuminated Manuscripts

BOOK LAMPS

Human beings used to tell stories sitting around the campfire. Then books became the main arena for storytelling. Now books as we know them may become obsolete, but we still like to have them around the house. These beautifully designed glow-in-the-dark books will light up your home while giving it a warm, literary feeling. Created by Bleu Mobley and his book object team, these *Illuminated Manuscripts* remind us of texts that we used to dive into and swim around in. They reflect the nature of inspiration, big and small ideas, and the natural world (if once or twice removed from the real thing). Like all good books, they help us navigate the darkness and take us beyond ourselves. Available through www.bookobjects.com.

INSPIRATION ↑   THE NATURALIST ↓

2006, bookobjects.com

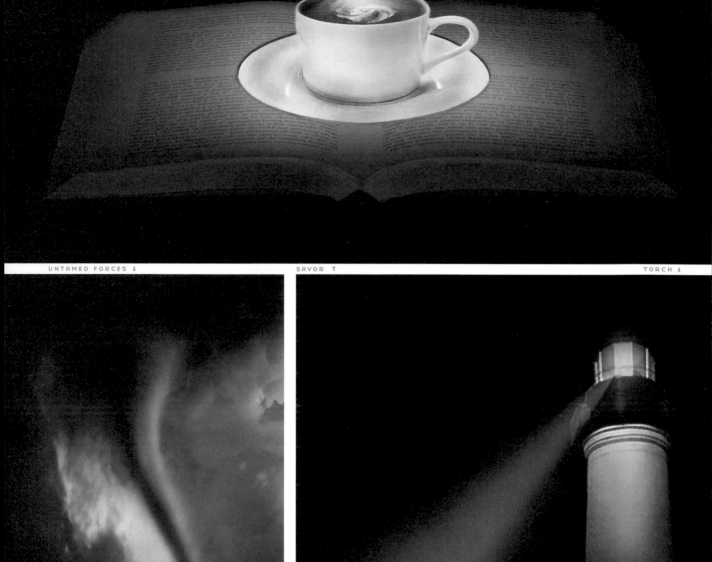

UNTAMED FORCES ↓   SAVOR ↑   TORCH ↓

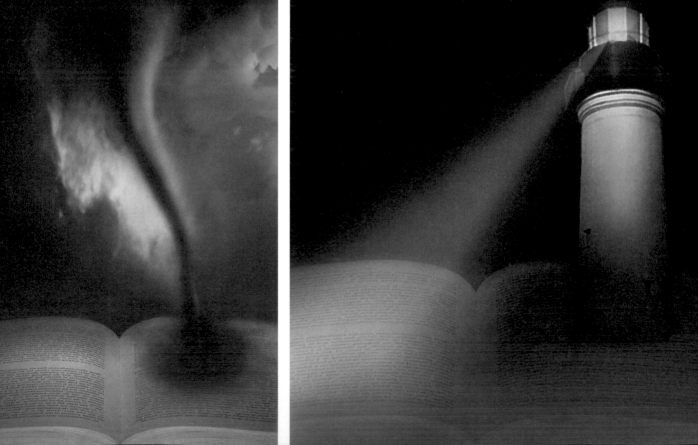

The phone rang, 6:30 in the morning. It was an old reporter friend based in ████████ with a lead on a story that he wasn't able to follow up on himself; a potentially explosive story, "that could rock the national political scene. It could be nothing. It could be huge."

I said good morning, then reminded this former colleague—who I first met at ██████ ████████████, and had since rubbed elbows with on the TV pundit circuit—that I hadn't reported on hard news in over thirty years, and besides, I never did inside the Beltway stuff. He told me it wasn't exactly a hard news *or* an inside the Beltway story. "It's more. . . a *below* the beltway story." I asked if he was talking sleazy tabloid kind of story, or what? "It might lead to sleaze," he said, "or it might not. If nothing else, it could be a great oral history project, which is another reason I thought of you. She's a very unusual person."

"Who?"

"The woman with the story to tell. You'd like her."

"Which is it," I asked, "a political story or an oral history?"

"It could be both, but it will take time and skill to draw her out. I don't have that kind of time right now. My father has Alzheimer's, and dealing with him is a full-time job in itself."

We exchanged anecdotes about caring for an aging parent. Regarding the lead, I told him I was busy with other projects, and if he hadn't heard, I'd retired from writing altogether. "I'm sure there are plenty of reporters who would give their eye teeth for a lead like that. Or get a rookie reporter to do the leg work, and you write it up."

"No," he said, "This is going to take someone with experience and guts, someone who understands you have to shovel through shit sometimes to get to gold. It's perfect for you!"

I don't like when people tell me how much guts I have so I can go do their dirty work for them. I was just about to hang up on the guy, when his voice took on a tone of desperation. He insisted we get together in person so he could tell me details he couldn't say over the phone. Feeling sorry for the old gumshoe, I agreed to meet, if he'd come to New York.

A few days later, at a Thai restaurant in the East Village, ███████████ told me about a White House maid who eye-witnessed some sordid goings-on involving the president.

"*Of the United States?*" I asked.

"Yes, Mr. Top Dog himself." The woman didn't want to go public with the story, just yet, but he felt certain that the right person could get her off the fence. "If it's not BS and she *talks* to you," he said looking into the rust-colored swirl of his Thai Ice Tea, "do us all a big favor and ghostwrite a book for her, just to get the story out. Or you could do one of your first-person narratives, like those portrait books you used to do." He tried every angle he could to whet my appetite for the story, but all I was hungry for was my Massaman Curry. Before we had a chance to order dessert his eyes darted in the direction of the street, signaling that he wanted to continue our conversation away from prying ears. We paid the bill and went outside. Standing by his car, he straightened out the lapel of my coat, brushed some flakes of dandruff into the snow covered street, locked eyes with me and said,"Listen,

Mobley, you hate this motherfucking president, don't you?"

"I don't like using the word hate. I hate the *things* some people do. That doesn't mean I hate the person. But in this case, yes, it's fair to say that I hate this president's guts."

"That's the spirit! And you *hate* what he and his administration have done to this country, and to the people in Iraq, and to our reputation around the world."

"Agreed. I think they should be tried for war crimes and for lying to the American people, and sent to jail for the rest of their unnatural lives."

"I saw your No Fly List article. You know the list is up to half-a-million names now?"

"Outrageous!"

"This story might be the only way to blow the bastard out of the water—get impeachment proceedings going, subpoenas, shake the whole goddamn White House upside down."

"The guy's a lame duck. Who's going to bother? Two more years and he's out."

"You know how much more damage he could do in two years? Nobody can churn a book out as fast as you. Even if it comes out right before the next election—it can keep him from having any coattails, and insure that his legacy is *crushed* for all times."

I reminded him that there were already stacks of books exposing the corruption and incompetence of the administration—prior to the last election, and they still got re-elected. I couldn't see what good one more exposé was going to do.

"Yeah, me and thirty other politico types read those books. But ordinary Americans aren't following that stuff. They need heroes and villains, winners and losers, scintillating distractions they can wrap their minds around in five-second headlines. They don't have the patience for complicated money trails; they're not going to read a 600-page book tracing the history of Iraq back to the Sumarians. This is Beef Jerky and Twinkies America sitting on the couch with a beer in one hand and a TV remote in the other. They can't follow a story about some unnamed person in the White House *outing* an undercover CIA agent as a way of retaliating against the agent's husband for writing an article accusing the adminis-tration of manipulating intelligence to justify going to war. What do Niger and yellow cake have to do with Iraq? I tried explaining that story to my cousin Louie. To him yellow cake is something you pick up at Baskin-Robbins. I explained the story to him as simply as I could. You know what he did? He threw his shoe at me for Monday-morning-quarterbacking the Commander In Chief during a time of war. I swear to God! All he knows is, we got hit—we hit the fuck back. When the narrative changed to 'we're bringing democracy to Iraq,' people like him didn't give it a second thought. The revision worked because it's based on the same premise: *We* are good. *We* are civilized. *They* are living in the Stone Age. *They* had a dictator. *They* are Arabs. *They* are uncivilized. And we have to show the world that we're not pussies. Period. You think Americans are going to get upset about a clause in the new Iraqi Con-stitution mandating the privatization of oil? *Privatization. Democratization.* What's the difference? Most Americans never read *our* Constitution, why should they read somebody else's? I wrote an article called 'Democratization or Swindle?' about where the Iraqi oil revenues are going—pretty much proving that the war was all about oil from the beginning. My article was cut in half so the paper could run three large pictures of Anna Nicole Smith after the Supreme Court agreed to take her inheritance case. In one picture, the twenty-six-year-old bombshell was kissing her ninety-year-old billionaire husband. Another picture, she's in a see-through dress, one arm around her new boyfriend, the other arm around her on-again off-again girlfriend. The third picture, she's getting into a car with her lawyer, looking a bit too much like Marilyn Monroe. How can oil proceeds in Iraq compete with that? Forget about trying to explain the deregulation of the banking and real estate industries, and why that will soon blow up into an economic crisis the likes of which we haven't seen since the Great Depression. The only stories today that get the kind of repeated coverage that can compete with sports, celebrities, and fear mongering are personal scandals. It's either got to be illicit drug use, infidelity, prostitution, homo-sexuality, child abuse, wife beating, or murder—basic ten commandment sins that your average Joe-and Sally Shmo can look at and say, *Oh my God, he did WHAT?!*"

"Listen ███████, you're talking to the wrong guy," I said, pivoting in the direction of the subway. "This has never been my kind of thing. I'm not even blogging anymore. I'm not even writing." He walked with me toward the subway, talking as if I was a hit man—the only one with the right weapon to do the job. Before I squirreled down the steps into the subway, I asked him, "Out of curiosity, what kind of things did this person see the president doing?"

"Here." He handed me his business card with a handwritten phone number on the back. "This is how you get in touch with her. It's not her direct number, but she'll get the message. What harm could it do to call? By the way, she's a big fan of yours. I'm a *nobody* to her. I'm just a guy who writes for a local newspaper. She's seen you on TV and has some of your books. That's another reason I know you're the man to pry this story out of her; right now her jaws are locked. Don't lose that card. The world is counting on you."

On the train back to Long Island, I proofread a term paper Frida wrote titled "New Traces of Feminism in Japanese Graphic Novels." I didn't know about things like that when I went to high school. After reading her paper, making very few corrections, I thought to myself, *The girl is good. Now she can be the writer in the family.* I put her paper in my shoulder bag, stretched out my legs and closed my eyes. Within minutes, the prideful thoughts about my daughters shifted to curiosity about the mysterious cleaning woman. *Forget it. Put her out of your mind.* I was content with the work we were doing at the Studio, and anyway, I always hated gossipy stories about the personal transgressions of politicians. To me, the peccadilloes of elected officials are irrelevant to their ability to govern, and therefore none of the public's business. The only instances when the public's right to know outweighs a politician's right to privacy is when it exposes gross hypocrisy, like when an anti-gay rights politician turns out to be a closeted queen. Even those stories make me uneasy, especially when they're dripping with salacious details, served on a platter of righteousness.

Later that night, I told Aconsha about my conversation with ███████. She'd heard me talk about how rabid he was at ███████. Whenever he got on the trail of a story that could destroy the reputation of a powerful person, he wouldn't let go until he saw it through to the end, which made Aconsha wonder "why he'd give up a lead if it was that good?"

"I'm inclined to take him at his word about his father. ███████ may be a lot of things, but I don't think he's a liar."

"Are you flattered that he thought of you?"

"It feels more like a burden than flattery."

Aconsha and I agreed that the journalism of personal destruction was distasteful, but we had to admit how delicious it would be watching this White House clan expire by scandal.

Before I went to bed, I emptied my pockets, and laid ███████'s card with the hand-written phone number on the nightstand. I turned out the light, and tried every trick in the book to get some sleep.

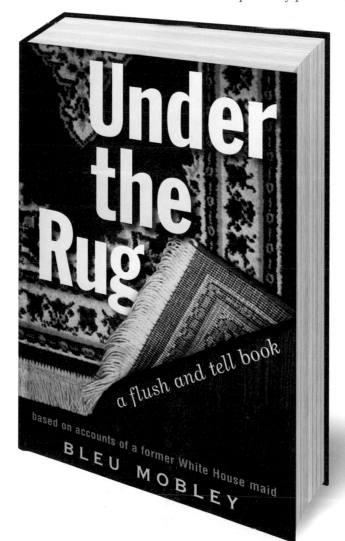

Under The Rug NON-FICTION

Being a housekeeper at the White House was the cushiest job Ms. X ever had. The pay was steady, there was a good health care plan, and except for her encounters with the First Lady, people were pleasant to her. Then one day, Ms. X overheard something she wasn't supposed to hear. She kept it to herself. Three months later she walked into the Oval Office and saw something she wasn't meant to see. Then she started finding things—in the course of her cleaning—that connected to other things she'd witnessed, which formed a pattern that told a heretofore untold story about the most powerful man in the world. *Under the Rug* is that story. It is a true story of unseemly behavior, indiscretion, and hypocrisy as told by Ms. X to bestselling author Bleu Mobley.

2006, Simon & Schuster, New York, NY

It doesn't seem to matter what happens to Ms. X—she will always be a proud American. The first time we met, she told me, "I know it is unfair I lose my job, but I still love this country. When I first come here, I didn't know one word of English, except I knew how to say coffee. Because I am allergic to coffee. I learned that word so I could say *no coffee*, and the word please. *Please, no coffee.* The first time I go to supermarket in America, I could not believe my eyes. Rows and rows of summer fruits in middle of winter. I thought, *WOW, I have die and arrive in paradise.* Only thing bad you will hear me say about America—the bread is no good. Bread here is mushy. It's full of air, sugar, and chemicals. Otherwise, this is greatest country in the world. Once in a while you lose job maybe for no good reason, but they don't put you on a list for the rest of your life or send you to prison camp for writing something against regime."

America gave Ms. X the freedom to raise her two sons and send them to college, even though being a cleaning woman was never her dream. The day after she arrived in this country—a refugee with images in her head of streets lined with gold—she got a job cleaning the boarding house where she was staying in exchange for a reduction in the rent. It was her first cleaning job ever, but she did such a conscientious job, the landlord told his neighbor, and before long she was cleaning six houses on that one block in Baltimore.

After her working papers came through, Ms. X went to a cleaning agency in nearby Washington DC hoping she could make more money in the nation's capital. The lady at the agency never saw a domestic worker with so many letters of recommendation; it seemed suspicious, so she sent her on some jobs to try her out. The reports of her performance were as glowing as the letters. The agency lady said, "I can give you as much work as you want."

"Perfect! I move to Washington DC right away. Make as much money as I can. One day I go back to college, get degree in social work." Within a few weeks, the agency was sending her on what they call *key jobs*, which are jobs that require cleaners to have keys. During the day, key jobs are in residentials. At night, they're in commercial spaces. "Which would you prefer?" asked the supervisor. "Both," said Ms. X, without hesitation.

Some of the commercial jobs had dozens of rooms, each with a different key. At one point Ms. X counted 167 keys in her possession. In the day, she'd let herself into apartments while the clients were out working. At night, she'd clean commercial spaces after all the workers had left. It was a lonely job for someone who wanted to be a social worker, but Ms. X made the best of it, "amazed by how much you can get to know a person just from how they keep their home or office." The pictures a person chooses to frame, the kinds of notes they write to themselves, the qualities in their handwriting, the food in their refrigerator, the kinds of phone messages that get left on their answering machines (you can't help but listen if the volume is up, who wouldn't?), the surface appearance of a desk compared with what's going on inside the drawers—"all these kind of things tell you more about a person than you might think."

Eight years after moving to DC, Ms. X, a single mother of two by then, was still working for the same agency. The new supervisor (the fourth in eight years) was a man with no sensitivity for how to treat his workers. "I could tell by how smooth and pale his hands look, he never work a day in his life except behind a desk. And if you're a woman, he don't think twice about special concerns you might have. Every client that comes to him needing cleaners, he accept without, how you say, discrimination. No background check. Nothing."

One night, Ms. X went to a new key job which turned out to be an entire floor of a large building undergoing renovation. There were nails sticking out of the walls, insulation falling from the ceiling. The floor was a foot deep in bricks, splintered wood and broken glass. The vacuum cleaner at the place didn't work, so she put gloves on, got down on her hands and knees and started cleaning. As the grime and construction dust began to seep into her lungs, she panicked that she wouldn't even scratch the surface before her four hours were up. She worked through the night—doing the best she could—until the construction workers showed up for their morning shift. She took two busses home, and burst out crying the second she closed the door of her apartment. It was the first time she cried since coming to America. This wasn't the life she had in mind when she escaped ███████████ for the land of opportunity. Fearing she would be fired, Ms. X called her supervisor and told him she didn't finish the job. He said, "There's nothing to finish. Just go back there every night for the next two months and do what you can." Ms. X told the supervisor she would only go back if he sent someone to help her. She couldn't believe such a brazen request came out of her mouth. Perhaps she said it because she had just become an American citizen.

The next night, Ms. G, an émigré from ███████████ showed up to work with Ms. X. As soon as they stepped inside, Ms. X saw that a few more walls had been knocked down and a new layer of rubble added to the mess. Working side by side, the two women swapped stories and Ms. G told Ms. X that a congresswoman she cleaned for gave her an application for a government custodial job.

One thing led to another and both women ended up quitting the agency and getting salaried cleaning jobs with the federal government. For Ms. X, the very idea of having a regular salary and regular hours and a signed contract with the *government of the United States* took some of the edge off that feeling of uncertainty that she carried around every day in the pit of her stomach—a feeling that she's had ever since she was eleven years old and there was a knock at the door and three soldiers barged into the house and took her grandfather away. After her grandfather disappeared, and her father was imprisoned for six months for writing an article that was deemed "anti-government," Ms. X learned that keeping your mouth shut was the surest way to stay out of trouble. It was a lesson that contributed to her reputation as *ultra-reliable* and helped qualify her for a low-level security clearance, first as part of a custodial crew in the Capitol building, and six years later the White House.

Sitting across from Ms. X that first time at a coffee shop in a suburb of DC, I saw a woman bursting with a story to tell, unsure of whether or not she should tell it. She kept her green parka on, zipped to the top. Her wide brim hat and long wavy hair shaded much of her face. In an attempt to break through the armor, I began telling the story of a man I knew from her country. A few sentences into it, she interrupted. "Pardon me, Mr. Mobley." Her voice was throaty and deep. "If you don't mind, I have a question."

"Please."

"If I tell you everything, can I be, how you say… *invisible?*

"You mean, anonymous?"

"Yes, anonymous."

"Of course. It's standard practice to conceal the identity of a source if…"

The sound of a siren wailed in the distance and grew louder and louder till we saw an ambulance speeding through a red light, followed by three police cars. "If you did write a book, what would you call me, the cleaning lady from ▮▮▮▮▮▮▮▮▮?" she asked. "No, if there's enough here for a book or even just an article, and I decide it's something I'd like to do, I'd come up with a name, Mrs. X or Mr. Y. Something."

She took off her hat and tucked the hair that covered the left side of her face behind her ear, revealing large almond shaped eyes that watered up every time she came close to releasing the story trapped inside. The next thing to reveal itself—a sensitivity to being described as a custodial worker. "When someone asks me where do I work, usually I say, 'The White House.' If they want to know more, I might mention, being on *domestic* side." By saying on domestic side, Ms. X could lead whoever was asking to think that she was involved in domestic policymaking. "Maybe they think I am with Department of Interior or Health and Human Services." If pressed further, she might say the word "cabinet" or "bureau," not mentioning that she *cleans* cabinets and bureaus, leaving it open for the questioner to think that she was a member of the president's cabinet or in the Bureau of Labor Statistics. Given a different set of circumstances (like better luck), "I would have gone to college and *easily* gotten one of those top-level jobs. Easily." I started to really like this woman who saw the humor in her not-so-humorous situation.

Hearing the things she heard that she wasn't supposed to hear, seeing the things she saw, knowing the things she came to know, triggered a three-way tug of war between her religious beliefs which command her to do what is right, her deeply ingrained habit of keeping secrets, and her status as a new American. "Reading the Bible since I was a little girl, you think I'd know the difference between wrong and right. I pray to God every day for Him to help me, and still I haven't a clue what is right thing to do. I am not a snitcher, Mr. Mobley. But I'm not a coward either. It's embarrassing, this situation. I'm embarrassed for United States of America, embarrassed for my president (I never had anything against the man), embarrassed for the great house I used to work in— *'The People's House.'* That's what ███ ████████ called the White House the first day of my orientation."

Ms. X searched my eyes for an answer to her dilemma. "I asked God, *When does a person's private life become public matter?* But God has not answered." She leaned closer and whispered, "Does His silence mean anything to you?"

"God isn't in the habit of talking to me about anything. But one thing I do know. . ."

Ms. X interrupted me again. "For two years I said nothing. At first I thought, *Oh, that can't be what I think it is.* Then I thought, *Oh, it's not such a big deal. The President is human being like everybody.* Then I thought, *This may be bad, but it is none of my business.* The more I saw and heard, the more I start thinking, *Maybe it is my DUTY to say something.*"

Out of a sense of duty, Ms. X requested a meeting with her supervisor at the White House. "I walk into his office, close the door behind me, and tell him some things I have seen and heard. A week later I get called back. I'm thinking he is going to ask more questions for investigation. Instead, I was 'let go' due to 'budget-cutting.'"

Ms. X wasn't transferred to another government facility or given a performance report with a list of areas that needed improvement, she was simply disemployed, wrenched from her means of livelihood, and from all I can tell, blacklisted from getting any federal jobs in or around the capital.

Fourteen months after she was fired, Ms. X and I had our first phone conversation. Between the bad connection and her speaking in fits and starts, it was next to impossible to hear what she was saying. I promised, getting together for coffee and a slice of pie wouldn't commit either of us to anything. During that first get-together, Ms. X didn't tell me the substance of what she had witnessed, and I made no offer to be her pen-man. But an unspoken bond was forged between us that day, and several days later we began a journey that neither of us planned on, asked for, or wanted.

And now, by opening this book and reading these words, you too may have crossed a line of no return. You probably would prefer to be elsewhere—in another book, something loftier. Or, if you're into sludge, surely there are other fleecings and cover-ups more deserving of your attention. But you're still here. You turn the page. A shaft of light slices through a room exposing a disreputable still life. Shame scampers for the shadows, denying its own existence. A cast of unseemly characters are hiding behind the curtains. You want to cover your eyes and ears, step outside the room, close the book. But you know there's more where that came from, and you most likely can see by now that Ms. X's telling makes it so much fun. In spite of yourself, you take another step toward the slimy maze.

I was alone in the Green Room awaiting the cue for my interview on an afternoon network talk show, thinking about what it will take to get more Americans—in this ultra-high-speed, multi-tasking world of ours—to read more books. Not junk books like the one I was there to hawk, but good books, great books. *The physical book really isn't the important thing.* This is what I was thinking about that afternoon. *The feel of a book in hand, the texture of the paper, the setting of the type—can be lovely things—but their real utility is to help carry the text from one thought, one place, to another. Portability! That's what's important about a book. Not the block of pages, not the stationary book, but the one in motion!*

"Mr. Mobley. We're ready for you." I snapped out of my trance and followed the producer's assistant into a room full of mirrors. The makeup artist seated me in a tall chair and tried his best to mask the bags under my eyes. I hadn't slept in days, preoccupied by the *Flying Book Project* I was working on up in Cambridge. Not only were we on the verge of a breakthrough getting the remote control mechanisms to work, I was just beginning to understand what the project was really about. The last thing I wanted to do was come back to New York to talk about *Under The Rug*. But I was under contract with the publisher to make appearances, and questions had already been raised about my methods and motives: How did I come to write *Under The Rug?* Could I really be trusted as an objective source since I was such a vocal critic of the president? Who was the enigmatic cleaning woman? *Where* was she? And couldn't she also have an axe to grind? My assignment for this appearance was to put those questions to rest once and for all.

Instead of reviewing my crib sheet of talking points, or looking in any of the mirrors to make sure I looked okay, I closed my eyes and resumed my inner colloquy: *Through the act of reading, the reader enables the words—and the words the reader—to escape the confines of their own bounded forms. Words take flight, bringing the reader along, out of his chair, her bed, their seat on the train. Airborne, we can see our own absurd. . .* "Mr. Mobley. As soon as she breaks for a commercial, we'll get you out there."

I was seated in a brightly-lit pink and olive studio next to the host, who was having her hair sprayed, her face blotted, and the collar of her blouse straightened. As I was getting miked up, I couldn't help but notice how much older she looked in person. She wore so much makeup, it was hard to tell if there was skin underneath. We shook hands and claimed to be longtime admirers of each other. *Five, four, three, two*—the producer pointed at the host. She flashed a sparkling smile, and reading from the teleprompter, recited a list of books, awards, some embarrassing accolades, then lobbed a softball question straight out of the publicity materials—whether or not I thought *character* was the most important factor in selecting our political leaders. Instead of hitting it out of the park, and segueing into a discussion about my bestselling Molotov cocktail of presidential gossip, I started talking about all the more worthy, wonderful, even quirky books that never get discussed on shows like hers. "How many of you," I asked, looking straight into the nearest camera, "ever read

Walt Whitman or Sylvia Plath or Langston Hughes? You've heard these names, but how many of you can recite one of their poems? A single line? Can you even name a title?"

The host sensed my disinterest in the book I was there to promote. "Okay, you don't want to talk about your new book." She picked up her copy of *Under the Rug* and tossed it under the coffee table. "What's on your mind today, Bleu Mobley? You want to insult my audience? Go ahead. Shoot yourself in the foot. You're my guest. Be my guest."

I was surprised by how quickly she changed from being sweet and bubbly to fierce and confrontational. "I'm not trying to insult anyone. I'm just *concerned*, that's all."

"I happen to know for a *fact* that I have a very informed audience." The studio audience leapt to its feet, fists pumping the air, chanting,

"Woo, Woo, Woo, Woo Woo!"

"Hey, I'm part of your audience too!" I said defensively. "I watch your show. I mean no disrespect. But let me share a little factoid with you, if I may."

"Go ahead."

"Of the two hundred thousand books published annually in this country, fewer than one percent ever become bestsellers. And of that one percent, only a fraction sell a million copies in their entire in-print lifespan. In contrast, a prime-time network television program that *only* pulls in a million viewers is considered a *FLOP* and is usually cancelled…"

"And *where* are we going with this?"

"Where're we going? It shows where most people go to get their information and their stories today," I said, lunging out of my chair, pressing my face into the nearest camera.

"And it's not books!"

The host broke for a commercial and asked if I was feeling all right. I grinned, "Couldn't be better!" Then (I don't remember this, but eye-witnesses claim that), I growled at her like a bobcat, at which point she snapped her fingers and two bouncers forcibly removed me from the set, my legs and feet flailing. Before I was exited out the studio doors, I turned my head and blurted to the audience and crew, "I'm sorry, I don't know what got into me today."

A year later I watched the tape of that show before the grand jury, and I could see what looked like foam coming out one corner of my mouth. I can admit now that I was in the middle of what has since been described as a "nervous breakdown," that I came apart in full view of millions of people, that my ability to distinguish between right and wrong had become skewed, that I made mistakes and took risks not worth taking. But I can't say, I *won't* say that this was a completely lost period of time for me. Even before my tawdry book left the printer, I realized that it wasn't going to topple the president, and *I* was the one whose little empire could be flattened. Whatever sense of purpose propelled me all these years, sputtered. My bibliography meant nothing to me. The more my ego unmoored from the illusory anchors of my persona, the more alive I felt (bizarrely enough). I didn't always feel *good* during that time, or happy, or safe, or in control, but I have never felt so alive!

My therapist thinks that my "emotional unraveling" began much earlier, around the time my mother died. And all the pill-popping was a way of not dealing with the loss directly. When I stopped the pills, and I announced my retirement from writing, only to turn around and write a trashy book that betrayed nearly everything I thought I believed in—something cracked. Sorrow and loss, love and anger, laughter and joy oozed out—along with lots of abnormal behavior:

- engaging a squirrel in a long conversation, thinking she might be the Buddha incarnate

- having nothing to say at a dinner given in my honor, inwardly berating the assembled crowd for their poor judgment

- screaming at a man for screaming at a meter maid for writing him a ticket, insisting that the man thank the meter maid for working such a detestable job so *he* didn't have to work that job; then going back and apologizing to the man for making such a scene

- sobbing uncontrollably while Frida practiced Eric Satie's *Gymnopédia*, my mother's favorite piece of music

- recalling a memory (that I had suppressed my entire life) of seeing my mother strapped to a hospital bed (I couldn't have been more than three years old), the terrified look in her eyes, the raspy voice of the doctor explaining to Aunt Chloe, "It's for her own safety." Remembering my confusion at the time, trying to understand how tying someone to a bed could make them better, eventually believing Aunt Chloe that Mommy wasn't really strapped to the bed, they were just playing a pretend game.

I went to the hospital that my mother stayed in close to a dozen times and asked for her records. I wanted to see how often she was put in restraints, what else they did to her and why. But all records of Rose Mobley were gone. As far as the hospital was concerned, she never existed. I left empty-handed, overtaken by a feeling of helplessness that must have only been a sliver of the helplessness my mother experienced. I lay down on a bench across the street from the hospital, looked up at the sky through watery eyes and had a vision of books unraveling: pages peeling free of their bindings, the wind catching each leaf, endowing them with the ability to float, bob, dive, somersault, *dance* through the domed proscenium. Into a cerulean sky, the idea for *The Flying Book Project* hatched. By some means, in honor of my mother, I would figure out a way to physically liberate books—setting them in motion across the sky. If nothing else, it could make for a grand art show.

I hurried home and rummaged through boxes of mildewing records till I found Ornette Coleman's 1972 *The Skies of America*. I dusted off the turntable, placed the needle on the vinyl, settled into my Backsaver chair, closed my eyes and listened to Ornette's soaring alto sax weave in and out of orchestral cloud patterns, evoking cries and celebrations of a paradoxical America. When the record was over, I called Samir to see if he still had connections to the electronic ink engineers at MIT.

Samir put me in touch with Hiroshi Kanagawa, who ended up directing the programming team that worked on *The Flying Book Project*. Years before working on e-ink and other "liquid media" projects, Hiroshi won tournaments flying model airplanes in Japan, and he'd been looking for an excuse to "play in the sky again." Hiroshi brought in Bishnu Rajbandari (known to everyone as The Raj) to be Chief Engineer. The Raj had an engineering degree from MIT, but his father—a master kite designer from Katmandu—is the one who really taught him the secrets of flight.

After a few months, Aconsha joined the team as the choreographer. She studied birds in flight: their patterns of alignment, cohesion, modes of steering. She called it "the genius of the flock," matched only by the protean performances of fish, those unschooled schools of synchronized swimmers. Aconsha's multi-colored notations for the project were works of art in themselves, full of flowing shapes, dashed and solid lines, arrows, arcs, swirls, whirls, and figure eights.

We premiered *The Flying Book Project* over Portland, Maine. Then we flew it over Philadelphia, Baltimore, and Richmond. Our initial idea was to launch the flying leaves with no publicity so they would appear as apparitions. But a smattering of traffic accidents purportedly caused by the sight of flying pages made us reconsider. After settling a few lawsuits (and voluntarily changing flight paths to avoid highways, busy intersections, and bridges), we decided to go public with some interviews.

The Flying Book Project *SKY LIT*

Worried about the decline of literacy in America, bestselling author and cultural critic Bleu Mobley had a thought: *If the people won't come to the books, maybe the books need to come to the people.* Fourteen months later, with the help of a team of engineers, students, and alumni from the Massachusetts Institute of Technology, he launched *The Flying Book Project*. Funded with Mobley's own life savings and bound together only by the thread of time and space, pages fly over cities and towns, swoop down Main Streets, along coastlines, over ballfields, bridges, and backyards. These spectacles of cascading classic and contemporary texts lift the spirits of people throughout the North American continent.

2006-08, Off The Shelf Editions/MIT Labs
Aquebogue, NY/Cambridge, MA

You don't need to be a meteorologist to see something is going on in the sky. Weather is for everyone. So too, *The Flying Book Project*. You needn't be an avid reader. You don't even need a library card. As long as you can see, and have a rudimentary ability to read, you are a member of *The Flying Book Club*.

In a suburb of Baltimore, a man in his early twenties fast-walks his girlfriend's dog down the street, worried that he's not going to make it back to his place in time to catch the FedEx man. While the girlfriend's basset hound is yellowing a car tire (at long last), the young man—an unemployed MBA grad with an addiction to video games—notices a movement of color in the sky. He looks up, wonders what he's seeing. Is it a flying banner? A very long kite? A hallucination? Are those *words*? What does it say? One banner/thingamajiggy (whatever it is) flies directly into his line of sight. It hovers in place for a few seconds like a hummingbird. He reads it. It turns, ascends. Another one glides into reading range. As one sequence of flying pages changes direction, dives, then soars past the horizon, another sails into view.

Barely believing his eyes, he takes out his cell phone and calls his girlfriend. "It's hard to describe," he tells her. "It's like wave after wave of flying flags with writing on them. Like giant pages. . . What do they *say*? Let me see. 'The spotted hawk swoops by and accuses me / He complains of my gab and my loitering / I sound my barbaric

yaws over the roofs of the world / The last scud of day holds back for me / It flings my likeness after the rest and true as any on the shadow'd wilds / it coaxes me to the vapor and the dusk.'" The young man rests his neck for a few seconds, switches the phone to his other ear. "Is that *awesome* or what? . . . I'm not *sure* what it means, but. . . *Yeah*, there's more. They keep coming. 'I depart as air / I shake my white locks at the runaway sun / I effuse my flesh in eddies / and drift it in lacy jags.' . . Yeah, hold on, there's more. They're moving further away from me. I have to catch up to them. . . Do I *what*? . . . No. I don't remember saying I *hate* poetry. Anyway, I don't think this is poetry. I'm not sure what it is. It's like an ad for something or something. Or some kind of art project. Hey, let me call you back."

In an interview at his Long Island home, Bleu Mobley—the best-selling author and artistic director of *The Flying Book Project*—described his intentions: "My hope was to create fleeting moments of wonder, to recapture the innocent experience of a child coming upon something for the first time. As a little boy, a friend of mine witnessed a field of moon flowers opening their glorious white petals to the light of the full moon. It took his breath away. I wonder what his reaction would be today if he came upon that same scene? I remember the first time I experienced a kiwi fruit. My mother let me hold it. Then she took a knife and sliced it in half. I was

flabbergasted that this nondescript hairy thing would open up into this beautiful, bright green silky inside with a perfect ring of black seeds. My mother cut the kiwi into quarters and handed me a section. When I bit into it, a sweet and sour circus of flavors exploded throughout my mouth, and the kiwi instantly became my favorite fruit. Unfortunately, kiwis were rare and expensive back then, and we were poor. I'm still partial to kiwi fruits, but now that they're everywhere and I can afford them, I haven't had one in years." Mobley had a distant look in his eyes. I wasn't even sure if he remembered my original question about his intentions. "Even the most sensuous encounters," he continued, "have a way of becoming neutered as we get older, through repeated exposure. So you can imagine what a challenge it is trying to rekindle the experience of being a new reader. Whatever my team and I came up with, it had to be at once recognizable and unfamiliar. It had to be a spectacle of some kind. We take so much for granted. Love. Reading. Life. Our capacity to imagine. But when *The Flying Book Project* swoops into view, for at least a few moments, we're reminded of all these things."

Before long, *Flying Book Project* sightings triggered text-messaging blasts informing people where to go and what direction the flying leaves were heading. Online discussion groups sprang up, creating forums for *Flying Book* photos, texts, and debates over which classic texts worked better in print versus "in the air," and which original texts were worthy of "air publication" and which were not. Despite all the publicity, there were people who never heard of the project, and some were convinced that the leaves were messages from outer space. We anticipated a little of that, figured, *What would be the harm if a few crazies in Nevada thought extra-terrestrials dug poetry?* But some people really freaked out that our planet was being invaded, so we bit the bullet, hired a public relations firm, held press conferences, put up a website with schedules, maps, study guides, disclaimers, and the *Flying Book* policy manual.

I never wanted my name attached to this project. Instead of writing *Flying Book* texts myself, I oversaw production and manufacturing, and was part of a team that accomplished far more than any one of us could on our own. I put together a panel and let them select the texts. They tapped the public domain first, using texts of writers like Ryokan, Rumi, Shakespeare and Dickinson. Then they selected from thousands of submissions composed specifically for *The Flying Book Project.*

As interest spread, we received requests from other countries, not only from their literary societies and private foundations but from government arts and humanities agencies. Could we bring *The Flying Book Project* to their part of the world?

It coaxes me to the vapor and the dusk.

I depart as air, I shake my white locks

at the runaway sun, I effuse my flesh in eddies,

and drift it in lacy jags.

under

your

boot-soles.

look

for

me

if you

want me

again

to grow

from the

grass

I love,

I
bequeath
myself
to the
dirt,

nevertheless

to you

good
health

You
will
hardly
know

but I
shall be

or what
I mean

who
I am

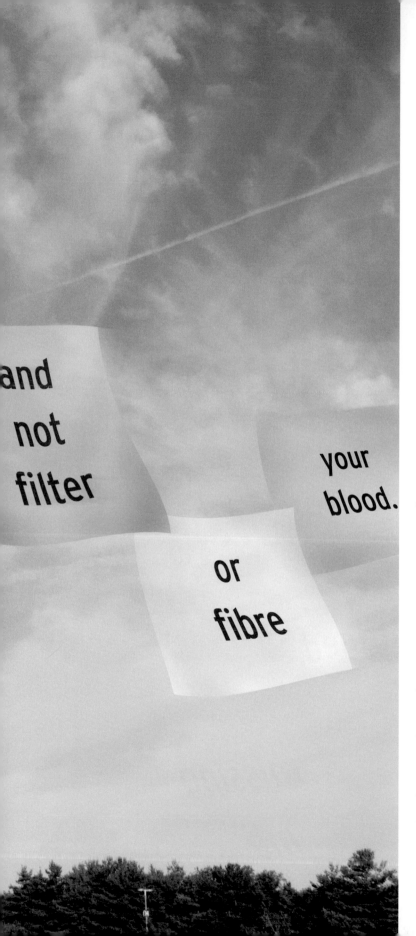

and
not
filter

your
blood.

or

fibre

It was all a bit over our heads, but globalizing the project made perfect sense: there was nothing inherently American about what we were doing, and having some money coming *in* appealed to Aconsha—who had good reason to worry that this project was bankrupting us.

At the same time, we were approached by commercial interests that wanted to sponsor *The Flying Book Project* with ads inserted between the poems. Though tempted (especially by one company that manufactured home solar power systems), I turned them all down. But then a New York ad agency teamed up with a national billboard company, and they just went ahead and ripped us off. We sued, but lost. As long as there are one or two changes to the design, a patent (apparently) means nothing. Competition trumps intellectual property rights. I didn't care that my idea was being used by others without giving me credit or paying royalties; what infuriated and saddened me was that I had spawned a medium that ended up cluttering the sky with logos and animated ad campaigns for everything from *Hamburger Helper* to political candidates— and there was absolutely nothing I could do about it but add my voice to the growing outcry calling for a total ban on the technology.

Failing
to
fetch me
at first

keep
encouraged,

missing
me

I stop

some

where

search

another,

waiting

Leaves of Grass

WALT WHITMAN

you.

for

9

DAWN

Instead of stirring the American public into a fever of repulsion and outrage toward the president, igniting a top-to-bottom investigation of all his misdeeds, crimes and misdemeanors, *Under the Rug* ended up being just one more pin-prick to a body politic that remained protected by an inexplicable bubble of immunity till its bitter, term-limited end. No matter how many scandals gyrated around him, the forty-third president of the United States managed to hold onto the reigns of power, swaggering up and down the steps of Air Force One, driveling facile quips into the laps of a stenographic press corps. Though he's ending his second term with the lowest approval ratings in the history of presidential approval ratings, he never was called before Congress to explain himself, he never was reprimanded by them or censured or special prosecuted or even named as an unindicted co-conspirator. Free of having to ward off any meaningful investigations of their administration, a few of the president's cronies in the Justice Department (most likely the same ones who inserted my name into the No Fly List) decided, while they still had the power, to have a little more fun with one of their least favorite pin-prickers.

The federal prosecutor whose lot was drawn for the job (a right-wing up-and-comer appointed by the president to the DC Circuit), convened a grand jury to *explore* whether or not any crimes were committed in connection to the writing of *Under The Rug*; the principal allegation being possible breaches of national security perpetrated by the White House cleaning woman. "Even under *normal* circumstances," the thirty-two-year-old, square-jawed prosecutor said in one of his non-press-conference press conferences, "*all* employees working in the White House are subject to security regulations that restrict what they have access to and what they can or cannot divulge to others. And the person in question would have had the *lowest* possible security clearance, subject to very restrictive guidelines. Under *normal* circumstances, violations of those guidelines are serious business, subject to federal law and prosecution. But during a time of war, any compromises to national security have the potential of being exploited to devastating effect. Lest we forget how recently our nation's capital was attacked by a diabolical enemy whose modus operandi is to use our vulnerabilities against us."

When asked by a reporter to respond to the charge that this grand jury was impaneled for the sole purpose of sticking it to one of the president's most ardent critics, the prosecutor dismissed the accusation with a rare smile. "By statute, our office is *completely* apolitical. Even if Mr. Mobley was the president's biggest fan, if he had information pertaining to breaches of national security, the grand jury would want to hear his testimony. Let me reiterate: Mr. Mobley is *not* suspected of any wrong-doing himself, and is only being called in as a witness." When asked if he thought Mobley's status could change, the prosecutor replied, "If he's a cooperative witness, and we have every reason to expect he will be, I don't foresee his status changing in regards to this case." Pushed by reporters to respond to further hypotheticals, the prosecutor said, "Who knows what the future might bring? It's *possible*, some time down the road, Mr. Mobley might be implicated as an *accomplice* to a crime. But that's speculation, and I'm not in the speculation business. As I said earlier, right now we just need to see where the facts lead. I'm sorry, but that has to be the last question for today. Let me remind you, for the duration of the grand jury proceedings, we will be enforcing a news blackout about everything taking place behind those doors. Have a good day. I'll talk to you tomorrow."

Behind those closed doors, I sensed a good deal of sympathy among the twenty-three grand jurors. At the end of my first day of testimony, one of them slipped me a copy of *The Boomerang Case*. I autographed it with the message, "And Justice For All." The next day the woman was gone from the grand jury, and the prosecutor warned me to cut the crap. I told him I was sorry, "I've been autographing books for thirty years and I didn't want to discriminate against the woman just because she happened to be serving on a grand jury." I promised the prosecutor I wouldn't do it again, but wondered why it mattered since I was only a witness and not a target of his probe.

When the prosecutor asked me how I wrote the "Articles of Evidence" (the one page chapter interludes in *Under The Rug*, each written from the perspective of a different inanimate object), I explained the concept of poetic license. When he asked if it was standard practice to use "poetic license" in a work of non-fiction, I explained that I never was one to adhere to standard practice. "The important thing," I said in a professorial tone, "was to get at *the truth*. Writing about a subject *or* an object in the third, second, or first person; or past, present, or future tenses, are stylistic choices. It's no different than a photographer choosing what lens to use or how to frame a picture. In the end, a photograph, a book, a movie— either reflects truth or it doesn't." When he asked if I possessed the actual articles of evidence that I wrote about, or if I even saw any of them with my own two eyes, I said, "I don't recall seeing any of them. Then again, I've never been inside the White House either."

I tried to be a cooperative witness, but when it came to answering questions about "the White House maid," I refused to answer on the grounds that my source requested anonymity. "You can ask me a hundred different ways, but that's a professional pact that I will not violate. A *sacred* pact." The prosecutor's impatience snapped into belligerence. "It may be a sacred pact to you, Mr. Mobley. It may even be a professional pact, but it is not a *legal* pact. I'm sure you're aware that there is no federal shield law protecting journalists or their sources. On the contrary, the law *requires* you to answer the question. Who is Ms. X?"

"I'm sorry, but I gave my word. Promising confidentiality to sources who have reason to fear retribution is something I learned about in seventh grade." I looked at the jurors and started telling them about Mr. Gutiero and *The Oracle*. The prosecutor interrupted my reminiscence. "It's nice to know that you were practicing journalism in middle school, but nowhere on your last *ten* tax returns did you list your occupation as journalist. Nor are you described as a journalist anywhere on the cover or inside this book," he said holding up a copy of *Under The Rug*. "Even if there was a federal shield law for journalists, which there *isn't*, you and your Ms. X would not be protected by it. Unless you are her lawyer or her doctor, she enjoys no confidentiality privileges with you."

"Then I'll take the Fifth."

"Why would you take the Fifth? I'm not asking you to tell us anything that could incriminate you. Unless there's something we don't know about that could. . ."

"Did you hear that?" I said, turning to the jurors. "See what he's doing? He's suggesting that by asserting my constitutional right not to incriminate myself, I am somehow incriminating myself."

"Okay, Mr. Mobley. Did you bring your lawyer with you today?" I nodded.

"Let's go into the hallway."

In the hallway, the prosecutor tells my lawyer that he's ready to offer me immunity.

"Could it be a trick?" I ask my lawyer in our stairwell huddle. "If I consider his offer, could it imply that I'm concealing something, then he can withdraw the offer and make me the target of his investigation?"

"It *is* a trick, but not the one you're thinking about," explained my lawyer. "If you accept immunity, then you can't be prosecuted. This is a good thing. But it also means you'll be compelled to answer all his questions."

"And what if I don't answer all his questions?"

"Then he can get the judge to hold you in contempt."

"What do you think I should do?"

"It depends if you have anything to hide?"

"You mean other than the identity of my source?"

"Yes."

"Mmm. *Maybe*."

"Maybe? Like maybe *what*? Like what are we talking about?"

I looked around the stairwell, and up to the ceiling. "I don't feel comfortable having this conversation here."

"Okay. I'm thinking you *should* take the immunity. I'll try to get you Transactional."

"What's that?"

"Full immunity. It means they can never prosecute you for anything you testify about."

"I like the sound of that. But I'm still not giving up the identity of my source."

"That's your decision. Just don't be surprised if you spend the night behind bars. I know where they'll send you. It's no picnic in there."

A few hours later I signed papers agreeing to *Use Immunity*, a more limited form of immunity that prevents anyone from using my grand jury testimony as evidence against me, but still leaves open the possibility of being prosecuted in the future as long as the evidence is derived from other sources.

The fact that my lawyer—whose specialty is intellectual property law—wasn't able to get me full immunity should have been a wake-up call. Now I know that intellectual property law is as different to criminal law as Gregorian chant is to punk rock; but at the time, I just thought *a lawyer is a lawyer*, and if you have one you trust, you stick with her.

When I re-entered the grand jury room the following morning as a partially immunized witness, the prosecutor handed off the questioning to his sidekick, a middle-aged, roly-poly, Assistant United States Attorney, who had a less combative approach, but referred continuously to the contents of an overstuffed three-ring-binder that had all kinds of detailed information about me, most of which had nothing to do with *Under the Rug*, or possible breaches of White House security regulations. Over the course of seven hours, in response to very leading questions, I admitted to:

- using assistants to help me write my books since 1992.
- requiring my assistants to keep mum about the specifics of what it is they do for me.
    (Though I made sure to add that all my employees were well paid, and nobody ever complained about keeping certain things confidential).
- being Dr. Sky Jacobs.
    (That is to say, using a pseudonym—just like many authors have used throughout the ages).
- disguising my voice as Dr. Sky Jacobs for interviews and his weekly radio program.
- issuing composite photographs of Dr. Sky Jacobs to the public.
    (I challenged the implication that by using the pseudonym Dr. Sky Jacobs, I fraudulently impersonated a doctor, since I [Bleu Mobley] have a PhD, and therefore the right to use the Dr. prefix. I never once wrote or said that Sky Jacobs had a medical or psychology degree. Any references to Jacobs being a psychologist or psychiatrist were made erroneously by others. Sky Jacobs never took on private patients, and any advice he gave was always given in general terms, never as specific medical or therapeutic counsel to individuals).

being the mastermind behind the free-market ideologue Blane Masters, also not a real person; hiring an actor to play him in public, and debating him once on TV.

- concocting the bogus Privatize Now Institute as an imprint for Masters' books.

- concocting a research group called *The Council For Bible Verification* to solicit release forms for *The* New *New Testament*.

- voting on the Lower East Side of Manhattan even though my primary residence is on Long Island.

> (Though I admitted to this, I questioned why it mattered. The U.S. Attorney shot back, "Would it matter if I told you that it's a felony to vote in a district where you don't reside?" I told him I was unaware of that law, and explained how I forgot to register the first year we moved to Long Island, so I went back to my old voting place, and after that simply never bothered to re-register. "The important thing," I added, "was that I always made sure to vote—to participate in our democracy. And anyway, I only voted *once* in each election." Nobody laughed. "My God, what is this?" I asked, wondering what else my pudgy inquisitor had in his bloated ring binder.)

I also admitted to:

- having a substance abuse problem (but not succumbing to it in 187 days).

- having had a nervous breakdown (and still being in a process of recovery).

- having a history of mental illness in my family (though it's none of anyone's god damned business).

Instead of looking at the prosecution team, I confessed to these things looking directly into the faces of the grand jury as if they were my personal judges—that long imagined panel of ordinary wise people made up of readers, moviegoers, TV watchers—moral arbitrators sitting before me with impartial goodness. If the man had asked me if I once kissed Monica Medollo, or if I thought my *Flying Book Project* might have caused some traffic accidents, or if I considered myself an imperfect human being—I would have said yes to all of it.

This interrogation should have been one of the worst experiences of my life, but oddly, expelling all these tightly wound secrets to this randomly selected quorum of souls turned out to be an unexpected relief. I felt grateful to them for not averting their eyes or appearing to take pleasure in watching me field these prying questions. Like me, they were pawns in the hands of political hacks who had hijacked the system to conduct a witch hunt. Each of those jurors had their own stories, their own imperfections and overreachings. They'd all taken some well meaning wrong turns in their lives—*I could see it in their eyes*. Undoubtedly, some of them would break their sworn obligation never to repeat anything they heard in the grand jury room, and in time, some of the things I confessed to would leak into the public—I already forgave them for it. They would soon be asked to pass judgment on me (like a set of teeth passes judgment on a ham sandwich), but I wasn't going to judge them.

Having immunized me, and gotten me to answer all these personal softening-up questions, it came time for the assistant prosecutor to deliver the sucker punch.

"Who is Ms. X?"

"I'm sorry, I can't tell you that."

My refusal to answer this question triggered an elaborate game of follow-up questions by both the prosecutor and his assistant, trying to bamboozle me into saying the name. After refusing to give up even a middle initial (let alone a gender or ethnic background), they threatened me. I stood my ground. They made good on their threat, calling on the judge to slap me with contempt-of-court charges.

So began my internment in this dungeonary pit stop that has lasted a whole lot longer than one night. Now that I'm coming up on my ninth month, I'm not as petrified as I was when I first arrived. As dismal and stultifying as the place is, I have carved out an existence for myself in here, and have made some of the closest friendships of my life. But it's time to end it. I can't expect Aconsha to put up with this for much longer—the faithful wife visiting her imprisoned husband the allotted five hours a month. I tell her how lucky I feel, a screw-up like me married to an incredible woman like her, and how sorry I am leaving her the way I did, surrounded in scandal and now debt. She agrees I was reckless with the money. She would have managed the finances differently, but she's still proud of me for what I'm doing. I tell her there's nothing to be proud of. She tells me there's a lot to be proud of. I tell her there isn't.

"There is."

"Isn't."

"Is."

"Not."

Since Frida is away at college, I've probably seen more of her than if I'd been living at home. But it can't be a good thing, visiting your father in a federal prison, even though she says that I'm her hero, and she brings me copies of petitions she's collected describing me as a political prisoner and demanding my release.

It's Ella I worry about most. She barely visits anymore, and when she does, she's distant. She doesn't hide her disappointment or her anger. I can't bear it. I've deserted her, and for what? For a principle that makes no sense to a thirteen-year-old.

The headline for her is simple: **MY FATHER DOESN'T LOVE ME ANYMORE**

She has a friend whose father left home for a more tangible cause—to go fight in Iraq. He got hit by an IED and has a prosthetic leg. "Isaac's dad had no choice," Ella tells me.

"He *did* have a choice," I tell her. "He chose to enlist. He didn't do it because he wanted to. He did it because he believed it was the right thing to do for his country. It was a brave thing to do."

"Then why'd you say it was a terrible waste?"

"Did I say that? I shouldn't have. We all make choices and sacrifices, but things don't always work out the way we hope." Ella turns toward the barred windows in the visiting room. My very expressive and affectionate child has grown chilly with me. A girl from her school has a father up in Sing Sing. "At least *he* killed somebody," she says, her aloof pose silhouetted by the glare of the afternoon sun. "He doesn't have a choice. He *has* to be locked up." There's a beautiful logic to what she says. Ella's a beautiful kid. Her willful resentment sledgehammers the fortress of my charade. At least now she thinks that I've sacrificed being her live-at-home dad for some holier-than-thou principle. What will she think when she finds out I'm a fraud, and sees images on TV of people throwing their FREE BLEU MOBLEY paraphernalia into bonfires? *I'm sorry Ella. Daddy screwed up, big time.*

"All you have to do," my lawyer says, "is tell them the name of your source, and you're back home with your family."

I'm ready to tell it.

I will go to the prosecutor and tell him,

I am the source.

That's what I'll say, because it's the truth. *I* am the source.

There was a person who had a low level job in the White House who came to me about writing a book, claiming to be a witness to indiscretions. But she, he, that person, backed out after only one interview. I wouldn't even call it an interview. It was a conversation over coffee. The person told me a few rather inflammatory things, but it was very sketchy. We set up a meeting for the following week. I waited at the address, and waited, and waited till I couldn't wait anymore. When I called the contact number I had, it was disconnected. I didn't know the person's real name or how to get in touch, and I never heard from him or her again. That should have been the end of it.

But it wasn't.

Instead of abandoning the project, or going out to find other sources who could confirm or deny the allegations, I went ahead and wrote a book anyway, filling in the gaps of the person's story.

In other words—I made most of it up, whole cloth. Or seven-eighths.

I came up with the title *Under The Rug*, designed a cover, and wrote the book from start

to finish in an eight-day nonstop frenzy, without help from any of my assistants. It was the first book in years that I wrote entirely by myself. After I began writing, I couldn't stop. I fell into a trance-like state, unable to distinguish between what I was imagining and what was real. Differences between night and day, fiction and non-fiction, ethical and feckless melted away. *That's* what was breached. Not—White House security! In the throes of my confused state I breached the sacrosanct line between journalism and fiction with hardly a second thought. All I had were *first* thoughts. Words poured through my fingers, scenes appeared before my eyes, objects took on human traits—the fragments of a story came together as if from on high. It felt as if I had little choice in the matter.

By the time I brought the manuscript to an editor that I'd once worked with, and told her that it was non-fiction, and asked her to "trust me on this," I knew that I had played fast and loose with the truth. But in my heart of hearts I believed that a greater truth was being served. I believed that I was morally justified fictionalizing a story that could take down the most powerful man in the world—a man who lied to bring his country to war, lied about torture, lied about spying on his own people, lied about the science of global warming and the fate of the planet, lied about so many things that imperiled millions of lives. I must have convinced myself that because *my* lying was done with integrity—as a selfless act that put my entire reputation and livelihood at risk for a greater good—it was okay. A tragedy had befallen my country and it was my job to rescue it from the brink. If I needed to show the emperor naked for people to see that he had no clothes—so be it.

Four months after *Under The Rug* was published, I checked myself into a clinic to be treated for a nervous breakdown. After years of being a highly functional neurotic, I finally blossomed into a full-blown psychotic. "It's happened," I told Dr. Michaels. "I've turned into my mother." He insisted that wasn't it. "Yours is a temporary condition, Bleu. There's no reason for it to become chronic. The thing is, your writing has…" he corrected himself, "I mean your *composing* has always been a way for you to fill the holes in your life. That's what words and books have been for you. You never had a father or knew who he was, so you wrote, sorry, you *composed* books imagining who he might be. You didn't understand marriage or know many people who had healthy marriages, so you looked toward your neighbors, that couple you admired, and wrote a book about them. You didn't believe in therapy, so when you experienced loss and encountered hard-to-figure-out conflicts, you invented your own therapist based on the things you do believe in: Zen Buddhism, contrariness, anti-materialism, individual choice. When you felt helpless about wars and other injustices you had no control over, you wrote stories that shed light on the effects of those things. More recently you've been afraid that words are losing their primacy in the culture. To fill the hole, you made books with televisions in them and coloring books with pictures of war atrocities. You tried to bring poetry to people who wouldn't seek it out for themselves by printing poems on toilet paper, and now you're making large-scale pages that fly 'over town and country' in order to enthrall people into reading. You're petrified that words are losing their meaning entirely as your government distorts language and does all the craven things that you've been railing against on television and in your political writings. But you grew weary of your own use of words as 'rhetorical weapons,' so your solution was to quit writing altogether. Just like that, you quit the very thing that enabled you to survive and thrive—and started making book lamps, book toys, and what do you call them, book *accessories*. You say that you're still 'composing' books. But they contain no stories! They're all form and no content. You think this freed you from something—from, as you say, 'believing in your own biography'—and now you're able to experience your feelings and memories and LIFE itself *directly* without having to carry pads and pens around, without having to turn any of it into a book. I follow your reasoning, but life is not always reasonable. I agree, it's a good thing that you're coming into contact with feelings that have been walled up inside you for years. You're grieving over your mother's death and also over her life. Your childhood is flashing back at you all over the place, and when your friend Carla died, it really stirred the pot. But your retirement from writing is not helping. I think you gave up writing so you could test this lingering fear of yours that you would one day turn into your mother and become an island of images. Unfortunately it's left you with little ability to process all these feelings you're having. If you were just a visual artist like your mom, it would be different. But you love *words*, and when you deep-sixed them from your work, it was like killing off the very thing that makes you who you are. Writing isn't just a career for you, it's how you make sense of the world—how you make it whole. Without it you faced the abyss and the randomness with no defenses."

"And what's wrong with that? I don't want to make something whole that's really broken just to make myself feel comfortable. I don't want to keep doing things because I'm used to doing them. Can't a person make a radical change in his life without getting psychoanalyzed to death?"

"Blame my profession if you want, but you're the one who checked yourself into a mental health clinic. I think you and I have been making good progress, Bleu. You've just hit a nasty bump in the road. Can I tell you what I think happened?" he asked, moving his chair closer to me.

"You're on a roll. Don't let me stop you."

"I think when your old newspaper buddy presented you with an opportunity to write again, to write another book that incidentally could rid the world of one of its top spoilers, you leapt at the chance, even though it made no sense for you to do it. Even when your source vanished and there was nothing for you to write about, you didn't walk away from the project. You thought you could save the world from a tyrant, but you were really trying to save yourself."

"Oh, that's heavy."

"I think what you really need to do, after you get some rest and some food into you, is start writing about yourself. A hundred books you've written about every kind of person and every thing under the sun, *except* yourself. Once you start dealing with that, you can move onto something else."

"Whatever a writer writes is a reflection of himself. Anyway, I'm a boring subject."

"You think you're boring? You should listen to some of my other patients."

It turns out, the shrink I picked to help me deal with my substance abuse problem has written three books himself.

They're not the most riveting books ever written, but I like the things he says about all these serotonin uptake inhibitors and anti-psychotic drugs making the problem worse for a lot of people who really need to find purpose in their lives, and love and friendship and community. As a one-on-one therapist, Dr. Michaels (Leonard) has a way of explaining things in neat little packages that you can take or leave with a grain of salt, but every so often he comes up with something very practical that really helps. Like getting me out of the looney bin I signed myself into, which he called counter-productive. "We're trying to get you *unhooked* from medication. Pills aren't what you need, or psychiatric interns searching the DSM for the exact name of your disorder. The *world* is crazy, and you have a way of taking too many of its problems onto your shoulders. I'm sure all that weight has something to do with your back problems. It's time to bring things home, my friend," he said putting his finger to my heart. As he approached me I could see myself reflected in his glasses, a wavering, ghostly figure. When he leaned back, I was gone.

Leonard drove me home from the clinic, and without divulging any confidences (he was the only person alive who knew how I had written *Under The Rug*), he explained to Aconsha the highlights of what I was going through. When she asked what to do about my not being able to sleep, he prescribed things like forgiveness and acceptance and embracing imperfection. "That all sounds wonderful," she said, "but how does he get to sleep on those things?" As soon as he left, Aconsha called a local Ayurvedic doctor asking for something that would help me sleep. Later that night after drinking the dreadful brew, I told Aconsha my shrink's theory about my insomnia. "He thinks it's caused by all the middle-of-the-night scenes I lived through growing up, when my mother was acting out, or being taken out of the apartment by cops or medics, with all our neighbors looking on. It's true, the nights were often difficult for me when I was a kid—and there were times when I was frightened (out of my mind), and lonely (fighting back tears or soaking in them), and falling to sleep was next to impossible—but I don't buy his theory. I just think I have an overactive mind. Sometimes a pipe is just a pipe."

When the judge threw me into this place, and then wouldn't release me, I thought for sure I would die—either from a relapse of nervous breakdown leading to suicide, or at the hands of a serial killer. I owe it to Chester for showing me the keys to my survival. *What good luck*, I thought, *to be rooming with someone like him*. As soon as I felt myself becoming dependent on Chester for friendship and protection, I found out he was the ringleader of a notorious white power gang. I chose not to believe the rumors about his brutality, and chalked my cellmate's lapses into hate speech up to bluster. From the beginning of the writing workshop, Chester would challenge the writings of anyone who was black, Latino, or foreign born—taking issue with their life experiences.

He wasn't the only one who made it necessary for me to keep clarifying the terms of what we were doing. "You can criticize the writing, but not the subject matter *or* the writer."

I had taught some lively classes at the college, but they never got as emotionally charged as the ones I've taught in here. A huge fight broke out one time over a love poem about a black man and a white woman. The reading of that poem resulted in broken bones, puncture wounds, smashed furniture, a lot of bruised feelings, and the warden nearly shutting us down. That's when I realized that the very same things that were saving my ass were fraught with danger. After the love poem rumble, I revised my teaching methods and posted a sign with strict guidelines for the writing workshop:

WRITING WORKSHOP PARTICIPANTS
MAY NOT CRITICIZE, BELITTLE OR ATTACK ANY OTHER WORKSHOP PARTICIPANT BECAUSE OF THEIR RACE, RELIGION, LACK OF RELIGION, CULTURAL UPBRINGING, PLACE OF BIRTH, SCHOOLING, LACK OF SCHOOLING, AGE, DISABILITY, SEXUAL ORIENTATION, LIFE EXPERIENCES, THOUGHTS OR FEELINGS.

WORKSHOP PARTICIPANTS ARE ALSO NOT TO:

- INQUIRE ABOUT THE CRIMES OTHER WORKSHOP PARTICIPANTS ARE ACCUSED OF COMMITTING (UNLESS THE PERSON VOLUNTEERS THE INFORMATION)

- ASK ABOUT ANYONE'S INNOCENCE OR GUILT

- THROW ANYTHING OR START A PHYSICAL FIGHT OR A FIGHT OF ANY KIND

- USE A PEN AS A WEAPON; BRING WEAPONS OF ANY KIND INTO THIS ROOM, OR USE WRITING OR ABUSIVE LANGUAGE AS A MEANS OF ATTACKING OTHER PARTICIPANTS

- SLOUCH OR SLEEP OR MAKE FACES OR NOISES OR BE INATTENTIVE WHILE OTHERS ARE SHARING THEIR WRITING

- READ ALOUD WHILE CHEWING GUM OR SUCKING ON CANDY, TOBACCO, OR ANY OTHER SUBSTANCE

For safety reasons, I decided it would be best to describe my role as a *facilitator* rather than teacher—to avoid being in a position of authority over a group of people who have major issues with authority. But this seemingly minor difference, between *teacher* and *facilitator*, not only improved the attitude coming at me from my incarcerated brethren, it transformed my own attitude and expectations. Instead of conducting a class, I became just another participant in a collective. We all have tasks, and mine is to ensure that everyone is making progress with their writing. Someone else makes sure the ground rules are adhered to. Others are in charge of supplies, time keeping, coordinating events. . .

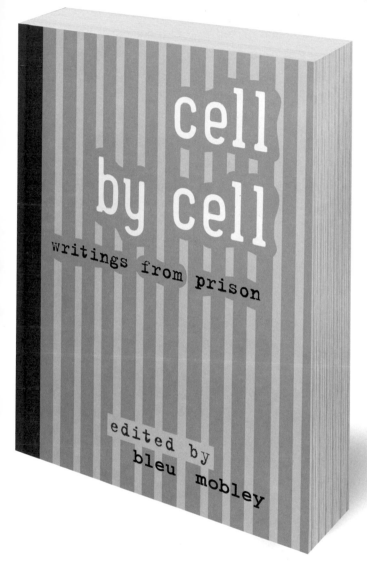

Cell By Cell

This collection features poetry and short prose by twenty-four in-resident members of the *Writing From Life* Workshop at a federal detention center near Washington DC. These searingly intimate, uncensored writings transcend bars and barbed wire, ink and paper, enabling the reader to practically hear the voices of these incarcerated men as they reflect on their lives in and out of captivity. Edited by in-residence workshop facilitator (and best-selling author) Bleu Mobley. Proceeds go to the *Cell By Cell Writing in Prison Fund.*

2008, McSweeneys, San Francisco, CA

excerpt [from the section *Scars*]   CELL BY CELL

THREE KINDS OF SCARS *Abrafo Cougbadja*

My happiest scars are from climbing coconut trees. When I was a child I would walk through the forest to the bank of the river, climb a tree with my bare hands and feet, drink my coconut, look out at the sunlight dancing on the river, and think, *It is good to be alive.*

I also have scars from when I was beaten by military police and tortured with a wooden stick and a metal ball on the end like the kind of thing people probably used in Medieval days. These are the first scars I got fighting for democracy in my country. I wear them like the flag of a nation that hasn't yet come to be.

Then there are scars inside my heart from losing my wife and never knowing if she is dead or alive. The first two scars are nothing to me, like a mosquito I can flick off with one finger. But the scar of losing the love of my life—no treetop view or medicine can help me to forget. Even my freedom cannot heal that wound.

THE THIRD DEGREE *Robert Earl Anderson*

Got this third degree burn on my hand from cooking bathtub crank with Charlene in Atlanta. Whenever I shot her the middle finger after that, she'd ask why I was giving her the third degree. I've got to laugh—all the stupid shit we used to do. Laugh to keep from crying.

- First we'd go to the hardware store, pick up a half-gallon jug of muriatic acid, otherwise known as the stuff you use to clean swimming pools.
- Then we'd go to the drug store to buy Benzedrex inhalers, otherwise known as those things you stick up your nose when your head's all stuffed up.
- Break a couple of inhalers and squeeze the juice out.
- Mix the muriatic acid in with the juice.
- Set a roll of toilet paper on fire in the middle of the bathtub.
- Hold the little pan of Benzedrex and muriatic acid above the flames.
- By the time the toilet paper burns away, it's ready to smoke. You can kick back, hitch a ride on an angel, and the stinging, stupid world fades to laughter and you're body-free.

Except *that* night, we were already wasted on something else. The shower curtain caught fire. I grabbed hold of the burning curtain. Charlene dropped the scalding crank all over her legs. Neither of us was in any condition to drive to the hospital, so we stayed there playing doctor and nurse from hell, making a bad situation a whole lot worse. *That's* what I see whenever I look at my hand.

IF THIS SCAR WERE A LADDER *Cashman Woodard*

If this scar were a ladder I would climb
To the universal clock, reverse time
Before I worked my grind, the crime,
Before this razor-tooth world tainted my mind
It's cliché, but they say we all choose our fate,
Can't relate, wasn't many choices to make
Either poison of the hood, venom, snakes

Nothin but to hustle, watching out for the jakes

When you're Black, that's reality, not a tough break—

"You lie in the bed you make"

I alone didn't land me in this cell bed awake

The system forces your hand

Won't allow you to live as a man

Ain't complainin, just saying THEY don't give a damn

Was a *plan* for me to end up right here where I stand

Another child caught on the Ave livin fast

Without guidance on a dangerous path

If this scar were a ladder let me climb again

To a new height, my life to begin

Learned a lot since the day I came in

This prison forcing me to travel within

I see the picture much clearer: I'm Black in AmeriKKKa!

Land mines, gotta always beware of em

Soldier up, time to know for sure who I am

Mind and spirit still free when the cell door slam

HARD ENOUGH DYING *Sergeant Tom*

First time I took her to the hospital was to get the lump on her head checked out. They got this fucking kid doing the biopsy. I say, Are you an intern? He says, Yeah. Well I say, Get the fuck out of here, in plain English. You don't know what the fuck you're doing. You know you don't know what the fuck you're doing. Your hands are sweating. You're starting to sweat all over just to put a fucking needle in. Her veins fell apart! I say, You're not going to *practice* on her. You've been practicing on her for forty-fucking-minutes.

Two weeks later I bring her in for the operation. We're waiting and waiting in the waiting-fucking room. I see the name tag of the attending physician. It says KELLY. I say, You know you got two l's in your fucking name. After seven fucking hours you say you're gonna admit her. Now you're telling me to take her home, right? She's gonna drop dead in the street or jump out the fucking window. She's losing her fucking mind. He goes down the hall. Five minutes later he comes back. Well, we're gonna admit her. Well by Jesus! A quarter to ten before they got her up to the fucking room. Eleven in the morning till a quarter to ten at night. Once she's lying in the bed, they're hitting her with blood. They're hitting her with this and that. They punched her with so many needles and tubes, she looked like a science experiment. I ask the surgeon, I thought you said the operation went well? Surgeon says, The operation itself was a success, only your wife is starting to fail. Jesus fucking Christ. HIS OPERATION was a success! (You could see the beautiful stitch job he did when we planted her. He should get a job sewing jeans for Calvin Klein in China.) It's only that *my wife* is failing. I don't argue that everybody's got to go some time. And maybe Paula's time really was coming up. All I'm saying is, it's hard enough dying without them killing you. I shouldn't have done what I did, but *somebody* had to show that fucking white coat what it feels like on the other side of his clipboard.

HER EYES *Chuck Zimmer*

the mother of the boy / *her eyes* / the boy i hit that night / her eyes are my scars / didn't even know i hit anything at first / had some beers after the softball game / no more than any saturday night / five pitchers between four guys / it was so hot that night / not just hot—humid / i remember the first cold mug feeling so good / tasted like water / by the fifth mug it was just starting to taste like beer / big athletic guy like me / i always thought / metabolism like mine / always thought i drove *better* after five or six beers / no kidding / smoother on the steering wheel / breezier making turns / less in a hurry / singing to my favorite tape / nice guy / i always thought / volunteered with big brothers / have a kid of my own / used to be his hero / his eyes to the world / it could have been *him* that night / but it was *her* boy rolling out from the curb on his skateboard / still some light in the sky / should've seen him / should've slowed down for the stop sign twenty yards ahead / her eyes / her devastation / her boy / i remember hearing a dull thud / that's all i ever knew of him / a dull thud / he was dead in an instant / didn't know what hit him / i replay it in my mind a million times / a million rewinds / a boy taken down in an instant / could've been my boy / she wrote me back—said she can never forgive / do i have any idea / any idea what i took? / she can never forgive what i did / but her faith allows her / her faith *instructs* her to forgive the person / i forgive you / she wrote / but not what you did / her faith / her eyes / her boy / my boy / her devastation / my scars.

THE JOLLY GREEN GIANT *Chris[sy]*

I could write a book about all the scars and aches and pains from all the plastic surgeries, silicone injections, having my hips done (just enough to make them a little curvy), the laser treatments on my face (which weren't bad because I never was that hairy), and having to do the BIG surgery in two stages instead of all at once (still waiting and saving for Part Two!).

I could write about all the times I got beat up as a kid for being a girlie-boy (my mother had to take me out of school by ninth grade to keep me from getting killed); how scarred I felt on the INSIDE as far back as I can remember, knowing something was wrong, knowing I'm *supposed* to be a girl, having everybody tell me I'm gay, and I'm like, "No, I'm Chrissy."

"No you're gay."

"No I'm Chrissy."

Until I was like, "Okay fine, I'm gay," just to shut them up.

I could write about hearing the whispers behind my back after I started the treatments and procedures, half my gay friends and half my straight women friends hating me because I'm turning the heads of the men *they* wish they could get, and half my lesbian friends going, *Who the hell are you?* Experiencing the really abusive side of men for the first time; either they want to get laid or they're showing me off like I'm their science fair project.

And being in here—Oh man, I could write a *dozen* books.

But the scar I want to write about, the one that tugs at the middle of the middle of me every day is the shame my mother and sister feel now that I *look like* who I am. After not seeing them for two years, I showed up to my brother's wedding wearing make-up and a miniskirt. (By then I was a B cup heading into a C). My new sister-in-law and all her bridesmaids were like, "Oh my God, she looks better than we do." Once he got the okay from them, my brother was cool with it. But my mother and sister said I RUINED the wedding. I'm a wedding *ruiner*. I ruined their box I could never fit myself into, that's what I ruined. After the reception, I was playing outside with my niece. She's calling me Uncle Chris, and I tell her, "Let's do something, honey. Let's just call me Aunt Chrissy from now on." It took me a half hour of correcting her, and she's been calling me Aunt Chrissy ever since. I asked my mother and sister, "Why is it, a nine-year-old girl can learn to call me Chrissy, but you guys can't? If you told me to call you The Jolly Green Giant, I would call you The Jolly Green Giant because you asked me to call you that. Because I love you." They know where I am. They can come visit if they cared to.

Memory Scars Serenade Me To Sleep Every Night *Angel Cardenez*

I remember my oldest brother Oscar teaching me about the Lucky. "Every time you break open a new pack, first cigarette you pull, flip it upside down and put it back in the pack. That's your Lucky. When you've smoked all the others and the Lucky's the only one left, force yourself to stop whatever you're doing and think about the good things in your life. It's your Lucky because it gives you luck. Only sad thing about it, it's your last cigarette, which is another reason why you savor it. Just like this breath could be your last. Got to make it count, brother. Live it. Breathe it to the fullest."

I remember Paul and Dolores taking me in after Oscar died. Paul said, "Here, read this... Now read this... Now this." They turned me onto ideas I never even knew existed. Dolores put a video camera in my hand and said, "Show me what you see." I said, "I don't even know how to..." Dolores shushed me. "Just go like this. Push that down like that, and aim." I remember Paul telling me to get rid of my weapon, and me telling him, "As long as there's one person on this earth with a tool, I gotta have mine. They point that thing at me, I'll do whatever they tell me. But if they go for the trigger, I'll get mine off just a little bit quicker. That's my philosophy." Paul shook his head like, you don't get it man. That's no philosophy. I rolled my eyes back at him like, no man, this is one thing *you* don't get.

My little brother Ro always quacked like a chick. His real name is Pedro, but we called him Ro. Every thought that flew through his head he had to share. Sometimes I just wanted to shut it off. I'd be like, "Yo. Don't take offense, but I'm not listening to you anymore tonight." I remember thinking, *Where'd Ro get that chatterbox gene from?*

I remember going for long drives with Dad and Oscar in "borrowed" cars, every window open, radio cranked way up, singing, laughing, hardly ever saying a word. Didn't know enough to be scared back then. Used to think death, anyway it gets you must be natural. I thought bullets flying through the air were a part of nature, like mosquitoes and pollen. What else would you think—your father gets gunned down when you're ten years old? Some kind of "business deal" gone bad. Your big brother, gunned down when you're thirteen. You're standing on the corner. Shots ring out. Somebody screams, "Oscar!" You turn around. Your brother, who you *adore*, who taught you almost everything you know, is on the ground. Somebody else running in the opposite direction.

I remember years earlier, before my mind was formed enough to understand, before we moved into the projects—a favorite uncle disappeared to a place called *Away*. In between swatting flies, bullets ricocheted through houses most people wouldn't live in if you gave them one for free. My entire youth, scored to a soundtrack of sirens advancing and retreating. On TV, white kids went to country summer homes to visit their relatives and go horseback riding. We took the shuttle bus to prisons, hospitals and graveyards. Barbecued on the edges of parking lots. Heaven was a fabulous family barbecue on the edge of an asphalt cloud. I remember Oscar saying, "All this heaven shit is bullshit." He hated anything Latin. He refused to speak Spanish. He'd tell our father, "That's not my language, man." He wouldn't eat the food or listen to the music. He'd say, "The Spanish conquered us with lies about heaven and hell and an almighty god and his favorite son, and our people took this god and made it their own, so much more than others. We fill our tiny homes with golden saints who blind us from the truth. They took our history, our land, our people. We should've fought harder."

Oscar didn't say much, but when he did, it always made me think. I remember him telling me one time, "Everything on this earth has an energy that cannot be destroyed. They can kill me. They can take my body, but I will never die. Maybe I'll show up in a rock some day or a buzzing lamppost or the wind—tickle your ear when a storm rolls in." I didn't understand what he was saying at the time. A week later he was dead, defending a corner. Took him years to establish that corner.

MY SCAR, BIGGER THAN YOUR SCAR   *Chester Clarkson*

my scar, bigger than your scar

my scar, is a daddy who wasn't ever there

my scar, a daddy was there

day and night, night and day

one left a hole. the other filled it with his fist

my scar, I had two daddies

my scar, four daddies, five daddies, six

my scar, a mother way too tough

my scar, a mother too laissez-faire

my scar, a mother doped up all the time

my scar, a mother way too famous

my scar, a mother for sale on every corner

my scar, a mother loved me too much

my scar, a mother really my grandma

my scar, my scar, my scar, the sugar made me do it

my scar, the TV made me do it

oh yeah, that's *my* scar

the computer game, the internet. the lyrics, porno

my scar, the gun made me do it

the bullet, the NRA

my scar, my DNA

my scar, your DNA

my scar, the NBA never signed me up

my scar, I was born a Rockefeller, the pressure just too much to bear

my scar, born with no underwear

my scar, goes back four-centuries-and-a-half

my scar, planted by a UFO

my scar, the way you look at me

my scar, had a panic attack and moved to Canada

my scar, someone wrote a book about

my scar, has its own section in the library

my scar, got panel-discussed on PBS

my scar, they added to the official list of diseases

my scar, has support groups all over the world

my scar, I'm all alone with it

my scar is bigger than your scar
I chicken-scratch it on pads of paper and bathroom stalls
I wrap myself in it 24 and 7
nurture it, curse it, feed it, weed it, bleed it, need it, milk it for all that it's worth
my littlest scar is bigger than all your biggest, baddest scars put together

my scar, my scar,
my scar, bigger than your scar

When I taught college students, I always tried to get them to see past themselves, to go outside and bear witness to a world they didn't know much about. But in here, nobody is going anywhere except the yard for an hour a day, or to court, or to be transferred to another joint, or if they're lucky, set free. The field of witness in here, by necessity, is *the self*. Many of these guys—even the ones who are just now losing the peach fuzz on their faces—have lived more, seen more, embody more emotion (pent up or otherwise) than a lot of professors emeritus I've known. Some of them may be ruthless, or out of control, but almost every one has taught me something. More than I've taught them.

Walter teaches me about silence. The first day he came into the workshop he said nothing. He wrote nothing. He just watched. The next day he wrote about being in solitary confinement for seven years at a maximum-security prison. During those seven years he read five books a week, and talked to no one. When they finally let him out of solitary, his mother came to visit. He and his mom were sitting there with the plexiglas between them, each with a phone in their hands. After twenty minutes, his mother said, "I came all this way. Why aren't you saying anything?" Walter didn't understand why she was asking that. He thought he had been talking the whole time, but it was all going on in his head. It took him years to rebuild his social skills. Now, with very few words, he's a fountain of stories.

Serge taught me about bad luck. He is an immigrant from Romania who killed a mugger in his cab with an unlicensed handgun. His volunteer lawyer told him if the scar on his neck from the mugger's knife was more substantial, more *photogenic*, he might have a better chance of getting off. Serge was just learning English, but he had a beautiful way with the language. His lawyer got him a deal: freedom for deportation. It's been over a month since they sent him back to Romania.

Chris[sy] teaches me about change. S[he] is the closest this wing of the prison comes to having a woman inmate. He was more than halfway toward becoming a she, when [s]he got caught siphoning thousands of dollars from the hair salon [s]he was managing. Even at black market prices, the whole procedure was costing more than eighteen grand. Chris[sy] was best friends with the owner of the salon, but [s]he needed the extra cash to complete the long-awaited transformation. After Chris[sy] was indicted, a state medical examiner determined [s]he was still a he. Soon as [s]he came here, guys went crazy for the babe in D block, so [s]he asked for protective custody. Fortunately, Chris[sy] is tough as nails, plus [s]he has a craft that is unsurpassed. Thanks to the prison's *Best Use* policy, which takes advantage of free labor when they can get it, [s]he's become the official in-house hair-cutter, and as far as I can tell, nobody messes with her/him anymore.

Sergeant Tom teaches me I can care for someone who I have every reason to despise. He tried to kill the surgeon who worked on his wife before she died. The poor surgeon probably did the best he could. Tom says he's sorry he did it. Seconds later he swears he would do it again if he had the chance. *"Except I'd make sure to fix him for good."* Tom's a tough guy whose eyes are often drowning in tears.

Chuck Zimmer teaches me that I need to forgive myself, because he's having so much trouble forgiving himself, and it's killing him.

Angel taught me about birthrights and birthwrongs and rebirths and tragic legacies. He was a kid gangster who turned his life around and became a documentary filmmaker, until his past caught up with him. Yesterday, the judge gave him fifty years. Angel's lawyer promised he will make an appeal.

I'm grateful to everyone in the workshop who allowed themselves to turn down the noise in their heads telling them that they're worthless, that writing is for sissies, that everything has already been written and said, and there's nothing that putting ink to paper will get them.

I ask them to write what they know. "Tell it like you're telling the best friend you haven't even met yet. Fire the prison guard inside your mind and let your thoughts run free." When the writing stops, they stand up one at a time and read aloud. Sometimes they whisper. Sometimes they shout or sing. And the rules and the barbed wire and the cinder block walls fall away, and with each recitation these men in their orange garb and their accents and asymmetrical faces restore my faith in the power of story. So many of them didn't think they had a story worth telling, or a life still worth living. I was one of them. We think the holes in our lives are unfillable, and our sins, our mistakes—unforgivable.

Yesterday I told the group that I was thinking about writing one last book—a kind of open letter of apology/explanation/gratitude to all the people I've disappointed. I told them it was part of what I needed to do to move forward with my life. Then I offered up the theme of apology for the afternoon. "Even if you're innocent," I said, "it might be a good thing to write an apology to somebody you may have caused harm to along the way." There were a few grumblings, but everyone settled into writing some kind of *mea culpa*, if only to themselves.

After the session was over I heard two newcomers to the workshop asking Chester what I meant by writing one last book. They never heard of Bleu Mobley before they came here.

"Does he really write books, professionally?" To them, I'm simply the facilitator. It's so refreshing.

"100 of them!" Chester bragged.

"Do you really believe that?" one of them asked.

"He seems like a cool guy," said the other one, "but how could one person write that many books? You sure he's not making it up?"

If only I did make up the story of my life in books, I would have given the reader something more to chew on: a real hero for instance, or anti-hero. I would have made myself a world traveler or a spy or astronaut—a woman for sure (not just higher counts of estrogen in my testes). Who wants to read a book about someone who stays married to the same person their whole lives? The marketing people can tell you, consumers of books prefer to read about *new* love, *new* flesh, torrid affairs. And look at this ending! What kind of crime is this to leave a reader with? Nobody is murdered. No one's kidnapped. Nothing *physical* has been stolen. I didn't even put a dent in the president's armor. Look at me, lying in my prison cot—a bankrupted bundle of contradictions with no intention of ever putting these stammerings into a book, thinking only...

of getting out of here... of lying in bed next to Aconsha,

just holding her, barely moving, the slow motion embrace of two fermenting

creatures loving each other, despite everything—in no rush, nobody watching over us.

Looking forward to having the time to give Ella whatever time she needs not to hate me. Got to make sure I'm out of here in time to see her play Annie Oakley in *Annie Get Your Gun*. It's a silly, anachronistic play, but a great role for her: tough, funny, romantic, and she gets to sing *Anything You Can Do I Can Do Better*. That would be something if the lights came on after the curtain calls and she saw me in the audience, sitting next to her mother. If I come around, she'll come around. Just can't rush her.

Looking forward to feeling something other than cement or metal under my feet, to breathing outside air for more than the allotted fifty-nine minutes a day, to giving the eyes in the back of my head a rest from their round-the-clock vigil, hearing the churn and bang of garbage trucks in the middle of the night, waiting on line at the Department of Motor Vehicles, getting telemarketing calls!

However tempted, I will not live to write anymore, or write to live; no more perpetual note taking, experience hoarding, idea stockpiling, or shrinking and expanding the world to fit between the covers of a book. If I have the time, it would be nice to keep painting. Just for the fun of it. Landscapes. Still lifes. Nothing heavy. I like painting more than I thought I would. The smell of the turpentine. The bounce of the brush against canvas. Not fussing too much with it. Just for relaxation. For work, I think I'd like to do something in a senior center helping old people in some way. Not as a teacher. See if there's a job treating people with dignity. Tease the inner gorgeousness out of the harder cases. I'd look forward to a job like that. Or, I could become a gardener, working with my hands in the earth, gloveless, planting seeds, arranging rocks in the language of geometry and chance—*facilitating*—delirious at the thought of the first buds of spring. That or become a fisherman. Being out at sea, teaching Ella the ropes. She loved being on that fishing boat that one time. The bellow of the foghorn. Keeping an eye out for seals and dolphins. They're a tight fraternity, those fishermen. I think you have to be born into it. Maybe they'd let me be a boat hand, or better yet a… *Oh Jesus*, look at the time. 5:59 a.m.

    The windowless morning has come around again.

    I hear the guard's footsteps at the end of the tier.

    He's turning the key to the master lock box—*chckachckachckachckachcka*.

    The cell doors are opening from one end of the block to the other, followed by the mad cavalry of feet running out onto grated metal floors. Having made it through another night, the most motivated of my fellow incarcerees rush to get to the TV room to see the morning news or the final sports scores, or to get to the laundry room, or wait on line to put their names down to be seen at Sick Call later in the morning—try to get some medical care out of the in-sourced physician assistant who hates his clientele for some reason, maybe because we remind him of his own unspeakable feelings of being trapped.

    Dressed in a sleeveless orange jumpsuit, hair moussed and aspiring, Chester is raring to catch up with his buddies. He tucks his head down toward the lower bunk to see if I had any luck catching some winks last night. His youthful face is filled with optimism for a new day. Fighting back exhaustion, I flash him a broad smile and pull the blanket over my eyes.

The Passage

painted by Bleu in prison

Thank You

To everyone who helped me with this project over its eight-year labor (of love) before birth:

Foremost to my wife and partner, Judith Sloan, who believed that the improbable (if not insane) premise of this work was worth pouring my heart and soul into, for her patience with all the time and attention I spent with Bleu Mobley, for her ideas and suggestions, her editing, and her partnership with *my* Life in Books, and the too-porous membrane between the two;

Melina Rodrigo Smyres for her artful collaboration with some of the cover and book object illustrations; Donna Chang for her meticulous dimensionalization of books and their covers; Jonathon Rosen for his virtuosic collaboration on the cover illustration; Michelle Martynowicz, Melissa Medina Mackin, Tatyana Starikova Harris, James Monroe, and Noah Woods for additional illustration assistance;

Michael Denneny, Jennifer Traub, Mark Puckett, Mary Lindberg, Vicki Dennis, Joe Regal, Mike Strong, Corrie Evanoff, and Matthew Hillyer for their insightful editorial feedback and assistance;

Chenits Pettigrew for collaborating with me on the poem, *If This Scar Were A Ladder*;

Gordon Goff for believing in this work, kicking off his new imprint with it; the help of the whole Goff team;

Frank J. Martinez Esq. and Andrew S. Rendeiro Esq. for their consultation on the legal intricacies of Bleu's story and stories;

Michaela Baldwin for her generous, almost all-knowing computer (and artistic) consultation;

Leonard Seastone for his hands-on help binding dummies, and for consultation;

Carol Barton for her expert consultaton on paper engineering;

Michael Premo, Ninotchka Rosca, George Braithwaite, Sultana Wakili, Doug Breismeister for posing;

Brandon Campbell for his help with animating Bleu's story (see my live presentation, web materials, the e-edition); Dick Kane and Robert Winn for their video and editing assistance (of same);

Colin McArdell, Andy Pratt, Thai Truong for consultation on the electronic publication;

Susan and Alec Meiklejohn for letting me stay in their house in Maine one winter to work on Bleu;

The Queens Council on the Arts, NYC Department of Cultural Affairs, New York State Council on the Arts, Joseph Leff and Purchase College/SUNY, Steve Hitt and the LaGuardia Performing Arts Center LAB Residency—for their support;

Howard Sanders, Jonathan Stuart, Nick Boys, Dennis Bernstein, Maria Rogal, Zoe Sadokierski, Steve Heller, Gary Hawkey, Ed Marquand, Garima Thakur, Brian Lehrer, Vicki Dennis, Nathan Lehrer, Simon Lehrer, and Ruth and Arthur Lehrer for believing in this project, consultation and support.

A LIFE IN BOOKS is set in Filosofia, Interstate, Garamond, and Scala. Additional typefaces and families include: Akzidenz Grotesk, American Typewriter, Amiral, Angel Tears, Atrament Std, Bancroft, Bank Gothic, Barbera, Base 9, Baskerville, Bell Gothic, Bembo, Birch, Blockhouse, Bodoni, Century Expanded, Clarendon, Cochin, Cooper Black, Copperplate, Covington, DIN, Fette Fraktur, Franklin Gothic, Futura, Giambattista One, Gill Sans, Giza, Goshen, Gotham, Goudy, Helvetica, IFC Railroad, Keystone State, Letter Gothic, Magda Clean Mono, Matrix, Memphis, Modula, Mrs Eaves, OCRA, OCRB, Officina, Quadraat Sans, Rotis, SF Movie Poster Condensed, Skannerz, Solex, Squarehouse, Steelfish, Swiss Rounded, Tema Cantante, Trixie, Univers, and Weiss. The book was composed on Macintosh computers at EarSay in Sunnyside, New York, and in Downeast Maine. The book was printed in China on acid-free paper using sustainable manufacturing processes.

Warren Lehrer is a writer and artist/designer known as a pioneer in the fields of visual literature and design authorship. His books, acclaimed for capturing the shape of thought and reuniting the traditions of storytelling with the printed page, include: *Crossing the BLVD: strangers, neighbors, aliens in a new America* (with Judith Sloan); *The Portrait Series: a quartet of men* (four-book suite); *GRRRHHHH: a study of social patterns* (with Dennis Bernstein and Sandra Brownlee); *French Fries* (with Bernstein); *i mean you know*; and *versations*. He has received many awards for his books and multimedia projects including: the Brendan Gill Prize, the Innovative Use of Archives Award, three AIGA Book Awards, two Type Director's Club Awards, the International Book Design Award, a Media That Matters Award, a New York Book Show Best of the Best Award, and a Prix Arts Electronica Award. He's received fellowships and grants from the National Endowment for the Arts, New York State Council and Foundation for the Arts, and the Rockefeller, Ford, Greenwall, and Furthermore Foundations. His work has been exhibited widely and is in many collections including MoMA, L.A. County Art Museum, The Getty Museum, Georges Pompidou Centre, and Tate Gallery. Lehrer is also a performer, and has co-written four plays, one opera, co-composed two audio CDs, and he co-produces public radio documentaries and audio works with his wife Judith Sloan. He is a frequent lecturer and presenter at universities, art and literary centers, and book stores throughout the United States and internationally. Lehrer is a professor at the School of Art+Design at Purchase College, SUNY, and a founding faculty member of the *Designer As Author* grad program at the School of Visual Arts. Together with Sloan, Lehrer founded EarSay, a non-profit arts organization dedicated to uncovering and portraying the lives of the uncelebrated in print, on stage, on the radio, in exhibitions, concert halls, electronic media, and through educational programs in public schools, community centers, and prisons: www.earsay.org